A Fateful Homecoming

Kim almost pushed the swing back too hard after all.

Steph was here, right *here* in Lightning Gap?

"I thought Steph got married?" Kim said. "Moved away with her new husband not long after I went to college in Atlanta?"

Auntie Venus took a drink of coffee, peering at Kim over the edge of her world mug. The kind of knowing gaze that would either discover everything or get you to say it out loud for her.

Kim fought revealing *any*thing as hard as she could.

"She *did* get married," Auntie Venus said, tilting her face up and to the left like she always did when she was trying to remember something. "Went to school down in Texas, but she ended up with a local boy. From over in Laurel Gap if I recall. They went up to Louisville for a while. But she's been back here for several months now. Started teaching at the start of the school year."

"That is an interesting bit of luck. Both of us back here now after years away. Might be nice enough to catch up with Steph, see how life's been treating her. Just out of curiosity, did she bring the husband back with her?"

Auntie Venus shook her head. "She sure didn't. Seems to me she got all of that out of her system before she got too old. Some might say that's a smart move. In her case, I have to agree."

KARI KILGORE

Protecting Her Own

Spiral Publishing, Ltd.

For Strong Mountain Women Everywhere

Protecting Her Own

CHAPTER 1

ater really did make all the difference when it came to brewing coffee. And Kim Mullins had never tasted anything as good as the water from her Auntie Venus's mountainside spring.

Kim closed her eyes and pushed her bare toes against the thick wool rug, sending the porch swing backward again. Her great aunt's house sat far enough up that they often got fog on these early spring mornings. Reason enough to get up with the sun as far as she was concerned.

Right now the air outside the screens surrounding her was pure white, with thinner patches revealing a flash of the pine trees in the front yard every couple of minutes. The fog managed to cushion sounds out of the air too, muffling the breeze, the musical creek close by, and the birds greeting the day. She probably had a solid hour to enjoy the sensation of swinging on a porch swing in the middle of a fresh, mineral-scented cloud before it burned off.

Not that the view of mountains all around them barely showing the first sweet blush of spring was a bad follow-up.

The coffee that surpassed anything she'd ever tasted back in Atlanta, in New York, or on a trip with Auntie Venus to Italy years ago filled a mug that really was too big for a single serving. In fact, Kim had used the huge purple and pink striped ceramic vessel as a soup bowl many times when she was a little girl.

Between the decadence of drinking coffee out of it and the warmth against her fingers, she'd started every day since her move back home on an entirely positive note. Having the perfect weather for bare feet, blue jeans, and a black hoodie alone felt amazing when late March would already be getting hot in Atlanta.

She might have to shift her routine once the hot weather really settled in a few months from now. A switch to cold coffee, maybe.

Even though it could still snow into May at this elevation in the southwestern corner of Virginia and March still had a week to go, days were pleasantly warm. Unlike they'd be in late October once winter made itself comfortable. Now was the time to enjoy the outdoor mornings.

The rug she pushed herself off of to keep the swing going —and to get an agreeable *gronk* out of the chains holding it up—had come from another of her Auntie Venus's adventures. Kim couldn't remember where, but she was determined to ask later on.

Much later on, once her aunt finally decided to get up. She'd been as much a night owl as Kim was an early bird throughout her whole life.

The rug had thick, soft pile, deep enough to really sink her toes into. Indigo blue around the outside, with a swirling pattern that gradually got lighter toward the middle. The fibers dyed violet, blood red, dark green, and even black were trimmed to different heights, irresistible for little girl fingers or grown woman toes. Kim had never seen anything like it.

That was the thing about Auntie Venus's house. It was full of things no one anywhere near Lightning Gap, Virginia, would ever find if they searched near and far.

The porch was built so the wooden ledge under the screened windows was extra wide, and shelves painted in as many different vivid colors as the rug lined the space under the windows.

And every inch held a different treasure from a different exotic corner of the world.

Bunches of statues of all shapes, sizes, and materials. Some fairly new from trips over the last few years, others obviously older than Kim herself at thirty-seven. The typical figures of round Buddhas and many-armed deities sat comfortably alongside stylized couples embracing and birds, snakes, and bears. Wood, metal, stone, even what looked like jewelry quality gems and minerals.

Most of the figures, human and animal alike, had an odd look to the head or the eyes or the ears making it clear they came from a different culture. Some strange enough that Kim suspected they may be even older than Auntie Venus at eighty-three.

Ceremonial-looking bottles and jars. Painted tiles and plates. Wands and crystals and crucifixes and peace signs. As long as they held meaning or memory, they all belonged here.

Kim hoped she would eventually feel the same way, like she had when she was a little girl whose legs were too short to push off in this swing.

She took another long drink of just-hot-enough coffee, nowhere near the scalding nonsense that came out of most American coffee shops, and shook her head at the silliness of her own wandering thoughts.

Of course her Auntie Venus welcomed her. The first time Kim mentioned wanting to take a break from city life in Atlanta on one of their weekly phone conversations, Auntie Venus had offered company and a place to live. The second time, Auntie Venus had admitted she'd love to have the company.

The third time, she admitted she needed the help even more than Kim needed the change of scenery.

Barely a month later—job respectfully resigned and city house on the market getting lots of interest—Kim made the big move.

Everyone had welcomed her, to the point that she felt more than a little uncomfortable with all the attention. Even with a great group of friends, satisfying job as a technical writer, and ten years in the same house, Kim hadn't realized how anonymous she'd been in such a huge city.

Some people knew her, of course, but the majority of folks

had no idea who she was. Millions of them wouldn't recognize her from Eve. That didn't count countless numbers more who came in and out of Atlanta every day, month, and year.

But back here? In and around the close-knit community of Lightning Gap, she wasn't Kim Mullins, skilled tech writer or good friend or any of the other roles that had defined her life.

Here she was Bill and Stacy Mullins's girl. Throw in all the grandparents and aunts and uncles and cousins, and Kim suddenly felt like nothing more than an extension of people she hardly knew any more.

What she was *most* known as, of course, was the grand-niece of the rather eccentric Venus Elizabeth Mullins Thompson McFall Kelly. She'd gone back to only Mullins after her third beloved husband passed away because she didn't plan on having another, don't you know.

Even with her great aunt's example to live up to, Kim knew she was the subject of much speculation after so many years living away in the Big City. Naturally.

And just as naturally, at least for her, she spent an unreasonable amount of time pondering the questions that must surely be flying around with her name attached.

Why had she come back home? Had she *failed* somehow? Was she running from something? Had she been *forced* to sell out and run back up here to the mountains? Did she have some kind of Big City Scandal hanging over her head, just waiting to reveal itself?

And most importantly, had she turned out as interesting and odd as her Auntie Venus?

The only scandal she could think of wasn't much to trade on these days, even in a small town. Being gay hardly turned heads any more. Not that she wanted the trouble with that subject that had only so recently slipped into the past. Not for herself or anyone else.

Hell, her family and everyone else around here had probably known long before she figured it out herself.

It was only that Kim would have happily traded being seen as exceedingly odd or even shocking if she could stop feeling so drearily...*ordinary*.

A low screen door squeak as comforting as the porch swing's gronk let her know Auntie Venus was up and about, and surely anything but ordinary. A few seconds later, a vision in shimmery pink silk pants that flared before fitting tight around the ankle, sky blue high-top booties, and an oversized fuzzy lavender robe appeared.

She had her thick silver hair braided as usual, with the end forward across her shoulder and caught up in an iridescent forest green clip. Kim only hoped her own heavy mop of brunette hair would end up with that lovely color over time.

"You're up early, Auntie Venus. I hope I didn't wake you."

Auntie Venus shook her head and smiled as she joined Kim on the swing.

"Lord no, honey, I doubt a boulder rolling down the mountain would wake me these days. I heard a big beauty of a storm last night, but I dropped right back off. You're quiet as a mouse in the mornings as far as I can tell. Just turned over with my eyes wide open is all."

Her cup was a black globe with the continents rendered in

glittering jewel tones. She took a good long drink of her coffee and hummed.

"I thought you were crazy talking about brewing coffee on the counter all night long when you first got here. But damned if this doesn't make a fine morning cup. Every bit as good cold as it is hot."

Kim's own expertise in swearing had largely been learned at her great aunt's knee.

"Well thank you," she said. "I never had such luck until I was using your good spring water."

They both glanced toward the steep mountainside close to the side of the house, barely visible through the fog. Covered in poplars, oaks, and maples that hadn't started budding out yet. The scattered rhododendrons and mountain laurels thick in the understory still looked like overgrown azaleas to Kim's eyes.

The spring that brought the amazing water made its way through the underlying stone of that mountain, and a trickle still filled a little pond circled with huge rocks of all different kinds and colors. Most of it had been harnessed to provide drinking water for the house before Kim was ever born.

She'd heard several explanations for why that water tasted so good since she was first old enough to ask. Auntie Venus's special mugs or glasses brought back from all over the world changed the flavor. The limestone rock the water filtered through, that did it. Some special formula of the soil held the secret.

Kim's favorite—and the one her great aunt held to herself—was the peculiar magic of Lighting Gap itself. Maybe even the namesake lightning. No one ever said more than that, but Kim had the feeling many of the locals knew more than they let on.

She wasn't sure she'd ever be considered a local again after so long living away.

"You got any work to do this week?" Auntie Venus said. "Your technical writing freelance work, I mean, from the folks at your old job."

Kim shook her head and gently pushed the swing back again.

"Not so far. They're giving me some time to settle in. I'll let them know when I'm ready to start. Why, you got errands for me to run in town?"

Auntie Venus lifted one shoulder in a half-shrug, one of the signs that she had something to say or ask, and was working her way up to it.

"Nothing to speak of for me, no. I hear they're doing one of those Career Day things at the high school next week. You remember the Holfields, David and Donna? You knew their girl Stephanie pretty well."

Kim raised her eyebrows and turned her head the other way, toward a stand of cherry trees and the road down into town.

Oh, she remembered Steph. *Too* well.

"The Holfields, sure. I remember Career Day, too. I'm missing the point where they go together."

Auntie Venus patted Kim's knee.

"Well, they think the high school will want you to come by and talk to the kids, of course. Tell them how you're able to work just fine from here or anywhere else in the world as long as you have your computer. Show them a good career they don't have to leave home for."

"Maybe," Kim said. "I've never done anything like that before, but it might be fun. I'm still...confused about where the Holfields come in."

"I thought you already knew. Stephanie is a teacher at the high school now, some kind of science I think her daddy said. He's right sure Stephanie will be excited to talk to you about coming down there next week."

Kim almost pushed the swing back too hard after all.

Steph was here, right *here* in Lightning Gap?

"I thought Steph got married?" Kim said. "Moved away with her new husband not long after I went to college in Atlanta?"

Auntie Venus took a drink of coffee, peering at Kim over the edge of her world mug. The kind of knowing gaze that would either discover everything or get you to say it out loud for her.

Kim fought revealing *any*thing as hard as she could.

"She *did* get married," Auntie Venus said, tilting her face up and to the left like she always did when she was trying to remember something. "Went to school down in Texas, but she ended up with a local boy. From over in Laurel Gap if I recall. They went up to Louisville for a while. But she's been back here for several months now. Started teaching at the start of the school year."

"That is an interesting bit of luck. Both of us back here now after years away. Might be nice enough to catch up with

Steph, see how life's been treating her. Just out of curiosity, did she bring the husband back with her?"

Auntie Venus shook her head. "She sure didn't. Seems to me she got all of that out of her system before she got too old. Some might say that's a smart move. In her case, I have to agree."

"You?" Kim said, smiling and leaning her shoulder against her great aunt's. She decided not to ask what her great aunt meant by Steph getting all of that out of her system. "You didn't leave a single one of your husbands, and not one of them ever stopped loving you. You were just stubborn enough to outlive them."

"Doesn't mean I don't understand what it's like to have your marriage fit you like a shoe with a stone caught inside. Stephanie seems real happy now, back here and teaching."

Kim didn't want to say how well she understood, how well her great aunt's words described her own relationships. A couple of those had been more like a *sharp* stone in her shoe, and a shoe that hadn't fit right in the first place.

The last one, and the longest one, had started out soft and easy, as comfortable as her great aunt's booties. But by the time she and Stacy managed to get away from each other, it felt more like running across shards of glass.

If nothing else, catching up with a friend from so far in her past might help her get settled in. Couldn't hurt to try.

"I know what you mean, Auntie Venus. Maybe I'll get in touch with Stephanie later today."

CHAPTER 2

S teph Holfield enjoyed being in her classroom pretty much any time. Classrooms, really, since she had the relative luxury of an instruction room out front and a lab in the back. The chance to sprawl out and get comfortable to her heart's content.

She took great pride in the instruction room, with its rows of two-student-sized black tables more or less in order, and two huge whiteboards up front waiting to be covered with multicolored words and drawings and formulas. The faint, ever-present paint thinner aroma of dry-erase markers lingered rather than the dusty chalk scent of her own school years in this same building.

A dully reflective black rectangle in the middle—four feet tall and eight feet wide—would display any sort of movie or graphic or diagram she sent to it from her laptop or tablet.

Essentially a huge smart TV her gadget-loving father still envied several months after she'd started this job.

Her own desk off to the side, between the front door and the doorway to the lab, changed according to what she was teaching at the time.

Right now a wooden box filled with thin partitions held what most people would call a bunch of rocks. Different colors, yes. Some shiny, other dull. Translucent or sharp-edged, soft or opaque. That was about as far as those Steph sometimes thought of as civilians cared to go.

To her, though, and the passionate rock hounds she knew all over the country, that humble little box her former mother-in-law made for her years ago held the keys to the mystery and majesty of the entire planet.

Igneous and metamorphic and sedimentary. Quartz and coal and granite. Gems and minerals, gravel and gold. Bright yellow sulfur and its flammable stink, off-white talc with a soapy, greasy feel. Formed by pressure or explosions or trans-formation, and even a few pieces of gorgeous forest green moldavite from an ancient meteor impact.

Her favorite was a slender, snakelike wand as long as her hand that looked like blackened dirt from the outside. Looking into the ends, both open about an inch in diameter, revealed a glassy, smooth dark gray finish lined with bubbles, abruptly closed off like the bottom of a frozen puddle.

A spectacular specimen of fulgurite she'd retrieved from a lightning-struck area near the Lightning Rock itself. Steph was certain the whole town was full of the unusual formations.

Since the first time she'd toured a huge cave as a little girl and picked up a box of rocks in the gift shop, Steph had never tired of collecting and learning and understanding, and later teaching about the slow march of time and weather and erosion all around them.

Even with all that joy of teaching and the excitement of seeing a good number of kids in each class pick up her own enthusiasm, Steph still loved these quiet hours when she had the place to herself.

The lab behind her classroom was already small by the standards she'd gotten used to in college and in her first years of teaching in a big school in Louisville, but it was well-equipped. Long white tables with drawers underneath stuffed full of tools and equipment, and more of the whiteboards along the wall that joined her classroom.

Two of the walls in her corner classroom perch on the third floor were full of windows, bringing in plenty of light to help identify subtle variations in structure or color, or with reading measurements on a scale or thermometer.

Outside those windows, Steph and anyone else who actually paid attention were treated to the view she'd missed during her years in Louisville. Probably more than just about anything else. Out the left side, a breathtaking vista of endless rows of blue and green and black mountains, beautifully sculpted by rain and wind and millions of years.

The low ridge on the edge of town blocked that view from most of Lightning Gap. Her exclusive access alone made the hike up three flights of stairs worth it every day of the week.

Out the right side, a much closer and higher ridge jutted

up, evidence of a more sturdy layer of rock that resisted the softening and shaping of the land below. Covered with trees and scrubby brush for the most part, that solid, curving wedge of mountain backed up the high school and the rest of town. Creating a sense of being sheltered and protected, even so high up above the rest of the world.

But Steph's favorite part—and the feature that drew many of her fellow rock hounds and weather nerds to Lightning Gap year after year—was the jutting gray leading edge of that ridge. Lightning Rock. The towering conglomerate peak of sandstone, limestone, glassy edges, and countless colorful pebbles formed the leading edge for the whole protective ridge.

The gigantic storm that rolled through the night before seemed to have swept all the clouds in its wake, leaving everything bright and washed clean.

As she so often had since she'd first taken possession of these rooms in the old brick high school a month before school started in September, Steph gazed out at the tower of stone to calm herself. To relax after the hectic morning of teaching and the rush to eat lunch.

She'd heard people in town and her own family talk about the magic of Lightning Gap and how it was somehow tied to that jutting stone since she was in pre-school. Every time she sat here and stared at it, felt herself connect to it in a fundamental way she didn't yet understand, she believed in that magic a little bit more.

She had a precious hour of *preparation time*, most teachers called it, and she understood why. The endless river of tests to grade and labs to set up and presentations to create sometimes felt like a tide she could drown in.

But she did everything she could to carve out this part of her day by herself, for herself.

She'd even reclaimed a tiny corner of the lab for just that purpose.

The oddly shaped half-hearted closet had been set up as a makeshift storage area by past teachers. Tucked away along the same wall as her desk, opposite the views of the rolling mountains below, the space was only a few paces across in either direction. A few rows of rickety wooden shelves were jammed against the inside walls, with the remaining wall an extension of the windows that looked out over the sheltering ridge.

Steph suspected the shelves were made of scrap wood from the shop department at the far end of the school. The heavy, scratchy brown fabric that had been tacked up as a curtain in front of the windows and across the narrow entry was surely a Home Economics reject, maybe meant for a class on making a duffle bag or something equally unappealing.

All manner of books and papers and samples and tools had been stacked into the little space when she first saw it. Some of it likely from her own high school days or even before that.

After cleaning a bunch of that out, she still used the shelves for storage of her own. More rock and mineral and gem samples and displays, and various weights and measures for the general science classes, too.

As for the precious bit of reclaimed space, she'd found a

compact but amazingly comfortable meditation chair that fit perfectly in the corner by the windows. The low-backed seat held a bronze-colored cushion, with little wings to support her knees if she sat cross-legged. She'd never quite managed a proper lotus position with each foot tucked on top of the opposite thigh, but she got close enough.

Steph had cleared the whole strange room of antiquated academic clutter, and the shelves closest to her of everything. Then she set up her own soothing oasis.

A small collection of rocks, of course, one that some of the new-age types she'd come across would assume she'd chosen for their energy or healing power.

Sharp-edged quartz and other clear stones in various colors. Gleaming lumps of pyrite, entirely unlike gold to her practiced eye.

Like the smooth, heavy, charcoal-gray bits of hematite, some simply felt good in her hands.

Others looked wonderful when the sun hit them, so she had those lined up on slender shelves right against the windows for their best glittering and prism-casting effects.

One great example each of meteor-created moldavite and lightning-created fulgurite completed her personal collection.

She'd replaced the ugly window curtains with midnight blue blackout blinds first thing, and left them open most of the time. The only exception was when she had a rotten headache or she'd had a particularly challenging morning.

No matter what her day had been like, Steph closed and locked the classroom's outer door when she retreated to her personal space in the lab. Mainly for privacy, because unless she had a need for darkness, she left the little closet's entry curtain open.

In that ugly bit of cloth's place, she'd hung a curtain printed with a deep-space telescope view full of every color, shape, and size of galaxy imaginable.

That way she could stare out at the spectacular ridge from inside her own peaceful and quiet shelter.

The first half of the day's classes hadn't been bad at all, so she settled into her mediation chair with the door open and the blinds raised out of the way. The morning's thick fog had burned away, leaving a beautiful clear blue sky dotted with perfect cotton ball clouds.

A wonderful view as a background for either reading or scribbling a bit in her journal. She'd added the plain spiral-bound notebook to the shelf a couple of weeks ago, curious what might happen if she finally took her therapist's ongoing advice to make her own investigations of what went on inside her own head.

She took a long drink of hot ginger tea, steeped on her normally hidden hot plate. Then she let out her customary long, deep sigh, her mental signal that she was on her own time now. Student and school time would be back soon enough. She'd be ready to dive right back in.

Just as Steph picked up her ink pen, she heard a knock at her outer classroom door.

No students should be roaming around during class hours, and the faculty and staff knew how much she treasured the time to herself. The fact that she never spent it in the faculty lounge jammed in with other teachers made that pretty clear.

The knock rang out again, loud enough that the biology class next door or the chemistry class across the hall were going to hear it.

Steph closed her eyes for a second. Much as she treasured and fought for her privacy, especially about her years in Louisville, the school administration had a description of her ex-husband.

No possible way that could be him.

She brushed out the wrinkles in her forest-green pants and straightened her burgundy blouse as she walked, and automatically glanced around the classroom. Nothing out of place or in need of attention. A quick check of her frequently misbehaving curly red hair, and she opened the door.

The neutral expression she always cultivated when faced with the unknown (and especially the potentially *unwanted* unknown) took a mighty blow, but held. At least she hoped so.

Waiting outside the door was one of the most potent ghosts out of Stephanie Holfield's past *before* Louisville. One she wasn't at all sure she was ready to welcome back into her adult life.

Kim Mullins, looking almost exactly as she had all those years ago in these same hallways. Thick waves of brunette hair falling around her shoulders, neat blue jeans and black button-up shirt. Huge brown eyes lighting up as they met Steph's, full red lips curving into a smile.

Oh no.

Steph wasn't ready for this particular ghost. Not one little bit.

"May I help you?" she said, gripping the door hard so Kim wouldn't see her hand shaking.

Kim's brow wrinkled for a second, and Steph saw the signs of years passing all at once. Kim's cheeks were more hollow, no longer holding the plumpness of youth. Lines marked her lovely eyes and around her mouth. That brow wrinkle seemed quite comfortable on her face, too.

"I...I'm sorry, I didn't mean to interrupt you, and I obviously did. I feel silly but I have to ask. You *are* Steph Holfield, aren't you? You went to school here, same as me?"

Steph gritted her teeth, torn between wanting to be honest and wanting time to regroup.

To decide if she was ready to reconnect with this part of her past.

"I am Steph Holfield, and I went to school here. I apologize, but I'm not that great with names and faces."

Despite her reluctance, Steph's heart sank at the way Kim blinked and drew back, clearly confused. That made perfect sense. She'd remember how well *Steph* remembered pretty much anything and everything she ever encountered. Whether she wanted to or not.

Including names, and faces.

"Okay, now I'm going to sound more awkward and weird than I feel, which isn't easy. I'm Kim Mullins. We...well, we were pretty close for a while there in high school. A long time ago."

A little smile crept out despite Steph's firm advice against it.

"Now I remember a bit more. You were more into English than science, right?"

Kim's smiled seemed pained, and Steph knew it wasn't because of the science. It was more because of the stupid, fake question.

"I wasn't bad at either one. Listen, I really am sorry to bother you. I was down here signing up for Career Day next week, and I thought I'd say hi. But maybe we can catch up another time."

Kim turned to go. In one of those lightning-fast mood shifts Steph disliked so intensely in herself, she felt awful about making her old friend feel worse.

"Career Day?" she said. "What will you be talking about? What are you doing these days?"

"I'm a technical writer." Kim turned back and crossed her arms. "Pretty much since college. Freelance for the last month or so, since I moved back here. HVAC and engineering firms before that."

"Wow," Steph said, her eyes widening. "You're right, that's not someone who's no good at science. That's exactly the kind of thing our students need to hear about, too."

Kim's tense features relaxed a little.

"Yeah, I thought so. I've never done anything like talking to a bunch of kids before, but I'm looking forward to it. Anyway, I'll let you get back to whatever you were doing. Take care, Steph."

And Kim was gone, walking along the hallway with the same graceful stride she'd had at seventeen.

All Steph could do was wish she could regain the confidence and certainty she'd had back then. She closed and locked the door again, and retreated into her little closet.

With the curtain closed and the black-out shades drawn this time.

CHAPTER 3

Kim drove along the cozy main street of Lightning Gap, reassuring herself that time had indeed passed. That new shops and stores had moved in, things that couldn't have existed when she was an insecure teenager in high school fresh from another awful humiliation.

No matter how she felt right that second.

The electronics store that carried smartphones was certainly new. Same with the lack of any sort of video rental store. The internet provider had taken the place of the last one to go.

Even the things she was glad had stayed open and in the same place had adapted with the changing times. Odds and Endings Bookstore was still going strong, thank goodness. But a good part of their business was now conducted online, or by selling ebooks to loyal fans who lived far away.

And venerable old Kay's Cafe, one of her Auntie Venus's favorite haunts, now advertised free Wi-Fi.

Close enough, then.

Whatever had happened back there with Steph sucked, and Kim was being perfectly reasonable to feel upset about it. And she was still unwilling to dwell on it all day long.

She turned out of town and headed up the narrow, winding road back toward her great aunt's house, determined to keep the bad mood at bay.

Her compact sedan wasn't quite up to the task of climbing even higher without wheezing a bit, but the last thing she was willing to consider right now was a new car. This little beauty had gotten her through the last few years in Atlanta just fine.

Kim was willing to take good care of her sedan for a while longer and put up with the slow ascents rather than taking on a car payment.

What on earth *had* happened back there?

Steph had recognized her, Kim was sure of it. The second she'd opened that door, her eyes lit up. And if she had been pretending, why? What could that possibly accomplish? Besides making Kim feel rotten.

It wasn't like she'd stormed into the classroom and demanded they resume the at first tentative or later passionate explorations of their youth. That hadn't even crossed her mind.

Not seriously, anyway.

After a remarkably steep curve that dragged her poor car's engine even more, she passed the last house before her great aunt's, wondering at how the yard there still looked empty after a massive oak had fallen sometime the previous autumn. The tree had been big and beautiful enough that Kim noticed even after living away for so long.

It *had* been a long, long time. Nineteen years since she left for college, and she'd only visited once or twice a year, if that. Maybe her memories of Steph really were a lot stronger than Steph's memories of her.

That idea made her feel more sad than embarrassed, but that didn't mean it wasn't true.

Kim tried to occupy her antsy mind with what she would talk about during the hour they'd given her for Career Day. Well, a solid forty-five minutes with time left for questions.

And that was more than enough to give her a creeping sense of stage fright and panic.

She turned off the paved road onto the gravel driveway that led across the mountain to Auntie Venus's house perched near the top of the same ridge as the big outcrop on the edge of town. That view was well worth the drive, but she was still grateful that this last bit of road winding through thick stands of trees on either side was mostly level.

The questions crowded into her mind very much like those overhanging trees.

What would she say next week? Make sure you have a nerdy eye for detail? A high tolerance for drawing sometimes shy engineers out of their shells? Maybe a translator's ability to turn geek-speak into instructions anyone off the street could follow?

Why had Steph pretended not to even *remember* her?

One last curve, and she saw the full three stories of the

back of her great aunt's house tucked into the rising landscape. Wooden siding aged to nearly black over the decades contrasted with the muted green of grass still mostly asleep for winter.

Neat arrangements of flower and garden beds tucked here and there, with the mysterious magic of Auntie Venus's early radishes and peas already bright and vivid against the dark soil.

Kim again resolved to figure the whole put-seeds-in-ground, get-food-out-later thing for herself.

She glanced ahead at the rounded graveled parking area beside the house just in time to hit her little sedan's brakes much harder than she wanted to on the driveway. Thankfully the skid didn't carry her quite far enough to hit the big brown SUV parked beside her great aunt's bright yellow pickup truck.

Kim let out her breath hard enough to fog up her passenger side window.

Even if she hadn't exactly been paying close attention to her driving, the last thing she'd expected was a vehicle parked squarely in her spot.

A Felten County vehicle, no less, with the stylized insignia for the county's most distinctive feature at the end of this very ridge in a circle on the SUV's back gate.

She backed up and parked behind the pickup, leaving plenty of room for whoever was here to get back out. The post-startlement shakes reliably started up about the time she made it inside the house and upstairs to the kitchen.

Having a surprise drop-in visitor spend time pretty much

anywhere else in the house was unthinkable. The kitchen was the obvious and beloved heart of the house.

Kim had heard tales of all the discussions about where to put the rooms in this wonderfully odd house her whole life, since her great aunt and her first husband built it before she was born. The slope of the land turned the three-story back of the house into one and a half toward the front where the porch was.

As far as Kim and everyone else was concerned, Auntie Venus's long-fought battle to get the kitchen, dining room, and living room upstairs and the bedrooms and laundry rooms on the partly underground floors was well worth it.

The wide open space she stepped into now had been modified over the years, removing walls and adjusting the layout as trends (and husbands) changed. Sure enough, her great aunt sat at the sweet little kitchen table in the middle of a bunch of wooden cabinets and shelves recently painted white.

Even though she sometimes missed the cozy kitchen of her elementary school years—with four tan walls and dark cabinets—Kim had to admit the changes made the whole upper floor feel much larger. The dark green stone floor and big windows up front made it feel like being outside.

Sitting at the table beside Auntie Venus was a guy about her age, wearing jeans and a golf shirt, with the same thick brunette hair as Kim's. His was trimmed into a typical short business cut, but with the same spiked-up bangs he'd had since high school.

Her first cousin Jay Murray, dropped by to marvel at the return of the wayward city girl at last.

"Kim!" He bounded to his feet and caught her in a big hug. "About time we ran into each other!"

"Hey there, Jay," she said, smiling to soften their usual teasing. "Good to *finally* see you. I've been right here with Auntie Venus the whole time. I'm sure you heard the news all around the county the second I got back."

He wrinkled his nose and shook his head, waving one hand toward Lightning Gap.

"I don't much pay attention to all that gossip unless I have to. Certainly not when it comes to my own crazy family, or pretty much anyone who lives up on this mountain. Come on over here and sit down. Auntie Venus baked up a mess of her best chocolate chip cookies despite my protests."

Auntie Venus winked when Kim looked her way, surely at the idea of Jay avoiding gossip under any circumstances. She'd changed into one of her usual colorful ensembles. Today a swirly gauze skirt made of scraps in every shade of the rainbow and a black long-sleeved sweater, with her silver hair twisted and looped on top of her head.

Kim sometimes wondered whether her great aunt actually needed any help, or if she just wanted the company.

"Oh yes, Jay *protested* all right," Auntie Venus said. "Protested his way to turning on the oven and fetching a bag of my frozen cookie dough from the deep freeze downstairs."

Jay waved his hand again as he sat, but his grin gave it all away.

"Well, you can't much blame me, not with your amazing cookies. I really am glad to see you, Kim, don't think I didn't care. I thought you might want a little bit of time to get yourself settled and adjusted. And I'm happy to report the gossip down at the town council didn't amount to much more than curiosity."

Kim sat, adding two of the cookies that were more dark chocolate than anything else to a bright yellow plate from somewhere in South America. Same place her Auntie had gotten the idea to add a touch of cayenne pepper to the divine cookies.

"I guess that's good news," she said. "Curious I can handle. It's nosy and prying into my business I was dreading moving back here."

"That may very well be the case out in the county," Auntie Venus said, pouring a glass of milk for her. "But you know that's not the way of it here in Lightning Gap. People are happy to have you back home is all. Just like me."

Kim chewed her perfectly sweet and spicy mouthful, then chased it with a long swallow of milk.

"I think it's worse in my imagination than anywhere else. Everyone was friendly out at the high school today. *Almost* everyone. How's the town council going, Jay?"

Jay raised one eyebrow at her, then half-smiled. He hadn't missed things like her little slip there, not even when they were kids.

"It's going. I was just telling Auntie Venus you coming back here isn't the only big news. You're a lot happier to talk about, though. You remember David Holfield, right?"

Kim tried not to scowl or sigh. She managed not to look at her great aunt, either.

"I remember him," she said. "Steph Holfield's father."

"Right, right. I remember you and Steph being pretty close back in school. Anyway, he's the county sheriff now, not sure if you knew that. There's been a guy missing from over in Laurel Gap for a few weeks now. Just vanished, or that's what they thought."

Auntie Venus shook her head.

"Not all that nasty business with those Phipps boys, is it? I think they've been at each other's throats since *I* was in high school."

"It might well be," Jay said, drumming his fingers on the table. "This is a Stan Phipps that's turned up. That's the big news, you see. He's not missing any more. Some hikers found him today, not far from the main road into Lightning Gap."

Kim's stomach dropped, and she pushed the plate with her second cookie away.

"I hope you're not about to share the gory details, Jay."

He held one hand up and shook his head.

"Course not, I wouldn't do that. I don't know much, to be honest. Just that he's no longer among the living, and no one knows how or why. All I will say is he didn't look like he laid down and went to sleep. He had some kind of...help along the way. With the shape he was in and where he was found, he was moved after whoever did this was finished with him."

"That kind of thing can't happen very often here, can it?" Kim said. "I don't remember hearing about any murders or whatever it is when we were kids."

"No, not at all," Auntie Venus said. "I've always heard it said that Lightning Gap helps keep us safe, and I believe it."

She took a deep breath and stared toward the front windows.

"I heard stories about a couple who died not too far from where Jay's talking about, but that was an accident. Ran off the road in a snowstorm, way back during the Great Depression. That was the baby a pair of local lovebirds took in when they were first married. They don't think Stan Phipps was murdered?"

Jay shrugged and held one hand up, tilting it back and forth.

"Not sure just yet. No one seems to know why he would have been over here in the first place. His family and work and everything else are in Laurel Gap. Sheriff Holfield probably knows a lot more by now than I ever will."

"I'm sure he does," Auntie Venus said. "How was your visit to the high school, Kim?"

So neither one of them had missed Kim saying *almost* everyone was friendly.

"It was fine. They got me set up for Career Day, for kids who want to learn more about writing. I'll get forty-five minutes to talk and look goofy, then fifteen to do my best not to sound foolish answering questions."

Jay pointed at Kim's plate and raised his eyebrows.

"You go right ahead."

He grabbed the cookie and got right back to talking.

"Career Day can be so much fun, I might have to swing by and see what you have to say. I've been down there a few times myself. Town council isn't much on its own, but they love to hear about running a hardware store for some reason."

Auntie Venus shook her head, like Kim expected she would.

"No, honey, I meant did you get to visit with Stephanie?"

Jay opened his mouth, then settled for filling it full of cookie and nodding.

"I saw her," Kim said. "Just for a minute or two. She seemed pretty busy, I guess."

Jay raised his eyebrows for a quick second, then stared down at his empty cookie plate as if he could refill it with his mind.

"What, Jay?" Kim said. "What do you know about her?"

"Steph? Nothing worth talking about. Nothing to *worry* about for sure."

He started to reach for yet another cookie from the big plate, but Auntie Venus slapped his hand right before Kim could.

"Gossip is one thing, Jay," Auntie Venus said. "But we've all known Stephanie since she was a little girl. I think Kim would like to know if she's okay. So would I."

Kim started to protest, but it was too late. They'd both already seen her face.

"Okay, I guess," Jay said. He stopped drumming his fingers or trying to snatch another cookie by folding his hands together on the table. "It's just...word is she had a pretty rough time of it up there in Louisville. Nothing she did, mind you. But that husband she hooked up with turned out to be a rough fellow to live with."

Kim's stomach twisted this time, remembering how Steph had pretended not to know her.

"Rough how?" she said before she could stop herself.

"I don't know much," Jay said. "Only that she has a protective order against the guy. With her dad being sheriff, word got around within law enforcement pretty quickly, then trickled out to county government, too. Not sure why or how long it lasts."

"Oh no," Auntie Venus said, shaking her head. "Poor Stephanie. I'm sure she was glad to see you then, Kim."

"Maybe," Kim said, grabbing the last cookie before Jay could. "We'll see how it goes."

She made a point of not looking at either her cousin or her great aunt. She didn't especially want to know how they felt at the moment.

Because if Steph had all of that on her mind, maybe she'd only been pretending not to remember after all.

CHAPTER 4

*M*uch as she hated to admit it, Steph truly did look forward to having an after-school snack prepared by her own mother, or her father. Even though Steph was the teacher now, and old enough to have been making them for her own kids for years now, if she'd had any.

And after what turned out to be a strange roller coaster of a day, she needed the little love-and-nutrition pick-me-up more than ever.

By the time she dropped her backpack loaded down with tests to grade, changed clothes, and made it to her parents' cheerily bright and cozy kitchen, the irresistible scent of roasting garlic hung heavy in the air.

She padded across the huge orange Mexican tiles in her sock feet, still scrubbing her fingers through her hair and against her scalp.

That was the strangest tension hangover she'd developed since leaving Louisville and Bobby and their marriage, but not the only one.

Her *hair* felt like it was knotting itself up throughout the day. Keeping it short and refusing to wear any sort of barrettes probably kept the problem from being worse, but only rumpling it and trying to rub the tension away really made it better.

The delicious in-floor heating working through her thin socks helped immensely. Almost as much as shedding her workday uniform for her favorite black yoga pants and over-sized purple sweatshirt that hung halfway to her knees.

She leaned her elbows on the tall green slate serving counter as always, much like she had when she was coming home from school as a student. Peeking to see what sorts of snacking delights were in store.

Her parents claimed they'd gotten deeper into their habit after she moved away, experimenting with new appetizer and hors d'oeuvres recipes purely for fun. That was possible, with all the different things Donna and David Holfield got into to keep themselves entertained.

Either way, Steph greatly appreciated such a simple, reliable ritual. And if the daily snacking routine made her parents feel as caring as it made her feel cared for, so much the better.

On the lower waist-high level of the island—the broad communal work surface for both of her parents and her little brother Ryan when he was home—two big round serving plates were covered with pieces of bread about half the size of a playing card. Dark pumpernickel and whole wheat, medium tan rye, and plain old white all scattered together.

Little tubs of cheese waited nearby, warming up to spreadable room temperature. Soft, rich brie and tangy, strong blue cheese, along with more ordinary blends of cheddar and mozzarella, so everyone could dress up their own. A jar of fig spread and one of hot, seed-filled mustard along with slices of apple spritzed with lemon juice to keep them from turning brown rounded out the spread.

Steph was sure one or both of her parents would walk over to the huge south-facing bay window to snip the perfect finishing herbs from their impressive terraced indoor garden. Finishing touches she enjoyed too much to guess at and ruin the surprise.

The stainless steel wall oven ticked to itself, finishing up the last of the grown-up version of a hearty mini-meal to celebrate getting through another day.

Steph fought back the temptation to lean over the counter and dig in early. That was something else that hadn't changed. Both parents got annoyed and pretended great and glorious offense when she did things like that. And she still fell into most undignified and decidedly un-grownup giggling fits at their responses.

Especially with the difficult and too-often painful events of the last few years, Steph loved anything that brought her back to comfort and familiarity.

She let out a long, slow sigh, letting her head drop forward in an attempt to loosen her shoulders and neck.

If she was so drawn to comfort right now, to the familiar, then why had she been so *horribly* rude to Kim?

"No sneaking, young lady!"

Steph turned to see her father standing behind her, still wearing his brown and green sheriff's department uniform, hands on his hips. He often had to go back out in the evenings, so he wasn't nearly as fast to get into slouchy garb as Steph was. That was one reason for these between-meal feasts: in case he missed dinner entirely.

At least he'd shed the gun belt and the Smokey Bear hat, leaving his curly, gray-streaked red hair flattened in a ring around his head.

"I didn't have a chance to sneak yet, Dad. You got in here before I could work up the nerve."

He stood beside her, one big warm hand on her shoulder, and leaned over the counter himself. He smelled like his leather jacket and fresh air and home.

"We both worked on this one," he said, smiling, "but your mother's going to try to take all of the credit. I dug up garlic out of the garden and everything."

"Last July," her mother said, standing in the kitchen door with basketful of pale greens. "What he *forgot* to say is he dug those up last July. I'm sure you remember helping me get them braided up for storage, Steph. Not that I don't appreciate the effort, David dear."

She dropped the bundle of greens into the deep bowl of the steel kitchen sink and turned just in time to playfully fend off her husband's attempts at a hug.

Steph's mother might touch up her black hair at the roots

a bit, but otherwise she didn't look anywhere near her early sixties. Her slender figure had filled out to a sweet plumpness, and the lines around her mouth and eyes were almost all from smiling. Same as Steph's father.

Steph knew she looked older than both of them right now. And she wasn't sure hoping that effect faded over time was good for her or not.

"I *will* give you credit for getting the garlic out of the oven," her mother said, plucking a tiny bundle of chives out of the greens. "Smells like it's ready to me."

Her father closed his eyes and raised his head like a hound dog sniffing at the breeze.

"It sure does. I'm on it."

He slipped on a pair of quilted oven mitts covered with bright red cardinals and dark green holly leaves. When he opened the door and the earthy scent got even stronger, Steph couldn't help pulling the hound dog act herself.

"Can I help with the garlic?" she said, knowing the answer but determined to keep asking.

"No ma'am, you may not," her father said. He slid the small baking tray with five little aluminum foil bundles onto an adorably dorky cork trivet the two of them made from actual wine corks. "You've been doing the hard work of molding young hellions into productive members of society all day. This is the least we can do to say thank you."

Steph rolled her eyes, deciding to venture into half-hearted argument territory today. Not nearly as robust as the argument shaping up in her mind about whether she should try to call Kim to apologize or not.

"Oh yeah, I'm the *only* one here doing hard work, Mr. Felten County Sheriff. Not to mention Ms. Works Constantly Transcriptionist over there."

Her parents met at the courthouse, of course, when her mother was a fresh, vivacious court reporter and her father just starting out as a green, boyish deputy. Since her mom adored doing transcription work from home in the weeks after Steph was born, she never even considered going back full-time.

"Well," her father said, carefully opening the little foil packets to reveal steaming garlic heads with their tops snipped off, "you make my job easier by doing your part to keep them from swerving into the criminal lifestyle. And your mother's easier by keeping them out of the court system. So sit, relax, and let us take care of you."

Steph gave up, scooting onto a cushioned barstool and resting her elbows on the counter and her chin in her hands. Exactly like she would have all those years ago.

"Okay then," she said, "tell me about *your* day, both of you."

She didn't miss the quick glance between them like she might have as a self-absorbed teenager. At least that much had changed.

Or maybe Steph had just grown way too suspicious since she last lived here.

"Nothing to speak of, really." Her mother set out three tall glasses with thick bottoms, then walked toward the bay window garden. "More work for depositions and such, couple of witness interviews. More dull than you'd imagine. I do have a possibility of work from the bookstore in town. A new writer-in-residence who wants to try dictation. At least that should be more interesting."

Her father grinned while he turned one of the garlic heads onto its side and used a butter knife to squish out the perfectly soft and roasted cloves.

"That's got my day beat," he said. "Served a few summonses. Piles of paperwork. Lectured a group of brand-new drivers about all the ways they can get it wrong, so maybe they'll get it right at least some of the time."

Her mother brought back a handful of mint leaves, then gave them a good rinse. She dropped the bunch in front of Steph, bringing the sharp aroma with her. Next came the three glasses, paper towels, and a tiny bowl full of plain white sugar.

She handed Steph what looked like a hand-length baseball bat with an extra thick end.

"Dry and muddle, please," she said. "And tell us about your day, Steph. I hope it was more interesting than either of ours."

Steph sprinkled the thumbnail-sized toothed leaves onto one paper towel and gently patted them with another. She knew her parents would enjoy this same preparation later in the evening and include the alcohol. Probably bourbon. When they thought she was asleep.

That had annoyed her at first, but she didn't mind now. She'd never had a problem with drinking herself, and usually didn't mind it with other people. But her parents knew Bobby and the people around him had been driven by alcohol (and other things) toward the end, in more ways than one.

Most of the time, Steph didn't care to remember how much of a role booze had played in all the madness.

"Pretty good day," she said. "The kids were more distractible than usual this afternoon, some kind of rumor going around. I try to ignore that stuff most of the time, but a couple of them were really upset. Thought you might have heard about it, Dad. The guy someone found not far outside town?"

He looked at her with one pale (but starting to get bushy) eyebrow raised, but she only raised her own in return.

She divided the mint among the three glasses, sprinkled a bit of sugar into each, and started muddling. The push, twist, repeat fell into an easy rhythm, and the sharp smell drifting up from the leaves was amazing.

"You know I'll just ask Ivy," she said, starting on the second glass. "She always knows the truth, and she's happy to speculate on the rumors."

Her father snorted and mashed out another head of garlic. Steph's mother laughed under her breath as she brought a bottle full of pink-tinted liquid out of the refrigerator.

"You *introduced* us to Ivy, dear," she said. "Introduced her to me before Steph was born, and took us both up there after. Same thing after Ryan was born. So you can't act all surprised and confused now."

"No, no, I won't pretend that wasn't me." He shook his head and started transferring all the little dishes and jars to the high counter. "I just wish that old mountain woman would keep some of her *wilder* theories to herself. The world has enough conspiracy nonsense from the internet without her adding to the local supply."

"I haven't seen her for a couple of months," Steph said. Muddling complete, she poured a healthy dose of her mother's rosewater syrup into each glass. "Not since sometime in December. Might be time to pay her a visit."

Her father performed his ceremonial duty of adding ice to each glass, then topping them off with carbonated water from his prized metal spritzer bottle.

"Fine, I'll tell you. But only because I don't want you traipsing out to Ivy's place alone. I wish she'd move into town to be honest, and please don't ever tell her I said that. She'd string me up by my heels. Yes, a couple of hikers found a body today. A guy missing from Laurel Gap for a while now. Stan Phipps. That's pretty much all I know."

Steph managed not to shudder herself, even though several of the students she'd overheard discussing the horrifying discovery had shivered almost constantly. She suspected they'd enjoyed it, the vicarious thrill of discussing such a horrible thing.

Thankfully they hadn't yet had reason not to.

"The kids had some pretty wild descriptions going," she said. "Nothing I want to repeat with all this great food in front of us. Sounded pretty outlandish to me. A couple of them even said someone else turned up missing. From down in Wolf Branch this time. The kids are sure it's some kind of kidnapping and murder ring hiding out nearby."

"Well, they were exaggerating that," her dad said. "At least the descriptions part. The body hasn't even been examined yet, so we're not even sure of the cause of death. Sounds like kids haven't changed much since I was one."

"And the part about Wolf Branch?" Steph said.

Her father paused, not moving for a few seconds. He drew in a deep, slow breath and let it out as he spoke.

"That part about Wolf Branch is true. Someone else is missing, for a few days now. Not many people know this, but that person was last seen right here in Lightning Gap. At a convenience store."

He paused, staring at Steph, leaving her feeling like she was in a courthouse witness box again without even trying. He apparently found whatever he was looking for.

"I'll tell you this before you hear a bunch more lies and rumors," he said, "and that it can't leave this room. I know you know that, but it bears repeating this time. Another man was reported missing today, from over in Bountyfield. From what I'm hearing from the Boun County sheriff, he's a lot like the bunch of guys Stan Phipps ran with. Before you ask or hear worse, word from his local buddies is he was supposed to be heading this way, but never showed up."

The deeper, much darker shudder Steph felt like she was always trying to resist worked its way out from her belly to her muscles, leaving cold chills all over her flesh.

"That's too much all at once, isn't it? I can't help wondering..."

Her mother set the plates full of little toasts onto the counter with a resounding thud.

"There's no reason to suspect that, Steph. None at all. He knows if he so much as crosses the border into Virginia, he'll get picked up in a hot second. Dipshit Bobby should have thought twice before he married a sheriff's daughter. Or even better, he shouldn't have treated *anyone* like that."

Steph nodded, taking one of the long-handled spoons her father handed around and stirring her drink slowly, watching the bits of green float through the bubbly pink.

"Virginia has an awful lot of border," she said. "And no one can watch it 24/7 for one dipshit who might be driving anything for all I know. Or look like anybody by now. Exactly how many murders have happened in Felten County over the last fifty years? Or in Lightning Gap?"

Her father stood beside her again, this time gripping her shoulder in his big, warm hand.

"Listen to me, Steph. Look at me." He waited until she did. "This isn't something I want you to be worrying about all the time, but I know you will. Still, what I'm about to tell you is something else that shouldn't leave this room. Okay?"

She nodded, unable to look away from his eyes.

"It just so happens that the Jefferson County Sheriff's office over in Kentucky is aware of certain protective orders. Very aware. Same with Metro Louisville Police. I wouldn't be surprised if a few Kentucky state troopers know a thing or two themselves. You probably already guessed this part, but Virginia law enforcement isn't exactly ignorant. Understand?"

"I do, but—"

"Listen to me, sweetheart. Listen. Bobby hasn't bothered to leave town since you got away from him. Not once. In fact, he seems to have cooled it with all his usual unsavory activities. And if he does leave town, I'll know about it before he hits the city limits. Got it?"

Steph let out a long, deep sigh, and she was sure a tiny bit of the long-standing, exhausting tension inside her relaxed.

Not all of it by any means.

But enough that she felt the difference.

"Got it, Dad. Thank you."

Her mother leaned in and kissed her cheek before she pulled Steph and her father into a hug.

"You're home, Stephanie," she said. "You're safe. And you can stay here just as long as you want to."

Steph was equal parts embarrassed and relieved when her stomach growled. Her parents tried harder to fight it than she did as they stepped back, but all three of them finally laughed.

"You might want to reconsider cooking like this," she said, pulling one of each kind of toast onto a smaller plate. "You might be stuck with me for a long time."

"As long as it takes," her mother said, grabbing her own plate.

"Don't worry about me going to see Ivy alone," Steph said. "I'll make sure someone goes with me. I promise."

She spread a generous dollop of the tan roasted garlic mush onto the dark pumpernickel toast, added a chunk of soft brie, and topped the whole thing off with a slice of apple. Heavenly.

On top of feeling better about the enforcement of the

protective order, she'd just figured out a great way to apologize to Kim. And to get to see Ivy in the process.

Maybe put a bug in the old mountain woman's ear about someone dangerous wandering around Lightning Gap.

Knowing she could plan to see her dear friend from so many years ago without the surprise—the shock of having her show up out of nowhere—began the gentle switch from apprehension to anticipation.

CHAPTER 5

 obby Faulks paced around the carefully arranged furniture in his corner office, taking care not to squeeze the handset of his phone too tightly.

It wouldn't do to have to replace it, even if he did take care of that himself.

Too many chances someone might notice.

And people who noticed things asked too damn many questions.

Besides being a bit larger than offices where most of the software drones toiled away in endless mediocrity, Bobby's personal workspace wasn't too far off from the usual specifications.

Spacious black wooden desk, which he adjusted to a standing desk for precisely twenty-five minutes out of every hour. Three big flatscreen monitors set to the perfect ergonomic measurements to keep him in the right posture at all times.

A few geek-friendly toys scattered across the clean surface of the desk. A silvery collection of tiny magnetic balls in a round high-sided container, currently arranged in a perfect pyramid. A grownup version of a fidget spinner, this one with many layers and levels and steampunk gears.

A couple of miniature statues from whatever movie, game, or tv show was popular with nerdy types, but not overly mainstream. Bobby changed those out once every quarter.

Partly to create the proper "I'm one of you" impression for anyone who walked in. Partly to give the politely tolerated visitors something to pay attention to so they wouldn't pay too much attention to Bobby.

Having anyone pay too much attention to him would never be to his advantage.

A long table against one wall held what looked like typical project manager clutter to the causal observer. Stacks of paper more or less organized, various colors of folders in a vertical holder at one end. A shelf above that held books about programming, miniaturization, product development.

All the things he actually did need in his solidly midlevel job, even if it created the impression he was determined to cling to archaic habits like printing everything on paper.

But the paper allowed him to keep everything carefully disarranged and artfully scattered enough to match what he saw in everyone else's offices. Same with the monochromatic abstract art on the other walls, and even the low-maintenance plants arranged in front of the windows.

All the better to fit in: a skill Bobby had developed from the time he was in high school.

He finally stopped pacing and set the handset back in the cradle much more quietly than he wanted to. He then set himself in his black leather and mesh office chair, turning it to look out the window over the shiny, healthy leaves of all the plants.

The view over the budding treetops at the edge of the office park didn't do a damn thing to soothe him. Neither did the bright spring-blue sky dotted with fluffy pure white clouds.

None of that or anything else about his corner office made much of an impression beyond awareness that other people were impressed *by* it all.

It was just so much set dressing to Bobby. Props on the stage of the life he'd created to make sure he was accepted. Regarded as typical.

Successful, yes. But overwhelmingly normal.

The same role Steph had been so good at playing until she realized the whole thing was nothing but an elaborately staged production.

Bobby swung the chair back around and picked up the handset, but he managed to stop himself before he dialed again. Accessing an outside line several times a day was a given in his job, and odds were high no one would care that he used a decidedly old-fashioned calling card to obscure the numbers he dialed.

Just a conscientious employee making sure not to put any long-distance minutes on the company tab. And making sure nothing showed up on any of his own mobile phones' records.

If he made too many calls in a day, though, that could draw more attention than he wanted.

After all, his latest contact back in the remote hillbilly hell he'd grown up in had made it abundantly clear neither phone calls or text messages were going to get any response.

Bobby leaned forward and activated his computer instead, pulling up the agenda for the afternoon meeting.

One his oblivious manager scheduled for right before the end of the workday, three days a week, without ever noticing how irritated everyone got at having to stay late. Listening to her drone on and on about things that could have easily fit into an email.

Again.

It wouldn't do to walk into that meeting still focused on how he seemed to have lost track of not one, not two, but possibly three former associates in Virginia. Old middle and high school friends, all of them, who'd been utterly reliable working for him in the past.

On jobs that had seemed vital at the time, and turned out to be almost obscenely profitable, even compared to his extracurricular activities closer to Louisville.

Perhaps most importantly, those jobs had been interesting.

Something he could pour his considerable energy and concentration into.

Bleeding down a good deal of his natural...intensity, so his coworkers, his neighbors, and of course his dear, innocent wife wouldn't notice anything *off* about him. Anything different.

Anything unsettling or strange.

That care and caution had served Bobby well since his college days, letting him build his artificial life as cover for his true self.

All those meticulous efforts had failed him at once over the summer when Steph miraculously got a clue.

And got herself back to Virginia and back into Sheriff Daddy's house, and away from him.

Bobby tapped his slender white gold wedding ring against the edge of his desk. An even number of taps, then an odd number. Like some mysterious ancient form of Morse code, the patterns soothed his agitation. Brought the inner unrest he simply wasn't used to into a familiar cold harmony.

He'd take the ring off according to *his* timeline. Not hers or according to Kentucky's quickie divorce laws that left him no say at all in his own marriage, or in the end of it.

It would be over when *he* said it was over.

By the time he gathered his notes—electronic and printed—for the worthless meeting, he'd also gathered his far more important thoughts and plans.

He was ready to deal with his unreliable associates in Virginia and his unreliable wife.

And ready to wait for a timeline that suited him to fall into place.

CHAPTER 6

Once Jay finally headed out—meaning all of Auntie Venus's absurdly good cookies were gone—Kim got herself settled in at her desk in the corner of the living room.

Or at least the old oak breakfast nook table she was referring to as her desk. She hadn't done much of anything there so far besides aimlessly rearranging what little she'd scattered around.

The surface was nicely aged after decades of serving Auntie Venus and each of her husbands, as well as hosting countless game nights for all the nieces, nephews, and cousins. Kim remembered quite clearly the night she'd caught Jay using one of the ancient jacks Auntie Venus let them play with to gouge his initials into the tan surface.

She felt a little guilty decades later for telling his parents, pulling them away from their adult game of bridge or poker or something at the much larger table. Eight-year-old Jay had sworn to never, ever forgive her, not for as long as he lived and breathed.

To no one's surprise, all was forgotten the very next day.

The deep, precisely made "J" was all that survived now, darkened with countless coats of wax.

Kim made sure her laptop never covered that sweet childhood remnant.

That or her ceramic coaster from a long-ago getaway to Key West, or the tiny filing cabinet that held all the business cards she'd collected before leaving Atlanta. Promising to let each and every one of them know when she was ready to take on freelance tech writing or maybe editing work again.

She hadn't even opened the drawers yet, and today wasn't feeling like the day so far.

A peach-shaped mug with Atlanta embossed on the side held her collection of pens and pencils. Besides that and a few rocks she'd picked up on other trips tucked into a brass bowl Auntie Venus brought back from England, the surface was empty.

Plenty of room for work. Someday.

She'd purposely pushed the desk against the wall rather than leaving it under one of the big front windows where Auntie Venus had kept it. That made sense at the time, the idea of not letting herself get distracted by the incredible views of the mountains out there.

She was starting to think moving it back might make even more sense. Maybe getting in the habit of sitting here, even if she did just stare out the window for a while, would help her start getting over her deep and intense feeling of burnout.

Or maybe she'd just try it all again tomorrow.

Her bank account was kind of insanely healthy after selling her house, and Auntie Venus stubbornly refused every offer of helping with utilities or paying rent. Kim was afraid her great aunt would cross over from mildly offended by the offer into hurt feelings if she kept on bringing it up.

So besides her own quiet insistence on paying for all the groceries and anything else she brought back from town without her great aunt along, taking the break she had while she had it may be the sensible choice.

She flipped open the laptop and was about to check her email for the first time in days, or maybe make an outline for her upcoming Career Day talk, when the house phone rang.

Kim jumped to her feet and dashed across the living room and into the kitchen. She had the black phone in hand before Auntie Venus stirred from her perch in a Japanese chair shaped like a giant cushioned bowl.

"Hello? Kim? This is Steph. Stephanie Holfield."

Kim blinked, trying to force her mouth into gear before the flush of decidedly un-grownup heat rushing through her shorted out her brain.

"This is... I mean, yeah. That's me. Hi Steph."

Auntie Venus's face shifted from bright-eyed and curious about who could be calling to a warm, secret kind of smile. She turned back to the huge hardcover book she'd been reading. Kim took the offer of privacy and wandered over toward the porch door.

"Hi Kim. Did I get you at a bad time?"

Kim managed not to blurt out something about "Do you

mean like the bad time when you pretended not to know me earlier today?" She managed to shake her head before remembering she needed to speak out loud.

The heat had turned into shaking hands not that different from when she nearly crashed into Jay's SUV when she got home.

"No, not a bad time at all. I'm just...kind of surprised you called."

"I know, and I'm really sorry about that." Steph took a breath loud enough to hear over the phone. "I don't know what I was thinking earlier. I think I was surprised myself. Startled, more like. I had no idea you were back home."

Kim laughed under her breath. She waved at Auntie Venus and stepped out onto the porch, her bare feet far more chilled by the floorboards than they had been that morning.

"To tell you the truth, I didn't know you were back home until this morning. I've only been here for a few weeks, so I'm pretty behind on things."

Too late, Kim remembered Steph's homecoming hadn't exactly been for easy or cheery reasons. She sounded sad when she answered, but not upset.

"Yeah, I've been back since July. Seems like forever and yesterday at the same time. Teaching let me get back into the Lightning Gap routine in no time at all. Listen, if you can forgive me for being so rude, I'd like to catch up. Whenever you have time, of course."

"Time I have." Kim was glad Steph couldn't see her blushing. "I haven't exactly gotten back into the swing of work yet. Still figuring out what comes next. Catching up sounds great."

"Good! I was thinking I need to drive out and visit with Ivy sometime soon, but we don't have to do that right away. Maybe we could meet in town? Grab coffee at Kay's Cafe? Or lunch?"

"Do you have time for lunch during the day? I mean, of course you have lunch, I'm not quite as out of touch with school as I sound. Not that we have to take hours and hours. A quick bite would be fine, too."

She held her breath, trying to fight off a giggling fit over how her own words were determined to elbow each other on the way out of her mouth. Thankfully Steph's soft laugh didn't sound mean at all.

Her laugh sounded like she understood.

"I have an open hour right after my lunch, supposedly for planning. That's what was...that's when you got there today. I can get away to have lunch sometimes instead of staying at school." She paused for a beat. "We actually only go for half a day tomorrow. So we'll have plenty of time."

"I think that sounds great. Tomorrow? Or is Saturday better? And back up a sec, did you say you wanted to visit with *Ivy*? You mean Ivy Gweddon? Way up on the mountain?"

"Tomorrow at noon works, at Kay's. Yes, that's the same Ivy. I won't be rude enough to ask if you remember her after the horrible way I acted today. And it's not like anyone could possibly forget Ivy."

Kim shook her head, looking along the ridge toward the hidden outcrop at the end of town. Clouds were rolling in purple and red and orange against the setting sun. Ivy's place sat much closer to the outcrop, and it made where Kim stood look positively suburban.

"Sure I remember Ivy. She was a trip, and I say that from the front porch of my Auntie Venus's house."

This time Steph's laughter sounded light and happy, and Kim's heart swelled at the joy of it.

"I'd love to see Venus, too. No matter what anyone ever said about her or Ivy, no one could dispute that they both do what they please. Role models the rest of us could stand to follow a bit more often."

"Well, I know she'd love to see you too, Steph. Maybe we can even get the two of them together, if either one will agree to leave her house. So noon at Kay's tomorrow. That sounds wonderful."

"Good. That's really good, Kim. I'll see you then."

Kim breathed in the cooling late afternoon air through her mouth, slowly smiling at the same time.

It wasn't like Steph had asked her out on a date or anything. And Kim knew all too well she wasn't in a place to even consider dating anyway. Not when she couldn't reliably manage to do something as mundane and safe as checking her email, or even considering getting back to work.

Still, she didn't want to question the warm, soft excitement bubbling up in her belly and chest all too much. The simple idea of seeing her friend after so long, even more so of knowing Steph hadn't actually forgotten all about her, felt plenty damn good.

CHAPTER 7

Steph sat on the robin's egg blue side of Kay's Cafe, her back to the wall, and a clear view of the whole adorable place.

The opposite side was painted in a warm pink she didn't know the exact name for, with the back wall nearly the same spring green that would soon explode in the mountains all around. All the tabletops and floor tiles and even the menus echoed the cheerful combination and variety.

She'd debated with herself before arriving whether she wanted one of the cozy booths or one of the more open tables toward the middle of the room. Her need to have a wall at her back finally overrode her desire to have a bit more privacy, so one of the gleaming Formica tables won out.

Thankfully the place wasn't too crowded even with school letting out early.

She'd been tempted by the fantastic old-fashioned soda

fountain older than her parents, and one of the real cherry Cokes she'd loved so much as a kid. Coffee had seemed like a wiser choice when she walked in. But now with her third cup of Kay's smooth, rich, chocolate-edged brew in front of her, she thought the soda might have been better.

Jittery caffeine overload was the last thing she needed for the first day she would spend so much time alone with just one other person. The first day she spent much time at all outside of either her parents' house or the school since she'd gotten home. Talking a mile a minute probably wasn't the best plan for lunch with Kim, either.

She shook her head, breathed in the rich aroma of baking bread, roasting meat, and undertones of garlic and onions. Kay never served up anything nearly as elaborate as Steph's parents did, and her customers would be furious if she tried.

A place specializing in the best possible versions of comfort food Steph had ever run across felt like exactly the right place to be today.

The art department at school had gotten a head start on the season with the seasonal window decorations they did in all the shops along Lightning Rock Road. Right now, bunches of bright yellow daffodils and pink cherry trees framed the view of the Victorian splendor of the houses across the street. The brilliant sunlight highlighted the lovely purple shades of the Odds and Endings Bookstore most of all.

Steph knew kids from the high school would add to their broad plate-glass palette over time. A little more each day as junior and senior art classes ventured over for their one-hour field trips. She remembered doing her level best to paint butterflies or robins, or even a simple bright yellow burst of forsythia.

After scraping off several failed attempts, she'd been relieved to take on the reliable shapes of Easter eggs, where her unusual patterns and color choices didn't make much of a difference. Just because she couldn't recreate much of anything with a paintbrush didn't mean she didn't love the vivid signs of spring after a long, difficult winter.

A flash of deep, earthy red passing outside the windows pulled her back to the here and now, and Kim's warm smile as she walked in made Steph happy to be right where she was.

"Hey Steph. Am I late? How long have you been here?"

Steph shook her head, trying not to stare at the lovely cool-weather flush in Kim's cheeks.

"I got here early, no worries. I think everyone at the high school was in a rush to get out of there extra fast on such a gorgeous day."

Kim shivered. "Gorgeous, yes. But so much colder than it has been. I guess our early spring decided to hold off for a while."

"Aren't you the one who loved cold weather back in the day? Always wearing short sleeves while the rest of us bundled up?"

"Well sure," Kim said. "I still do, or I did before I moved back here. I think all those years down south thinned my blood or something. I swear that crazy storm last night pushed all the warm away. That's why Auntie Venus made me bundle up like this. I'm never sure where in the world her clothes come from, but I think this is from Peru."

She rubbed at her arms, and Steph noticed the different colors covering the sweater. More earth tones of blue and green and purple woven through the red, all in patterns that were mysterious and strange to her eye. The overall effect was harmonious, though, and brought out the highlights in Kim's auburn hair.

"It's beautiful. Suits you very well, too."

Kim rolled her eyes and looked away, but she was smiling.

"I appreciate you saying that. It's been a while since anyone has."

Steph realized she'd been so caught by surprise by her friend's appearance that she hadn't asked what brought Kim back. She understood too well what an abrupt change like that could mean. And how awkward it was to be asked.

"How is your Auntie Venus? I can't remember the last time I saw her."

"She's tough and ornery as ever. Assuming you haven't seen her since high school, she probably doesn't look much different at all. More of that gorgeous silver in her hair would be about it."

They both looked up and grinned as Kay herself waltzed over to take their order. She had to be close to both Venus and Ivy's age, but her perfectly waved hair was the same remarkably natural shade of strawberry blonde as always. Steph had overheard her once, saying she'd never go gray as long as Clairol stayed in business.

Kay's uniform had evolved over the years from a full-skirted Fifties diner style to a tunic and comfortable pants, but it still featured a sweet coordination of the cafe's pink, yellow, and blue style.

And as if anyone would ever wonder who she was, she wore a big heart-shaped enamel name tag to match.

"What a nice surprise, seeing you two girls in here together again!" She was short enough to lean over and pull Steph and Kim each into a one-armed hug, squeezing their faces against her considerable bosom in the process. "Venus said you were back home, Kim. It's great to see you."

Kim winked up at Kay with the same easy charm Steph remembered.

"I wouldn't say I was back home until just now, Kay. Not until I got a hug from you."

Kay let out her big, infectious laugh and pushed at Kim's shoulder.

"That's one thing I'll say for all you kids who find your way home to Lightning Gap. You always remember how to make an old lady feel loved. Now, what can I bring you to return the favor?"

Steph barely pretended to struggle with her choice. Any time Kay was offering her outrageous fried chicken, that was going to go into Steph's belly. Kim pretended almost as well before she asked for the country-fried steak.

They each ordered salads to start. Steph at least wanted to make an effort to cushion the chicken on the way down. So once Kim ordered herself a raspberry Coke, she ordered the cherry Coke after all as a reward.

Kay grinned like a kid as she headed back to the kitchen.

"Now that's what I like to see. Neither one of you afraid to enjoy your food. And I'm going to make damn sure you do."

They managed to wait until Kay disappeared through the swinging steel door before they laughed together.

"I don't see how anyone could walk in here and *smell* the food," Steph said, "and not decide to eat themselves silly."

"That's one reason I hadn't been in yet. This place becomes a habit after the first visit. Hey, do your parents still do the big afternoon snacks thing?"

"Were you there for that? This part I honestly don't remember."

The young woman working the soda fountain—Steph thought it was Kay's daughter-in-law—brought their drinks then. Kim didn't answer until after she took a long swallow, so Steph felt obligated to do the same.

Freezing cold, extra strong and fizzy, with the sweet cherry in the ideal balance with the bitter bite of the soda.

They both smiled and sighed.

"Even living in Atlanta," Kim said, "I never found any Coke that good. Your parents, yeah, I stayed with you a few times our junior year. And you had a whole group of people over once or twice. We certainly weren't eating pizza rolls at your house."

"No, though I loved those things when I was where I could get them. Mom and Dad still cook like that. They still call it an after-school snack, too. They refuse to let me help them, but I'm wearing them down."

Kim rolled her eyes over another long drink.

"Auntie Venus is the same. Do you ever wonder...never mind."

Steph scowled. "No, don't do that. What were you going to say? Whatever it is, it's okay."

"I was...what I should say is I sometimes wonder if Auntie Venus didn't need any kind of help as much as she wanted the company. Which is fine with me. She's decided she likes my cold brew coffee better than her usual, but otherwise she insists on doing everything."

Steph stared at her glass and Kim's, noticing how the cherry flavor made the brown liquid look a bit more like blood than the raspberry did.

"My parents won't let me do much of anything either. No rent, and they won't let me do a thing to help around the house. That may be self-defense in the kitchen, since I never have been much good at that. But still, I want to do *something*. Thank goodness I have school to keep me focused and more or less sane."

She waited as long as she could before looking at Kim, which turned out to be about ten seconds. Kim had the same predictable, irritating expression Steph had spotted on way too many faces over the last few months.

The curious worry about her, with a massive dose of reluctance to ask if she was okay. Mainly because the answer might be too unpleasant, or simply drag her through too much pain and discomfort. All tied up with a big bow made of uncertainty about whether they should say anything at all.

She couldn't blame anyone who felt that way. She'd spent

the last few months of her marriage feeling exactly the same way about herself.

She wanted to reach across the table and touch Kim's hand, the most natural response in the world at a hard moment like this.

But because it *was* Kim, and their past rose up so strong around them, she couldn't.

"Okay, let me get this out in the open," Steph said. "I'm wondering about you, why you came back. What you did while you were gone. And I'm sure you're wondering the same about me. Maybe we can both be brave enough to admit we wonder. But maybe we don't have to expect to tell every story during one lunch. We can just...catch up."

Kim blinked and smiled at the same time, and Steph was sure her hand twitched forward on the table.

"I'd love that. So yes, I'm wondering about why you came back, too, Steph. If that comes up later on, or if you want to talk about it, that's good. For now, tell me the thing you miss most about Louisville."

Steph only hesitated for a second.

"That's easy. The river, the Ohio River. It sort of sprawls slow and wide through the city most of the time, except when it floods. I loved watching it change with the seasons. Sometimes day to day. There's nothing like that near here, not until you get to the Grasppe around Wolf Branch. Now your turn. What do you miss most about Atlanta?"

Kim waited while a young man Steph recognized from school but not from her classes brought their salads.

"It might sound strange, but I miss all the different areas

of Atlanta. It really is like a whole bunch of small towns that butted up together over the years. Decatur is different from East Atlanta, which is different from downtown and Midtown and Roswell and Ansley. And even within those, the neighborhoods and sometimes the blocks look and feel like you're in a new place."

"We both did the same thing, did you notice?" Steph said. "We talked about things rather than people. For Louisville, I miss the mix of Southern and Midwestern. The very proper hats and dresses and the mint juleps at the Kentucky Derby up in the stands, for example. So *very* Southern, don't you know. But the infield is all beer and party and just having a good time. I enjoyed the way those two go together."

Kim swallowed her bite of salad, leaving Steph free to try her own. The greens were bright and fresh and peppery—the kind of thing her parents would love to experiment with.

"The thing about Atlanta is no matter what you're into," Kim said, "no matter where you're from or what you want to be, you can find it there. People from all over the world right next to someone who's lived their whole life on the same block. Huge Jewish and African-American and gay communities, too. It's easy to find the place you feel at home. The people you fit in with."

An odd flush moved through Steph's middle when Kim said *gay*. That word suited Kim naturally, easily. It felt like a part of her. Steph had struggled on and off since she'd left Lightning Gap, wondering if that might be part of her as well.

Another aspect of her *self*, maybe, one of the many she'd found, lost, and later suppressed as the years passed.

"So we both found places we love," she said. "And yet we're right back here in Lightning Gap. I did miss the mountains the whole time I was away. That part of Kentucky feels wide open somehow. Like you can see forever, and everyone can see you. Having the big ridge, the way it sort of surrounds the town, that makes me feel safer."

Kim nodded. "I missed the snow. The seasons. It gets cold down there once in a while, but only for a day or two. Especially up here on this mountain, you know what time of year it is, no doubt about it. And Lightning Gap will earn its name during certain times of the year, just like clockwork."

"Kind of," Steph said, rolling her eyes. "That's been strange, all through the autumn and winter, even into the spring. I've always taught a good solid unit of meteorology. A good bit for high school kids, anyway. I think the kids here are more than halfway convinced I just make it up. Storms rumbling through out of season, too hot or too cold. I just lean on the *predicting* part and move on."

"Auntie Venus would say you'd make a perfect world traveler then. Expect the unexpected and make it part of the fun. That's the other thing about living away. I really did miss the people, you know? Auntie Venus most of all."

Steph smiled, looking forward to seeing Kim's great aunt more than she expected.

"How is Venus? She was always sweet as she could be to me."

"Auntie Venus is great," Kim said. "Stubborn as ever, even if she's not traveling quite as much. She acted like she needed help at home when I was thinking about making some kind of change. I do a few things for her, sure. But I honestly think she just wanted the company."

"And your parents, they moved to Hidden Springs, right?"

"They did, about ten years ago. They love it, being so near the college there. But I don't think they're ready for me to live with them any more than I am. So this works out a whole lot better all around."

Kay and her young waiter brought out a truly intimidating amount of food then, with fried chicken and country-fried steak and bright orange carrots and buttery mashed potatoes, and even big fluffy biscuits to clean up after everything else. Every single bit of it steaming hot and smelling fantastic.

"Told you I'd get you welcomed back in style," Kay said, beaming at Steph and Kim's gasps and wide eyes. "You'll want to save room for dessert, too. Blueberry pie, cherry cobbler, apple stack cake. Big banana pudding without a bite out of it yet."

"I hope you've got to-go boxes ready then," Steph said even though her stomach was growling. "I'll have to get back in practice."

Kay dropped a dramatic wink of her own. "I bet you'll manage more than you think. But I've got you covered either way. You girls enjoy."

Kim held up a fork in one hand and a spoon in the other and stared down at her food with enough determination that Steph laughed.

"You still thinking about going to visit Ivy today?" Kim said. "Assuming I'm invited, I might be better off walking up the mountain instead of driving. That way I'd have some chance of burning all this off."

Steph tried to remember if she'd mentioned going today or not, and it turned out she didn't care. Now that she'd gotten past the initial nervousness, she *did* want to spend more time with Kim, and that was the question that mattered.

"I'm up for going this afternoon if you are. We can even take her some of Kay's apple stack cake to fuss about, since it would never, ever be as good as hers. That way we'll have to drive, so it won't matter how much we eat. Because I can tell you right now I have no intention of walking out of here today without a big serving of that cherry cobbler."

Kim paused with a forkful of mashed potatoes halfway to her mouth.

"I just remembered why we got to be friends in the first place. Banana pudding for me, and you're on."

CHAPTER 8

Kim didn't mind one bit letting Steph make the long drive up Lightning Ridge Road to Ivy Gweddon's house, for more reasons than she wanted to admit even to herself.

The easiest was Steph's sedan was built for it, with all-wheel drive and what Kim called a grownup engine. The thought of trying to coax her own little car up the mountain with two people inside didn't sound like anyone's idea of fun.

Especially two people stuffed entirely silly on Kay's incredible food.

As it was, Kim was relieved to be able to fall back on the goofy bits of their friendship rather than being mortified every time either of them belched. A shared giggle was so much more fun.

The road past her Auntie Venus's house might not have

been all that steep compared to the initial climb, while this one ran more or less level. But Lightning Ridge Road was much...wilder. Thankfully Steph's mountain driving skills hadn't deteriorated the way Kim's had over years of city driving.

What seemed like constant twists and turns with massive trees growing right next to the asphalt combined with the lack of lines on that asphalt to make the trip feel like driving into another world.

Or maybe going back in time.

Sort of like sitting beside Steph in a car did all by itself after so much time passing.

And with so many memories of everything they'd gotten up to once the cars of their youth were parked.

That was the other problem Kim was relieved she didn't have to face. Her mind kept wandering back to those days, to those heady evenings alone with Steph. The sensations that had never been stronger or more intense with anyone else since.

Trying to focus on a challenging drive wouldn't have been the greatest idea, and letting her mind go too far in that direction after one lunch certainly wasn't. Instead she focused on the land changing all around them.

Even the understory was different under the huge trees this far up. Rather than the open forest floor with not all that much growing, the space was full of vast patches of mountain laurel like overgrown versions of the azaleas back in Atlanta. Unlike the huge flowering bushes scattered here and there around Auntie Venus's house, these were dense and packed together.

Between that and the far more intimidating and inter-laced rhododendron thickets, it was tough to see very far, much less try to walk.

And the trees themselves grew so close to the road that the branches managed to block out a bunch of the light, even with no leaves out yet.

The heavenly, spicy scent of the whole apple stack cake Kay had happily packed up for them filled the car. She'd also flat out refused to let them pay for more than a single slice no matter how much they protested.

Despite her very contented and verging-on-overly full belly, Kim was glad she'd insisted on getting generous slices for herself and Auntie Venus to go. Maybe by the time supper-time rolled around, she'd be able to at least sample it.

She'd gorged on nostalgia-laced banana pudding for dessert instead. The only thing she wanted more of at the moment was the tiny taste she'd had of Steph's cherry cobbler.

"This *road*," Kim said as Steph cruised through yet another sharp curve. "I always wondered if they built it with this many curves because they ended up with extra concrete or something and wanted to use it up instead of hauling it back down the mountain."

Steph grinned at her for a quick second before looking ahead again.

"Ever seen an aerial view of this road? Or the whole ridge formation?"

"Well, no. Not that I remember. I know it's a lot of the same rock as Lightning Rock, right?"

"The same conglomerate, right. And that's *why* the road is built the way it is. It's tough to see with all the trees and undergrowth, but we're driving between a whole bunch of big outcrops of the same rock, all along through here. The ridge is broad up here, more than a lot of them are in our mountains, because of all the outcrops."

"Really?" Kim peered out her window, trying to spot what Steph was talking about. "I can't see any of them for the trees and brush."

"They're a ways back. The road builders followed the natural path where the mountain eroded, so they wouldn't have to blast nearly as much. These are still here because they're much harder than what was around them. Better for rocks not to be falling on the road all the time, too. That made it into a bit of an adventure to drive, but it was a smart choice."

Kim turned to look at Steph, at how her smile matched the excitement in her voice.

"Is coming up here to see Ivy all these years what got you into rocks? Geology, I mean."

Steph laughed, and Kim couldn't help grinning in return.

"It didn't hurt, I'm sure. It really started the first time I got a box full of them at a cave gift shop, remember those? There are some amazing caves over in Boun County, and near Wolf Branch and Estonoa. I never thought I'd get over how many different kinds of rocks there were in those boxes. You know, all of *sixteen* in my first set. Remind me to show you some of the aerial views, you'll love them. And my rather more extensive rock collection."

"I'll do that. Do you bring students up here for field trips?"

"Sure, I did once. I come up here a lot on my own, too. I brought a class last year before it got too cold. The honors geology group was willing to put in the time to hike. They're mostly seniors, so they're a bit more serious, with at least a little bit of sense. For general classes it's so much easier to get to Lightning Rock in town."

She laughed, and Kim smiled in return.

"For one thing we can *walk* to the Lightning Rock instead of trying to wrangle either a bus or a bunch of hormonal freshmen or brand-new teenage drivers. Can you imagine? If we made it up here in one piece, we'd spend the whole time worrying about them getting distracted and falling over the cliff, or slicing themselves to bits trying to climb on all these jagged rock formations. Some of the edges are sharp as knives."

Kim snorted and shook her head. "I'd rather not imagine. I know how crazy *we* were driving when we had half the chance."

She stopped herself from adding something about how they were usually driving in one car rather than caravanning together in a big group. But Steph seemed to pick up on the idea anyway. She was silent for a long moment, and the air between them felt uncomfortable for the first time since they'd sat down at Kay's.

"Did you say you come up here on your own?" Kim said. "Aren't you afraid you'll run into a bear or a bobcat or something? I've always heard rumors about mountain lions back in the mountains."

"Oh yeah, I've heard those rumors about mountain lions myself. I'm sorry to say that's really unlikely, but I have to admit I hope it's true. Don't worry, I keep...well, I'll just say I'm safe as long as I can get back to my car. Dad insisted, and for once I didn't argue. You know, once I moved back."

Kim tried not to groan when she realized she'd moved them from touchy conversational ground to downright rudeness.

"I'm so sorry, Steph. I didn't mean to make it should like you *should* be afraid."

"I think I'm the one who made it awkward," Steph said, talking too fast now. "Don't worry about it. The real field trips up here these days are for grownups. That's why I know the road so well. We get groups of geologists and rock hounds all the time coming up to check it out, especially Lightning Rock. It doesn't behave the way it should."

"Doesn't behave? What do you mean? How is a rock supposed to behave?"

"It's the lightning. We get too much of it for one thing. I know you remember the huge storms? If you got back a month ago, we haven't had one since. The one last night was a gentle shower compared to those. I mean the *really* big ones, where the lightning strikes so much?"

Steph slowed as they neared a gravel driveway off to the left, in the middle of one of the curves. It was so narrow and dim with trees thick overhead that it would have been easy to miss.

"Yeah, I remember those storms," Kim said. "My great aunt's house shook with the lighting and thunder. We got big storms in Georgia, but nothing that...well, that violent."

"Well, that's the thing. We get normal storms, sure, like last night. But the big ones are off the charts, at least in one way. We get way too many lightning strikes. That's how the town got named, of course. What I've wondered more and more is *why*."

Kim had lost all track of direction, but she thought the broad turn to the left Steph followed would lead toward the Lightning Gap side of the ridge rather than away from it. The level road was well-maintained, but even more narrow than the paved road.

She couldn't imagine something like a big delivery truck or a school bus trying to squeeze through the oaks, poplars, and pines crowded along the sides and soaring overhead.

"Something about the Lightning Stone being higher than everything else, isn't it?" she said. "Or the shape of the valley? I'm sure I wasn't paying attention in those classes as much as you were."

"No one was paying as much attention as me in those classes. Just look where I ended up. That geography explains part of it." She glanced at Kim as the car topped a small rise in the road. "Please tell me I'm not the only one who's heard about some kind of...magic around here."

Goosebumps raced up and down Kim's arms. "You're not the only one. I've heard it my whole life, too. Do you...you're a science teacher, Steph. Do you actually believe there's something to that?"

Steph stared at the road ahead, and Kim followed her gaze. What looked like a one-story building with a dark green metal roof angled up like a steep ski jump, making a narrow wedge of a house.

Ivy's house.

"Yeah, I'm a science teacher," Steph said. "Specializing in geology with a healthy dash of meteorology, of all things. That's about as solid and reality-based as it gets, really. Rock solid, you might say. The rocks do what the rocks do, and they don't change unless we do something to *make* them change. Or something in nature makes them change. Quick like lighting or a volcano, or slow like wind or water. No room for magic there at all, is there?"

She parked in a wide spot at the end of the long gravel driveway, beside a sturdy and well-cared for burgundy Jeep. Covered with broad unpainted wooden boards weathered dark with time, the house gradually rose from one story at this end to three on the far side. Kim loved how the tallest wall was made almost entirely of windows that overlooked all of Lightning Gap and the massive valley beyond.

Steph shut the motor off and gripped the steering wheel, still staring out the windshield. A thick berm covered with blueberry and huckleberry bushes, taller elderberry bushes with long delicate branches, and shorter gooseberry bushes covered in sharp thorns kept any errant drivers from inadvertently taking the plunge.

"All of that may be true about geology," Kim said, "but you believe there may be magic anyway."

Steph looked into Kim's eyes, with a smile that managed to be shy and challenging at the same time.

"And I believe there may be magic anyway. Ready for Ivy?"

"You know, I really am. If I remember her correctly, she's a serious dose of magic and reality all mixed up into one."

Kim leaned into the back seat to retrieve the cake—carefully and properly wrapped in a dish towel—making sure she had a solid grip. When she stepped out of the car, she nearly dropped it anyway. She barely managed to set it on the sedan's roof.

Ivy Gweddon stood behind the car, having somehow gotten herself out the door, across the short gravel walk, and into place without seeming to make a sound or cast a shadow. She wore the same sort of tan clothing Kim remembered, pants and a jacket and a rounded hat made of sturdy canvas. She stood a little shorter than Kim, and she was built just as solidly as her clothes and her house.

From the looks of the clothing and Ivy's nearly unlined face—all high cheekbones and big blue eyes—not a day had passed up here since Kim was seventeen years old.

Magic, or something stranger.

Steph turned quickly enough to scrape the gravels with her feet, but she didn't seem surprised by Ivy's abrupt appearance at all. She grinned and gathered Ivy in a big hug.

"It's been way too long, Ivy! I'm so glad to see you."

At the sound of Steph's voice, a series of loud, rapid-fire barks erupted from the front of the house. A lanky red dog built like a slender bloodhound came loping around the corner. Her tail curved high and proud over her back, and her huge eyes and mouth were lined in jet black.

She also shook her head and stretched, obviously just woken from a nap in the sun.

"Yeah, this is my newest guard dog," Ivy said, her voice confident but gentle. "Watch out, BeeGirl will cuddle and kiss you half to death. What brings you up here at long last, Steph? And is this really Kim Mullins standing right here in my yard?"

"This is indeed Kim," Steph said, with a smile that warmed Kim's full belly. "Just moved back from the big city. We met for lunch, and it occurred to me it had been way too long since I saw you. Even longer for Kim, so I figured it was time."

BeeGirl bounced over to Kim and immediately started living up to her reputation as an enthusiastic kisser. Kim didn't mind one bit, happy to take the time to give the soft, floppy ears a good scratch. BeeGirl wagged her tail so hard she whacked herself in the ribs.

"Any time is a good time." Ivy walked around the car, now making noise on the gravel like everyone else did, and hugged Kim while BeeGirl turned her considerable attention to Steph. "Welcome home, Kim."

Ivy's grip was warm and firm, and she smelled like fresh bread and some kind of earthy herbs.

"I'm glad to be back. Is BeeGirl the same kind of dog you had before?"

Ivy squatted and rubbed the dog's head and neck, shifting BeeGirl's loose, supple skin back and forth.

"Course she is. I've been lucky enough to have a bunch of different dogs in my life and known a whole lot more. But there's nothing sweeter on this earth than a redbone hound. That being said, you might want to grab whatever you've got perched on the car there. The only thing BeeGirl loves more than attention is anything she can wrangle into her belly."

CHAPTER 9

Steph settled herself on Ivy's huge porch, trying not to stare too much at either the bird's eye view of Lightning Gap, BeeGirl flirting shamelessly with Kim, or how Ivy didn't look like a single day had passed in twenty years.

The porch was screened all around, with the bottom sections shorter than most. That meant they could comfortably sit in a charming and mismatched collection of rocking chairs and still see the town spread out far below. Steph easily spotted the streets and buildings, probably because she'd spent so much time studying aerial views.

The same aerial views she hoped Kim actually did want to see rather than pretending.

Steph's chair was a more modern version, with precisely milled joins between all the wooden bits and no signs of warps or repairs. Tufted cushions made of soft green paisley fabric protected her from the wood. In fact, cushions on all the chairs were made of the same fabric, along with lap blankets hanging over the backs of several.

Even the huge dog bed on the porch's neat wooden floor —complete with a tall cushioned rim on three sides—was covered with the same fabric.

She had to admit the matching cushions kept furniture from at least five different eras looking like they were meant to be grouped together.

Kim sat in a much older chair that looked handmade, with careful repairs to the delicate curved arms and especially long rockers on the bottom. She wasn't rocking, because BeeGirl had captured Kim's knee, groaning and tilting her head from side to side. Kim's sweet smile showed how much she was enjoying delivering exactly the perfect scratches to the hound's sleek red head and black-tinted ears and chin.

Ivy slowly rocked in her own chair that Steph knew was more than fifty years old. More squared off in design, with enough thick layers of white paint that some of the curvy accents on the legs were disappearing. Ivy had the quiet, peaceful smile that said she was well contented with her situation right that minute.

She sipped from a heavy wine glass full of elderberry wine so dark it almost looked black. She'd given Steph and Kim what she called the beginner's wine. Barely fermented, much closer to juice than wine, with a sweet-tart flavor and earthy undertones.

Steph hadn't yet gotten old enough for the "expert"

version Ivy enjoyed. Or maybe she just hadn't gotten brave enough to ask for it yet.

With the drive off the mountain still ahead of her—possibly after it got dark—today was not the day.

BeeGirl drew in a huge, hitching breath, then let it out in a sigh so big her cheeks flapped. Unperturbed by everyone's laughter, she ambled over to her cushion, walked in a tight circle five times, and curled up with a satisfied grunt.

"My work here is done," Kim said. "Think I'll get a couple of years off my time in purgatory for making her sigh like that?"

"If that's so," Ivy said, "BeeGirl has surely cut more than a few decades off for me. Between her and all my other dogs over the years, even I might do okay in the hereafter. Now, I'm awfully glad to see you two, and even more glad Kay sent that spice cake. We'll have to break into it later. What else brings you all the way up here?"

"Mainly to visit with you and BeeGirl, honestly," Steph said. "It's been too long. And so you could see Kim. But yeah, there's another reason. Have you heard much about the guy that was missing from Laurel Gap recently?"

Steph noticed Kim looking sharply at her. She wasn't sure if she wanted to know why or not.

"Course I heard about that," Ivy said, rocking again. "Heard he turned up dead, too, not too far outside of town. Just because I'm a hermit up here doesn't mean I'm completely unaware of the world."

"Well, no, I didn't think you were," Steph said with a

laugh. "I wanted to make sure you knew is all. Dad said they're not sure what happened to the guy yet."

"That's what my cousin Jay said, too." Kim was red-faced, but she kept talking. "Some hikers found him. Stan Phipps was his name."

"Same as I hear," Ivy said. "That poor kid came up in a rough way of life. He was bound to end up in trouble. Still, a thing like this is unusual for anywhere near Lightning Gap. Your dad think so, too, Stephanie?"

Steph rubbed her arms against the chills. She trusted her father, but she still wasn't sure how well a protective order filed in another state would work.

Her father didn't know Bobby the way she did.

Or some of Bobby's friends.

"He thinks about the same, yes. Dad also thinks we're all perfectly safe. To tell you the truth, Stan Phipps might have been a piece of work. But he thought he was safe, too. I had to make sure you knew about what happened so you could do whatever you need to."

"Sounds to me like you, your father, nor anyone else knows much about what happened," Ivy said. "But I appreciate the warning all the same. I know she doesn't look a bit like it right now, but BeeGirl is quick to let me know if someone's around this place. A redbone hound is a better judge of character than any person I've ever met. And I'm plenty capable of handling any trouble from there."

Kim leaned forward in her chair, producing a creak from the old wood.

"What do *you* think happened, Ivy? If I'm remembering right, you usually know a lot more about what goes on in these mountains than pretty much anyone else."

Ivy's mouth twitched up in a quick smile.

"I generally do know a thing or two. But that's mostly because I've lived out here longer than most folks down in town have been alive. I haven't seen or heard more than your father, Stephanie. Or your cousin, Kim. On the other hand…"

She took a sip of her wine and closed her eyes for a few seconds.

"Can't say I agree with your dad that it's perfectly safe."

Steph drained her glass, wishing she had a bit of the stronger version. Ivy's words focused a fear that had been drifting around the bottom of her mind since she finally slammed the door in Bobby's face and kept going.

"Why is that, Ivy?"

Ivy rocked for several seconds. Long enough for Steph to breathe in and out twice, and share a worried glance with Kim.

"One thing about living where we do, and even more being from here, part of families with deep roots in this land. We're safe here. I'm sure you both heard that when you were growing up. I sure did. And I'm going to bet you heard it a lot more when you decided to come back, didn't you?"

Steph blinked. Even if she wanted to, she'd never had an easy time trying to fool Ivy.

"I heard it just yesterday," she said. "And plenty before that, even before I decided to come back."

"So did I." Kim nodded slowly. "My parents haven't lived

here for years, but they said that to me. And I don't have to tell you Auntie Venus said the same."

"I'm not a bit surprised," Ivy said. "Thing is I knew you'd *both* be back, probably before you did. Not because of what you might think, either. I know what some people say about me. How I'm supposed to be some kind of old mountain witch or some other such nonsense. That's not it, though I'd be damn proud to say so if it was."

She rocked in silence again, half smiling at BeeGirl twitching and barking in her sleep. Steph thought the rising and falling sound was eerie, as if BeeGirl were having a nightmare instead of any kind of good dream.

"It's something I recognized in you," Ivy said. "Something I know in myself and in a whole bunch of other people besides. Your great aunt Venus has it, Kim. Much as she loves going off all over the world, I always knew she'd come back home. Some people, when they leave, they take the very air of Lightning Gap along with them. Some little part of the magic. That always draws them back safe."

Steph did her best to keep her shiver from showing, but Kim and her sharp eyes seemed to notice. Kim always had caught things other people didn't.

Steph hadn't exactly been safe when she left Lightning Gap. And she wasn't the least bit sure she was safe now.

"But you said you don't agree that we're safe now, Ivy. Why do you think that?"

Ivy shrugged and shook her head.

"It's hard to argue we're absolutely safe with a murder happening just a short walk outside of town, isn't it? And now someone else has come up missing, from down in Wolf Branch. Word is they were last seen here in Lighting Gap."

She looked at Steph with one eyebrow raised, obviously wondering if that matched what she knew. Steph nodded once and Ivy went on.

"I don't know what all you two have heard, but that Phipps boy wasn't killed somewhere else and dumped here. I'm told there was more than enough disturbed ground all around him to make it clear his life ended where he fell. Where he was found."

"I didn't hear *any* of that, no," Kim said, her voice low and tight. "Not a whisper that someone else was missing. I don't think Jay knew about that at all. The only thing I heard about Stan Phipps is he didn't just fall down or freeze to death or anything easy like that. Jay said he wasn't...in the best condition when he was found."

Steph's full belly twisted, and she stared out at all the mountains rolling away from them. Ivy knowing about the second missing person was almost as bad as neither of them knowing about the third.

But not as bad as the images her mind wanted to conjure about how bad the body was.

Bobby had never actually gotten around to anything as violent as what happened to that guy found in the woods, not with her. He'd managed more than enough harm without drawing Steph's blood.

But he'd threatened her the night she decided to leave, even before she said a word to him about it. He'd threatened her in enough graphic detail that she knew she'd never have to work to imagine awful things happening to her again.

She'd lived it out in his words, and in her own nightmares.

"Jay told you the truth," Ivy said, jolting Steph out of her uneasy memories. "Stan Phipps didn't meet his end in an easy way. No matter how rough he lived his life, he didn't earn anything like that. What I'm telling you is for such violence to happen so close by here means something is...off. Out of place. Pushed out of true."

Cold settled into Steph's bones, bad enough to make her teeth want to chatter. She didn't want to give the awful thought any space inside her mind, so she tried another awful thought instead.

"I don't mean this to sound as terrible and mean as it does," she said, "but was it because he wasn't from here? He never lived here at all. And the other person, they're from Wolf Branch. Is that why such a bad thing could happen?"

"That doesn't seem right to me," Ivy said, shaking her head slowly. "Doesn't *feel* right is more honest. I've never felt anything like what's wrong right now before. I might even say the mountain sounds out of tune, or maybe one note in a hundred is wrong. But that one note is enough to sour the whole song."

Kim stared up at the plain yellow pine boards of the porch ceiling, then rubbed her face.

"I tried not to, but I have to ask. When did this start, Ivy? This feeling like something was broken?"

"You trying to ask me if I think it's because you came back home, Kim? Or because Stephanie did?"

Steph let out a small, bitter laugh before she could stop it.

"Kim just beat me to it. I was wondering the same thing."

The expression in Kim's eyes was so relieved, so grateful, that it drove most of the chill out of Steph's body. The warmth that rose up instead wasn't quite as uncomfortable as it might have been a few hours ago.

"The answer is, don't either one of you *dare* go thinking such things," Ivy said, fixing each of them with a fierce stare. "Hell, for all we know, you coming back kept whatever's wrong from getting worse, or happening sooner. Both of you being back here is a *good* thing, and that's all there is to it. Now tell me this. Did you feel safer once you settled in back home?"

Kim met Steph's gaze again, and the warmth intensified. Almost to the same heated curiosity and exploration they'd shared all those years ago.

They both nodded.

"Then what do we do?" Steph said, barely above a whisper. "What *can* we do? Will this mean Lightning Gap isn't as safe as it should be from now on? That it's spoiled forever?"

Ivy waited long enough to answer that Steph felt like she was going to scream.

"I'm sorry to say this, but I don't know. Like I said, old as I am, this is outside my experience. There might be clues to the whole thing there in the woods where that boy met his end, but that doesn't feel right to me. I'd say we'd be better off finding someone in town who might know more than I do."

Kim looked up, her eyes bright.

"We should all talk to Auntie Venus. She knows a bunch

of Lightning Gap history, and her friends do, too. I'd bet they would at least know where to look."

Steph wasn't sure she'd ever seen Ivy grin so big.

"I haven't seen Venus in longer than I'm going to admit to you or anyone else. I believe you're right. If the two of us can't figure it out we'd sure be able work out who to ask."

"Then what are you doing for dinner tonight?" Steph said before she lost her nerve. "Maybe Kim can call and see if Venus is up for company."

Kim raised both eyebrows and grinned as big as Ivy.

"I'd be glad to, but I'm sure it won't be a problem. She's been trying to get me to go out and socialize more. I've told her a hundred times that I'm not the only one who stays home too much."

"Now that you got my whole evening planned," Ivy said, throwing up her hands, but she was smiling. "You're welcome to use my phone right there in the living room. Venus used to like visiting with my hound dogs, maybe she won't mind if BeeGirl joins us."

"I don't see why not," Kim said, getting to her feet. "I'd sure like BeeGirl as my dinner guest. I'll be right back."

When the screen door closed behind her, Ivy turned to Steph and winked.

"You sure do stir up a storm when you come for a visit, Stephanie. Hope you don't mind me saying so, but you look like you've had a rough time of it. Doing better since you got back?"

Steph closed her eyes and leaned back, letting the rocker

carry her backward and forward. When she looked back, Ivy was smiling again.

"I'm doing a little bit better every day, Ivy. Much better today."

Ivy nodded once. "I'm glad to hear it. I always thought Kim was good for you, and you the same for her. Maybe we can all work this trouble out and bring some peace for both of you."

CHAPTER 10

Kim breathed deep and slow as Steph parked in the graveled space beside Auntie Venus's house, only a few feet back from where Kim usually parked herself.

Much discussion on the drive down about whether they should retrieve Kim's little sedan first had ended with a fairly reasonable compromise. Stop by here first, just in case Auntie Venus needed anything from town for dinner. That way they'd cut out at least one return trip.

Even if she didn't need anything, Steph insisted this still made more sense than her driving down, driving back up, then driving home.

Kim wasn't sure she agreed with any of that logic, but she wasn't about to turn down the chance to spend more time with Steph. She also put herself under strict orders to not read too much into Steph wanting to spend more time with her.

Time would tell how that turned out.

The sun had crossed over the house from the right side to the left on the way to disappearing behind the far end of the ridge. Kim still spotted the gouges she'd made in the gravel yesterday, driving and too caught up in thinking about Steph.

And now here she sat in Steph's car.

Steph, who naturally didn't miss the skidding mess, either.

"Do those gravels always get torn up like that? I can get someone to help you out with a better roadbed."

"No, no, that was all me. I came around through here yesterday, not paying enough attention. Nearly plowed into the back of my cousin Jay's SUV. A county model, even."

Steph stared at her wide-eyed for a second, but her twitching lips gave her away.

"You almost crashed a *Felten County* vehicle? Think of the waste of taxpayer money. And a council member's car, too? You'll end up as a bad example in my dad's new driver lectures."

Kim stared wide-eyed right back until Steph gave up and dissolved into laugher.

"I should probably sit in on one of your dad's lectures after driving in Atlanta for ten years. I'm sure speeding and tailgating aren't the only bad habits I've picked up."

Kim got out and backtracked enough to kick down some of the ridged gravel.

"I meant to get all this smoothed over," she said. "Got in too big of a hurry to meet you for lunch, I guess."

"I'm glad you did." Steph ducked her head, but not before Kim saw a sweet flush spread across her cheeks. "Come on, we better make sure we're not heading right back into town on a grocery run."

Auntie Venus met them at the kitchen door, most likely on her way down to the garden boxes. Today brought a relatively sedate outfit of chocolate brown pants and a jacket, but they were made of rich, heavy silk. The exotic cut and angular drape reminded Kim that the clothes had come from a long-ago trip to Bali. She'd outgrown her matching sunflower yellow version before she started high school.

A long gardening apron made of patchwork squares of odd fabrics—including several things Kim had outgrown—covered the silk.

"Oh *there* you are!" Auntie Venus exclaimed as if she hadn't seen Kim for months. "And I'm so glad to *see* you, Stephanie. If you're willing, I've got plenty for both of you to do, starting with bringing me a good solid handful of those white radishes. The kind that aren't all that hot. The ones you like, Kim."

Steph stopped Auntie Venus from careening back into the kitchen by grabbing her in a big hug. By the time Steph let go, all of them were giggling.

"I'm glad to see you, Venus. Now, since Kim knows what radishes to get, what can I do? Do you need anything from town?"

Auntie Venus stared at Steph with a puzzled frown for a few seconds, then shook her head.

"No, I can't think of a thing we don't already have here. Maybe you could run down to the deep freeze and bring us up four pork chops. They're over on the right."

Steph nodded once, winked at Kim, then walked out. Kim tried without any measure of success to hide her smile.

"Here, you'll want this to keep from getting dirt all over yourself," Auntie Venus said, slipping the apron off. "Looks like you've had a good day with Stephanie. I haven't seen you smile like that since you moved back home."

Kim slipped the loop of the apron over her head, then reached back to pull the ties forward around her waist. One of the apron's many deep pockets would be plenty deep to hold enough radishes.

"It's been great to catch up," she said, focusing on tying a sweet little bow rather than looking at her great aunt. "I needed to get out and stop feeling sorry for myself."

"You sure did, and I'm proud of you. Seeing your friend is doing you a world of good. Same as it will for me to see Ivy. Whatever else happens between you and Stephanie will turn out just the way it's supposed to."

She turned on her heel and headed back into the kitchen, leaving Kim laughing under her breath as she stepped outside on her radish errand.

When she'd first come to her own terms with being gay, she'd imagined other people had no earthly idea. Which she found out more and more was entirely untrue.

Getting herself used to exactly no one being all that surprised took longer than anyone *else* needed to adjust.

Just like back then, what she needed now was a bit of time to herself, and a stern bit of self-talk to hopefully get her quickly re-growing crush on Steph under control.

The bright white rock pathway to the garden beds crunched under her feet, and the evening breeze rolling down the mountain brought the promise of rain sometime soon. Kim had never had much of a weather sense in Atlanta, certainly not living downtown in the middle of all that concrete.

But something about being back home in Lightning Gap brought her meteorological awareness back full force. Nothing she'd ever studied so much as a natural sense she'd only stopped using for a while. When she thought about it on purpose, she decided the rain would actually be in a couple of days, and a good-sized storm would come along with it.

She barely had time to kneel beside the wooden box, knees on the row of concave rocks surrounding the whole thing, when she heard the clear sound of a heavy vehicle's tires crackling and popping along the driveway.

The sharp, unbelievably fast hound dog barks made it clear Ivy had arrived. So much for a bit of quiet time to herself, or her cautionary self-lecture.

Kim let her fingertips sink into the soft, almost fluffy soil around the long green radish leaves, feeling for solid shapes. She didn't know as much about gardening as she wanted to, but she loved the ritual and routine of it.

The bright green leaves against the black soil. The

shocking red as she gently pulled the long radishes loose, and the final white rounded tip. The earthy, rich scent of growing things.

The Jeep parked not far behind her, and Ivy called out the window between bursts of BeeGirl's joyful greeting.

"Okay if I let her out? I've got a leash, so it's no problem either way."

Kim dropped about ten of the radishes into one of the apron's wide pockets and got to her feet, brushing her hands together. Ivy was still in the Jeep, and she had her arms around BeeGirl's sleek, red, furry neck. Ivy's whole body shifted with all the wags.

"Sure, as long as you don't think she'll get lost trying to chase after a squirrel or something. We don't have cats or anything. Not yet."

Ivy leaned forward to push the door open, and BeeGirl seemed to launch herself straight out into the air. She hit the ground with a grunt, but it never slowed her momentum. She charged so hard she crashed into Kim's knees.

"You just saw me, you big goofball. Not even an hour ago. Have I changed so much you don't recognize me?"

BeeGirl paused in her exuberant wagging dance long enough to stare at Kim, head held to one side, as if to wonder how humans could ask such silly questions. Especially when there was greeting and exploring to do. She happily restarted her grin, wag, and dance routine when Kim knelt and held out her arms.

"BeeGirl, you calm yourself down," Ivy said, standing not

far from Kim with her hands on her hips. "You're going to knock Kim right over into that garden bed."

"She's fine. I gotta say, having someone this glad to see me is doing wonders for my self-esteem. I hope you like radishes. I'm not sure what Auntie Venus is going to do with them, but we've got plenty."

Ivy leaned forward and peeked into the apron's pocket. She'd changed out of her sturdy tan work clothes, but her midnight blue pants and shirt looked almost as tough.

"I always thought that was one of the best parts about Venus traveling so much. She's always happy to share whatever she learns when she gets back. Anything I can do to help?"

Something about her words or maybe her voice set BeeGirl off and running toward the front of the house, hellos concluded. Kim got to her feet again, now brushing at her knees.

The liberal coating of red hound dog hair might have to wait for a change of clothes.

"This was all she asked me to do, but she might have come up with something else by now. She sent Steph down to the deep freeze the second we walked in the door."

"I brought Kay's stack cake," Ivy said, "and a big bunch of the shiitake mushrooms I grow up at the house. Might have grabbed a couple of bottles of wine and something stronger on the way out, too."

Kim grinned as they walked toward the house. BeeGirl passed by behind them, letting out a half-growl, half-grunt with each leaping stride as she started into another rapid circuit of the house.

"Auntie Venus will put that all together into something amazing I never would have thought of."

Ivy detoured to her Jeep and retrieved two big bags made of faded denim. She kept hold of the one that sagged and clinked, handing the other to Kim. It was stuffed full of something, but it was surprisingly light.

Ivy raised her head and whistled so loud Kim jumped, but it brought BeeGirl trotting right to her side. She grinned and panted up at both of them with her tongue lolled out of her mouth.

"That run will keep her calmed down pretty good," Ivy said, opening the back door. "Hound dogs pretty much have two speeds. Run and sleep. Once she gets a good drink of water she'll pass right out."

Steph stood beside her great aunt at the long kitchen counter with the intent air of a student. As far as Kim could tell, the subject of the impromptu lesson was onion slicing. Steph held one hand on the counter beside Auntie Venus's onion-laden cutting board, her long, delicate fingers tucked under in imitation.

"Hey Ivy," Steph said, and to Kim's delight she blushed. "I've already sworn Venus to secrecy about the cooking lessons. I'm utterly clueless. My parents would be heartbroken that I decided to learn from someone else."

"They'll never hear a word of it from me." Kim fetched a wide, flat bowl and filled it with cool water. She added a rubber placemat and a towel to at least try to protect the dark green stone floor while BeeGirl milled around her legs.

"Lord, honey, don't worry about the floor," Auntie Venus said. "I expect I could drop a sledgehammer on it without hurting a thing."

True to Ivy's prediction, BeeGirl drank down most of the bowl, then wandered around looking for somewhere to nap. With Ivy's laughing permission, Auntie Venus directed BeeGirl to hop right up on the couch and make herself at home.

And true to Kim's prediction, Auntie Venus put all three of them to work on an absurdly good dinner of pork chops with mushrooms and onions, radishes sautéed along with their leaves, and buttery mashed potatoes. BeeGirl didn't even pretend to turn up her nose at a healthy dollop of potatoes added to the bag of kibble Ivy brought.

Turned out both Kim and Steph had room for a bit more food after all.

Once everyone slowed down and managed to put away at least small(ish) slices of Kay's stack cake, Auntie Venus brought out the most beautiful shot glasses Kim had ever seen.

Shaped like little half globes that fit in the palm of her hand, the gleaming black glass was etched in swirling patterns that revealed glittering gold underneath. The gold followed through inside.

"Where did these come from, Venus?" Steph said as she held hers up to the light in her fingertips. "They're lovely."

"Would you believe I found them in a thrift shop in

Atlanta? I stopped by when I was heading home from one of my visits with Kim just a couple of years ago. Kind of a shame to hide that blueberry liqueur of yours, Ivy. I can get something else."

A quart-sized canning jar that was every bit as plain as the glasses were gorgeous sat in the middle of the table, filled with indigo liquid. It had waited while the four of them got through two bottles of elderberry wine that was stronger than juice, but still on the mild side.

"We can see it just fine in the jar," Ivy said as she poured a bit of the liqueur into each sparkling black glass. "Now this stuff packs a real punch no matter how smooth it tastes. To tell you the truth, I didn't expect to be sharing this wonderful dinner with all of you when I had my afternoon tipple. If I have much of this fine blueberry hooch, BeeGirl and me will be claiming one of your guest beds."

Kim picked up her glass at the same time as everyone else, holding it close to her nose. The thick, almost syrupy liquid smelled like it had a bit of a kick, but the primary aroma was an intense blast of pure blueberry.

"You know you don't even have to ask, Ivy June Gweddon," Auntie Venus said. "Neither do you, Stephanie. This old house has plenty of room. I'll make sure to give every one of you a good dose of my hangover prevention tea before we head off to sleep, so don't you worry about that either. As far as what to drink to, I can't think of anything better than good food and good company."

She held up her glass and everyone else did the same.

"Good food and good company."

The liqueur tasted much like it smelled. A faint warning alcoholic hit, then what felt like an incredible explosion of concentrated fruit, complex and sweet and absolutely delicious. Dangerous indeed.

Kim wasn't surprised she and Steph only took sips, while Ivy and Auntie Venus finished theirs. Nor when the two of them exchanged a meaningful look and a nod.

"Now that we're all well-fed," Auntie Venus said, "I get the feeling we've got something to talk about that wasn't proper dinner conversation. Why don't you all fill me in?"

CHAPTER 11

Steph held her breath for a moment, perfectly balanced between wanting to know more about what might be going on in Lightning Gap and wanting to hold on to the blissful warmth of the day.

The strangely familiar comfort of spending so much time with Kim, as if not a day had passed and nothing had changed between them. The fact that so many things had changed *about* them only made their connection stronger.

Ivy gave her the same feeling of security and adventure with a thread of danger underneath as always. Even with Steph's newly born desire to keep herself out of risky situations when she possibly could, Ivy still delighted her.

Of course BeeGirl had won her heart from the first sweet wag.

Her impression of Venus as so brave and confident, so

exotic and worldly, hadn't changed a bit, either. Moving away for so long didn't make a bit of difference.

Having a belly full of good food for the second time that day made up for missing her parents' grand snack experiments for the first time since she'd gotten back home. They'd sounded more excited that Steph was staying out than disappointed. She suspected they would quite enjoy their alone time.

Add wine and Ivy's blueberry rocket fuel to the mix, and it was no wonder Steph felt like she floated on a toasty cloud of friendship.

Maybe more, depending on how things eventually went with Kim.

But she couldn't pretend worry and fear didn't gnaw underneath it all. The whole idea of this get-together was to get an idea of what was going on with two people missing and one dead, in a town where things like that truly didn't happen.

Knowing someone else was already missing—and keeping it to herself—only turned the whole thing up to painful levels.

She glanced at Ivy and Kim in turn, shrugged, and told Venus most of what she knew. Starting from the quietly excited rumors at school but stopping just short of telling her father's secret. No need to share her paranoid speculation about that or anything else until she had reason to.

When she finished, Venus closed her eyes and shook her head, a fine network of lines showing around her mouth and forehead.

"Looks to me like you have the same feeling I do," Ivy said.

Venus opened her eyes and stared down at her empty glass.

"That the Phipps boy wasn't some kind of accident. And that he won't be the last. I hate to speak a terrible thing like this out loud, but I'm afraid the poor soul from Wolf Branch simply hasn't been found yet."

Steph clenched and unclenched her hands under the table, determined not to be rude or seem unhinged. Or let everyone know how frightened she actually was.

"I don't like any of this," she said slowly and carefully. "But I don't understand what you're saying. Why are you so *sure* it's going to get worse? I remember what you said about the mountain feeling wrong, Ivy, but it didn't make sense to me."

As soon as the words were out of her mouth, she wished she could yank them back. She knew very well what it felt like when a bad situation was about to get so, so much worse.

She jumped when Kim touched her upper arm.

"I know what they mean, Steph," Kim said. "I knew when it was time to come back home. It felt like I was about to start making the same mistakes over again. With work, with...relationships. No matter what I tell people—including you, Auntie Venus—there was no logic to it. In my bones, I knew."

Steph leaned into Kim's touch. When Kim shifted to gently stroke her hand, Steph held on tight. Even though the contact was too much.

Not too fast, or too pushy. The warmth and the way their fingers still fit together felt like finally, truly coming home.

But sitting beside Kim and with two such amazing

women, and knowing that all of them loved her, Steph couldn't pretend any more.

After she'd struggled with herself and with Bobby so long and so hard and finally gotten herself away, she couldn't bear this kind of fear and violence in her life again.

Not right here at home.

"I know that feeling too," Steph said, her voice quivering not much above a whisper. "That's how I made the changes I did. I escaped, even though there was a while I never believed I would. I don't know if I can stand this kind of thing happening again. Not here."

"That's why we have to make damn sure it doesn't," Ivy said, leaning forward until Steph looked into her flashing, furious eyes. "I don't know what's wrong. What's broken, or at least out of place. But I'm not willing to ignore it or pretend I haven't noticed."

Kim squeezed Steph's hand and leaned closer until their shoulders touched. The old, lingering heat between them was more soothing than romantic for the moment.

Exactly what Steph needed.

"Me neither. I just got here. I'm not about to let it all go to hell."

Venus refilled her and Ivy's glasses with the liqueur and topped off Kim's and Steph's.

"Sounds to me like you came to the right place. And we're all ready to face this thing head-on. I say this is a fine time to dig into some of the real history of Lightning Gap, see if we can find something to help us. I can't think of a better place to start than Odds and Endings."

Steph smiled as a little bit more of her worry slipped away. She'd turned to the Seagons—the wonderful and strangely ageless couple who owned the Odds and Endings bookstore —more than once when it came to the odd weather around Lightning Gap.

Even with that and her own love of meteorology, she'd struggled to keep up with the strange patterns of off-season electrical storms over the past few months.

She knew history teachers often depended on the Seagons and their incredible bookstore as well.

Kim laughed as she picked up her glass, not letting go of Steph's hand.

"I loved that bookstore as a kid. I'd love to pay the Seagons a visit for any reason."

Steph picked up her own glass and held it up, ready to tap with the others.

"To Odds and Endings. And to figuring this thing out and putting a stop to it."

CHAPTER 12

The one change Bobby made after Steph deserted him was in his office at home. The one part of the house he'd managed to keep more or less to himself, and *for* himself, with minimal interference.

The space was less than half of what he enjoyed at work, with one puny window that looked out over their boring suburban backyard. Neatly trimmed green grass, tame maple and dogwood trees, ordinary rounded flowerbeds with predictable, low-maintenance specimens tucked inside.

At nearly midnight on a Friday, all Bobby saw was the irregular orange glow of streetlights and the city in the distance.

The room itself had changed little from the day they'd moved in. Same flat brown carpet, same nondescript tan paint on the walls. A standard flat, frosted white light fixture in the middle of a matching white ceiling.

Perfect for a nursery, the borderline manic realtor claimed, widening his eyes at both Bobby and Steph. Bobby had wondered then as much as now what sort of self-respecting parent would shove all the clutter and crap that came with children into a room little better than a closet.

But he'd laughed along when Steph did, noticing how her laugh had an artificial edge. A slip-up Bobby would never make.

He'd claimed the room as his own before they'd ever moved in, offering to turn a useless space into a home office rather than taking up one of the four bedrooms. A tiny white desk barely big enough to hold two monitors and a charging station for his preferred model of cellular phone wedged against one wall, with just enough space left over for a matching bookshelf and a chair.

Uninspiring, certainly. But adequate for needs too personal and private to risk doing at his real office.

Steph had of course managed to make her presence known. The chair was a gift from her, for one thing. An absurdly expensive brown leather monument to conspicuous consumption he never would have allowed at his office, no matter how comfortable it turned out to be.

Bobby adjusted the lumbar support to a different position, leaned forward to stretch some of the tension out of his upper back, and resumed scrolling through news reports from a cluster of insignificant little towns back in Virginia.

He'd never trusted the internet connection at work as much as the private browsers he had set up at home.

Steph had intruded even more with silly knickknacks she

was convinced would make the tiny space feel more pleasant. A huge framed photo of his parents' house back in Virginia, supposedly in the family for ages. One of Bobby's more effective fictions.

Pictures of him and Steph on their honeymoon in Bermuda or on some other expensive vacation. Even cheap, tacky snow globes she somehow believed were endearing.

And Bobby never bothered to let her know how much he resented her intrusions, her assumptions about what would make him feel at home.

The night she'd run sobbing out the door and back to Virginia, he'd hauled every scrap of it out to a remote dump site he was familiar with. Far into a scrubby wooded area just over the Indiana border.

Remote enough that he didn't hesitate to reduce everything to the smallest possible pieces and burn every bit to smoking cinders.

No one ever noticed, or bothered to report it if they did. Just like anything else that happened at that dump site.

His vigorous activities that night helped keep him from getting in his own car and taking action to retrieve Steph. Aside from the immediate satisfaction, even in the moment he knew nothing good would have come from that.

Now his office suited him so much better, far more than he'd ever let anyone see out in the world. Nothing but the smooth, tan walls, all Steph's nail holes repaired and painted over and invisible.

The blank white desk. The empty brown carpet and

useless, pitiful excuse for a closet shoehorned into a room that already wasn't much more than a glorified closet itself.

Only the monitors, charging station, nondescript black box of a computer, and that stupidly expensive office chair remained to show anyone had ever spent time inside.

He had added a second charger to accommodate both of his phones. No need to hide the second one from a wife who might suddenly develop reasonable powers of observation. Not any more.

Bobby switched from the dull news reports to the potentially more interesting feed from local law enforcement, laughing out loud at the idea of this cramped architectural miscalculation ever serving as a nursery.

The harsh bark of laughter sounded perfectly right inside the empty house.

Not that he and Steph hadn't made a gratifying habit of at least practicing all the different ways he could have gotten her pregnant. He never would have chosen her as his nod to normality if she hadn't been willing, eager, and skilled in that particular spousal duty.

Her impressive physical attributes would have surely made nice-looking children, especially combined with his own less flashy but more than acceptable appearance. She remained a bit on the skinny side to be sure, but with good-sized tits to make up for that, and hair perfect for passing along. Their offspring would have been healthy, intelligent, and attractive enough to add to his credibility and his cover.

Bobby ran his fingertips through his short brown hair, pressing hard enough into his scalp to leave pulsing little sensations behind. Working at home freed him from worries about keeping his corporate-neat appearance intact.

No matter how many times he'd mentioned kids, or how many times he'd heard Steph talk about having them, she'd never been willing to do anything about it. She'd quietly and stubbornly kept her birth control implant throughout their marriage.

When he asked her why—only at appropriately playful or tender moments—she would only say she wasn't ready. Or it wasn't time yet.

Then she changed the subject.

He'd wondered more and more since she left if some part of her hadn't sensed who he really was. How much his fake air of normality covered up.

If somehow in that one area if nowhere else, Steph had suspected her charming husband's true nature.

An ordinary two-line note in the Felten County report yanked his attention away from his thwarted interest in fatherhood. He leaned forward and clicked through to the full report.

Heat stirred in Bobby's middle as he read about a random missing person case and its unfortunate resolution. One Stanley Gene Phipps of Laurel Gap, Virginia. Found dead just outside of Lightning Gap, Virginia.

Cause undetermined (or at least unreleased), foul play undetermined.

The first of Bobby's associates who'd failed at the simple task of keeping an eye on his wandering wife.

Failed at continuing to live too, apparently.

A couple of quick searches—one public, one decidedly private and likely illegal—turned up nothing about the other two pathetic fools. At least so far.

Exactly what he should have expected from those three, not a brain cell shared between them.

Except for one of them, theoretically still in the land of the living. He and Bobby had shared a certain...compatibility when it came to their games of choice back then.

He could admit inside his own office, inside his own head, how that one going missing was a surprise.

An unpleasant one.

Bobby closed the search window and shut down the computer. A glance at both phones showed no messages or anything else to worry about.

He sat back in his top-of-the-line chair and kicked off enough to spin in a slow circle.

The news about Stan Phipps wasn't much of a surprise at all. Not even what he'd call worrisome.

Frustrating, sure. Something to keep an eye on going forward.

The corpse outside his disloyal wife's hometown was mostly...interesting.

The most interesting thing since Steph left.

That was enough to capture and hold Bobby's considerable attention.

CHAPTER 13

Much as Kim wanted to invite Steph into her own bedroom, or join her in the guest room, the other feeling she got loud and clear was that would be a mistake. Maybe not always, and maybe not for long.

But for tonight, and especially with two other women in the house, she'd be better off giving Steph time.

She wasn't sure she was ready hear what Steph had really gotten herself away from in Louisville, anyway.

Finding her something to sleep in, though, and taking it down the hall to the guest room was more or less inevitable. Especially after Auntie Venus made it clear that's what she was doing for Ivy as she settled into the guest room on the second floor.

So with the tingles and blueberry fire of that last drink still rippling through her—along with the mellow, bittersweet warmth of Auntie Venus's hangover tea—she gathered up a pair of shorts and a t-shirt and headed over.

Her own bedroom and one guest room were on the bottom floor, along with the beloved and always-full deep freeze. Washer and dryer, too, which was one of the few things she'd managed to convince Auntie Venus to let her handle.

This level hadn't been remodeled nearly as often or as consistently as upstairs, which left it looking much like it had when Kim was a kid. In fits and starts, anyway. That meant pastel flowery wallpaper and flat blue carpet in the hall, and beds decorated with earth toned fluffy comforters and far too many pillows.

After a quick knock and Steph's quiet answer, Kim reminded herself to take it easy and walked in.

Steph had kicked her shoes off, but otherwise she looked the same as she had at dinner. Maybe with her cheeks a bit flushed from the alcohol, which only made her irresistible curly red hair and fair skin look even better.

She sat cross-legged on the gigantic brown comforter with a huge, thin book in her hands. A book with an embossed cover with a stylized image of the Lightning Rock. Kim recognized their senior high school yearbook and tried not to groan.

"Where did you find that thing?" she said, dropping into a brown chair shaped like a cushioned box. "I thought I had them all safely hidden away."

"You must have missed one." Steph flipped the book open on her lap. "It was on that shelf over there calling my name."

The plain wooden shelf on the wall opposite the bed was stuffed full of more yearbooks and even family photo albums that were surely much worse.

Kim tossed the t-shirt and shorts onto the bed and smiled, but she half-covered her eyes with one hand.

"How bad is it? I don't think I've looked since I left home."

Steph shrugged as she flipped another page.

"No worse than they are now, though I guess the page layout is a lot easier." She drew back and smiled. "There you go. Got us both at once so it's all over with."

Kim got up and sat as far away from Steph as she could despite her best instincts. They both leaned against the wall as they had so many times during the time captured in the yearbook.

The image was of the Science Club all gathered to test out the bridges they'd built out of toothpicks. A bizarre collection of...well, spindly or overly thick or just plain odd toothpick contraptions sat on a long table in the gym, with the group of builders sitting on the bleachers behind it.

Kim's eyes went right to herself and Steph in the back row. Shoulders and heads together, grinning back at the camera. Both of them with longer hair and the same black t-shirt with a white atom on front as everyone else.

At the height of their relationship back then. Emotional and physical.

Both of them certain no one suspected a thing.

"What a bunch of nerds," Kim whispered, blinking back tears.

"Yeah. Thought we had the whole world in front of us for

the taking. We're not exactly old maids or anything now. But everything feels much more...I don't know, narrowed down."

"I didn't exactly expect to be living back here. Pretty much in my Auntie Venus's basement, no less. Couldn't hack it in the big city and had to scurry back home."

Steph leaned her head forward and mock-glared at Kim.

"How long did you live in Atlanta?"

"I went to college there. So since I was eighteen."

"You mean you lived there longer than you did here? Nineteen years? And you call that not being able to hack it? Or, maybe you just decided you needed a change."

Kim leaned over and turned the page, thankfully to one with no pictures of either of them.

"Well, if you want to look at it that way. I guess so. If I could only figure out exactly what change I need, maybe I'd make some progress."

Steph snorted. "You're way ahead of me, anyway. I'm back with my parents, and I don't have any plans past getting through the next day."

Kim's hand twitched with wanting to touch Steph. She knew she should change the subject back to safer ground. But then Steph had brought it up.

"At least you're working, doing something you love. Listen, you know you don't have to tell me anything you don't want to. But are you okay, Steph? Now, I mean?"

Steph turned another page, nodding slowly. Kim had the feeling neither one of them was looking at the yearbook any more.

"Since you said *now*, I can say I'm okay. Because I can

compare it to before, you know? Now I'm working, sure. But I'm on antidepressants, and I talk to a therapist online twice a week. Three times if I need it. Compared to where I was a year ago, though, you bet your ass I'm okay."

Kim closed her eyes, not sure what to say or do. Brushing back Steph's hair and maybe holding her hand again felt like the most natural thing in the world.

It also felt like Steph really needed to take the lead in anything like that, just as much as she did in talking about her past.

"I'm so sorry, Steph. Whatever happened, I'm sorry."

Steph looked at Kim again, this time with her head leaned back against the wall.

"I appreciate that. I know you didn't ask, and a lot of people would rather I didn't tell. So I'll just say the guy I married turned out to be a world-class asshole. Not just to me, either, but I guess I was the safest outlet for it. His favorite for sure before it was all said and done. I think Bobby liked to scare people and get control over them for fun in the beginning. Then it...took over everything else in his life."

Kim clenched her jaw, wishing she had some other way, any other way through this. She didn't want to hear another word. But she'd never hurt Steph's feelings by saying so.

"Did he...hurt you?"

"I used to try to justify the whole thing so I could answer no to that question. Can you believe that? I tied myself in knots trying to focus on how *at least* I had a place to live. How *at least* he held down a great job. How *at least* I never had broken bones, or all that many bruises, even. He never drew blood, not once. Not from me."

Steph drew in a shuddering breath.

"Now I think all of that is only true because I left before he worked himself up to really focusing on me."

She closed the yearbook and set it down, creating a little rectangular valley in the absurd puff of the comforter.

"I haven't really talked to my parents about this. Nothing more than the bare bones of it. No one besides Bobby, the police, and my therapist know anything close to the truth. I'm sure Ivy's concoctions have something to do with me talking now. So does sitting here with a friend."

Kim managed a smile and touched Steph's arm for a quick second.

"We always did tell each other everything, didn't we?"

Steph laughed under her breath and stared down at her hands in her lap.

"Sure, for a long time we did. Until the very end." She pressed her lips together and shook her head once. "Never mind that. Another time. Honestly, Kim, if you don't want to hear this, it can be another time, too. Or even never. I have my shrink appointments already set up for next week."

Kim rubbed her mouth so she could take a second to check inside and see how she felt.

No, she didn't want to hear this.

Yes, she was terribly curious to know what Steph meant about the very end of their high school relationship. Her own feelings about that were...complicated. Working through that together at some point would surely be a good thing no matter how it turned out.

Most importantly, though, yes, she wanted more than anything to be Steph's friend again. And to be a good friend, even when she was scared of hearing this particular truth.

"I told you I'm here if you want to talk, Steph. I meant that. When *you're* ready, I'll listen to anything you want to tell me."

CHAPTER 14

Steph closed her eyes, shutting out the insanely fluffy comforter, the so-called earth tones she'd gotten sick of decades ago, the potentially mortifying yearbook.

She concentrated on the cool wall against her back. The soft bed underneath her. The quiet security of being in an underground room, something she'd loved her whole life.

The lingering fruity taste of the blueberry hooch she'd probably had a tiny bit too much of. That mixed surprisingly well with the refreshing dose of Venus's warm hangover tea.

Thankfully the brain fog effect of all the alcohol—hopefully without the headache to come—was tempered by her second pleasantly full belly of the day.

And the solid, familiar, and entirely new sensation of Kim sitting beside her. The faint, clean scent of the clothes she'd tossed onto the bed, and the way her hand warmed Steph's whole body in one too brief touch.

Steph didn't need the words of her shrink or any of the books she'd read to know getting romantically involved with someone new was a terrible idea right now. Someone *not* so new couldn't be much better. Especially someone who'd just made a huge life change of her own, for reasons Steph didn't yet understand.

But that same wonderful therapist and her parents and the few friends from college back in Austin that she was still in touch with kept encouraging her to make new friends. And to rely on the ones she already had. The friends she still had.

Being married to Bobby—and living with years of him making sure she lost contact with more friends than she could possibly make—taught her how much those connections mattered.

The strongest connection she'd ever had outside of her family waited, right now. Someone she might want to spend a whole lot more time with, when they were both ready.

So maybe it was finally time to open her mouth and start talking.

"I met Bobby when I was on summer break from college my senior year. All us geology majors were supposed to be exploring interesting sites near where we lived so we could report back. Sort of our own field studies that we could practice, share with each other, and use to learn about different parts of the country. Anyway, I'd done all I could with Lightning Gap at the time, so I headed over to Laurel Gap."

She glanced at Kim to make sure she wasn't already zoned

out, or didn't have that deer-in-the-headlights, please-stop-talking look Steph knew too well.

Kim only nodded.

"I've often thought I should have gone to Bountyfield instead to check out all those weird new caves. I still need to do that. So, Bobby seemed very sweet at first. I'm told sociopaths usually are quite charming. Well, he charmed me all the way down the aisle and off to Louisville to start our new lives together."

She held her left hand up, relieved to see no trace of the tan line or indentation her wedding ring had left behind for so long.

"That was good at first, too. Marriage. He got a good job, middle management at a tech company, on the way up, and fast. I was teaching in a great school system, and I loved it even more than I expected. I think the *normal* got to him. The successful, happy married couple routine. He needed other people to bleed off his...impulses. That way he could keep me in the dark longer, I guess. So he started finding those people. Gamblers. Addicts. Immigrants who needed to protect their status, or keep it hidden. Anyone he could hook and get under his control."

Steph picked up the shirt Kim had brought and ran her fingers over the soft fabric. Dark green that would look great on her with her hair and coloring, too.

She wondered for a second if Kim had thought of that when she picked it out.

"Once he had his targets, the game was officially on.

Bobby wasn't into physically hurting people, not very often. What he got off on was screwing with people's minds. Making them do or say things they wouldn't normally do. Making them believe they were crazy, or worthless, or so desperate for his help that they'd put up with anything he did or said."

She glanced at Kim again, this time looking for the "Well, I would *never* put up with that kind of behavior" expression.

Not a trace of it. Kim only looked sad.

"I'm still not sure how he managed to get me. I would have sworn to you before it all happened that I'd spot someone like that a hundred miles away. Someone who was only out for control and manipulation would set off every single alarm I had. Or so I thought. Turned out I was every bit as easily manipulated and maintained as anyone he met off the street. Easier, probably. He knew all my weaknesses."

"That can happen to anyone, Steph. They're good at it. Master monsters."

That surprised a laugh out of Steph, one she was profoundly grateful for.

"He certainly turned out to be a master monster. As the years passed, he graduated to forcing people to pay him for his little schemes. Not because we needed the money, we were fine there. More than fine. It was more because he could make them do it. That fed his ego. The less they had to give, the more it jacked him up. Everything started to change about three years ago when I found his stash."

She laughed again, and the sound and taste were bitter.

"I was after Christmas ornaments of all damn things. We

had this weird storage shed built against the side of the house for stuff like that. But when I went to get them, everything felt...out of place. Like it was all there, but every bit of it had been shifted by a few millimeters. He never would admit he'd done a damn thing, of course, but I'd swear he did move everything just so I'd notice."

Steph gathered her courage and put her ringless left hand flat on the comforter peaks and valleys between them.

After a second that felt like a hundred years, Kim covered it with her own hand.

"I believe he moved the stuff so he could escalate with me. Why else would he have put the money out there, right in the middle of the ornaments and stuff? Right where I would find it. My fingers brushed against this slick plastic thing when I pulled out the box of lights. He'd stuffed all the cash into a cold bag. You know those cheap things you could get at the grocery store years ago? Not the good ones anyone would have actually taken care of."

"Yeah, I know. The silver ones."

"That's it. Who knows where in the world he found one. So I pulled out one of those silver cold bags shaped like a huge, hard brick and wrapped in duct tape. I had no idea what it was, but the fact that I *didn't* know cracked the perfect little denial shield I'd built up around myself. I brought it inside to ask him about it. Didn't open it or anything. Just put it on the kitchen counter. Everything went to hell when he got home."

Steph closed her eyes, making sure she didn't let herself

get too far back into that horrible night. Her shock when Bobby screamed at her, then anger when he accused her of spying and trying to steal from him.

His fury that had her cowering in a corner without him even lifting his hand toward her. The way she'd ended the night curled up in a ball right there on the floor, in the middle of all that money after he sliced the bag open and threw it at her.

Sobbing after the awful, cruel things he'd said.

"From then on, he still kept his other targets. In fact, he started getting bolder with them. Enough that a few finally found the courage or just got so scared that they walked away. He didn't much care by then, you see. He had me to take their place. By the time Memorial Day came around that year, he had me believing white was black, up was down. That I forced him into all that borderline criminal activity somehow. That I deserved everything he could throw at me, and everything he supposedly held back because he was so *merciful*."

She opened her eyes and risked a peek at Kim. Her eyes were red and her brow drawn down, but she still held Steph's hand.

"I got comfortable with the fact that all of his failings were entirely my fault. I accepted it all, took responsibility. He successfully followed the abuser's playbook and cut me off from my friends up there too, and more from my family then I want to admit. In my mind, either I'd driven him to it or I'd let him down. Including the fact that we never had kids. He brought it up from time to time, but he played it off like he was just curious. Like it didn't matter to him either way. He never admitted until the end that he saw that as one of the *duties* I'd failed at. Thank the gods I escaped that extra layer of nightmare, being forced to co-parent with him."

Steph took a big breath and blew it out through her lips, one of the best tricks she'd learned over the last few months. Blowing all the words and thoughts and memories away.

Every time she did it, the corroded, polluted places inside her ran a tiny bit cleaner.

"What changed for you?" Kim said, squeezing Steph's hand. "What made you finally walk away?"

"I ran into one of Bobby's old marks. Or he came and found me, I should say. A sweet, gentle guy from Senegal. Ansou. One of the immigrants who had the bad luck to run across my husband when he was new to the country and desperate to do everything right. Bobby caught Ansou alone on a moving job, said he saw him stealing things out of the truck, which of course he wasn't. Ansou was so afraid he'd get deported that he went along with Bobby's bullshit for a couple of years."

Steph turned her hand over and laced her fingers through Kim's.

"Bobby did the same thing to people in conference centers, hotels, restaurants. Men, women, Americans, immigrants, white, black, everything in between. As long as he could find even a sliver of insecurity or fear or weakness, he'd start chipping away until he could get his fingers in and start digging. Ansou finally walked when his wife arrived from Senegal and helped him get his confidence back."

"That's horrible. What did he say to you?"

Steph stared at the narrow wooden boards of the ceiling, knowing her face was turning red with shame. Understanding how it all happened—how she'd been manipulated too—didn't take away all her feelings of responsibility after all.

"He showed up during the summer, back in July. Met me in the parking lot at the garden center. By then I was making up for my complete lack of a social life by obsessing over working in the yard. Ansou was an American citizen by then. Thank goodness Bobby didn't manage to mess that up or scare him into going back home. He asked my name, then asked me why I didn't make my husband stop. I pretended not to know what he meant, but in my heart and my gut I knew."

Kim shook her head. "He can't blame you for what Bobby did. That's not fair."

"No, he didn't blame me. We stood there in the sun for almost an hour, and he told me the whole thing. I cried the whole time. Partly because I felt awful for Ansou and ashamed at what Bobby had done. But mostly because I couldn't pretend Bobby wasn't doing the same thing to me any more. When I got home that night, he was furious. Worse than with the brick of money."

"Did he know you talked to Ansou?"

"I don't think so, I really don't. Honestly, I think he felt the change in me. He sensed that I'd finally woken up, or at least started to. I believe that was the closest he came to actually hurting me, physically hurting me. He didn't touch me, but he told me all about what he'd do when he did. In gory, disgusting detail. Even his *voice* sounded different, Kim, like someone had taken over his body. Or the man I thought I knew had left it. Anyway, *I* left that night. Slammed the door in his face, got in the car, and didn't stop until I got to Lightning Gap."

CHAPTER 15

Kim struggled to keep still, did her best to keep her breathing somewhere near even and calm. She only managed not to clench her fists because Steph held one of her hands.

The truth was she'd never been more angry, more bursting with gut-twisting fury, in her entire life.

She expected Steph to be as shaking and red-faced as she felt. But Steph actually looked and felt calm. Her breathing was slow and deep, her grip on Kim's hand light.

Kim had no idea how she possibly did it.

"God, Steph. I'm so sorry. And I'm so glad you came back home."

Steph rested her head on Kim's shoulder, saying more than any words could have.

"Did you ever..." Kim stopped with a little shake of her head. "No, wait. Listen, if you don't want me to ask *any* questions, I won't. And if you don't want to answer anything specific, just tell me."

Steph nodded, her red curls shifting against Kim's shoulder and neck, raising chills all along her arms.

"I'll tell you. Go ahead and ask, Kim. I just dumped a gigantic pile of yuck all over you. The least I can do is answer a question or two."

"Okay. Don't forget I wanted you to tell me, okay? I feel weird about asking this one because I know who your father is, but you *do* have some kind of protective order against this asshole, right? Please tell me you do."

"Oh, I do. Dad helped convince me to get that ball rolling, but more people than you'd believe came forward once the word got out. Turns out Bobby got all kinds of sloppy in the end. Picked his targets too close together. Where they could find out about each other."

She laughed, but the only trace of humor in it was far more bitter than sweet.

"He was drinking by then, too. A lot. I don't think I mentioned how one of his favorite games was buying alcohol for people, did I? Not because they were underage or anything like that. He did it to help them hide their drinking from people who cared about them. To help them keep lying, and keep feeding their addiction."

"And then the addiction started feeding on him." Kim clenched her teeth, remembering friends who'd fought that battle long and hard. And some who didn't make it through.

"Bobby's demons rode him the whole time, but yeah. I think booze is the one that might prove too much for him someday. His own family crap helped drive him to that, to tell you the truth. Kind of fitting, really, as much as he got off on twisting the knife in other people."

Kim resisted the urge to put her arm around Steph, to do what little she could right that second to make sure Steph knew no harm was going to come to her.

Not while Kim drew breath and could put a stop to it.

Not to mention Auntie Venus, Ivy, and BeeGirl all more than willing to do the same.

"Is he...did he go to jail?"

"Not yet. Much as he escalated toward the end, he was very good at staying just this side of breaking the law. Breaking morals or crossing ethical lines? Absolutely. But his self-preservation instinct is way too strong for him to randomly break the law. I won't say he wouldn't have, though. If I hadn't gotten out."

"Last one for right now, then I suppose we really should get some rest. Was Ansou one of the witnesses? For the protective order?"

Steph shifted and sat up, and once Kim saw her happy, confident smile, she didn't even mind the separation.

"He was one of them. That day in the parking lot, he gave me an email address. One of those free ones, not anything that could easily be traced back to him. He told me to let him know if he could help me. Or help keep Bobby from hurting anyone else. He not only showed up, he brought several others with him."

"And he's safe now?" Kim said, not the least bit guilty about sneaking one more question in.

"He is, with his wife and a brand-new baby boy. I don't know *where* he is, and I don't want to know. But I know he's safe and doing well."

Kim leaned forward, looking up at Steph.

"Same as you. Safe and doing well. Thank you for telling me, Steph. I know that can't be easy."

Steph shook her head, then tilted it to the left and the right.

"I wouldn't say it's fun, no. But it gets easier every time I tell it. I think it bleeds a tiny bit of the poison out. Like using a little needle to start draining a nasty infection. I'm sorry to hit you with everything at once like that."

Kim squeezed Steph's hand, then let go and scooted forward to the edge of the bed.

"I said I would listen, remember? As much of a hermit as I've been since I got back home, I don't say that lightly. Just wait until I'm ready to share *my* tales of woe from the last ten years."

Steph got up in one smooth motion, taking the shorts and t-shirt with her.

"I'm ready when you are." She leaned over, kissed Kim's cheek, and walked to the bathroom door. "I'm glad we had the whole day together. Strange to say after everything I just told you, but it's been wonderful. Night."

"It sure has. Night."

Kim stood as Steph pulled the door closed behind her. She picked up the yearbook, resisting an oddly strong urge to flip through the whole thing and find all the pictures of the two of them together.

She only resisted for an instant. She tucked it under her arm instead, closed the guest room door quietly, and got back to her room as fast as she could.

Muttering to herself the whole way.

"Forget everything you're thinking about, Kim. Put it right the hell out of your head. No way Steph is interested in a relationship with you or anyone else after what she's been through."

She flopped belly first onto her own bed, much like she would have done back in high school even on a decidedly more modern purple comforter. The smooth cotton was much warmer and noticeably less fluffy than the near-antique in the guest room. The yearbook still closed in front of her barely made a dent.

Hell, she wouldn't be surprised if Steph *never* wanted to get involved with anyone again. Not after that nightmare.

The best Kim could offer would be her true and sincere friendship, and that's exactly what she would do.

No matter how much she might want more herself.

And of course when she flipped the book open, she was staring at the same image of the two of them. Thick as thieves, Auntie Venus might correctly say. No one who knew them would have said otherwise.

On the day that photo was taken—even with the way rumors flew with high-school fuel injection—Kim remained convinced she and Steph were the only two who knew exactly how close they were.

She flipped several more pages, her brain softly noting the other kids that were part of her life back then for whatever reason. More nerdy science club buddies, fellow athletes from her days on the track and volleyball teams.

Other school newspaper writers, drawn to the power and drama of words and information no matter how minor their reporting of vital high school issues seemed to Kim's adult mind.

A reasonable number of kids she didn't much like at the time and hadn't seen since. Some who felt the same about her. Thankfully nothing all that harmful or serious.

A few girls who'd played a role in her youthful fantasies and tentative explorations, a few guys who'd done the same with Steph. Giggling with Steph about those awkward attempts had been one of Kim's first lessons in being a good friend rather than some kind of teenaged stalker.

Or a confirmed psychopath like Steph's ex, doing everything possible to keep Steph isolated and alone.

Kim brushed away a tear before it could fall on the glossy page.

She flipped another page and let out a breathy laugh.

This time she and Steph weren't even the focus of the photo. The Drama Club was posed on the lawn in front of the school, each of them in a different costume from one of their productions that year.

Several students were seated on the concrete and brick steps behind them, basking in the sunlight and warmth of a spring day lunch hour.

She so clearly remembered the details of that day, the *sense* of it.

The low mutter of conversation around her, laughter from

the group in the photo shoot. The scent of lilac drifting on the soft breeze. The cold, fizzy, bittersweet burst of Coca-Cola across her lips and tongue.

The warmth of Steph's leg pressed against her own, their shoulders and arms together. Lingering heat and thrills of excitement coursing through Kim's heart and belly and lower down. Echoes of the intense explosions between them the night before.

The first time they'd properly made love.

Still the most erotic experience of Kim's life.

That day was when they'd abandoned worrying about anyone knowing about the two of them after weeks of sneaking around, encouraged by other openly gay couples they saw in the hall each day.

Between that and crossing such a huge emotional and physical line together, hiding didn't make sense any longer.

Kim shook her head and flipped the pages, stopping to dash away tears that slipped over before they could soak in and leave a mark of how she felt right now rather than a memory of how she'd felt then.

She stopped at a much safer section full of the various sports teams. At least she wasn't the only one who looked strangely adult and endearingly gawky at the same time.

Or the only one destined to make questionable choices in the near future.

Her relationship with Steph had intensified over those last few heady weeks before graduation and the end of summer. Before it all came to an abrupt and painful end thinly disguised as a sensible and mutual decision.

Unlike so many teenage sweetheart stories she'd heard from gay and straight friends alike, no outside forces conspired to push them apart as August turned into September.

Only the forces of quite reasonably deciding to attend two different colleges in different states.

And convincing themselves they owed it to each other to start the next phase of their lives without such hot and deep attachments. Free to figure out who they were, or who they wanted to be, or who they wanted to be with.

Youthful reasoning that sounded and felt insane to Kim after spending the day with Steph after years apart.

Never mind that she vaguely remembered being the one to finally suggest their split.

"Maybe not your best thinking," she muttered. "Especially since you were the one who didn't stay in touch."

She closed the yearbook and dropped it on the bright Turkish rug beside the bed as she sat up. A quick shove with her toes scooted it underneath where she wouldn't have to see it first thing in the morning.

She'd deal with finding it under there at some unspecified date whenever that date arrived.

Kim had already done quite enough digging into her past for one long and possibly sleepless night.

She'd never in her life imagined she'd be grateful for such a grim business.

But she breathed a sigh of relief at the idea of heading to Odds and Endings for a Lightning Gap history lesson in the morning.

CHAPTER 16

In an entire lifetime of walking into the sprawling old Victorian glory of the Odds and Endings bookstore, Steph never failed to let out a happy sigh.

Followed immediately by a deep breath, taking in the scents of every kind of book she could think of short of rolled papyrus.

At least she hadn't spotted any of those.

Yet.

Every inch of space inside that could hold shelves did, many custom-made of gleaming wood that was a remarkably good match for the beautiful original floors. Others were made of airy decorative cinderblocks or steel that spanned huge stretches without needing supports underneath.

Every one of the rooms on three main floors and all along the hallways too.

The walls were the same wonderful vivid purple as the

exterior, but the color only showed through in peeks and gaps. Everything else was a riot of different hues and sizes and textures.

Because the shelves were all stuffed full of endless variety and the promise of a million different kinds of escape. Hardcovers and paperbacks from shiny and brand-new to older than Steph's grandparents. A room on the second floor full of comic books and graphic novels from every era.

A huge selection of slim yellow spines from the glories of the pulp years. A magical collection of children's books in the delightful fourth-floor turret room that Steph loved even more now than when she wandered those miniature shelves as a kid.

All sorted and organized and lovingly cataloged by the same couple for...longer than Steph knew.

She turned to Kim and got a return smile that made her heart sing. And something about being in this bookstore with both Auntie Venus and Ivy made Steph feel like the world had properly settled on its axis for the first time in decades.

Just as she wondered where Mr. and Mrs. Seagon had gotten to, she caught another scent joining the various aromas of books. That could only be Earl Gray tea and fresh ginger crisp cookies.

Sure enough the diminutive but powerful Carabelle Seagon turned the corner at the end of the hall, carrying a delicate china tea service on a wooden tray that should have been too heavy for a woman her size.

Not to mention a woman who had to be at least in her eighties.

Mrs. Seagon wore a typical outfit for a woman her age, perhaps, a comfortable dress with mid-length sleeves and a skirt that fell just past her knees. But as with at least some part of everything Steph had ever seen her wear, the dress was the same shade of fabulous purple as the exterior of the house.

And close beside her as he always was, Arthur Seagon carried another wooden tray. A plate piled high with what had to be his special cookies took up most of the space. Scattered around the edges were bundles of ribbon of all textures, colors, and sizes. They were cut about six inches long, and many of them had buttons of every description tied onto one end.

He wore his usual dark pants with a lighter shirt. As dependable as his wife's clothing, but fading into the background beside her, and beside his own sparkling blue eyes.

The Seagons both looked up with such broad, surprised expressions that Steph was afraid the cookies and the tea were going to land on the hardwood floor.

"Oh, you're all here!" Mrs. Seagon exclaimed, her oddly smooth face lighting in an irresistible smile. "And you did bring your sweet hound dog, Ivy, what a *pleasure* to see her. We were just heading downstairs to get everything set up."

Ivy grinned and kept a firm hold on BeeGirl's leash, while BeeGirl just about wagged herself into two pieces.

"We thank you for inviting her. Don't worry, I'll make sure she doesn't run you down."

Steph and Kim strode forward side by side, past several

book-stuffed rooms and shelves that fairly creaked with their loads.

"Can we help you with that?" Kim said.

"No, no, of course not," Mr. Seagon said, his smile as broad and bright as his wife's. Mrs. Seagon sounded like the locals, with a soft, musical mountain accent. Mr. Seagon on the other hand had a much thicker, slower cadence to his words that spoke of time spent somewhere farther south. "You're our special invited guests. Good to see you, Ivy, Venus. The bookstore will be opening soon, so we should get going. I would appreciate it if you could open the basement door, Stephanie dear."

Kim stared at Steph, her brow drawn down in confusion.

"You haven't seen the basement?" Steph walked to the end of the hall, beside the carved and inlaid table where the tea normally resided. "Wow, are you in for a treat."

She turned right at the end of the hall, toward what looked like just another of the shelves crammed full of books. Unlike secret passageways in the movies—where the trick was only revealed after touching a specific sequence of books or some other overly involved routine—the shelf was fairly easy to open once you understood the trick.

A dark spot on the far left side of polished shelf looked like nothing more than a bit of knot wood. Just under Steph's waist-level since she was so much taller than the Seagons. She pushed gently with her fingertips, amazed as always at how smoothly the disguised button sank inward far enough to feel, but not quite far enough to see.

Just as smoothly, the shelf to her right receded back into

the wall and the shelf in front of her rolled over to take its place. A row of mellow lights set into the angled ceiling in front of her illuminated a sturdy wooden staircase on the way down to the basement.

"You've got to be kidding me," Kim breathed, her face wreathed in a delighted smile. "A secret *doorway*, and I never heard a word about it? How long have you known about this, Steph?"

Steph laughed, with more than a little of the joyful excitement from the night before making an appearance in her belly.

"Don't worry, I wasn't keeping it from you when we were prowling around in here as kids. Mr. and Mrs. Seagon were kind enough to let me in on the secret when I needed help with Lightning Gap history. The kind of history that generally isn't for sale, even in a bookstore this wonderful."

Mrs. Seagon made a picture-perfect curtsy without a wobble from the tea service.

"We're always more than happy to help teachers, of course. Especially those who focus their lessons and their own study on the wonderful *natural* features of our town."

She and Mr. Seagon headed down the stairs, leaving Kim staring and shaking her head.

"What about you, Auntie Venus?" she said. "You don't seem too surprised by the sudden appearance of a hidden staircase. Don't tell me you knew about this, too."

Steph fought back a giggle as Venus executed an impressive bow of her own, complete with a sweeping wave of her arm toward the basement. The exaggerated long points on the sleeves and around the bottom of her deep burnt orange jacket brushed the hardwood floor, and the copper bracelets on her wrist jangled. Her silver hair swung forward loose and curly and gorgeous.

"Then I won't tell you, my dear niece. I'll just agree with Stephanie that you're in for a delightful surprise."

Kim turned toward Ivy, hands on her hips and eyebrows raised. Rather than an elaborate response, Ivy only shook her head. A reaction as ordinary and comfortable as her usual brown work clothes and constant redbone hound companion.

"If we told you young folks all our secrets," she said with a wink, "you wouldn't need us around any more."

Kim rolled her eyes and followed the Seagons downstairs.

Steph started down, then stopped with her hand on the displaced bookshelf.

"How did you two know? I never heard a word until I asked the Seagons."

The two women glanced at each other. Steph didn't see an actual wink, but she would have sworn it happened anyway. A gesture as secret and invisible as the disappearing staircase. Ivy patted her shoulder on the way downstairs.

"I'm sure you'll have cause to find out someday, Stephanie. I suspect you and Kim both might be the type."

Steph waited for a grinning Venus to waltz after Ivy and BeeGirl before she stepped through herself. She touched a decidedly more mundane and ordinary brass button set into the wall to close the bookshelf door behind her.

She skipped down the steps, eager to revisit the basement treasures with expert guidance and assistance. Rather than any trace of a hangover after the first time she'd had enough alcohol to feel tipsy in months, she felt light.

Almost buoyant, as if she could float down the stairs or all the way up to the turret room and dance around the fairy lights strung outside the huge windows all around.

Whatever Venus put in her hangover prevention tea not only kept the aftereffects of drinking at bay, it seemed to have revitalized Steph, woken her up more than a quick breakfast and multiple cups of coffee could explain.

Telling her parents or a judge or her therapist about her time in Louisville had only left her drained and exhausted. With furtive, deep feelings of shame she hadn't quite managed to shed despite denying it out loud over and over again.

Talking to Kim about that past—sitting close and holding hands the whole time—lifted Steph's clammy, sticky certainty that she'd been responsible for Bobby's actions in a way she couldn't explain.

Very much like being with Kim all day long, sleeping in the same house with her, had rekindled the sweet, hot attraction between them. Steph had no idea what she wanted to do about that yet, or whether she should even be thinking about such things so soon after such a painful divorce.

But she was glad to have the decision and the possibility ahead of her now instead of behind.

She rounded the corner at the bottom of the stairs and giggled before she could stop herself.

Kim stood in the middle of what Steph was convinced had to be the most warm and welcoming study on the face of the earth. Eyes wide, lips parted in a dazed smile. Looking around as if she'd just woken in the middle of a scene out of a favorite childhood fairy tale.

Steph felt that way every time she was down here.

A seemingly never-changing fire was laid in the huge fireplace, one of the biggest Steph had ever seen. The flames danced and sparkled against the painted tiles, lighting up the rich green and purple. Even when she'd been down here in July and August, the room was never anything but pleasantly warm.

The Seagons, Ivy, BeeGirl, and Venus had already arranged themselves around the gorgeous old brown leather chairs and sofas, each of the humans with their own delicate cup full of tea. BeeGirl perched on a matching brown cushion, happily gnawing a huge dog biscuit.

Steph couldn't be sure without asking—or perhaps taking a sip—but she was convinced she smelled bourbon in the air to go along with the lovely smell of countless shelves full of books.

Venus did have a bit of telltale flush in her cheeks.

But what caught and held Steph's attention as always was the books.

She spotted modern versions down here too, some that she'd heard of as bestsellers out in the rest of the world. But more than she could imagine trying to catalog were surely ancient, surely rare examples of nearly every advance in printing technology.

The shelves here reflected the value and rich variety. Spines of every width, height, color, and texture. Leather embossed with luxurious gold, rough paper edges hand-stitched.

And that was only in the shelves Steph could see. She knew this basement was full of corners and nooks and rooms just out of view, and she'd always had the impression it was too big for the space the house itself took up.

Steph shivered in delight at the idea of digging into even older and more obscure history of Lightning Gap. Meaning more books than the fantastic ones she'd seen so far.

Maybe even some of those hidden rooms, too.

She finally noticed Kim had stopped staring around the room in open-mouthed wonder, and was now staring back at her. The light in Kim's eyes made Steph shiver all over again.

Steph walked over and stood beside her in the middle of the room, resisting a surprisingly strong urge to grab her hand. She settled for a shoulder bump instead.

"What do you think, Kim?"

Kim let out a breathless laugh.

"I can't believe every single one of you has kept this from me for so long."

In the midst of the answering laughter, she winked at Steph. This time the shiver turned into warmth dancing along Steph's nerves. Taking extra time and attention along the best nerves of all.

But when she sat close beside Kim on one of the soft-as-butter brown leather sofas, Kim scooted away against the arm instead.

Thankfully Mrs. Seagon spoke before anyone had a

chance to notice Steph's startled expression. At least Steph hoped so.

"Well, we're delighted to welcome you to the heart of Odds and Endings now, Kim. I don't think anyone would be surprised if we see both of you fine young women down here much more often." She smiled at Mr. Seagon, grasped her hands together in her lap, and turned toward Venus and Ivy.

"Now, why don't you tell me what sort of history you're in need of, my dears?"

CHAPTER 17

Kim did her best to focus on the question Mrs. Seagon had just asked, and how badly she wanted to know the answer to that question and so many more.

Most of all how she could have spent endless hours in this building with no idea a vast, glorious collection of rooms and books and who knew *what* else was hidden away under her feet.

Or why she'd moved away from Steph just then instead of moving closer, when all she'd wanted to do last night (and in shockingly vivid dreams) was get closer.

Her eyes were repeatedly drawn back toward the exquisite fireplace, the adorable little antique tables between the couches and chairs, and of course, more books than she could possibly read in several lifetimes.

She wanted to kick her shoes off and explore the contours

and ridges of an incredibly lifelike picture rug under all the furniture with her toes.

Kim was certain if she had a good swallow of whatever she could smell that was much stronger than Earl Gray tea, she'd be able to convince herself that the rug truly was a neat path through an overflowing flower garden. Complete with full-color birds, several species of bees, and a dizzying array of butterflies.

More than anything else, she wanted to catch everyone distracted so she could wander around what felt like a vast, hidden basement and explore. She saw a few rooms branching off of this one, but that didn't *feel* like all of it.

Not even close.

She dragged her attention back to Ivy and Auntie Venus, but not for any sort of rational, adult reason. She simply didn't want to get caught not paying attention. The risk of never being invited down here again because she was too busy daydreaming was too big a chance to take.

"I'm sorry to bring up such an unpleasant business," Auntie Venus said, "but I'm sure you've heard about the missing person turning up just outside of town."

Mrs. Seagon pressed her lips together and shook her head.

"Yes, such a terrible thing. Not the sort of goings on we're used to here in Lightning Gap at all. Those *poor* hikers. Out to enjoy a beautiful spring day and coming across something so horrible and ugly."

"Unusual, yes, thank goodness." Mr. Seagon tapped his chin with his fingertips. "But not unprecedented. Strange things have happened here over the years. The good kind of strange, of course, and plenty of it. But the bad kind of strange, too. And plenty of things that were simply bad."

"We met during an age of great difficulty," Mrs. Seagon said, gazing at her husband. "Right here in this house. A time of pain and sorrow that reached all the way here on its way to grieving the entire world. Then we were married during another. I've often wondered if times like that are when Lightning Gap learned to protect those who live here."

Kim watched them, trying not to be too obvious. But doing her best to figure out...not what Mrs. Seagon could be talking about, though that was part of her confusion. She couldn't find the answer without knowing how old they actually were.

And she had no doubt her Auntie Venus would be *loudly* displeased if Kim was rude enough to come right out and ask.

But she did promise herself to find out somehow.

Mr. Seagon smiled and took his wife's hand.

"I think Lightning Gap always knew how to do that. People took a bit longer to finally settle here and figure it out. Even with all of that, one poor soul may not be anything more than a tragic accident. Each and every one of you are sensible, or we wouldn't all be here together. So share with us what we don't yet know or understand."

Kim took a sip of her cooling tea to stop from laughing or groaning, or even meeting Steph's gaze.

She'd too often felt anything but sensible over the past month. She still had no idea what had truly possessed her to volunteer for Career Day besides wanting to see Steph, or what on earth she was going to say to those poor kids.

The barely sweet, citrusy brew didn't look or smell especially strong, but she somehow still felt like it was going to clear years' worth of cobwebs from her mind. But with a good bit more of this tea, she might actually be able to figure it out.

"This part isn't pleasant," Ivy said, "but it's pretty easy to explain. Someone else has gone missing, from down in Wolf Branch this time. Last seen here in Lightning Gap."

Mr. Seagon winced and turned his head to the side, while Mrs. Seagon only closed her eyes for a second. When she opened them again, she focused on Auntie Venus.

"And the part that's hard to explain?"

"I get the feeling it won't be all that hard to explain to you," Auntie Venus said as she looked around the room. "Not here in this precious place. We're afraid—Ivy and me for sure —that something else is wrong. Not only the one missing from Wolf Branch and the poor Blevins boy. Something is wrong all around us."

Instead of the puzzled looks or nervous giggles Kim half-expected, the Seagons only looked gravely at each other.

"Such things have happened here before," Mrs. Seagon said, rubbing her husband's hand in a sweet, absent way. "But not for a long time. We're not immune here in Lightning Gap, or even in this house. We're just...protected, you might say. If something is wrong, we'll do everything we can to figure it out."

Kim sat far away from Steph (and she still wasn't sure why). But she still felt her friend tense up before she spoke.

"There's more to what's going on. Someone else is missing. From Bountyfield this time." She stared at the fantastic rug under their feet and nodded, almost to herself. "Last seen in Lightning Gap. My dad always says two might be a coincidence. But you have to consider the possibility that three makes a pattern."

"Even if it has shifted from a coincidence to a pattern," Auntie Venus said, "it could be one we shouldn't interfere with. Like when people tried to stop all forest fires from burning and the brush grew up so high it made the fires worse. And some kinds of seeds couldn't sprout at all without the fire. This may be a pattern that has to play itself out."

"When did you find that out?" Kim said. "I didn't think you'd seen your parents since yesterday morning." She fought the urge to cover her mouth with both hands, settling for lacing her fingers together instead. "No, I'm sorry. That's none of my business."

"I wasn't exactly supposed to tell anyone about that," Steph said, now concentrating on the dancing flames in the fireplace. "This didn't seem like the time to be keeping secrets."

Ivy finished her tea and flashed a warm smile at Steph.

"I've known your parents a long time, Stephanie. I believe this is one case where your father would understand. Might want to clue him in on everything else that's going on when you get home, though."

Steph grunted, glancing sideways at Kim with a quick smile.

"I will. Maybe not *everything*."

Kim grabbed for her tea again, wishing even more for a good swallow of whiskey or bourbon or whatever else the Seagons were spiking theirs with. Between this surreal meeting in a room she'd never suspected, so much time spent with Steph after so many years, and her own puzzling resistance, she needed some way to catch up and settle her whirling mind.

"You may already know our town got its start during a time of great sickness," Mrs. Seagon said. "The 1918 flu made it all the way here. The Great Depression took a toll as well, though not as badly as in many places. People here still sicken and die, of course. But strange patterns, as you said, Stephanie, are noticeable. I suspect if this has happened before, someone wrote it down and stored it here."

"Well then," Mr. Seagon said, standing effortlessly as if he were thirty years younger than he looked. Maybe fifty years younger. "We can all get started. Our writer-in-residence and the person she's working with are out today doing research. They both say their apartments stand ready for any investigations we might need to make."

Mrs. Seagon stood beside him, just as sprightly. "There are almost as many books in the apartments as out here, and they're always getting switched out. Mr. Seagon and I will handle that. I hope you understand. We form a certain...bond with our regular houseguests. The rest of the basement is yours to explore, of course."

They paused beside the fireplace, in front of a low table Kim hadn't noticed in her efforts to take everything else in. The wooden trays sat nested on top, with little piles of every kind of ribbon imaginable neatly spaced along one edge. She'd mistaken them for napkins at first glance.

Each of the Seagons picked up a bundle—leaving four more behind—and something on the ends clattered.

"Don't forget your bookmarks," Mr. Seagon said with a wink. "It wouldn't do to fold the pages down, you know."

The two of them walked arm-in-arm toward a door at the bottom of the stairs. An ordinary wooden door that was surely as old as the house.

The size of the basement itself looked like that door couldn't shelter much more than a closet until the Seagons walked through. Kim caught a glimpse of a big sitting room with a kitchen beyond before they closed it.

Kim turned to Steph, and they each said "Apartments?" at the same time.

"Why sure," Auntie Venus said. "Where else would the writers and their...special guests stay?"

She gathered her collection of bookmarks and walked toward one of the side rooms, shaking her head.

"Did the Seagons say 'houseguests'?" Steph said, standing beside Kim. "I thought they lived somewhere else."

"No, they live right here," Ivy said. "Mrs. Seagon, Carabelle, always has as far as I know. They have their rooms on the second floor like they have for years."

She rubbed BeeGirl's head, getting only a soft doggy snore in response. Ivy walked off to a side room in the opposite direction, picking up a colorful bunch of bookmarks along the way.

"I'm more confused than when we walked down here,"

Kim said, crossing her arms. "I feel like we've passed into some kind of alternate reality."

Steph moved closer on the sofa, until she was near enough that Kim felt her warmth.

"I'm confused about some things. Starting to get clear on others."

She reached for Kim's hand.

Kim froze, unable to think or feel or do anything past remembering the way Steph's eyes had looked last night, talking about her ex-husband. How frightened and tight her voice sounded, when it didn't sound cold and lifeless.

Much as she might want to, she couldn't be the one to add even more change to Steph's life. Not even one she was certain would be a good change in the long run.

She patted Steph's hand, but nowhere near the fond, affectionate gesture she'd seen between the Seagons. To her own dismay, this was more like indulging an insistent child, or a suitor she really wasn't interested in.

Before she could get really worked up and angry at herself, Kim got up and grabbed one of the two remaining bundles of ribbons. She realized the clattering sound was a variety of buttons knotted or sewn onto the ends of many of them. She pretended to focus on the shelves beside the fireplace.

Kim managed to count to five before she glanced back at Steph.

Just in time to see her hurt expression as she grabbed the last bundle of ribbons and turned away.

CHAPTER 18

Steph gritted her teeth as she walked away from Kim, determined to keep her embarrassment and confusion to herself.

She turned left into a cozy and gorgeous reading nook tucked under the stairs, one she'd admired but never spent time in before. Two adorable loveseats the exact dark green as the juniper bushes outside her parents' house fit perfectly into the space. Every possible inch inside—extending well past the width of the steps overhead—was loaded with books, of course.

A curvy Art Deco coffee table with geometric patterns of inlaid wood had her wishing for more tea, solitude, and an unlimited time to settle in and read.

Mainly meaning she didn't want to worry about Kim walking around the corner and surprising her.

The same way she'd surprised her showing up outside her

classroom door. Slipping herself far too easily and comfortably into Steph's life, and her heart.

Again.

She shook her head and stepped around the coffee table, up close to the multicolored wall full of spines demanding her attention. She held the delightful little knot of buttons in one hand and ran her fingers down the length of the ribbons. They were as varied as the books all around her.

Wide and narrow, smooth and velvety. Decorative, wavy edges and sharp borders. Shimmering and flat and iridescent, and more colors than she could have imagined.

They weren't down in the bookstore's wonderful basement for some kind of flirty half-date nonsense, after all. They were here to figure out what was happening in Lightning Gap, and whether they should or even *could* do anything about it.

Not to mention the fact that she'd been worried enough to spill her father's confidential sheriff business for the first time in her life. She was surprised and relieved to not feel the least bit guilty about that.

Steph tucked the ribbons into her pocket and ran her fingertips over the books in front of her, focusing on the smooth, scratchy, rough, slick contrasts more than the titles or the colors. Local authors, most of these, and most focused on history. This was a fine area to begin her search.

Never mind that it was also a fine place to hide.

Kim's apparent change of heart not only hurt, and made Steph feel more of the churning heat of shame than she wanted to admit for crossing a line she'd convinced herself didn't exist. It didn't make sense. Seeking her out at school, then spending the day together, then that intimate conversation Steph still could barely believe happened last night.

They could have been back in high school, sharing details they never would with another living soul. About things that may have felt like life or death back then, even if they were mostly embarrassing now. Nothing as tough to talk about or admit to as Steph's disastrous adventure into marriage.

Or her months and years spent as the willing, silent victim of a master manipulator.

She was nowhere sure enough of her own mind or motivations yet to know whether she was the one doing the manipulating now, on herself.

Misunderstanding Kim's intentions the night before. Or overreacting to Kim sitting far away and...patting her hand like the head of an overeager puppy.

She shook herself and changed positions, kneeling on one of the loveseats so she could get a good look at the shelves arranged behind it. Several of the spines held the stylized O & E logo that meant they'd been written by one of the writers-in-residence.

Many were about the area itself, more nonfiction than the rest of the basement. About coal mining, logging, the railroads. All the many groups of people who'd settled the whole region over time, from the few Native Americans who passed through, to bunches of Scots and Irish, to freed slaves, to workers from all over Europe and the Middle East.

More of a melting pot than most folks realized.

Several of the towns were featured too. Lightning Gap,

obviously. But also Wolf Branch, Holly Creek, Hidden Springs. Even Laurel Gap.

Where the recently deceased Stan Phipps had come from. And Steph's own ex-husband.

And one of the currently missing folks.

Steph pulled the slender volume down, her fingernails rasping over the rough cloth of the burgundy cover. A fairly typical genealogy and history book. Full of old photographs, local names, records of when they first settled there.

She frowned when she saw no listing of Faulks, Bobby's family name, in the index. He'd always claimed they'd arrived in Laurel Gap around the time of the Revolutionary War, and she'd never been worried enough about it to verify his claims.

Nor that interested, to be honest. Steph's sort of history went back millions of years. Not decades, or even centuries. About all she knew was Laurel Gap was much older than Lightning Gap.

Still, it seemed strange that his family wasn't there at all.

She flipped through the faded pages, squinting a little at the slightly blurry print. Her breath caught at one of the black and white photos. Nothing more than a row of old houses, white clapboard and picket fences.

That was the house Bobby grew up in, right in the middle and too clear to mistake. The odd arrangement of high, narrow windows in between the typical old double-hung versions was unmistakable. Again, he'd claimed that had been their family home for at least two hundred years.

The smudged-looking text below the photo declared it the

McReynolds house when the book was published only fifty years ago.

Steph shook her head, not sure what it could possibly mean, or why on earth she cared. She had no plans to return to Laurel Gap, and certainly no plans to ask Bobby or anyone else in his family about the odd discrepancy.

It would be far from the only thing he'd lied to her about, though it may have been the first. And for no good reason she could think of.

She heard her father's voice in her head, talking about how the strangest thing that seemed unimportant might be the most important clue. How learning how to trust that faint whisper in the back of your mind changed everything.

When it came to solving crimes, making tough decisions, or knowing what would make you happy in the end.

She slipped a wide, mud-brown ribbon that felt sandpapery against her skin into place, set the book on the coffee table, and went back to searching.

CHAPTER 19

Bobby ended the call when the drawling redneck voice started, making a sad attempt to be clever instead of just suggesting he leave a message.

Again.

He stared down at his smartphone. His formerly private one that Steph, his co-workers, and anyone else in his normal life had never or would ever call. Last year's model, just like his public version.

The only visible difference between the two was the slim-fit case for his day-to-day phone was outlined in cool gray. The more important, personal one in blood red.

When the screen finally locked itself and went black, he pulled a blue microfiber cleaning cloth out of his pants pocket and wiped his fingerprints away.

Not because he was worried about anyone finding this phone, or matching his prints up with anything he didn't want to be associated with. That was too absurd an idea to even consider. He was far too careful for that.

Hands-on was generally not his sort of game. Not for the past few endless months, anyway.

He simply didn't see any good reason to allow the disorder of leaving either of his perfectly good phones covered in grease and dust. He could admit letting his fingerprints become...commonplace wasn't a good plan, either.

Starting down that road never led to anywhere good.

He'd had that lesson inadvertently reinforced only a few minutes ago, while he was outside. The grass hadn't quite started growing yet in the lingering cool spring. But a heavy winter full of snow and rain had played hell with his careful job of mulching around the flowerbeds.

Being out there cleaning that up and neatening the gravels edging the walkways fit right into his usual lucky timing. He'd barely managed to keep himself from waving at the cop who just *happened* to cruise by for no apparent reason.

But Bobby knew she'd been watching him as closely as he watched her.

Big Bad Ex-Husband: verified safely at home and properly miserable yet again.

He neatly folded the cleaning cloth and slipped it back into the pocket of his appropriately aged and worn blue jeans, then turned his excess of orderly attention to the kitchen island in front of him.

Spotless charcoal gray granite. Almost a perfect match for his usual work wardrobe and the cellular phone linked to his name, this address. Not so much for his weekend uniform, which required him to pair a brown button-up shirt with the jeans.

The color palette of the granite suited him better, much like the texture did.

Cool. Even. Sturdy and predictable. Simple to keep clean.

And much like his clothing, not the nicest they had in the showroom. Not the cheapest, either.

A reflection of a certain status in life. A certain level of achievement.

But not flashy and showy enough to attract more attention than was necessary. Even on a Saturday morning, Bobby had no interest in dressing like either a corporate tight-ass or a suburban slob.

Appearances did matter.

Just like the front lawn, everything in the kitchen was in its right place. Clean and correct. Nice but not too valuable dishes washed and put away inside oak cabinets. Solid and efficient glass cooktop scrubbed and gleaming. Refrigerator well stocked, but stopping well short of hoarding.

Nothing to see here.

But if someone like a nosy neighbor (or police officer) did happen to see it, nothing to remark on.

Nothing to remember.

In fact, he'd kept everything exactly the way it had been before.

When Steph still lived there.

All her girly little touches. Matching cardinal-on-pine-tree potholders, useless copper cake pans hanging on the wall, ceramic cooking spoon holders painted to look like fire hydrants.

All of it frivolous, yes. But Steph had contributed a useful touch of normal. That's why Bobby had brought her into his life and his plans in the first place.

Before she lost her mind and risked destroying everything he'd worked so hard to build.

Bobby rolled his broad shoulders forward, then back, settling the tension with the motion.

This was nothing but a temporary setback, not being able to reach his...associates back in middle-of-nowhere Virginia. A bump in the road. A condition that wouldn't hinder his overall plan.

The fact that this same setback had happened three times didn't enter into his plans or calculations.

Not even knowing for certain one was deceased, and the second officially reported missing.

He knew how to work around annoyances like this. Hell, he expected it from years of playing with the local drunks and drug addicts every day.

They often expired on him and had to be replaced.

Never by his hand, though.

Always by their own in one way or another.

All of those backwoods rubes had gotten themselves lost, and at least one of them had gotten himself killed. Without managing to do the easiest task Bobby had ever assigned to anyone, and for the most generous rewards he'd ever dangled in front of someone's greedy eyes.

So it didn't matter.

Except...

He might have expected this kind of flakey behavior from the first two. Stan and Eugene had never been any sort of brain trust. As far as Bobby was concerned, they spent their time as a living example of people who wouldn't know where to lean or squat unless someone told them.

Dusty, though, Dusty had always been different. Not as ambitious or maybe not as focused as Bobby. Maybe just not quite capable enough to get himself out and away where he could create a life and persona normal enough to hide behind.

But not stupid by any means. Dusty was the one person—besides his playmates—who knew anything at all about what Bobby got up to when it was time for entertainment or blowing off steam.

Not all of it, no. No one on the planet knew *all* of it. But more than anyone else.

Partly because the two of them had learned some of the games together back in Laurel Gap.

Bobby had trusted Dusty enough to let him be the general ringleader back in Virginia. Sending him in to get his hands dirty like this wasn't the normal procedure.

Any more than keeping an eye on his formerly sweet, loving wife, learning her habits and patterns and routines, was normal.

It was simply necessary before that situation could be dealt with.

He got up and pushed the black barstool back under the

overhanging edge of the kitchen island, then tapped his neatly trimmed fingernails on the granite.

The important thing to remember was he had work to do here. His business in Virginia could wait. The business of the useful wife gone astray.

She still hadn't gone any further than back to Mommy and Daddy's house, that much was clear.

Bobby knew where to find her when the time came, Sheriff Daddy hovering and just itching to interfere or not.

It might even be better if he did the finding himself rather than utilizing some redneck uneducated hillbilly he made sure to stay in touch with from a long time ago.

Some hick so desperate for money or attention or a steady supply of his preferred poison that he'd do anything Bobby asked.

No matter how shady or strange.

Even the smartest of the uneducated carried a risk.

Much like the pathetic fools he so easily found all over Louisville and Lexington and even in Cincinnati.

Didn't take any effort to locate them. Weak minds tended to make themselves known.

Even less effort to get them on the hook.

Reeling them in and getting whatever he wanted out of them had grown almost...boring.

Someone who resisted, now, that was different. That was *interesting.*

Bobby might even say that could get downright *exciting.*

One of the rare things he hesitated to admit to himself was he still got a quick thrill of excitement when he wondered how the hell Stan Phipps had ended up in an untidy, lifeless pile right outside of Lightning Gap.

Even his most advanced and penetrating searches online hadn't managed to turn up any real details.

He'd managed to keep his fascination with those sorts of *details* entirely to himself for most of his life. That side of him had only surged into his reality over the last year or so.

He pointedly refused to glance toward the shoulder-high cabinet where he and Steph always kept the alcohol. The kind that didn't need to be cold, anyway. More potent than beer or wine.

Party supplies, mostly. Brought out only when she had her chirpy teacher friends over, or when he felt obligated to host his own quietly geeky co-workers for appearance's sake.

Barbecue, Babble, and Booze, the two of them called such gatherings. One of the few things they honestly had in common. The sort of shared secret he knew normal couples had in abundance.

Disliking The Three Dreary Bs.

As in "Fair warning, time to break out The Three Dreary Bs. Fourth of July coming up."

Up until the last year, Bobby had avoided the hard Booze component himself. He'd seen too many people in his family have trouble with it. He could manage beer for whatever reason, even though he knew a lot of people who couldn't.

He had never been willing to take the risk himself.

He enjoyed playing with those people too much not to know their challenges quite well. Games with the pitiful souls attempting to sober up from some addiction or other were some of his favorites.

But something tipped him over the edge into taking that risk, at a fucking New Year's party of all things.

Maybe spending the day of the party encouraging a desperately sober couple to return to their carousing ways. Listening to them talk wistfully about how huge quantities of good old Kentucky bourbon *changed* them.

Took away all their insecurities and inhibitions.

Made them and everyone around them fun instead of depressing and dull.

Bobby understood all too well the thrill of finding something exciting, something *interesting*, in an endless blur of boring.

Maybe it had been his looming fortieth birthday.

Maybe Steph's continued refusal to discuss having kids. Not performing the simple task of providing him with another layer of protection, another reinforcement in his cloak of civility.

Whatever the reason, Bobby had finally given in to the offer of a shot of tequila of all things.

And another.

And a few more.

The first two or three had seemed like a good idea. The next nine or ten had seemed like a *great* idea.

And on and on, until Steph had basically shoved him into their bedroom and told him to stay there.

He had, but the very next day he'd gotten himself a more

reasonable amount of booze—to blunt the hangover, he reasoned.

But slow sips of fine bourbon (but not too fine) did more than dull his head that pounded like a rotten toothache.

That New Year's Day over a year ago, Bobby finally understood why some called it liquid courage.

And that courage led him to get more...aggressive in his games.

He didn't actually do the dangerous things he'd so often daydreamed about. Not then. But he started saying the dangerous things out loud. To people who believed he *would* do them.

The games got more exciting than even he could have imagined after that.

When his drinking and his escalating internal demands led to a springtime surge of finally *doing* the dangerous things, Bobby realized he was getting closer to crossing a line he could never turn back from.

One Steph had inadvertently saved him from when she left. But not before he gave in to his years-long urge to explain everything to her. To make sure she understood how many of those dangerous things he'd struggled so mightily to keep himself from doing.

To her.

How hard he'd worked to protect her.

From him.

Bobby ran his fingertips and then his nails along his scalp, hard enough to make his eyes water and his heart race.

But he was careful to go back and rearrange his short

brown hair. Neat but not too short. A nice balance between corporate tight-ass and IT relaxed. He needed to move comfortably in both worlds, after all.

And he needed to move right now.

Find a new game.

He'd abstained from drinking or playing in the eight long months since Steph made her surprise escape. He'd never figured out whether the drinking drove him to the Dangerous Things, or if his desire for the Dangerous Things drove his drinking.

He honestly didn't care.

The restraining order Steph managed to convince a rather gullible judge to grant didn't give Bobby much of a choice when it came to calling a temporary halt to both.

The order hadn't mentioned his more dangerous activities —even though a few of his more recent playmates had shown up to testify.

Bobby knew Sheriff Daddy well enough to know he had to be careful, and he had been.

Now he deserved a reward and he was going to take one.

He had his eye on a scrawny young man at the AA and NA meeting across town. Newly arrived in town from the wilds of eastern Kentucky, newly sober. Still had that longing look in his eye when he talked about the bad old days of booze and drugs, though.

He'd come right out and said he missed the tight companionship of a true drinking buddy more than anything else.

Neatly identifying himself as the new distraction Bobby needed.

Until it was time to get himself down to Lightning Gap and take care of business for himself. Remaining single wasn't an option he wasn't willing to consider, any more than he was willing to try to keep up the charade of a happy marriage when his wife was more than 350 miles and a torturous six-hour drive away.

But he couldn't locate and cultivate a...replacement until he'd dealt with the original.

If his dear old high school friends couldn't even manage the simple task of keeping an eye on the wayward wife, he was perfectly fine not rewarding them for their lack of effort.

Much as Bobby enjoyed his little recreational mind games, sometimes it was worth the risk to get hands-on after all.

CHAPTER 20

Kim sat cross-legged on the floor, in a compact room as far as she could get away from Steph, pretending to examine the books in front of her. She'd retrieved several hand-stitched volumes from the little side room she'd discovered.

A room that had nothing but shelves in front of the stone walls. No chairs or tables, and only soft overhead lighting rather than the cozy lamps all over the rest of the basement and the store upstairs.

Even the carpet she sat on was an ordinary light brown, somewhere between an old shag and a modern flat version. Thank goodness the padding underneath was generous.

This room smelled different, too. Hints of that wonderful book scent, of course, and a lingering warmth of wood from the fireplace out in the main room. There was a trace of...age here. Dust, and a dryness that didn't exactly feel sterile or threatening.

More like Kim was breathing in the aroma of time itself.

Time that seemed to have drawn itself out and stretched like melting taffy since she'd been so rude to Steph.

She laid her collection of ribbons across her thigh and picked up one of the books, curious and wanting to distract herself.

Maybe even do what they were here for and find some kind of hint about what was going on around town.

The board inside the dandelion yellow fabric was still solid and firm, the matching yellow stitching around the spine neat and tight. Someone had made this carefully, and everyone else who touched it had taken great care.

Kim opened the cover gently, making sure she didn't put stress on those delicate, ancient threads.

Inside sharp printed black letters declared this *Arthur's Record of Days for the Year 1931.*

Kim blinked, numbers flashing through her mind. That couldn't be Arthur Seagon. He was hardly a young man, but being old enough to write in 1931 would make him well over a hundred years old. Had to be more his father's age, or possibly his grandfather.

If any years were going to be tough in Lightning Gap, surely The Great Depression would qualify. She'd enjoyed twentieth century history during high school and college, to the extent that she'd considered teaching rather than technical writing.

If she was on an honest-with-herself streak, she still considered it sometimes.

She turned another page and smiled at the faded blue type and soft edges of the close-spaced text. Several letters were blurred, and ghostly images of mistakes showed up in a few spots.

When had anyone last seen or used an old typewriter eraser, much less modern correction liquid? Still, being able to read words put down so long ago—the time travel of old writing—enchanted her as always.

So of course she got pulled right into the story of a terrible car crash when there weren't all that many cars on the road. The blizzard that helped cause the crash, and killed almost everyone in that little car. Everyone except one tiny little girl.

And how badly Arthur wanted to take that baby in and raise her with his sweet "C" by his side.

Kim jumped so hard she let out a little squeak when someone spoke from right behind her.

"Oh, I didn't mean to startle you," Auntie Venus said, but Kim heard how hard she was trying not to laugh. "I was just coming through to check on everyone. Find anything that caught your attention?"

Auntie Venus was indeed pursing her lips to keep from smiling. She had several books under one arm—some as old as the ones in front of Kim, others looking far more modern and official.

"I'm not sure it caught my attention for the right reasons, but this is certainly interesting." Kim flipped back to the first page and held it up for her great aunt. "It says there was a car crash right outside of town, everyone killed but a little baby. In January, in a big snowstorm no one expected. Do you think…"

Kim paused, surprised at how Auntie Venus's eyes lit up.

"Why, what did you find?" she said.

"Well, I don't want to say just yet. It might be nothing at all. But I wonder if your car crash wasn't near where that poor Stan Phipps was found?"

Kim shook her head, staring back down at the book. She plucked a slender silver ribbon with adorable tiny loops of gold along its length out of her bundle. She couldn't help smiling at how perfect the glittering red button looked tucked against the top of the book.

She shifted to get up, and only then realized not one but both of her legs were numb and sound asleep.

"I couldn't tell from what's written here. But there's only the one road out of town. Damn, I'm going to have the most awful pins and needles."

Auntie Venus took Kim's ribbons and books and set them with hers on a nearby shelf. She held out both hands.

"Oh, I'm sorry, hon. I hate when I do that. Let me help you up."

Kim shifted onto her hip, then up on one knee. Her legs felt like dead wood from the knee down.

"I don't want to pull you over, Auntie Venus. Then we'd both be hobbling around."

"I'm stronger than I look," Auntie Venus said, smiling. "Or would you rather I call Steph in to help you?"

Kim did grab her great aunt's hand when her right foot

wobbled underneath her. She tried to keep her voice from getting louder and failed miserably.

"I'd rather you didn't. Sorry, I'm fine. Just give me a minute to let my feet wake up."

"I wasn't exactly talking about your feet, Kim, even though I how rotten that feels. Everything okay with you?"

Kim squeezed her eyes closed as the awful prickly sensation spread through her lower legs. Not a damn thing to do but wait it out.

She didn't miss the words her great aunt left unsaid.

"Everything okay with me and Steph, you mean? To tell you the truth, I don't think she needs a bunch of old high school crush drama in her life right now. She's dealing with a lot. I'm probably not in the best place for anything like that either.."

"Maybe not. I know such things are none of my business, and you can feel free to tell me so. But I didn't see a high school crush last night at dinner, or this morning. What I see is two grown women who've had a bit of a rough time, which is after all what your thirties are all about."

Kim stood on one foot, then the other, trying to shake her tingling flesh back to life.

"My thirties? You mean I have *years* left of not knowing what the hell I'm doing?"

Auntie Venus shrugged, but her expression was kind.

"Sorry to be the one to break it to you, but yeah. Life starts to make a whole lot more sense when you hit forty, and again about every ten years after that. All I'm saying is don't put too much pressure on spending time with Steph again.

But don't cut yourself off from what could be a good thing. Okay?"

Kim forced herself not to argue. And not to tell Auntie Venus all the awful things Steph had told her last night. That would be a perfect way to mess up their friendship and anything else that might be a possibility.

Someday. In the distant future.

She gathered the stack of books they'd both picked out—holding her barely used ribbons against her thumb—feeling a little guilty when she noticed how many ribbons were tucked into her great aunt's selections.

"I'll do my best, Auntie Venus. Got somewhere we can flip through these, maybe make some notes? And where I can sit in a normal chair, obviously. What did you dig up?"

They headed back toward the big fireplace, but thankfully Steph wasn't there yet. Someone had moved a taller than usual coffee table into the middle, exactly the right height so everyone would be able to see without bending over.

No one else was there, but the fire was still comfortably warm, and the empty tea cups they'd left behind were now full and steaming.

"Sounds like something similar to what you have," Auntie Venus said. "An accidental death in the 1940s, and another in the 1950s. Then I didn't see anything else until the 70s."

"That's not very much for so many years. I know people died in between, but it seems like something else could have happened in all that time."

Auntie Venus sat on one of the loveseats with a sigh, and

Kim joined her, happy to avoid any awkwardness about sitting beside Steph or not.

"I suppose we'll know more when we see what everyone else is coming up with," Auntie Venus said. "But that's what I've always heard about Lightning Gap. Takes care of her own and all that."

Kim handed over her great aunt's stack of books and opened another of hers. Another of the mysterious Arthur's record of days for 1933, this one covered and stitched in pale pink. The random entry—typed in the same soft blue as the first—mentioned making a drive up north to settle the final business for the baby.

"Takes care of her own," Kim said, brushing her fingers gently over the letters. "You mean keeps them...us...safe while we're here? I have plenty of scars and clear memories of a broken collarbone to make me wonder about that little saying."

Auntie Venus brushed her silver curls back over her shoulders and picked up one of her own books. The spine looked machine made rather than hand-stitched, but unlike the homemade ones, the tan fabric cover was frayed and loose around the edges.

"I don't think that would have been doing you any favors, would it?" she said. "Protecting you from *every*thing? That's no way to grow up and learn how to go through life. I remember when high schools stopped teaching driver education classes for a long while. People could just turn eighteen, pass the test, and hit the road. Didn't work out very well. It's better to practice making small mistakes instead of going right to the big ones."

Kim shrugged, opening another of what she was sure were carefully typed diaries. The 1947 edition. The type was a good bit more precise and sharp, and the ink in a more modern black. She wished the words weren't quite so clear.

"What year did you say you found?" Kim said. "Sometime in the Forties?"

Auntie Venus shuffled through her books, coming up with a modern one bound in shimmering green. She flipped the page open to reveal an inky black bookmark ribbon with a crystal on top that looked like a frozen drop of blood.

"It was...yes, 1947. A few kids...well, they got into a fight. I mean kids as in young men in their early twenties. One of them had, my goodness, he had a knife. Three of them were gone before anyone knew what was happening. The one with the knife, he died in the hospital down in Hidden Springs a few days later."

Kim swallowed hard, thankful it had been a while since breakfast. Her book mentioned the same incident. It was somehow much harder to read about in Arthur's matter-of-fact, calm retelling.

"It says here no one ever could find parts of two of them." She shuddered. "The ones fighting weren't outside of town this time, but over by the fairgrounds. Almost at the foot of the Lightning Stone. It stormed like crazy that night, so people hunted in the mud for hours. The rumor is the...bits and pieces are still there."

Auntie Venus looked at Kim with one eyebrow raised.

"What book do you have there? I may regret looking at it, but that's a lot more detail than what I have here."

She took the slender volume Kim held out and turned it over in her hands, talking under her breath.

"This place always shows you what you most need to know."

Before Kim could ask whether she meant Lightning Gap itself, Odds and Endings, or something else, Ivy strolled back in with her own armload of books. BeeGirl finally stirred herself enough to thump her tail on the floor.

"Glad to see I'm not the only one who's finding things," Ivy said, settling into the armchair closest to her hound dog again, within head-rubbing distance. "And guessing I'm not the only one who has no idea what she found."

"Not much pattern to it," Auntie Venus said. "Not yet. Kim and I both grabbed books that mention 1947, but that's all."

Ivy paused for a long sip of her tea before she pulled out a thick book bound in black leather. Several ribbons peeked out the top, each with a different color of flat, plastic button snugged down against the pages.

"I imagine there's a reason for that. I think I hear the Seagons heading this way, so we're about to find out more."

Kim knew exactly what her great aunt was going to say, but she couldn't think of a way to stop her. Or to refuse.

"Kim, why don't you see if you can find Stephanie so we can get started?"

CHAPTER 21

Steph barely managed to notice the low murmur of voices from the room beyond her sweet little reading nook. The others, probably, getting back together to discuss whatever they'd found.

She then promptly returned her full attention to the life she was living vicariously in a late 1990s October. A life worlds away from what her own had been back then—five years old and happily enjoying her last year of pre-school before she went to first grade with all the big kids.

The young women and men in this story were much older then, and they had a much rougher life. Growing up tough and flinty in small-town Ohio, getting kicked out of high school for good before they made it through their junior years.

Deciding to reject everything their families and their school district and the state had to offer. Coming up with perfectly good reasons to leave instead, especially because the state's offers would surely escalate to jail and later prison.

They decided to take their chances in a world none of them liked or wanted to be part of, and depend on each other.

Roaming around the Midwest. Working their way gradually toward the Southeast. Aiming for bigger cities like Nashville, Atlanta, Miami.

Running one scam after another. Doing whatever it took to refine their efforts enough to create some semblance of a comfortable living.

Swindling and stealing from others to make it all possible.

None of this was presented as a noble tale, of misunderstood or ill-treated kids making their escape into a better life. Or the experience of a grand epiphany leading them all to become heroes, or even anti-heroes. Not even close.

Steph wouldn't have gotten so caught up in anything that resembled a modern-day Robin Hood.

No, this was getting into the *heads* of the wayward kids. Their twisted, disordered ways of thinking. And much to her surprise, those thoughts were making a strange kind of sense.

She got so deeply into the story again—heading from Nashville toward Knoxville—that she missed the soft footsteps, and the first couple of attempts at gentle throat-clearing.

When Kim finally tapped on the wooden shelf at the end of the reading nook, Steph jumped hard enough that the pages flipped closed, losing her place in the book.

"I'm sorry," Kim said, and she really did look like she meant it. "I tried to warn you instead of sneaking up on you."

Steph managed to smile as she held one hand over her pounding heart.

"No, that's okay. I probably shouldn't have spent so much time reading when we're supposed to be looking for clues. Something about this basement does that to me every time. Everyone else ready?"

Kim glanced over her shoulder, then turned back.

"Everyone's out there, not sure if they're ready. The Seagons just came back out. Looks like you found quite a bit."

Steph looked at the book in her hands, confused for a second before she remembered the stack on the coffee table. Eleven of them, and each holding at least one of the adorable little ribbon bookmarks. Most held several.

"I don't know if any of it will help," she said. "But I found a bunch, yeah. Then I spent the last...I have no idea how long reading instead of searching. Not the best use of everyone's time, I suppose."

Kim shrugged, her cheeks flushed, and Steph went right back to feeling awkward and kind of dumb. And the same clammy, queasy shame washed over her as when Kim patted her hand by the fire.

"I don't know about wasting time," Kim said. "I sat in another room back there and read until both my legs were sound asleep. I could barely walk getting out of there. Listen, Steph, about earlier..."

Steph shook her head, leaning forward to stack up her books. She started to return the disturbing story of the rambling, troubled kids to the shelf, then dropped it on top of the pile.

On a day like this, she tended to assume everything that happened had a reason. Even if she didn't understand it yet.

"There's nothing to worry about, Kim. I was being immature, especially with a bunch of other people down here. We've got more important things to concentrate on."

Kim leaned forward to take some of the books, and their fingers touched. Steph closed her eyes for a second, fighting down the surge of hot excitement at the contact along with another burst of shame.

"Still, I wasn't being fair," Kim said. "I just don't want to cause you any more stress than you're already going through, with Bobby and all. I'm sure the last thing you need is me hanging around like some lovesick kid."

Steph stared down at the books in her arms, then up at the narrow, age-dark wooden boards of the ceiling. Her therapist had warned her against even considering getting involved with someone new too soon.

Less than six months after escaping Bobby had to be too soon by anyone's measure.

But having Kim walk out of her life so soon after they'd reconnected would surely do more harm than good.

"Okay, you have a point. I'm not exactly what anyone would call recovered. Hell, I'm not so sure I'm even what most people would call stable. The truth is I don't want you to disappear again, Kim. I know it's only what, less than twenty-four hours? But it's been great spending time with you again."

Steph knew her face was burning red, and she didn't care. She looked up and into Kim's eyes. They were overly bright, but happy.

"It's been great spending time with you, too. How about this? We work on getting to know each other all over again, as *friends*. And we'll see what happens from there."

Steph blew air through her lips, letting out a breath she hadn't realized she was holding.

The rational, good girl part of her loved that idea. Put all that confusing, difficult stuff aside for now. Maybe for a long time, or forever.

And be good and listen to her therapist for straight A student extra bonus points.

The part of her who'd loved not only being friends with Kim, but all the things the two of them did together, *hated* it. That same part that couldn't stop wondering how the hell she'd fallen for Bobby and his fake charm and his very real lies in the first place.

That part of Steph wanted very much to drop the books, grab Kim, pull her into the cozy little reading alcove, and remind her what was so fantastic between them in the first place.

Everyone else could just mind their own business, sip their spiked tea, and wait.

She smiled instead.

"You got it. I could use a friend for damn sure. Let's go see if all of us working together managed to uncover anything."

Ivy, Venus, and Mr. and Mrs. Seagon were all arranged by the fire, talking quietly and passing books back and forth across a table that hadn't been there before. Steph wondered again at how the Seagons in particular didn't look any different from when she'd visited Odds and Endings when she was a little girl.

She was relieved and a little sad when Kim joined her great aunt on one of the loveseats, where they'd sat together earlier.

Once Steph sat beside Ivy and got a good look at what they were sorting through, she forgot all about teenaged or late-thirties awkwardness. Steph's heart beat faster, driving heat through her whole body.

"Did we all get books from 1947?" she said, pulling one of her books out.

Everyone stopped what they were doing to stare at her, like kids in her classes when she told them a pop quiz was on the way. She tried to fight it back, but a nervous giggle escaped her.

"I don't know when they were printed," Ivy said. "But I don't think that's what you're talking about, is it?"

"Well, no," Steph said. "I found things in other years, too, but I see books about the 1940s all over the table."

Mr. Seagon nodded slowly, a sad expression sitting uneasily on his round face.

"That awful business out at the Lightning Rock," he said. "When all those poor boys died. One of the worst tragedies to happen here, in memory or in history."

"Not likely in anyone's memory," Steph said. "Not from that long ago. And I have to say I haven't heard about any of these things in the Lightning Gap history I know of."

"You wouldn't, dear," Mrs. Seagon said. "We don't hide anything down here in our lovely basement study, not by any means. Quite the contrary. We keep everything we can to make sure the information is always available for those who need it. But so few people want to remember such awful events. So they slip away."

"The same happens all over the world," Venus said with a sad smile. "If people don't hide bad memories away, too many people choose to *turn* away. Unfortunately, that makes them want to keep anyone else from knowing the truth, no matter what that takes. That's one reason why a collection like this is invaluable, Carabelle. The human desire to forget and make sure everyone else does too is why they're so often secret."

Kim leaned forward, elbows on her knees, rubbing at her temples.

"Hang on, I pulled books from more than the 1940s, and I know you did too, Auntie Venus. Do we have more in common besides one year?"

A few minutes of shuffling, sorting, and Kim taking notes gave them too many matches to be any kind of coincidence. Besides the distressing event in 1947, violent incidents popped up in the 1930s, 50s, 70s, and 2010s.

The shared awareness of finding so many unpleasant events before they knew what to look for was bad enough.

What left Steph queasy and rubbing at her mouth was the matched set of news items from the late 1990s. About a group of disillusioned kids from the Midwest, traveling out from Ohio in an aimless circle of petty crimes that gradually increased in depth and daring.

Until they decided to head southeast, targeting big cities along the way. Aiming for Atlanta, and then Miami.

The supposedly fictional story that had so firmly captured her attention and time made no mention of small town stops along the way. But then she hadn't read far enough to get to this particular stop.

After they'd picked up an unwilling hostage in Knoxville and decided to pay a visit to his hometown.

In Lightning Gap.

"Are these..." she began, then stopped to clear her throat. "Do all of these things we're finding involve a local? Someone born in Lightning Gap?"

Almost everyone turned back to their books, verifying details. Ivy got up to fetch a thick book from the shelves beside the fireplace, cross-referencing from the list of births and deaths.

Rather than taking notes from what everyone found or checking her own books, Kim stared at Steph. Distress and fear painfully clear on her face.

She knew her parents would have looked at her exactly the same way.

No one else seemed to know why the idea of a native crossing paths with a dangerous outsider horrified her to her bones.

CHAPTER 22

K im forced herself to look away from the terror and shock on Steph's face, to concentrate on what had to be an antique spiral-bound notebook she'd found as she wandered the basement. It seemed a shame to mark up the slightly yellowed pages, just over the length and half the width of her hand.

But trying to keep up with the flood of names and dates on her phone would be impossible.

Nearly as impossible as pretending she didn't know exactly what disturbed Steph just now. She resisted a nearly overpowering urge to hustle Steph up the stairs, into her car, and back to her parents' house where she had a much better chance of staying safe.

She drew in a shaky breath. "Okay, listen. I think what we're looking for is someone from Lightning Gap being...

attacked. Targeted. Probably by people who aren't from here. That would be my guess, anyway."

Ivy looked up, her expression sharp.

"So you think that Phipps boy isn't part of the pattern after all?"

Before Kim could figure out how to answer without putting Steph on the spot, Auntie Venus shook her head.

"He may still be a big part of the pattern. Those young men in the 40s weren't from here, but they did attack two who were before they met their end. And that unfortunate group of women and men in the 90s were from Ohio, but they had a young man from Lightning Gap with them. Stan Phipps may not have been the target."

Steph covered her eyes with one hand, her red curls falling forward as she lowered her head.

"He may have been the first warning," she said quietly. "Sent from somewhere else. For someone else."

Mr. Seagon tilted his head and frowned.

"A warning? The first one? I'm not sure I understand. Warning who, or of what?"

"Not warning the other two who've gone missing," Ivy said. "That wouldn't make sense. It's not like there's a reason to keep people from coming to Lightning Gap."

Steph looked up into Kim's eyes, her expression too cold and neutral. As if she'd shut down every trace of her emotions. All the breath left Kim at once, but she managed to catch enough to speak.

"That depends on *why* they were coming to Lightning

Gap," she said. "If they were planning something unpleasant. Something bad for someone who is from here."

Auntie Venus sighed, then turned a sympathetic, worried gaze toward Steph.

"Planning to harm one of our own, you mean. And the warning was for anyone who came after, trying to do the same thing. Or maybe, a warning for the one sending them."

Steph tried to smile, but the pain and tears in her eyes turned it bitter.

"It's okay, Venus. I think the time has passed for trying to keep my secrets. Or protect my dignity or pride or some other such nonsense. That's at least three of us who think this may have to do with my ex-husband."

In the long silence, interrupted only by the strangely cheery cracking of the fire, Kim wished she had sat beside Steph after all. She wanted nothing more than to put an arm around her and try to offer some kind of comfort.

Knowing the only comfort in the long run would probably involve jail or violence rather than hugs only made her want to step in front of whatever was coming.

Ivy flipped the book on her lap closed with a sharp snap, then sat back with her arms crossed.

"I've known you your whole life, Stephanie, and your family a lot longer than that. Not a one of you are the kind to volunteer something private like that unless you have a damn good reason. I know that every bit as well as I know every single person in this room and a hell of a lot more besides will do whatever it takes to protect you, all talk of Lightning Gap itself doing the same aside. What do you need to tell us?"

Kim watched Steph's shoulders and chest slowly rise and fall. She picked up her tea cup in hands that shook less than Kim's did in that moment.

"The truth is I didn't expect to have to explain this to anyone once I got back here. I figured the small town rumor mill would take care of all of that for me." She glanced up and smiled, then returned to staring into her tea. "I won't get into the unpleasant details, but I didn't just leave my husband in the usual sense of trying to work it out, planning to leave, dividing things up, all of that. I left late at night and with only what I was wearing. I *ran* from him. I escaped."

No one spoke, but Ivy put her hand on Steph's shoulder.

"He didn't want the divorce, but thank the gods he couldn't fight it in Kentucky. The fact that he more than qualified for a protective order helped it go quickly. He bought out my half of the house to keep it quiet, and it was over."

Her voice broke at the end, and she sipped at her tea.

"Except maybe it *isn't* over. I didn't know this Stan Phipps. I've never even heard of him. But he's from Laurel Gap, just like my ex. I don't think I'm the only one who feels like this could be because of me."

Mr. Seagon blotted his eyes with a sky-blue handkerchief.

"I'm so sorry that happened to you, Stephanie. No one deserves something awful like that. Least of all someone as sweet and kind as you are."

Mrs. Seagon was dry-eyed, but her voice was soft.

"They surely don't," she said. "I'm not disbelieving you, not at all. Everyone in this room understands how important it is to heed a feeling, especially about something like this. Do you have more making you believe this, dear?"

Steph started to shake her head, then froze, scowling at the stack of books in front of her.

"Nothing I can point to, though the second I get home I'm going to ask my father for more information about the other two who are missing. See if they may have crossed paths with my ex. There was one thing, something I saw in the first book I put my hands on. It may not mean anything."

Kim jumped when Auntie Venus put an arm around her and squeezed.

"I realize you and Kim are new to our little group," she said. "New to the heart of Odds and Endings, and how that connects to the heart of all of Lightning Gap. So I'll tell you plain and true that the last thing you should be doing is trying to talk yourself out of whatever you found."

"She's right," Ivy said, nodding. "I'm sure you both noticed the collection down here isn't exactly organized to fit a computer or even an old card catalog. But I've never known anyone who had an honest need who didn't find their answers in this basement. You have a wonderful scientific mind, Stephanie, and it will continue to serve you well. When you're here, you have to get comfortable relying on other ways."

Steph's gaze met Kim's again, and Steph let out a soft laugh.

"If I have to rely on other ways, I'll need all the support I can get." She picked up a thin hardcover book, with what looked like a scratchy burgundy cover. The book fell open to a dirt-colored ribbon that looked like cheap velvet.

"My ex... This isn't easy, but I need to make it simple. His name is Bobby Faulks. So, *Bobby* always claimed this house had been in his father's family for generations. At least two hundred years. But this book shows it as belonging to the McReynolds family only fifty years ago, and for generations before that."

She held the book out to Ivy, who took a quick look and passed it on to Mrs. Seagon.

"I know that sounds like a minor thing," Steph said, rubbing her fingertips through her hair. "A silly thing. No other house in Laurel Gap looks like that, though. And, well, it caught pretty hard at my attention when I picked up the book."

"Then you're right to mention it," Mr. Seagon said, holding the book out to Auntie Venus. "You met his family, in that house?"

Steph shrugged. "Sure, a few times. We didn't go out there all that much. He has an older brother and sister I never even met, not even at our extremely small wedding. To tell you the truth, I came back here to Lightning Gap to visit without him most of the time. He was always busy at work. Or he claimed he was, anyway. I never thought much about it until now."

Kim took the book, and the cover was indeed unpleasantly rough against her hands. The house in the black and white photo was pretty much standard-issue old house as far as she could tell. A two-story box with wood siding, close to several others of a similar style.

Most of the older houses in Lightning Gap were more like Odds and Endings, with fanciful Victorian design and color and tons of accents. The house in the photo was plain and ordinary as could be in comparison.

Except for the unusual arrangement of windows, with some narrow and too high to see out of wedged between the traditional rectangular ones. The houses around it had the usual arrangement. She doubted Steph had made a mistake after seeing it even once.

She touched the muddy ribbon, and tried not to shudder at the way it caught at her fingertips. She called back to her years of constant investigation and interpretation as a technical writer.

When it was more important to understand than to worry about how her questions might sound.

"How did his family act?" she said. "Did they seem to be hiding anything? Or uncomfortable around him? Or you?"

Steph opened her mouth and stared up at the ceiling for a few seconds.

"They seemed...quiet. Friendly enough, but they didn't say much. 'Bobby talks enough for all of us,' his mother would say. I always felt welcome, though. It seems arrogant, maybe, but I'm going to say it. I got the feeling they were glad to see me. Glad to see someone *with* Bobby, I mean. I guess I never considered it all that unusual."

Auntie Venus smiled, with a wistful, remembering air.

"So you didn't get the overly inquisitive variety of in-laws. I loved all three sets I was lucky enough to have, mind you. But they never did tire of inquiring into our lives." She paused, glancing at Kim, then Steph. "Especially when it came to the subject of potential grandchildren who were never going arrive on the scene. That only stopped once I got solidly into my late forties."

Steph smiled, a real, honest one, and Kim reminded herself to thank her great aunt for breaking the tension.

"No, they didn't pry about that." Steph's smile faded and disappeared. "In that case Bobby was disappointed enough for all of them, as it turned out. Thank goodness I stood my ground on that front, at least."

Kim turned to Mrs. Seagon, once again desperate to change the subject away from Steph's painful memories.

"I don't want this to sound rude, but is it possible whoever wrote this book got the name wrong?"

"You're not the least bit rude, dear, but no. I knew Renee Fleming quite well, and I'm proud to have several of her history books in our collection. She was as careful and meticulous a researcher as anyone could ever want."

Before Kim put the words together herself, Ivy said it for her.

"So we know this Bobby Faulks has always been dishonest, to go along with being enough of an ass to treat Stephanie badly. Whatever else Stan Phipps may have gotten up to during his life full of questionable judgement, he may have had no idea what he was being asked to do. Or why."

"One of the things I learned about sociopaths," Steph said, "psychopaths, whichever term you prefer, is how very charming they are. I spotted several books about them upstairs, but I'd already read them all over the summer. Stan or anyone else working for Bobby probably doesn't have any idea *why* he's asking them to do anything. His superpower is making them *want* to do it for him. Desperately wanting to, would be my guess."

"So we're not going to get help from the other two," Kim said. "Assuming we could even find them." She waited until Steph looked her way, then smiled. "What I think we should do is coordinate the years we found, see what those events have in common. Then try to figure out if these two missing and one dead relate to Bobby after all."

Mrs. Seagon stood with a quick nod.

"I'll get in touch with a few friends of mine over in Laurel Gap and see what they have to say. And Kim, I can see you're doing a fine job of handwriting with your notes. But wouldn't you prefer to use a tablet, or even a computer? We always have spares on hand for our resident writers and our guests these days."

A quick laugh escaped Kim before she could stop it. The idea of something as modern—and as mundane—as electronics existing in such a firmly old-fashioned space had never crossed her mind.

"That would be wonderful, Mrs. Seagon. Thank you."

CHAPTER 23

Steph eased open the kitchen door of her parents' house, hoping for the first time in her adult life they wouldn't be home. She rolled her eyes at herself as she gently pushed it closed and leaned against it.

A grown woman who couldn't manage to remember that this was *her* house again, and for the foreseeable future, was exactly the one who would be sneaking around on a Saturday afternoon.

Much to her surprise, the cheery kitchen actually was deserted. The huge green slate island stood clean and empty, and nothing simmered on the cooktop or roasted in the oven. No aromas of bread or chicken or the family favorite of garlic lingered in the air. Only a faint trace of lemon, maybe for afternoon tea.

She couldn't hear a thing except the sound of her own breathing.

She kicked off her shoes and stepped onto the floor, the orange tiles toasty against her sock feet.

"Mom? Dad?"

Nothing.

Steph wished again that she'd gone with her initial idea of inviting the whole crew over for an early dinner and massive gabfest. She could have easily blended herself into the background between Ivy, Venus, and Kim, and maybe even Mr. and Mrs. Seagon keeping her father busy with an endless stream of questions.

BeeGirl would have happily helped with the distraction game.

No need to focus on how the whole bunch of them had found out about the latest missing person, not with all that excitement.

Both cars were out front, so they should be home. Steph padded through the kitchen and toward the side deck, the new pride and joy of the whole house. And the deck was a good guess on a sunny weekend day when it wasn't quite warm enough for gardening or fishing.

Sure enough, she slid open the sliding glass door to find Donna and David Holfield sitting together in the afternoon sun. A buddy of Steph's little brother Ryan had built them an oversized wooden lounge chair over the summer, which Steph and her mother had covered with overstuffed navy blue cushions. Now the senior Holfields could sprawl and relax and snuggle together, and very often did exactly that.

All the other quite comfortable but single-seater outdoor furniture now sat around the edges, looking sort of sad and abandoned. A big rounded pitcher full of lemonade sat on a table nearby, with two half-full glasses and one empty one.

The view of their neat lawn, still mostly hibernating garden, and forest rising up behind wasn't quite as grand and impressive as Ivy's overlooking the whole valley, but Steph adored it as much as they and Ryan did.

Both turned toward her at the same time with matching expressions of surprise shifting to welcome. That went nicely with their matching charcoal gray sweat suits and black house shoes.

"Hey, finally made it back," her mother said, smiling and holding out one hand. "You must have had a great time with Kim. I'd say you needed the break."

Steph gripped her mother's cool fingers for a second, then stretched out on a smaller version of their giant, cozy chair. The cushions were every bit as soft and cozy.

"I did. Kim, and Ivy and Venus, and the Seagons this morning. Not to mention Ivy's latest dog BeeGirl."

Her father raised a disapproving eyebrow at the mention of Ivy, but his smile gained ground at mention of the Seagons, then won out entirely at BeeGirl.

"I've never known Ivy not to have a sweet redbone hound by her side. Where did you see the Seagons? How are they?"

Steph took the glass of lemonade he poured for her and settled back.

"They're good. Energetic as ever, that never seems to change. We all went to Odds and Endings this morning, before they opened. They let us go roaming around the basement looking for books."

Her mother blinked and leaned back.

"The basement, huh? Hardly anyone gets down there besides the book club. The ones that work with the writers each year. What made that happen?"

Steph took a long drink of her lemonade, enjoying the ideal balance of tart and sweet as much as she did the few seconds to collect her thoughts.

All the planning in the world hadn't made her any better at trying to sneak things past her parents when she was a kid. Trying to get better at it now seemed like an especially pitiful waste of time.

She decided not to bother trying to sneak. But she would avoid telling everything if she could.

"We were looking for...patterns. Other times when bad things, dangerous things, happened in Lighting Gap. Kind of like what's happening now."

Her father stared straight ahead at the trees for several seconds, obviously doing some thought-gathering of his own.

"What makes you think there's a pattern happening now, or in the past?" His voice was calm and level, as if he was asking her if she'd seen any good movies lately. But he continued to look away rather than meeting her gaze. Yet another habit she recognized from her childhood years of getting into trouble.

"We found a lot of similarities, Dad. Several times when people here weren't as calm and safe as they usually are. Going all the way back to the 1920s, and quite a few since then. They all seemed to involve people from outside of town. Over and over again."

He finally looked at her, and his eyes were more curious than upset. Exactly what Steph had been hoping for.

"The same kinds of things happened every time? Any relationships between the people over time? Anything else seem to match up, like the number of years between?"

"No, not really. I couldn't find a math pattern that made sense, and I was definitely looking for one. But one thing was more common than I wanted to admit, to myself or to you. Most of the time, the original threat was from someone from outside. Toward someone who was from here."

He closed his eyes again and let out a long, slow sigh before he raised his head and looked at her. The sunlight caught the gray in his hair.

"You think the pattern is focused on you now."

Both he and Steph ignored her mother scowling at them.

"I don't know what to think," Steph said. "But you're the one who taught me how to follow my curiosity. How to trust that sense of something interesting. Something I should look into. And sometimes, yeah, my sense of something wrong."

He pinched the bridge of his nose and shook his head.

"What did the Seagons say?" Steph's mother said. She glared at her husband when he started to protest. "And Venus and Ivy?"

"They all...*we* all found the pattern. The dates that matched in all our different books, and the same things jumped out at us, even though we didn't look together. Ivy and Venus both say it feels like something is wrong. Out of tune, one of them said. Like the next wrong thing is on the horizon."

"So you're both willing to listen to them rather than me?" Steph's father said. He didn't sound angry, thank the gods. Just frustrated. "Are you all haring off on some kind of wacky adventure to try to solve the problem before the cycle starts all over again?"

Steph tried not to laugh when her mother smacked her father's thigh.

"You sound like a closed-minded, high and mighty ass, David. You know as well as I do there's often something to what the Seagons have to say. And you and your whole family trust Ivy for a good reason. Venus is just about the smartest person I've ever met. You're really going to tell me you don't think Lightning Gap has unusual qualities?"

He crossed his arms with a grunt.

"*Qualities*? Like what? The great schools? The charming location? The fresh air after our spectacular lightning storms?"

"No, Dad," Steph said. "Not like that. What I think Mom means is the way Lightning Gap takes care of her own. According to the Seagons, it always has, going back to when people first settled here."

He shook his head again, then uncrossed his arms and threw his hands up.

"Sure, fine. I've seen and heard of things around here that could be called *unusual.* Especially compared to what I hear from other county sheriffs. This town stays peaceful for the most part, yes. But when something finally does happen, most of the time it's pretty bad. I'm just not ready to make a leap from that to you being the target, Steph."

Steph's shoulders unknotted, and she took another drink of the lemonade to clear the sour, anxious taste out of her mouth.

"I'd rather not either, to tell you the truth. Maybe you can help me with that. Maybe both of you can. What's catching at me is Stan Phipps and my...and Bobby being from Laurel Gap. It makes sense to me to figure out if they ever crossed paths. Same with the other two."

"Well, that I can help you with," her dad said. "One of them, anyway. The second one, from Wolf Branch. He turned up earlier today."

Steph's stomach knotted up.

"In the same spot as the first one?"

He shook his head slowly.

"Not hardly. He got picked up way over in Holly Creek. Sheriff Crabtree called me this afternoon. Can't say the guy is in the best shape, mentally for sure. But he's alive."

"What the hell was he doing over there?" Steph's mother said. "He disappeared from here, didn't he?"

"That's what it looks like so far." Steph's dad shrugged. "No one is saying otherwise. And from what Larry says, the guy isn't making any kind of sense. They've got him held for observation, hoping he'll clear up. No traces of drugs that they can find. But he's either comatose or screaming right now."

Steph rubbed her arms, trying to tame the chills.

"I'm afraid that doesn't make me feel *less* like all of this goes together," she said. "Can we check on it? Please? See if they all knew each other? Or Bobby? I honestly think it would make me feel better."

"Sure, why not." Her father got to his feet and stood with his hands on his hips. "Sheriff Grant over in Wolf Branch has already been in touch today, too. Still no word on their missing person. But he'll have plenty of information. You know people in Kentucky are still keeping an eye on him, right? And people in Virginia are keeping an eye *out* for him. You're safe here."

"I know they are," Steph said. "I trust you. I wouldn't mind if someone swung by the house, of course. But I know."

He nodded and held out one hand to Steph's mother, pulling her to her feet.

"I've got my courthouse records," she said, "and a person or two I could get in touch with. I'm guessing Carabelle Seagon has a list of contacts at the ready herself?" Steph started to get up, but her mother waved at her to stay still. "Just stay put, we're going to start dinner."

"She does have a list, yeah. I knew you'd be able to get more."

Her father laughed and put his arm around his wife's shoulders for a second.

"I doubt very much that I'd have more than Mrs. Seagon. Different, but not more. I'll take a minute to dig up what I can. What I want *you* do to, Steph, is think about whether you really want to go down a road like this. Magical thinking, I guess you could call it. I'm not sure it would suit your scientific mind as well as it does others."

"I will, Dad. Thank you. You too, Mom."

Steph didn't miss another of those secret glances between her parents, and a nod her father probably believed was subtle. He stepped back as her mother patted her shoulder on the way by.

"Don't thank us yet, sweetheart. This may turn out to be a whole bunch of nothing. Or maybe a mess you wish you'd never gotten into."

When she closed the door behind her, Steph's father sat on the huge lounge chair again, elbows on his knees.

"I'm sorry I was being such a bear, Steph. I probably shouldn't, but I'm going to tell you why. I checked in with one of my buddies up in Louisville yesterday. One of the ones who helped us so much over the summer. Anyway, she took a ride by your old neighborhood this morning. She had eyes on him, working in the yard. Okay?"

Steph's breath caught in her throat. She wasn't sure if she was more upset that she'd gotten her dad worried, or more touched that he'd taken her so seriously.

Maybe someday she'd stop feeling so overwhelmed when someone treated her like she was sane after everything about her marriage made her wonder if she'd been crazy.

"Okay. I appreciate you checking, Dad. And for letting me know. That really does help."

He turned his head and rubbed the back of his neck.

"Yeah, well, it helped me, too. Much as I truly do hate to admit I was wondering about him. That's probably why I was so grumpy. I guess I should go in and apologize to your mother now. Not sure I should admit she was right to smack me a good one, but she was. Love you."

"Love you too, old man."

She couldn't see from where she was, but her weather sense told her a bunch of clouds were piling up to the west. Time to enjoy this soft springtime air while she could. Steph leaned back in the chair when he went inside, enjoying the cool breeze and the warm sun on her skin.

Trying to take her parents' very good advice and her father's reassurance, and remind herself that she was safe.

Digging into anything that might possibly lead back to Bobby was the *last* thing she wanted. The idea of him staying put in Louisville and still controlling some kind of hillbilly spy ring was horrible to the extreme.

After everything she'd seen, heard, and read over the past couple of days, the only thing that felt worse was the idea of pretending nothing was going on at all.

But at least for now, with her parents and so many other people on the case, she could turn her attention to another losing battle.

Her failing efforts to stop worrying about the *other* significant ex in her life. To stop wondering if she was willing or able to keep up the "just friends" arrangement after the night they'd had.

At the moment, Steph couldn't manage to close her eyes without wondering where Kim was and what she was doing.

And wondering if Kim was thinking about her, too.

CHAPTER 24

Kim managed to distract herself helping Auntie Venus clean up, for a while, anyway.

They had dinner and breakfast dishes to wash and put away. BeeGirl's red hair to sweep up. Guest room beds to change, and the usual Saturday laundry to get started.

When Auntie Venus declared the cleaning finished enough for the day, she settled herself into her great cushioned bowl of reading chair with her latest novel. She'd even changed into a strangely tame black silk pantsuit she'd brought back from Bali ages ago, and caught her hair back in a simple braid.

A clear sign of relaxation.

Kim had long-ago learned to trust her great aunt's insistence on a mental break so she could let everything they'd discovered that morning percolate and sift and arrange itself in her brain. Even though Kim rarely managed to give herself that break.

That led directly to Kim's desire to review the notes she'd emailed to herself from Odds and Endings, which had indeed been much easier to keep track of on a borrowed laptop rather than an ancient spiral notebook.

Which left her attempting to settle herself at her battle-scarred old desk.

It made perfect sense to sort through everything in her notes the same way, make sure she hadn't made any errors. See if she remembered anything else she needed to add in. Get things more clearly and firmly in her mind, so the mysterious and wonderful process of intuition could take over.

She made it as far as opening the files and staring into space.

Steph's hurt expression after Kim honest-to-goodness patted her hand (what the hell had she been *thinking*?) floated through her mind. Even if now wasn't the time for a new romantic involvement, or the resumption of an old one, Kim didn't have to be a shit about it.

Making her dear high school friend feel bad for suggesting the very thing Kim had been thinking wasn't going to help anybody.

She pushed idly at her collection of travel rocks, trying not to make enough noise to annoy Auntie Venus, or draw hard-to-answer questions.

The clusters of names, dates, and awful events on her screen was more frustrating than helpful at the moment. The only pattern to tease out and follow pointed to outsiders who threatened natives coming to bad times, if not a bad end.

None of that helped them figure out what to do right now. Or whether Stan Phipps had been an unusual accidental death, or the start of something darker. More sinister.

Something with Steph still caught up with her asshole of an ex-husband, whether she wanted to be or not.

Kim ran her fingertip along the neat letter J her cousin had carved into the surface of the old oak table with a jack from their games so many years ago.

Jay had said something about what Steph had gone through, hadn't he? The day he devoured mass quantities of Auntie Venus's chocolate chip cookies.

She pulled out her phone and scrolled through to Jay's phone number, finally remembering.

He'd known about the protective order, that was it. Apparently everyone in local law enforcement and local government did, too.

He'd known about the second missing person early on, so he might know more by now. Or more than he'd said that day.

She tapped to call, then hit the end button to stop.

"Auntie Venus? I'm sorry to bother you. Would you mind terribly if I called Jay? I was thinking he might know something about what's been going on around here with his government connections. And well, with what you might call his gossip skills."

Auntie Venus peeked up over the edge of her hardcover book with one eyebrow raised, but Kim could tell she was smiling.

"Gossip skills. That's a perfectly polite way to describe one of Jay's many well-honed talents. And complimentary in the best sense of the word, especially in his line of work."

She lowered the book to her chest and stared out the window for a second.

"That's a fine idea, Kim. A fresh perspective from someone who might know more, especially while everything is clear in our minds. There's still a good bunch of cookies down in the freezer if you want to use that to sweeten the deal. I think I'll leave you young folks to it, but I wouldn't mind a cookie or two myself."

Kim was across the room in a flash, resisting a surprisingly strong urge to touch Auntie Venus's forehead to make sure she wasn't feverish.

"Are you feeling sick?"

"Lord no, honey, I'm fine. Just had a busy day and a long night, then a busy day again today. All of it good, mind you, but tiring. I'm feeling a little achy and sore, too, probably another storm on the way." She sighed, then smiled.

"To tell you the truth, what I want to do is sit still and read for an hour or so. Then I'll go down to my own office and go over everything we found this morning. See what I can put together and who I might be able to get in touch with."

She looked at Kim for a long few seconds.

"Worried about Stephanie?"

Kim thought about brushing off the question, or giving a quick answer and walking away. As if that had any chance of working with her great aunt, or with herself. She sat on the chair's matching round footstool.

"I'm worried about her, yeah. About what we found at Odds and Endings, what all that might mean. That part scares me half to death. And…I'm worried about hurting her feelings, too. Getting into things that she might not be ready for. I might not be ready, either."

"I thought it might be something like that," Auntie Venus said. "Now I don't know what happened between her and that husband. That *ex*-husband. I know sometimes it can take a while to heal and get over a terrible thing like that. I also know you've cared about her for a long, long time. If you're meant to, you'll figure out the way forward together."

Kim lowered her head for a second, then smiled as she got to her feet.

"Thank you. I hope so. I'll leave you to your novel, and I won't forget your cookies."

Jay agreed before she quite finished asking, and before she even offered the bribe to sweeten the deal. He knocked on the kitchen door before she had them out of the oven.

His weekend ensemble consisted of a green t-shirt that was big enough to be comfortable, and blue jeans that were old and worn enough to match. His thatch of brunette hair was a bit more disheveled than usual, but it still had his signature flipped up bangs at the front.

And bless his heart, he was carrying a carton of milk.

"Kim Mullins," he said, stepping inside and giving her a one-armed hug. "Smells like paradise in here, and you and Auntie Venus can stand in for the heavenly chorus."

Kim took the milk, shaking her head.

"Jay Murray. Still every bit as full of shit as when you were in diapers. Thank you for bringing milk. We're just about out."

The usual catch-up chatter around the kitchen table continued after Auntie Venus took her cookies and disappeared to her own office. The remains of their sugar and spice and chocolate feast scattered across whimsical plates from Morocco this time. The edges curved inward almost like a four-leaf clover, and the middle was covered with loops and swirls of bright colors underneath the crumbs.

Despite three cookies surviving the feeding frenzy, Jay crossed his arms and stared at Kim

"While I appreciate Auntie Venus's cookies any time of day and at least twice on Sunday, the curiosity is getting to me. What did you mean you're wondering about the unpleasant parts of Lightning Gap's history? And about Steph's ex-*husband*?"

Kim nodded, pushing the crumbs on her plate aside so she could trace the patterns with her fingertip.

"We spent the morning at Odds and Endings. Researching. Me and Steph, Auntie Venus and Ivy Gweddon, and her sweet dog BeeGirl, though she mostly slept. Ever been in the basement there?"

Jay's eyes widened and he smiled.

"Once or twice, sure. There's no better place to study the town and how it got here. When we were planning the grand reopening for the post office once they finished restoring it a couple of years ago, Mr. Seagon welcomed us down there to get copies of photos of the original."

He leaned closer with a conspiratorial wink.

"Word is things get very interesting down there when they welcome a new writer-in-residence. And I'd swear the Seagons have been frozen in time my whole life. Not sure if it's living in that house with so many books or just the side benefits of a long, happy marriage."

Kim snorted. "I've never seen one Seagon without the other, or without books. So I'd say that could go either way. I'd never been down there until this morning. It was the strangest thing, Jay. All we had to go on was the one death and one missing person. But we all came up with the same list of dates and nasty incidents."

"Not that strange, maybe. You know as well as I do that bad things don't happen all that often here. So everyone notices when they do. It's not perfect, by any means. People will be people and act like idiots just like anywhere else."

He put another cookie on his plate but didn't take a bite.

"Still," he said, "crime here is almost non-existent compared to the rest of Felten County. And Felten County is an oasis of peace compared to just about everywhere else. Steph's father could probably tell you a whole lot more about that, if he wanted to."

Steph's worried but defiant expression when she told them about the third missing person that morning floated through Kim's mind. Sheriff Holfield *was* willing to talk, at least to the right people. Or with the right evidence.

"It's not so much that we all found the same things," Kim said. "What struck me as strange is most of us didn't know about the crimes we found. Like you said, we should all notice because it's unusual. But only the Seagons seemed to know about most of them. I guess people don't want to remember things like that, but it seems strange how they all disappeared."

"Is this stuff you're comfortable with me seeing, Kim? I know this was kind of a closed group, I get that. If I have an idea what you're talking about, it may help." He scowled for a second, then rolled his eyes. "I *know* what you're thinking before you say a word. Believe it or not, I do know how to keep my mouth shut when it really matters. I won't talk to anyone else unless you say it's okay."

Kim glared at him for a few seconds, unable to resist stringing him along a little. Jay had revealed a few things about her when they were kids that she hadn't appreciated one bit.

"I'm not sure I would have made this decision, but Auntie Venus thinks it's a good idea for you to see everything. So you get by on that technicality. Come on." She stood and waved toward her desk. "You can bring your cookie if you want, but don't you dare spill milk on my laptop."

Jay carried one of the kitchen chairs over, then made a show of scooting his plate and little glass of milk to the very edge of the old breakfast nook table before he sat. He grinned and traced the outline of his own first initial much like Kim had.

"Wow, I must have been digging down hard that day. I can't believe this is still here. You were so pissed at me, I thought you'd never get over it."

"I remember you being pissed at me because I snitched on

you." Kim opened her laptop and pulled up the list. "You swore you'd never forgive me as long as you lived."

"Well, I switched over to never forgetting instead a long time ago. It's a lot less stressful. *This* many? Are they all murders? All violent?"

Kim scrolled through the list, giving Jay time to glance over them.

"Almost all ended up with someone dead, yeah. The first...well, what everyone seems to think is first, was a car crash back during the Great Depression. That one didn't seem to be because of anything but driving in a blizzard. Struck me as odd anyway, though. Like they were running from something. Driving into a mess like that doesn't make sense on our modern roads, much less back then."

"Then what do *you* think was first?"

Kim turned to face him, not sure how much she was going to say until she opened her mouth.

"The town started pretty much at the same time the 1918 flu really hit. From what I saw just glancing through, the losses were pretty bad. A bunch of kids sheltered at Odds and Endings after their parents got sick. Or after they died. It was a doctor's house then. Someone in Mrs. Seagon's family, I think."

"So everything here got started during an awful time," Jay said, shaking his head. "I always heard 1917. I just never put it together with that flu hitting at almost the same time. Now, you tell me how you think that's related to Steph's ex. And I'll tell you about the second missing person. And the third."

"You mean the third one who came from Bountyfield?"

Kim said with a wink of her own. "We heard about that this morning. I probably wouldn't admit this to anyone else, but I'm not sure if I hope the news about the second person is good or bad."

Jay leaned close enough to nudge her shoulder.

"Look who has secret sources now. I'll just pretend I don't know who could *possibly* have inside law enforcement information. I guess you'll have to decide whether the news about number two is good or bad for yourself. They found him, over in Holly Creek, believe it or not. Seems he's alive, but quite a bit worse for wear physically. Mentally, too."

Chills raced over Kim's arms at the idea of someone disappearing from Lightning Gap and mysteriously showing up almost eighty twisty and hazardous miles away. Especially someone people had been searching for. Mental trouble on top of all that was almost too much to think about.

"What do you mean, mentally?"

"Well, I hear Sheriff Crabtree has the guy held at the hospital. Not because they suspect him of committing a crime, but because he may be the victim of one. He's either screaming his head off or staring into space. He's not exactly beaten up like you might expect, but he's scratched and bruised all to hell. Almost like he walked across the mountains to get there."

"And no idea what happened, or how he got there? Or why he was here in the first place?"

Jay shook his head, then broke off the edge of his cookie and held it out toward Kim. She took it and nibbled out a hit of pure, intense dark chocolate.

"No one's gotten a coherent word out of him that I know of. What I don't know is whether whoever reported him missing has any idea what's been going on. That might be a question for your secret source."

Kim drummed her fingers on the desk, only half hearing Jay's last words.

"Mrs. Seagon said she would be getting in touch with friends of hers over in Bountyfield. Auntie Venus might know folks over there, too. And yeah, smartass, it's possible Steph's father might have heard more. I don't want to out her for telling us about it, you know?"

Jay tilted his head to one side, then the other, with a strange little frown on his face.

"I could see what you mean there, but didn't you say this has something to do with her ex? That's what you said on the phone, remember? Not having her and probably her dad involved doesn't make sense with what little I know about Steph's ex-asshole."

Kim put her bit of cookie back on Jay's plate, then leaned forward and rubbed her eyes.

"No. No, it doesn't make sense. Listen, are you busy tonight? I think Auntie Venus wants a break, and I got the feeling Ivy and BeeGirl wanted to stay in and figure out what they could. Maybe it is time we talk to Steph. Maybe that will help me get it clear enough in my head to explain it to you."

Her phone buzzed in her pocket with what turned out to be a text message from Mr. Seagon, copied to everyone who'd been at Odds and Endings that morning. Kim knew before she finished skimming the first paragraph that she'd be talking to Steph tonight. And to Auntie Venus and probably Ivy as well.

"This all just got a hell of a lot more interesting," she said, handing the phone to Jay. "A lot faster than I expected, too."

"I'm all yours tonight," he said, eyes widening as he read. "I happen to have a very close friend who works in the hospital out in Holly Springs who owes me an information favor. I'll share as long as you fill me in on what you know about a guy stupid enough to lose Steph in the first place."

Kim groaned and sat back.

"We can compare notes about the ex all night long, and I'll tell you all about why we think he matters. As long as you pretend I wasn't stupid enough to lose Steph myself years before they ever met."

CHAPTER 25

Steph tried to pick up her half-empty glass of lemonade, but her hands were shaking too badly. A text message from the Seagons followed immediately by a call from Kim shattered every bit of the calm she'd regained in a few minutes of relaxing on her parents' deck.

And now she had to go marching inside and not only fill them in on what was going on, but also ask if Kim and Jay could join them for dinner.

She had to admit she'd told everyone about the third missing person.

She gave up on the lemonade and got slowly to her feet.

No, she wasn't going to cower out here and pretend nothing was happening. Then maybe pretend surprise when Kim and Jay showed up, like a guilty teenager.

She was going to face this whole thing like the guilty *adult* she was. And deal with whatever the consequences turned out to be.

By the time she got her nerves settled enough to head inside, her father met her at the sliding glass door. Face pale, eyes and mouth tight. A tantalizing whiff of cooking onions followed him out.

"Listen Steph, I just got off the phone with Ivy. She's on her way here, planning to pick up Venus on the way." He stared up at the clouds gathering as the sun tracked its way down toward the west. "Sounds to me like there's more of a connection between our three missing persons than we'd found yet."

Steph put her hand to her chest, not sure if she was relieved or that much more afraid.

"Something the Seagons found?"

He nodded with a grim smile.

"Of course it was. The two of them have more connections than all the law enforcement in Felten County, Boun County, and Sutherland County put together. I have no idea how they did it so fast, but the Seagons got into school records, or got someone to do that for them. All three of our missing attended the same high school for a few months."

Steph closed her eyes and took a deep breath before she looked into her father's eyes.

"It was in Laurel Gap, wasn't it? And they went to school with Bobby, too. Right?"

"You're right about Laurel Gap, and yeah, they're all around the same age as Bobby. I want to say we would have uncovered it eventually, but it might have taken a while. I guess two of our three disappearing men had…family trouble, or maybe it was trouble of their own. Anyway, they changed schools more than once before they finally got enough done to graduate. I'm sorry, sweetheart."

Steph blinked. "Sorry? For what? Now that you have the information, you're acting. Not flying off the handle and acting before. That's what I've always heard you say."

"I'm sorry because I lied to you earlier. At least I didn't tell you all of the truth. When you mentioned people feeling like something was off in Lightning Gap? Like it had slipped out of tune somehow? I've been feeling that without realizing it. Other people around town and around the county have, too."

He scrubbed his hands over his face and through his hair, messing up his red and silver curls.

"Law enforcement types used to say it was the phases of the moon, when people acted up like this. Or low pressure giving them headaches when the weather changes. Nothing serious usually, not like robberies or anything violent. More like an increase in minor violations. More people speeding. Running stop signs and red lights. Not quite getting into a fight, but getting restless. Less considerate and more unruly. On edge. I've been seeing that here over the last couple of weeks. In the county and even in town."

Steph started to protest, then she turned away and walked toward the edge of the deck.

She'd been seeing the same thing at school, hadn't she?

It wasn't just the kids acting up over the rumors on Friday. They'd been…well, restless for a little while now. Talking out of turn, not paying attention. Silly things like using their phones or even passing notes where she could easily see them. Kids she'd had all year who hadn't acted like that before.

Steph herself had needed her afternoon breaks in her little meditation closet in her classroom more than usual, too. Not only because her students had been more of a handful than usual.

Because she'd been feeling the scrape and shift of something wrong, too.

And after being back here for a month, Kim finally decided to drop by and say hello, unknowingly turning everything up even more.

Her father joined her by the deck rail, both of them leaning on their elbows.

"You're right, Dad. I hadn't put it together yet, but I've been feeling the same way. Seeing it at school, too. I guess it never occurred to me that it could be more than...I don't know, spring fever." She turned to look at him.

"I'm sorry to sound so blunt, but did it sneak up on you, too? Or, like you asked me and Ryan so often when we were growing up, did you make the decision to lie?"

He kicked at the wood under his feet.

"A little of both, I think. I caught myself thinking of that old saw about the full moon. The data flat-out don't support it, and I know that. But my mind went there anyway."

"Maybe things work more differently in Lightning Gap than we know."

He grinned at her and stood upright.

"Maybe. Anyway, I am sorry. It shouldn't have taken Ivy

or the Seagons or anyone else for me to take you seriously. I still don't know that this has anything to do with Dipshit Bobby Faulks, as your mother is right to call him. Ivy didn't mention his name in what they found today. But I'm listening, okay? And I'm still not going to let *anything* happen to you."

He held out his arm for her to link hers through, and he and Steph walked toward the door together.

"Okay," she said. "Want me to fill you in on what we found, or did Ivy pretty much cover it?"

He grunted. "Ivy covered a hell of a lot. More than I wanted to be aware of, to tell you the truth. I'd love to hear what feels important to you. You're pretty much my favorite, you know."

"Yeah, I know." Steph opened the door, then paused. "Did Ivy mention Kim and her cousin Jay are on the way over here too? That's what I was coming inside to tell you, but I got distracted and forgot."

"No, Ivy didn't mention that. Well, if we're having four more for dinner, this is your big chance. We could use your help if you're feeling up to it."

Steph blinked back tears that came up out of nowhere. She tried to hide it by turning away as she closed the door.

"Of course I can help. If you're willing to put up with me not having any idea what to do in the kitchen."

"Well, that's our fault, isn't it?" He shrugged. "You weren't interested when you were a kid, and that was fine. Neither one of us were going to force you or your brother to pick up more of the basics for sustaining life. Ryan wanted to learn, you didn't. But now, you've been offering to help since you got back home."

"I figured you were looking out for me. I wasn't exactly in the best state of mind when I got back."

They stopped beside the huge green island, where Steph's mother had just gotten out a much bigger pile of frozen shrimp and fresh spinach than the three of them could possibly eat.

Steph's father stared at her for a long moment.

"That's changed now, hasn't it? Your state of mind. Feels like all at once somehow. I'm still not going to push you where you don't want to go, but I can see the difference in you. You seem...calmer now. You seem ready."

Steph resisted the impulse to scrub her fingers against her scalp. She wasn't feeling that knotted up tension at all, honestly. What she was fighting now was a habit more than a compulsion. She didn't miss the sensation of her hair tangling and twisting itself all day long, either.

If her parents could let their understandable urge to protect and take care of her slip a bit, she could let go of a strange old ritual she might not need any more.

She leaned up and kissed him on the cheek, smiling at his scratchy weekend stubble.

"I think you're right. I don't know what's coming, and part of me wants to doubt anything is going to happen at all. But I feel like I'll get through it."

CHAPTER 26

The one good thing Bobby could say about the endless, frustrating drive between Louisville and backwoods, best-forgotten Felten County, Virginia, was traffic got lighter the closer he got.

Once he departed the seething mess of I-64 for Mountain Parkway, he could relax his focus on the swarms of other vehicles and drivers who obviously didn't suffer from any worries about road safety. Conditions would soon deteriorate when his route stepped down to the narrow twists of 23, and arguably even worse drivers than on the interstate.

Trying to anticipate the quirks and failings of an old junker of a van that had never been as well cared for as Bobby's vehicles was sure to make the final few hours even more of a headache than usual. Thankfully the headlights seemed to be one of the few systems that were in perfect working order.

But for now, he had the well-maintained road nearly to himself under a partly cloudy, half-moon sky.

With any luck, his oblivious passengers wouldn't stir before he got to Lightning Gap and dumped them and their worthless van in a convenient junkyard.

How they figured out where they were and got themselves back to Louisville—or not—wasn't Bobby's concern.

He glanced at his phone on the off-chance that either of his two still-living redneck associates had managed to return his calls. Cellular signal would soon be spotty at best for the rest of the way.

Nothing at all, exactly as he'd expected. No one had tried to call either his public phone—currently tucked into the charger at his house in Louisville—or this one.

If Steph's Sheriff Daddy or anyone else got curious enough to run a trace on the cellular network, they'd find ample evidence that he was as safely tucked in at home as the phone was.

If anyone bothered to call his public persona, he'd get the call forwarded to him in seconds.

Between that and the dusty rust bucket of a van, which had carried him out of Louisville as a reclining back seat passenger, Bobby had no expectation of anyone knowing where he was or where he was heading.

The price of two bottles of bottom-shelf bourbon (obtained legally in a Louisville liquor store) and a handful of powerful sleeping pills (obtained less legally from one of Bobby's Lexington suppliers) seemed a pittance in return for such freedom.

His two new playmates had been pitifully eager to believe he was giving them oxy or benzos once they'd rediscovered the joys of bourbon.

His supplier could always be trusted to obscure any identifying markers on pills or capsules. Of course by then, the happy couple couldn't have managed to focus well enough to read or recognize much of anything.

It had been their quick surrender more than any organized plan on his part that sent him hurtling toward Virginia and Lightning Gap for the first time more than a year. Since months before Steph made her escape.

That and a few sips of their liquid courage to keep his mind going full-steam ahead when he realized how much they were going to let him do, as long as he let *them* do what they'd been missing so badly.

Just as he'd expected, a couple of hours of brooding had given him more than enough ideas of what to do once he was in Virginia and reunited with his vanished spouse.

Bobby fiddled with the badly installed aftermarket radio, quickly giving up on finding anything he could stand to listen to for more than a few miles. As he picked up his phone to turn on music or a podcast or an audiobook or anything remotely interesting, it rang in his hand.

He drew in a sharp breath through his nose at the number flashing on the screen. A call from the sheriff's office in Walton County, Virginia, kept him from reacting to the sudden inhalation of stale cigarettes, rancid sweat, and truly disgusting farts embedded in the van's interior.

He was reasonably sure he hadn't been in Walton County

since his long-ago days of playing mediocre high school baseball. None of his useless collaborators were from there, either.

But someone there knew this phone number.

And whoever was calling might have information Bobby would regret not knowing in a few short hours.

Answering seemed like a better risk than not.

After his curt half-grunted greeting, a pleasant-voiced man who sounded like he'd spent time somewhere besides Walton County spoke.

"Mr. McReynolds? Robert McReynolds? This is Sheriff Crabtree down here in Holly Creek, Virginia. Sorry to bother you, but I'm hoping you can help us out with a situation we have here tonight."

Bobby held his breath for a second, slipping back into his childhood self. When he was every bit as hillbilly and rough-edged as his unreliable old *friends* still were. When he even spoke in a higher pitched, and always much louder, range.

His skin crawled at the sound of his own voice when he finally let it pass his lips.

Not from disgust, not exactly. More from fear that someone overhearing him would recognize all of the less socially acceptable tendencies he'd worked so hard to keep out of sight.

"Evening Sheriff, this here is Robert McReynolds. You're not bothering me one little bit. I'll be more than happy to help you if I can possibly manage."

Bobby didn't miss the subtle shift in the other man's voice. An easy adaptation toward the same higher pitch and unrefined accent.

"I sure do thank you for that. What we got here is a man that was found earlier today, out on the edge of town. He wasn't what you'd call beat up, but he was very much the worse for wear. I'm afraid he wasn't able to talk to us, either. No signs of drugs or alcohol, nothing like that. It was more like he couldn't catch hold of who he was or how he'd gotten there. Until just a few minutes ago when he cleared up a bit."

"That surely is strange, Sheriff. I'm right glad he seems to be doing better. I'm not real clear on how I might be able to help you out yet. He have a name you might be willing to share with me?"

The sheriff gave a brief *mmmmm-hmmmm* of agreement, and a quick pause like he was double-checking.

"Of course, that would make this whole conversation make a lot more sense, wouldn't it? Driver's license says he's Eugene Hunsaker, with an address out in Laurel Gap."

Bobby's jaw and shoulders and gut knotted up, and his stomach slid into an unpleasant mess of relief and fury.

Unreliable associate number two had finally reared his dumbass head.

But why now, and why all the way over in Holly Creek?

And how had any of that led back to Bobby? Or more accurately, to Robert?

"I know Eugene, sure," he said. "Haven't seen him in years, but we catch up over the phone from time to time. Hate to hear he's gotten himself into such a state. But I'm still not real clear on what I can do to help you, Sheriff."

"I was hoping you might know how he got into such a state, to be honest. Whether he's had this kind of trouble before. He doesn't have much of a medical history that we could find."

"I don't seem to recall Eugene ever talking about any kind of trouble like this. Course a whole lot of folks keep that kind of thing to themselves, don't they? I'll still do what I can even if I don't have any idea what that might be. I hope you don't take this the wrong way, but it does seem strange to call me with that going on. Mind if I ask how you came by my name and number?"

"I don't mind a bit, Mr. McReynolds. The way I got to you was he cleared up some this evening, enough to ask where he was. When I asked if there was someone I could call, he said your name clear as anything. 'Tell Robert, tell Robert, gotta tell Robert.' He managed to unlock his phone, but I'm afraid he's slipped back into his mind again now."

Bobby noted the mile marker sign streaking by, doing quick calculations in his head. He still had a good thirty minutes of cell signal, so that wasn't a worry yet. Or an excuse to drop off the line.

But assuming this sheriff was telling the truth—which he was unless he was a liar as gifted as Bobby himself—Eugene hadn't said a word about what he was doing in Lightning Gap. Loyalty was one of the rare signs of intelligence he could be counted on to show.

Another was an eerie knack for faking the symptoms of just about any kind of illness that didn't require a blood test. Eugene had often demonstrated his ability to turn himself green and sweaty on demand when they were in high school.

This seemed...extreme, but not unbelievable.

What Bobby needed most was information. And this talkative rube of a sheriff might sound more educated than most, but he seemed to be in the mood to give it.

"You needing someone to get in touch with his family? Or someone to sign for him, something like that?"

"We couldn't find any family of his close by, I'm sorry to say. The last of them passed away a while back. Do you happen to know if he has anyone else we should call? Maybe close by who might be able to take him in?"

Bobby forced the huge grin off his face before he answered. He doubted Eugene or anyone else would have mourned the last of his family passing away. A big party would be the more appropriate response.

Sort of the way he felt about his own not-at-all-dearly departed father.

"That's a real shame about his folks," he said. "I'm right sorry, I don't know of anyone else back there, Sheriff. Been living away a long while myself."

"Okay, I understand. I'm hoping since he came around once, he might be a little bit more clear-headed if he wakes up again. Listen, I sure do appreciate your time, Mr. McReynolds. If you think of anyone who might be able to help, would you mind to let me know? I'm afraid Mr. Hunsaker here might take a while to recover."

"That's all right, Sheriff Crabtree. If I can come up with anything, I'll give you a call right away. I just wish I could have figured out some way to make this right. I sure do hope you can get everything worked out for the best."

Bobby rolled down the van's window a couple of inches

when the call ended, contemplating tossing the expensive phone out into the eastern Kentucky night. But since one of his missing associates had managed to show up, the other one might do the same.

Maybe even with information about Steph that would make this trip much easier and more productive.

Even with his option of forwarding calls from this phone to the older model in his briefcase or to a new one he picked up along the way, Robert's digital tether might come in handy.

He settled for turning it off and breathing in the cold, humid air, scented with a nearby coal fire.

Every breath in pulled Bobby Faulks and his carefully built and maintained shield of normality back to the forefront. Every breath out pushed Robert McReynolds and his inability to hide much of any damn thing back into the past where he belonged.

Bobby had sparked into life when Robert's dear old mother remarried during his last year of high school. No one questioned her changing her name, of course. Even though she continued to live in the grand old McReynolds house to this day.

No one questioned how much Robert had changed when he visited from college the next year, or complained when he asked them to call him Bobby instead. No one even minded the fact that he dressed, wore his hair, even spoke differently. They were just so glad he seemed to be settling down. Finding his place in the world.

Him losing his disturbing mannerisms and habits—the

way the air in the room felt cold and sharp as broken glass when he walked in—that didn't bother his family, either.

He'd been a little surprised that no one got upset when he legally changed his name before he finished college, but he shouldn't have been. He'd never been close to his much older brother or sister, and the fact that they existed meant he'd never been close to his father.

One son and one daughter was enough as far as Harry McReynolds was concerned.

He'd never considered Robert the Unwelcome Surprise Baby his problem or his responsibility. And he'd never tired of making sure Mrs. McReynolds understood that.

No wonder his mother—by then so happily Mrs. Faulks—never protested her son's transformation from Robert McReynolds to Bobby Faulks.

The expensive little matter of doing so with a new Social Security number in hand never came up in conversation.

So of course no one in his family or anyone else ever caught on that he maintained identification in both names, and in two very different parts of Kentucky.

Worth every pretty penny to make that happen, too.

What mattered most was no one anywhere near Louisville had met or even heard of Robert McReynolds, and they never would.

Steph had only met him one time.

The night she left.

That few minutes with Robert had been enough to erase years of a perfectly happy marriage to Bobby from her ungrateful mind.

With one final breath and his transition complete, Bobby rolled the window back up.

He still had a few hours of driving ahead of him, and his unfortunate cargo in the back would make it hard to find somewhere comfortable to sleep. Hotels tended to frown upon such things.

Bobby might have to call upon Robert before he got to Lightning Gap—and Steph—after all. Dumping the van near a town big enough to have a motel and a used car lot would solve all kinds of problems.

A good night's sleep and a stop for a change of clothes, and he'd be ready for his reunion.

Steph and Robert were certain to have a fantastic time together.

Then Bobby would be free to find someone more... compatible with his and Robert's interests.

CHAPTER 27

Kim couldn't help wondering what cosmic turn of events had her spending most of a second day with Steph after so many years apart.

And what cosmic asshole made so much of that time happen while they were in the middle of a whole bunch of people. Especially people who were paying way too much attention to the two of them.

Steph's house (technically her parents' house) was every bit as calming and pleasant as Kim remembered. Same with the unbelievable good smells that floated through the huge kitchen.

Steph's parents were every bit as reassuring and welcoming, even while they were bustling around making all those enticing aromas happen. Donna and David—as they'd insisted on being called the first time Kim met them—hadn't changed much more than the house.

They'd both put on a comfortable amount of weight, and he'd let a bit of silver sneak into hair the same curly red as Steph's. Donna's hair was as black as ever, expertly touched up to be sure, but looking fantastic.

Besides being far more sexy and attractive in her late thirties than she'd ever been in high school, Steph didn't have anything to worry about when it came to how she'd likely age in the future.

Despite all the familiarity with Steph's house, as if Kim had last been there a week ago instead of almost two decades passing, she was startled and pleasantly surprised with how warmly Donna and David greeted her. Big hugs and genuine smiles that even had Steph looking confused.

Kim caught glimpses of what looked like too much shrimp for five, a gigantic bundle of greens, and a big pile of some kind of grain going into a steamer. If her memories of meals, and even snacks, with the Holfields was accurate, she was in for every bit as much of a treat as around her Auntie Venus's table the night before.

She was drawing breath to ask how she could help when Steph put tall glasses full of clear, sparkling liquid in her and Jay's hands. Before they could even ask what the mint-scented drinks were, Steph hustled them away from the massive green granite island and out onto a deck off the kitchen.

The deck looked new, with the wood still dark and sharp-edged. It definitely didn't have the lived-in grooves and comfortable soft places than either Auntie Venus or Ivy's porches did. Several black metal chairs, tables, and a long footstool sat around the edges, all overlooking a forest view that would be spectacular once springtime showoff season really got going.

But the obvious place of honor was a huge wooden lounger piled up with big blue cushions. Kim thought she and Steph would fit comfortably with room to spare for Jay.

If it were up to Kim, though, Jay would sprawl on the smaller version of the lounger close by and leave the big one for her and Steph.

"Sorry to rush you like that." Steph let out a huge breath. "Good to see you, Jay. We can go back in and offer to help in a minute, but I think the chefs of the house already had all they could handle with my dubious efforts to pitch in. Did you know Ivy and Venus are on their way over?"

Kim blinked and shook her head. "Um, no. Auntie Venus was holed up in her office when we left. Looking over all the stuff we got from the Seagons today and not planning to go anywhere, I thought."

Steph raised one eyebrow and smiled.

"You saw the same text message I did, I'm sure. We all got it. I get the feeling Ivy called Mrs. Seagon, then Ivy called Venus and my dad. I expect we'll be hearing a lot more than we read in that text message, and that was plenty."

Kim laughed before she could stop herself. This situation was fascinating and strange and more than a little bit scary, but funny didn't fit any of it.

"I suspect we may have a bit of new information to dump on top of the fire, thanks to Jay and his special investigative skills."

Jay ducked his head, but not before Kim caught his smile.

"Oh, you know how it is," he said. "Keeping up with how things are going with our friends and neighbors outside of Felten County is part of my job description. And my special investigative skills are one reason I'm so damn good at my job."

He did indeed settle himself on the single lounger, pointedly facing the double version. She and Steph glanced at each other, then each of them too obviously tried to figure out which of the chairs around the edge of the deck would work instead.

"Oh my *lord* have *mercy*," Jay said in an exaggerated Southern drawl from nowhere near Lightning Gap. "Would the two of you *please* stop playing coy and sit? We've got things to talk about before the grownups get here!"

Steph flashed a half-smile and curled up against the back of the big lounger, her legs tucked up to leave plenty of room at the foot. Kim considered for a quick second, then sat there instead of reclining beside her. Later would be plenty of time for all the things flitting through her mind.

She hoped.

"Okay, finally," Jay said. "What I found out has to stay under wraps, but I suspect we'll hear something about it soon. Turns out missing person number two isn't missing anymore. One Eugene Hunsaker turned up all the way over in Holly Creek late this morning. He's been either spaced out or screaming the whole time."

Instead of looking as surprised as Kim felt at receiving that bit of information, Steph only nodded.

"Sorry to scoop you, Jay. But my dad filled me in on the

mystery man not long before we got Mr. Seagon's text. I was going to tell you when you got here. Sheriff Crabtree over there is one of his big buddies."

Jay leaned forward and raised his eyebrows.

"Did your father mention the mystery man woke up a little while ago? Enough to ask where he was, and even unlock his phone so Sheriff Crabtree could make a phone call on his behalf?"

Steph's eyes widened. "He didn't, no. Did he… Did your top-secret source say who the guy called?"

Kim started to say they didn't know yet, but Jay nodded.

"I got a text about two minutes ago with that very information. Someone named Robert McReynolds."

Steph sat up and grabbed Kim's hand hard enough to hurt.

"McReynolds, you said? Are you sure about that?"

Jay held out his phone, one of the huge, almost tablet-sized models. Kim recognized the chat app as one Jay told her was encrypted and safe from anyone's prying eyes or snooping electronics.

Something about reading the name inside a bright yellow message bubble brought the morning's conversation at Odds and Endings back to Kim full force an instant before Steph spoke.

"I *knew* that caught my eye for a reason. Remember what I said about the house, Kim? The one Bobby always said had been in his family for generations? The Faulks family? It was listed as the McReynolds house."

Kim fumbled for her cold glass and took a sip, trying to

open up her dry throat enough to talk. The fizzy lemon and mint concoction seemed to open up her whole mind as well.

"There's no way those two names are an accident, Steph. Bobby Faulks and Robert McReynolds? And that same house. Is he smart enough to do something like that? Sneaky enough?"

Steph squeezed Kim's hand before she let go to rub her fingertips against her scalp, leaving her red curls in disarray.

Her eyes looked more cold and determined than upset.

"Absolutely. He's smart and sneaky enough to do a hell of a lot more than that. If he could find any advantage in it, or any way to hurt someone else, he'd do it just for fun. There might be a reason I never met his brother and sister, too. Do you know anyone who could trace both names, Jay? See if they're matched up somehow?"

Jay sat back, looking unsure of himself for the first time.

"I do, sure, but maybe not on a Saturday evening. I can ask. Do you think Auntie Venus or Ivy might be able to find out, Kim?"

"Maybe. We can ask when they get here. But I think our better bet might be going right back to Mrs. Seagon. Sorry Jay. Her contacts probably have a few decades of gossip on yours."

He held up both hands, palms out.

"You'll never hear me even pretend to play down the powers of either one of the Seagons. What are you thinking, Steph? That your ex changed his name or something?"

Steph stared up at the darkening sky, her eyebrows drawn close together, lips and chin trembling.

"I don't know, I don't *know*! I'm not mad at either of you, please don't think that. But I left him...eight...*months*...ago. All I wanted then and all I want now is to never see or hear another word about him as long as I live. And now *everything* I hear somehow twists back to him."

She pulled her knees up and wrapped her arms tight around them, both fists clenched so hard her knuckles showed white and her hands shook.

"I don't care what it takes or how we do it," she said, her voice harsh and low. "Not any more. I just want Bobby or Robert or whatever the hell his name is to stay the fuck out of my life."

Kim's body moved before her mind had a chance to interfere, scooting over beside Steph. She wrapped her arms around Steph and pulled her close.

Tears ran down Kim's cheeks at the way Steph relaxed against her. At how Steph's body trembled, feeling so fragile in her arms.

Not sad tears, or tears that said Kim wanted comforting. More than one of her own exes had made that mistake when she was nowhere near this nuclear level of upset.

These were bitter and hot, drawn from fury rather than sadness.

With enough heartbreak for Steph mixed in to twist Kim's rage even hotter.

"That's why we're here, Steph," she said, her own voice shaking.

She jumped when she felt Jay's arms around them both.

He'd moved almost as fast as she had, wedging himself in close by Steph's other side.

"That's exactly right," he said, rubbing Kim's back. "I don't know what he did to you and I don't give a shit. We'll do whatever it takes to make this stop."

CHAPTER 28

Steph fought it as hard as she could.

But two people holding her tight, both making it clear they were on her side, that they believed her. People who would do whatever it took to make this madness stop was too much.

She caught one long, hitching breath before everything made a horribly painful attempt to burst out of her all at once.

The fear she'd lived with since the day Bobby yelled when she found *his* money in *their* house.

Three years of confusion and growing unreality as he twisted and mangled her sanity.

The horror and heartbreak of what Ansou told her in that sweltering parking lot, and what she heard from so many more after.

Her gut-wrenching certainly her life was at risk the night

she finally left, when a stranger she'd never met before who looked like her husband described exactly how he'd end her life. In excruciating detail, making it clear just how much she'd suffer along the way.

Steph hadn't cried, not really, since she thought she'd shed enough tears to hold her for at least a hundred more years. On that last endless drive, when she fled alone from Louisville to Virginia.

Not when she got to her parents' house, not when she told them as much as she could manage the next morning.

Not when she had to repeat the whole thing to an attorney, then to a courtroom back in Louisville. Facing Bobby that day had been awful, but she'd had her parents by her side.

Not when the divorce was final, or when she struggled to understand it all in hours of talking to her therapist.

Not even with Kim when she'd said more than she'd ever managed to before.

After so many hours and days and weeks and months of keeping the whole rancid mess inside, Steph couldn't hold onto it anymore.

The idea of having to deal with him again, even one last time, made everything that had gone before feel tame and easy.

Steph wasn't sure she was strong enough, not for whatever was coming. No matter what her father or Kim or Jay or anyone else said.

She heard Jay whisper, but she couldn't catch the words over the sounds grinding their way out of her throat. He squeezed her tight before his arms withdrew.

Steph only turned toward Kim, wishing she could shrink down into nothing and disappear.

At least for a little while.

After a time Steph couldn't track even if she wanted to, Kim whispered close to her ear.

"Can you take a drink, Steph? I know that always helps me when I... Anyway, it may be a little flat now, but it's still cold."

Steph was honestly surprised to notice she'd finally stopped crying. Only the feeling of a gigantic storm passing remained, with the swollen eyes and throat to go with it.

She sat back a little, grabbing the collar of her shirt as she moved. Her face had to look horrid after all that.

Letting Kim or anyone else see her nose running was a step too far.

She didn't want Kim to leave, though, or even move her arm away.

"It's okay," Kim said. "Here."

Opening her sore and aching eyes showed a handful of her mother's favorite blue tissues right in front of her nose.

"Jay brought the whole box out. He claimed I was having a sneezing fit. He's back inside, but I can send him a text right now if you need anything at all. Like something fresh to drink, or maybe something stronger."

Steph shook her head and sat up without moving away, taking the offered tissues and pressing them to her nose. It had indeed been running like mad, and her congested voice confirmed it.

"I'm okay now. Well, I'm better, anyway." She swallowed a bit of the no-longer-fizzy lime and mint fizz, frowning at how the citrus drew a sharp, painful line as it went down. "I'm sorry."

Kim shifted lower until she was looking Steph in the eyes.

"I won't tell you not to say that, because you're a grown-ass woman and you can say and feel what you want. I'd *never* tell you what you're feeling is wrong, or not true. What I will tell you is as far as I'm concerned, you haven't done anything I feel like you should apologize for."

She held out another bundle of tissues, which Steph took and held to her eyes. She considered holding the cool glass against them, but asking Jay to try to sneak out a damp washcloth might make a lot more sense.

"Thank you for that, Kim. Thank you for everything. I don't know what happened to me just now, but I'm glad you were here."

Kim smiled a little and leaned closer.

"Well, I'm nowhere near a trained therapist, but I'd guess you had some poison you needed to get out. That's never much fun, I know. I hope you feel a little bit better."

Steph breathed in slowly, filling her lungs more that it seemed she had for months now. Maybe for years.

"I do," she said. "Still furious at that asshole Bobby, or Robert, or whatever the hell his name is. But yeah, I feel better. Are Ivy and Venus here yet?"

"They just got here. Jay said there was some kind of misunderstanding over dinner, and the two of them brought enough food from town to feed ten people. There's quite the apology circus going on inside, with everyone wanting to share but trying to avoid making each other feel bad. Jay's having the time of his life."

A giggle snuck out before Steph could stop it, and Kim smiled in return.

"Good thing we're hiding away out here, huh?" Steph said. "Maybe we should just stay right where we are."

"You won't hear a peep of argument out of me."

Steph wasn't sure if it was the twinkle in Kim's eye, the idea of missing the oh-so-Southern apology-fest, or the warmth of Kim's arm around her. Most likely it was the glorious calm inside her, the feeling of being washed clean of too much built-up hurt and upset and shame.

Whatever the reason, she was glad to take the internal feeling of ease and permission.

She leaned forward and kissed Kim, the lightest touch of their lips.

Feather-light, to be sure, but loaded with too many years of longing and imagination.

Passion and fire swept both of them up as hard and fast as Steph's tears had.

And all she knew then was Kim's lips, her tongue, the feel of her face and hair and back under Steph's hands. The deeper, bruising kiss, somehow more than the teenaged abandon that swept them both up so completely before.

Not discovering how every nerve lit up throughout her body for the first time, a torrent neither one of them could handle. This was coming back to that intensity with experience, with certainty. After years and other loves and lovers between them.

This was realizing they'd been in the right place to begin with.

And coming home was better for having left it.

Long before Steph was ready, Kim pulled back, cheeks flushed, breathing as hard as Steph.

"This is... I shouldn't do this, Steph. *We* shouldn't. Not that I don't want to, I've wanted to since I saw you in your classroom. Hell, since we were both *in* that classroom as kids."

Steph laughed under her breath. She pulled Kim close and whispered with her lips close enough to brush the deep cup of her ear.

"I remember. Every single touch, every single sound. The taste and feel of every part of you. No one has ever fit me better."

Kim's arms squeezed tight, and Steph gasped when Kim's lips and teeth brushed the sensitive part where her neck joined her shoulders.

But Kim drew back again.

"Oh god, Steph, you have no idea. What even thinking about you does to me, much less looking at you. Touching you." She moved again, pushing herself farther away on the huge lounge chair. Still there, but no longer touching. "I know you think... I don't have any way to say this that won't make me sound like a condescending ass."

She turned away and tilted her head forward, sending her thick brunette hair falling across her shoulders. It was everything Steph could do to not reach out and brush it back. Then lean over and kiss the exposed neck and shoulders and everything else she could reach.

The main thing that stopped her was what Kim said. What Steph *knew* she would say next.

"I've had friends in recovery," Kim said, still looking away. "From more than one thing. I know you're not trying to break out of an addiction. You already did break out of your own version of hell. But one thing I learned from them and from myself lately is it takes time to get through this. To get better. To heal."

Steph tried to keep the sinking feeling in her gut and in her heart from pulling her right down through the deck.

Even as she tried a half-hearted protest, she knew Kim was right.

The much worse struggle was trying to keep herself from feeling stupid and ashamed for not realizing that herself before Kim had to say it.

"I've *had* time, Kim. Time away from him, time to myself. It's not like we met for the first time this week, you know. We didn't have a nasty, mean breakup either. We just had... different paths in life we needed to follow."

Kim turned back, already shaking her head.

"I remember it differently. I remember it being mostly my dumbass fault." She touched Steph's lips with her fingertips, stopping her from arguing again. "What I want more than anything right this minute is to forget all my learning and logic and reason. I want to fall in love with you all over again and see how this is for us now. As adults, not two kids with no idea what we were getting into."

Steph's heart wanted to speed back up at that, almost as much as her lips and hands wanted a lot more privacy than her parents' deck offered. Her mind knew Kim wasn't finished.

"I don't want to hurt you," Kim said, moving her hand down to Steph's shoulder. "I'm afraid I'm going to, though. Right now, by getting up and walking away. Or much worse in the future if we get into this thing between us too fast. Too soon. Do you understand?"

"I don't like it." Steph slowly moved away, drawing her knees against her chest again and wrapping her arms around them. "And it does hurt. I can't say I don't understand, though. The worst part is I feel like an idiot, because I do know better. That's not your fault, not one bit. But it's the truth."

Kim leaned close enough to bump her shoulder against Steph's.

"You did hear the part where I said what I want is to be with you, right?"

Steph rolled her eyes. "That's what they all say. No, I get it, I do. Honestly, I haven't talked to my therapist about getting into another relationship at all. Now is obviously the time to bring that up. It never crossed my mind before. Not until I saw you again."

Kim's eyes went wide and she tilted her head to the side.

"You mean when you *pretended* you didn't *remember* me? Is that your idea of flirting now?"

As so often happened during their years of friendship, a giggling fit took them both at exactly the same time. Before it could devolve to the point of renewed tears for both of them, Kim recovered enough to pull her buzzing phone out of her pocket.

"That's Jay, wondering if we're sufficiently recovered to come sit at the grownup table. The festival of apologies has drawn to a close, and they're wondering where we are."

Steph managed to catch her breath through the last lingering bit of giggles, floating up like joyful little bubbles from her belly.

The aftermath of a good, hard laugh wasn't all that different from a good cry, really. The sensation of feeling clean and refreshed and simply better were hardly different at all.

"I suppose he's right. We've been hiding out here long enough. Avoiding all my rising troubles in the real world."

Kim grabbed her shoulder before she could stand.

"Waiting on more than friendship between the two of us is one thing," she said. "I meant every word about being here for the rest right now. I know Jay did too, and everyone inside will be right beside us."

Steph nodded and smiled, covering Kim's hand with hers for a second. She'd have to put on that same brave face inside, too. For her parents and Ivy and Venus, and probably for the Seagons again soon.

But she took her brief moment, standing and facing away from Kim, to let all her worry and fear and more than a little anger come through on her face.

Her ex, wherever he was and whoever he was, might not have any idea what he would be facing if he tried to force his way into her life again.

But Steph knew better than anyone else in Lighting Gap what they'd all be facing from him.

CHAPTER 29

Kim kept herself out of the way beside the sliding glass doors out to the deck once they got back inside, watching everyone else get themselves situated while she caught her breath.

Well she tried to, at least.

She had the feeling all she'd be able to manage tonight was keeping anyone else from noticing how upside down her insides felt after that kiss.

No, upside down didn't come close to covering it. Drifting loose and entirely disconnected was more like it. Cut free of their moorings by the turbulence set up between her heart and parts of her a lot lower down.

Parts that had taken over her whole body at once, including the lump of useless goo taking up space between her ears at the moment.

"Get a grip, Kim," she said under her breath. "Observe and remember. Ask questions later. Much later."

The mantra that helped her focus through countless new product meetings in her tech writing days probably didn't stand a chance against an emotional stormfront like this.

But she had to try something or else risk making an utter fool of herself in one way or another.

The Holfields had a big dining room just off the kitchen. She remembered sitting around the long oak table with cabinets full of dishes and glassware all around, celebrating birthdays and anniversaries and graduations. If everyone got cozy, twenty people could join in around that table.

Even though the room was hardly formal, and rarely used that way, she understood why the door stayed closed this evening. Something about the strangeness of the topic at hand—and the urgency—felt better at the much smaller table a few steps away from the giant kitchen island.

She was pretty sure Steph's little brother Ryan had put this one together with leftover bits of lumber from his other work, or else that he'd collected the wood from other families in Lightning Gap. The surface was as level and smooth as any bought in an expensive furniture store. But the wood shifted colors and grain patterns, from bright pine to yellow poplar, on to mellow oak and dark cherry.

The joins were seamless, creating a work of art to Kim's eye. She loved the way Steph's family used it every day rather than isolating and protecting it.

That beautiful surface was already mostly covered with sturdy serving dishes from the kitchen, alongside returnable blue metal containers from Chez l' Éclair in town. A much fancier destination than Kay's Cafe, to be sure. Kim hadn't had reason to stop by since she'd moved back.

More suitable for date night rather than a quick comfort food stop, but not so expensive that picking it up for dinner was overly extravagant. She'd heard friendly rumors that the owners and Auntie Venus had been especially close in their younger years.

Right now, her great aunt and Steph's mother sat across from each other around the food, each of them with a glass full of the same fizzy concoction that had once been in the glass she still held. Auntie Venus still wore her sleek black pantsuit and her single braid. But she somehow managed to look fabulous anyway.

Ivy, Steph's father, and Jay lingered by the kitchen island, talking and finishing up some kind of elaborate appetizer with figs, blue cheese, and honey.

A big white bowl full of kibble and another full of water were arranged nearby for BeeGirl. The redbone hound sat politely in front of her own dinner, but her body, nose, and all of her attention were focused on the kitchen table instead.

Sheriff Holfield watched Steph walk through on her way to her bedroom, but he didn't say a word. He glanced at Kim without stopping his preparation work, raising his reddish eyebrows in an obvious question. Surely about his daughter.

She wasn't completely sure what he was asking, or how she should answer. Kim herself couldn't get her thoughts and feelings about Steph into any kind of reasonable order.

She smiled and nodded, then they both watched Steph

walking back in. She still looked tired and a little pale, but her eyes and nose were no longer red and puffy.

The tiny bit of control Kim had regained over her renegade insides evaporated when Steph flashed her a quick half-smile on the way to her father's side.

Like the wonderful cousin and stellar friend he'd always been, Jay grabbed a big clear pitcher and headed her way.

"Steph seems to be doing better," he said, refilling her glass halfway with what looked like faintly green water. "I'm not so sure about you."

Kim started to take a sip, but he put a hand on her wrist to stop her.

"Probably not what you're expecting just yet. That needs a hit of seltzer water to make it drinkable. Or maybe you need a good swig of gin to go with it."

"I last gave up on anything being the way I expected a few days ago. As for the gin, I'll pass for now. Might settle me down, or might make me way too honest."

"Anything I can do about it right now? Before we all sit down, stuff our faces, and find out how much more strangeness we're walking into?"

She turned to face him, closing off her view of the room. And her view of Steph.

"You've had friends in recovery, Jay. Right?"

"Oh yes. I'm not sure how I avoided that fate myself to tell you the truth. It's kind of a miracle that any of us do."

"Then remind me of the rule about not getting involved in a new relationship for a year. That's what they say, right? That's what I've heard my friends in recovery talk about."

Jay looked toward the kitchen for a second, then back at Kim. She kept her eyes on him instead.

"I've always figured we all should be in recovery from something," he said. "Pretty much all the time. Trying to work out who we are and what we should be doing. How we can do better in the future. I don't know if Steph's as mixed up as someone who just got off drinking or drugging too much."

He stopped for a second, pressing his lips together and thinking something over.

"Right this second, it seems to me like she's several months out from whatever made the earth shift and crack open under her feet and sent her back home. It's you I'm more worried about."

Kim scowled, wondering if the gin might be a good idea after all.

"Me? I don't think I've taken nearly the hit she has."

He lifted one shoulder. "Maybe not. But you have stayed hidden away in Auntie Venus's house for a solid month. Pretty much until a couple of days ago, right? After a big move and a huge change in your life. All of it by choice, I'm sure. Without restraining orders involved unless you've kept that *extremely* private. But that's not what anyone would call a minor adjustment."

"You don't understand. It's not the same. Not at all."

Jay only stared into her eyes without saying a word, while Kim tried not to resent him for seeing right through her with no effort.

"All right," she finally said. "You have a point. I'm probably not ready for...whatever might happen with Steph. I know I'm not ready for whatever we're supposed to be talking about at dinner. Still going to pass on the gin, though. For now."

"I don't think any of us are ready for this. But we're going to stuff ourselves silly and do the best we can. Just tell me one thing. You two weren't crying the whole time out there, were you?"

Kim tried to keep her face from heating by sheer force of will, which of course only made the blush climbing her chest and throat and cheeks that much more intense.

"You could say we were...getting reacquainted. And yes, before you ask, that's thrown what little equilibrium and balance I might actually have built up over the last month out the window. Probably for a long damn time."

Jay's smile changed his face so subtly that only someone who knew him well would have caught it at all. Kim had no doubt.

"That could be a good thing, Kim, once you're both ready for it. Assuming we all make it through the next few days, of course." He looped his free arm through hers and turned them both toward the middle of the kitchen. "Let's get in there and figure out what we're up against."

Kim didn't imagine that Steph ended up sitting across from her at dinner by accident for a second. Not with Jay and Auntie Venus and Ivy all but encouraging the choice already made between them, and Steph's parents not objecting in the least. She simply considered herself lucky to have such a dizzying array of food to choose from.

As far as she could tell, the Great Southern Apology Convention had ended with a typical compromise. Rather than having anyone's feelings hurt—or anyone's food set aside for another day—everything had been brought out together.

That fig and cheese appetizer she'd seen earlier came first, of course. That she could keep track of, along with the unreasonably good garlic toast served alongside it. After that, Kim slipped into a daze of grilled shrimp and perfectly roasted chicken, early spring greens cooked with onions, and carrots glazed with ginger and chipotle.

After a few remarkably dramatic sighs, BeeGirl gave up and ate most of her bowlful of kibble. She took a few hopeful steps toward Ivy, only to be sent to her cushion set up in the corner.

Between the meal and trying to keep the more adult side of her imagination under some kind of control, Kim didn't need the gin or anything else by the time the remains of Ivy's stack cake, Auntie Venus's light-as-air cinnamon spice cookies, and Chez l' Éclair's namesake dessert made an appearance.

Kim felt more like she'd indulged in a generous hit of marijuana rather than any kind of booze. And she knew what created that feeling was constantly trying to avoid looking at Steph, alternating with the hit of excitement and pure desire every time their eyes met.

Steph seemed to understand exactly what was going on, too. She was ready with either a smile or a wink every time Kim glanced her way.

Finishing the food, the parade of carrying the remains of the feast back to the kitchen, and settling back around the table was almost a relief. Kim would have something else to focus on, for better or worse.

She politely declined when Ivy's potent blueberry liquor made the rounds.

Steph's father did take a slow, appreciative sip, then he smiled at Ivy.

"I have no idea how old I was when I first tasted this. Too young, I'm sure. I do know it's been too long since the last time." He leaned forward with his elbows on the table, glass still in hand.

"Now, I don't have any kind of illusions that I'm in charge here. Not in this crowd. I'll do my best not to revert to sheriff behavior. But I would certainly appreciate it if all of you would help me figure out how I can keep my little girl over there safe. Besides what I trust she still carries in her car."

Now it was Steph's turn to blush as she nodded, and of course she only looked more beautiful than ever when she glanced at Kim.

Jay brushed back his hair, leaving more than his bangs standing straight up.

"You all understand none of what I have to say tonight is in my official capacity as a member of the town council, right?"

Steph's father snorted out laughter and shook his head.

"You really think I'm saying or doing anything tonight as an elected Felten County official?"

Jay ducked his head and smiled, looking about eleven years old.

"Fair enough. What have you heard from Walton County

tonight? Anything new about their mysterious prisoner? Eugene Hunsaker, isn't it?"

Steph's father sat the half-full glass down, sat back, and crossed his arms, somehow looking more like someone in law enforcement than ever.

"I know Mr. Hunsaker woke up for a few minutes. Woke up, cleared up, whatever you want to call it. Asked to make a call, as a matter of fact. Should I pretend to be surprised that you know about that, Jay? And that it's reasonable that you know?"

"I wouldn't argue if you felt that way, no. Anything about that call strike you as odd?"

"Sure. Neither Sheriff Crabtree nor I could work out why a man who seems to have been dragged through half of southwestern Virginia wanted to contact someone from Kentucky. It made more sense to both of us that he'd be looking for someone from Wolf Branch to come get him."

Ivy glanced at Steph. "Did they tell you who he wanted to call?"

"Someone named Robert McReynolds, over in Eastern Kentucky. Still a few hours away. He checked out pretty much clean, just a few minor moving violations. Little bit of credit trouble. Nothing serious enough to catch my attention."

Steph's face went pale and cold, and that did catch her father's attention.

"What are you not telling me?" he said.

An eternity passed in the few seconds before Steph answered, leaving Kim wishing she could step in front of her and make it all stop. Or that she could at least hold Steph's hand.

"I saw something yesterday," Steph said. "A photograph that made me think Robert McReynolds and Bobby Faulks could be the same person. More than a photo, not just that. Jay has someone he thinks can find out more in a couple of days. I think it's worth looking into."

Kim held her breath when Steph's father sat up straight and started to speak, but Jay jumped in instead.

"I did talk to someone, a couple of them. One who could create a foolproof fake identity in no time if they wanted to says Robert McReynolds checks out. Valid from everything reasonably available online. The other, the one I trust more in this case, is Carabelle Seagon. She says Mr. McReynolds—the one who currently holds that identity anyway—is nothing but a ghost."

Jay stared down at the patch of gleaming yellow poplar under his hands on the table before he looked back up, his face worried and more afraid than Kim had ever seen him.

"We both believe Bobby Faulks *is* Robert McReynolds."

CHAPTER 30

$\mathcal{S}$teph froze, caught in the terribly uncomfortable certainty that her heart, lungs, the very blood in her veins had seized up solid.

She'd tried to convince herself that finding out Bobby had an entire hidden life as a tormentor of vulnerable people had been the worst surprise she could have gotten from him. That night back in Louisville when she cowered in terror as he told her all about it certainly should have been enough.

The fury and disgust only a couple of hours ago made perfect sense, when Jay linked those two names together.

But hearing it said out loud like that, and with Mrs. Seagon to back it all up, turned the whole idea into a brand new shock.

Not just that Bobby could have pulled something like that off, or even that he would want to.

Neither she nor her father or mother or anyone else had

seen this coming. And all the law enforcement protection in the world wouldn't work if they were watching for the wrong man.

"I'm afraid I know the answer before I even ask," her mother said, her face tight but her voice strong. "Any chance you or Mrs. Seagon could be mistaken? What did you see yesterday, Steph?"

"The house, the one he told me he grew up in. The one he took me to visit his family in. He told me his family had lived there for generations. But the name in one of the history books at Odds and Endings was McReynolds, not Faulks. He must have made all of that up."

"Well, he left a lot out," Jay said. "But he was telling the truth. A boy named Robert McReynolds did grow up in that house. After his father died, his mother remarried. Young Robert changed his name to Faulks, just like she did. What no one knew before today is he kept both Robert and Bobby alive, and living separate lives."

Steph watched her father shift in his chair, keeping his hands flat on the table. He managed to resist his telltale arms-crossed posture, but Sheriff Holfield had undoubtedly returned.

"You're telling me he set up a fake identity so good it fooled our background check *and* your hacker friend's best efforts? I know he works in tech, so I'm sure he could manage if he wanted to. But none of this comes easy, or cheap. Why the hell would he want to go through all that?"

Steph shrugged and threw up both hands.

"Because he could is one answer. The more important one

is he probably did it just in case. Bobby was extremely careful about who he appeared to be. He fooled me for years, remember. I never even suspected he might have changed his name. But having a hidden identity is exactly the kind of thing a monster like him would do because he might need it someday."

Kim laid her arm flat along the table and tapped several times with her index finger. She'd been alternating between avoiding Steph's eyes all through dinner and thrilling little quick glances.

Now she stared right into them, but the effect was chilling rather than arousing.

"What if we're all missing his *real* reason? This might not be my secret to tell, but I think we all pretty much know you have a protective order against him, Steph. Which means everyone is watching out for Bobby Faulks, right? Is anyone watching out for Robert McReynolds?"

Steph's whole body went cold, as if she'd stepped inside a huge freezer. From the pale, shocked looks her parents shared, they felt the same way.

Her father pushed back his chair with a harsh scrape, pulling his phone out of his pocket.

"I need to make a couple of calls. As sheriff, in this case. Jay, as Steph's father, I'm asking if your hacker friend might be willing to dig deeper into this. Bobby was seen in Louisville this morning, and his cell phone was still there as of a couple of hours ago. Between the two of us we should be able to locate wherever the hell Robert McReynolds is right now."

Steph closed her eyes, fighting to keep the table and the floor and everything else from tilting out from under her.

She remembered too clearly how rotten cellular signal was on long stretches of the drive through Eastern Kentucky and big parts of the drive toward Lightning Gap on the Virginia side. The truth was *Robert McReynolds* could be anywhere right now, or he could simply have his damn phone switched off.

No matter what name he used, the man she knew was more than smart enough to have a third phone, or a tenth, if he decided it was necessary.

If he'd left early this morning—after the ill-advised police drive-by that probably gave him the all-clear—he could be in the yard outside right now and no one would be the wiser. Even BeeGirl was sound asleep and snoring at the moment, just like all the humans had been when it came to Bobby and what he was capable of.

Steph startled and almost let out a yelp at a hand on her shoulder.

Kim sat beside her, mouth set and angry rather than soft and smiling.

Steph had never seen her looking more beautiful.

"Hang on, Steph," Kim said. "The men are off making their calls, but we're not going anywhere."

Steph blinked, realizing Jay had left the room along with her father. Her mother was on her other side, Ivy and Venus across the table. The women had moved to surround her without her noticing. All of them as angry and as determined as Kim.

Venus reached across and patted Steph's arm.

"We have the electronics and law enforcement experts on board," Venus said, nodding to herself. "That's all well and good. But we all seem to have lost sight of what we were here to talk about in the first place. What we *need* is experts on Lightning Gap. I'm not about to try to drag them out of their house this late in the evening, but maybe we can get the Seagons on the phone or a video conference or something."

A laugh from her own throat caught Steph by surprise, and all she could do was smile.

"I had classes online all through college, and I set up conferences like that in my classroom constantly. I still get the idea the Seagons could run circles around me when it comes to ways to communicate that I never even thought of."

Ivy had a smartphone out before anyone else could move. Steph tried to remember if she'd ever seen anything remotely electronic or modern in Ivy's house, but she had the call connecting in a heartbeat.

"What?" Ivy said, scowling. "You think an old mountain woman with a hound dog can't be part of the modern world, too? Hello, Arthur, sorry to bother you so late in the evening. Got a couple questions for you and Carabelle if you have a minute."

She stood and walked toward the kitchen door, an instantly alert BeeGirl hard on her heels.

"I'm sorry to bring up something this distasteful, Steph," Steph's mother said, "but you knew him better than any of us ever did. He certainly had me fooled, and your father. What do you think we should be doing? Or watching out for?"

Steph leaned her head to the side (toward Kim), and rubbed her forehead.

"He had me fooled most of all, Mom. I understand that's not my fault now. Most of the time. People like him are brilliant at manipulation, and even better at hiding it. He might have left this morning and be anywhere by now. If he has a fake ID that good, he could have gotten on a plane, but I don't think so."

Kim leaned forward enough to look into Steph's eyes.

"You don't think so because he's afraid of flying or too cheap or something like that? Or you don't *feel* so?"

"You're right, I don't *feel* so. The times I got even a glimpse of the real Bobby—maybe I should say the real Robert—were when I found out something about him. Something he didn't want me to know, or didn't expect me to find out when I did, anyway. That's when his mask slipped, at least around me."

Her mother sat forward with her elbows on the table, hands covering her face.

"And this morning a police officer saw him working in the yard. From what I remember about your rather quiet and calm neighborhood, anyone in law enforcement just randomly driving by like that wouldn't go unnoticed."

Steph shivered with a rush of prickly goosebumps.

"If he was outside working in the yard, he noticed. I promise. So yeah, he may very well have been set off by that, or any number of other things." Then a deeper cold washed over and through her, chilling her to her bones.

A beat later, Kim put her hand to her mouth, eyes wide.

"Wait," Steph said, a light, airy voice all she could manage to force out. "This Eugene Hunsaker guy, Dad said he went to school in Laurel Gap, and he's the same age as Bobby. And he asked Sheriff Crabtree to call Robert McReynolds today. After months of nothing from me or anybody else, I can promise you he'd see that as the *authorities* all of a sudden checking up on him twice in one day."

Her mother swore beside her, pushing back her chair a bit more quietly than her father had.

"You mean the same Eugene Hunsaker who was last seen in Lightning Gap, went missing, and turned up all the way out in Holly Creek looking like a bear dragged him there?"

Kim moved closer and put her arm around Steph's shoulders. Steph was grateful for the trace of warmth against the growing deep freeze inside.

"I don't know if Dad had a chance to tell all of you," she said, "but the other two missing men? They went to high school all over the place, but they were together in Laurel Gap at the same time for a while. Not just one of them. I'd bet more than I could stand to lose that school records will show Robert McReynolds was there at the same time."

A low *woof*, prancing footsteps, and a cool hound dog nose nuzzling into her hand let Steph know Ivy and BeeGirl had returned.

"Arther and Carabelle both want to talk," Ivy said, holding up her phone. "Might be kind of hard for everyone to see on this little screen, though, so I told them I'd call them right back."

Steph's mother stood at once and headed toward her bedroom.

"I've got a big tablet, hold on just a second."

Jay came through the deck doors then, causing BeeGirl to abandon Steph so she could greet the newly returned human. He squatted to rub her ears and accept a flurry of kisses all over his cheeks and chin.

"Nothing so far," he said. "Robert McReynolds appears to have been living and working around the same few hundred square miles his whole life. Born and raised there, from everything a quick search turns up. But I've got the best...shall we say information hounds I know digging into it. If there's anything to find, they'll find it."

Ivy grabbed a couple of paper towels on her way past the island and handed them to Jay.

"She laid some pretty good ones on you, might want to run one of these under the spigot first."

Jay grinned and scrubbed his face, while BeeGirl reattached herself to Ivy and followed her back to the table.

"I'm fine," he said. "Feels like the best exfoliation scrub I've had in weeks. Did Sheriff Holfield hear anything yet?"

"*Sheriff* Holfield will make you wish for something as gentle as exfoliation," Steph's mother said, "if he hears you calling him that, Jay. Certainly when you're a guest in our house. Come on, I've got the Seagons right here, almost big as life."

She turned off the overhead lights and arranged a huge tablet computer—almost as big as two sheets of paper standing side by side—at the end of the table. Steph hadn't ever used what she thought of as more of a portable television herself, but her mother was right about the dimensions.

The Seagons were already on the screen, their smiling faces nearly the same size they were in person.

"There you all are," Mrs. Seagon said, beaming. "Jay Murray, too, so lovely to see you. I understand we've *all* learned more since we last saw each other this morning. And we're not alone in feeling time is running short."

CHAPTER 31

Kim held herself perfectly still as Steph shifted, then leaned back against her. Kim took a breath and did her best to relax as much as she could under the strange and stressful circumstances.

If she needed more of a reminder why it was not a good idea to get back into an intense relationship with Steph, simply being in this group right now should be plenty.

An ex threatening enough to warrant a restraining order should be plenty. Especially one who was turning out to be more dangerous and more sneaky than anyone imagined.

Jay's unappreciated but accurate warning about Kim's own state of mind, that should have been enough, too.

And still, sitting here with her arm around Steph, in full view of Auntie Venus and Ivy and Steph's mother, that had to count for something.

That had to *mean* something, and not only to Kim.

Steph hadn't protested or made any effort to move away.

Before Kim could really get into her overthinking and obsessive analysis habit—potentially creating far more worry and awkwardness than would make sense to anybody—Carabelle Seagon started talking.

"We're all agreed that Bobby Faulks and Robert McReynolds are almost certainly the same person. A possibly dangerous person we need to pay close attention to and locate as soon as we can. But we have one murder, one mysterious disappearance with an even stranger recovery, and another still missing. We believe that would be the best place to focus our efforts now."

Everyone around the table nodded without hesitation. The truth was until Steph's father got back or Jay heard from his sources, that was all they *could* do.

"Besides the unusual violence within Lightning Gap," Mrs. Seagon went on, "have any of you found a different pattern to the events we discussed today? Anything else that links them together?"

Everyone glanced at each other, and Kim apparently wasn't the only one who felt sheepish about their lack of progress.

"I'm afraid not, Carabelle," Auntie Venus said. "We've been concentrating on the threat to Stephanie. The one we should be able to see and hear, that is."

"That's perfectly sensible," Mr. Seagon said, nodding. He leaned sideways, exposing a bookshelf mostly filled with books, with a few trinkets and photographs tucked in. "I'm sure we don't have to tell you those things likely go together.

The threat to our own, and whatever Lightning Gap may do about it."

Steph's father spoke, surprising everyone. He'd come back in without making a sound.

"I don't know how I feel about any of that. Not yet. I do know Bobby's cell phone is still sitting right there in Louisville. According to cellular records, Robert McReynolds was last on the network not far from where he lives in Eastern Kentucky a couple of hours ago. His phone's been offline ever since."

He took a long breath and let it out through pursed lips, then walked over to sit beside his wife on Steph's other side.

Kim had to blink back tears when he rested his hand on her back, then Steph's, on the way by.

"I hate saying these words out loud," he went on, "but I'm convinced he's not in Louisville anymore. A patrol car is headed out, just to make sure. You'll know as soon as I do. For now, it makes more sense to focus on this Robert McReynolds. And we can't skip over what you said just then, Arthur. I need to know what you meant by whatever Lightning Gap may do about it."

Mr. Seagon moved too close to whatever camera they were using, then held up a much smaller tablet of his own. This one was covered with the columns and rows of a spreadsheet, the whole thing full of data.

"I wish I could tell you specifics, David," Mr. Seagon said, his round face unusually solemn. "Besides all these dates and numbers. One thing Carabelle and I have learned over our long lives is while we think we can predict what happens, what that most often leads to is surprises. That's one of the joys of living, and especially living in Lightning Gap."

He turned the tablet toward himself and tapped a few times.

"Stephanie will understand from her challenges teaching this year that even knowing how something as simple as the weather behaves up here isn't certain. Of course we get our biggest storms—the ones that matter—when we need them. But beyond that, the long shape of our ridge and the Lightning Stone confuse a lot more than they conform."

Kim smiled along with everyone else when Mrs. Seagon shook her head and leaned forward.

"Arthur is getting a bit long on words, as he often does on this subject. The important thing is we've identified a certain...instability in the weather. It of course operates on a cycle as all such things must. A strange cycle. We've been studying it for years, but today is the first time we realized the unusual weather patterns coincide with the dreadfully violent outbursts we identified today."

"So you could use the weather to predict these problems?" Steph's father said, arms crossed in full sheriff mode. "To know when people were going to act up?"

The Seagons looked at each other with their heads tilted at exactly the same angle.

"No, I don't believe so," Mr. Seagon said, shaking his head slowly. "I honestly think the behavior drives the unruly pattern. Not the other way around. That may be impossible to know."

"Assuming it goes that way," Ivy said, "you might be able

to take extra care once an unusual pattern settles in. Keep an eye on things, maybe."

Kim felt Steph's shoulders rise slowly, pause, and relax.

"One of those cycles," she said quietly. "The unruly ones. It got started last year, didn't it? Around the middle of October. We're in the middle of it right now."

Both of the Seagons broke into wide smiles, which Kim normally would have returned. She was too strongly aware of how rigidly Steph sat now, how stiff and unmoving she was.

"That's *exactly* right," the Seagons both said. "We didn't catch it when it began. But once we looked back today, the shift is clear. Our normal big storms happened in mid-October rather than after Halloween, and we had more storms than usual throughout September. The winter brought lightning storms five times, twice during snowfalls. I'm sure you've all noticed how unusually cool and rainy this spring has been, with a spectacular display of electricity in the sky just this past week."

Kim didn't look at Steph, but she noticed when her mother did. Followed by her father and Ivy, then Auntie Venus and Jay.

"So we hadn't had a weather pattern like this for years," Steph said in a louder voice. "Or any of this uneasiness or violence. But it all started up not long after I returned home."

Ivy leaned forward herself, pointing at Steph, eyes flashing.

"I told you before and I'll tell you again until either you hear me or my voice gives out. None of these things are because you came back home, Stephanie. Not a one of them."

Steph sat forward then, and Kim let her arm drop.

"Oh, I agree, Ivy," Steph said, nodding. "Sounds like everything was fine in July and August, and most of September. I got back in mid-July, remember? In fact, I'd be willing to bet things around Lightning Gap didn't start to get *dis*orderly until pretty close to the date my divorce came through. That and the protective order."

Kim didn't like the edge in Steph's voice, how loud and fast she was speaking. But she knew better than to argue or offer comfort at the wrong time. That too often made everything worse.

Her mother showed no such hesitation.

"I know you're an adult, Steph, and I'm sorry to speak this way when we have company. But I won't sit here and let you try to blame yourself for any of this. Dipshit Bobby or Robert or whatever the hell his name is treated you horribly for years. Now it turns out he lied to you on top of it all, and he's got all of us worried half to death."

She paused, scowling. "Did you hear what I just said, Steph? *He* has us worried, *not* you. Every last bit of this is on him."

Arthur Seagon spoke into the uncomfortable silence.

"I don't mean to intrude on your private family matters, but I expect we're all in this together at this point. Donna and Ivy are probably right. This phenomenon does seem to get sparked outside of Lightning Gap, so to speak. By threats to someone from here. The timing you mention only reinforces our theory."

Kim rubbed her temples, trying to force her brain into gear.

"Are you saying the lightning does something? The storms? Is that what you mean by the town protecting her own?"

Mrs. Seagon's eyes sparkled as she shrugged, not the least bit disturbed by not knowing. Kim wished she understood that trick.

"That may be the case," Mrs. Seagon said. "Or it may be true sometimes and not others. Or we may very well be on the wrong track altogether. What I believe we can be sure of is the unfortunate young man who passed away and the two who were missing are part of the cycle as well."

Jay leaned so far forward his chin nearly touched the table, both hands on his head, fingers hidden in his lively bangs.

"I can go along with that," he said. "We just don't know why. Or why the one they found over in Holly Creek wanted to make the call he did. We don't even know how he got over there. I'm sure no one's suggesting the wind picked him up and dumped him that far away."

Uneasy laughter from everyone, even the Seagons, made it clear that while no one was suggesting such a thing, no one was quite comfortable with saying it was impossible just yet.

"So we're making more progress than we think," Auntie Venus said. Kim was dismayed to notice she was sitting as stiff and uneasy in her chair as Steph had been. "And we're still not sure what to do about any of it. Have you had any more word on the third young man who was missing, David?"

Steph's father shook his head, staring up at the ceiling.

"Not a word. I'm not sure if I should be relieved by that, or more worried." He looked at everyone in turn, then got to his feet with a groan. "I can't believe I'm saying this, but I've never been one to argue with hard data. If this link between weather and violence holds true, I'm not going to argue. Any of you checked the forecast lately?"

The Seagons both had expectant expressions, but they didn't say a word. Kim held out for a few seconds before she pulled out her phone. Everyone else did the same a second later, even Steph. Only her father waited along with the Seagons.

A curious excitement surged up from Kim's belly when she scrolled through the hourly forecast.

"Everyone else seeing increasing clouds overnight and tomorrow?" she said. "Warmer tomorrow, but getting colder when the sun goes down?"

Steph turned toward her, holding up her own phone. She still looked scared, and angry. But her eyes were bright.

"That and the barometric pressure is high and steady. But it won't be by this time tomorrow night."

Auntie Venus shook her head and slipped her phone back into her pocket.

"Mine says the same, but I don't need it for this. I've been getting little aches and pains all day long. The kind that tell me a big storm is on the way. Worse than the one this past week."

"I'm getting the same thing," Steph's father said. "On my phone and in my bad shoulder. Here's what I'm going to do about that. This is hardly acceptable after-dinner talk, but I'll follow up on the autopsy for Stan Phipps in the morning. I'm not that concerned about the tests that can take weeks. Our folks do good work, but we're a small rural area, and this isn't a normal case. They might not be looking for the right things."

"Did you find out anything about where he is?" Steph said. "Or where he isn't?"

No one had to wonder who she meant.

Her father held up one hand and tilted it back and forth.

"The patrol car in Louisville didn't get any response at the house, so I'm going to put out an alert on Bobby's description in our area right now. I believe I can work with Larry Crabtree to attach Robert McReynolds to that same alert. Especially once I get a look at his ID photo. I hope we hear more from your friend overnight or soon after, Jay."

Jay glanced at Auntie Venus, then at Kim before he spoke. "I expect an update any time now. I'll send you all a text the second I hear."

Steph took a second to look into everyone's eyes. She looked at Kim last. The corner of her mouth lifted a tiny bit, unknotting a little of the worry in Kim's chest.

"I don't know what to say about all of this," Steph said. "I'll probably have a hell of a lot of questions once everything settles down. I don't know how to thank all of you, but I'll figure it out."

The Seagons nodded, and Carabelle held her hand over her heart.

"You're most welcome, Stephanie. I don't wish this kind of

distress on anybody. I do wish I could tell you not to worry, and it breaks my heart that I can't. You take care tonight. I hope we can trouble one of you for an update tomorrow. Rest well, all of you."

She leaned forward and ended the conference, leaving only a photo of the Lightning Stone against a brilliant blue sky on the huge tablet.

In the flurry of agreements and movement and promises, Kim focused on her great aunt across the table. She seemed okay, chatting with Ivy, BeeGirl's head in her lap. But she still had that stiffness to her back.

The sure sign of an incoming storm.

Kim stood beside Steph.

"I won't ask if you'll be okay here," Kim said. "I don't think you'd be safer anywhere else in the world. I think I need to get Auntie Venus home."

"It has been a long day for all of us." Steph leaned closer. "I'm in serious need of sleep, but I'm not convinced that will happen at all tonight. Not between all this insanity and trying not to think about you."

Kim laughed, soft and low.

"You won't be the only one. On either count. I'll have my phone on all night."

Steph darted forward and kissed Kim's cheek before she went to say goodnight to Ivy and Venus. A purposeful throat clearing let Kim know who was behind her before she turned around.

"You two seem to be getting along quite well," Jay said.

"Will you need a ride back, or have you decided on a sleepover?"

"Not tonight on the sleepover, much as I wouldn't mind. This is probably going to be the safest place in the whole county for Steph or anyone else. I'd appreciate a ride very much. Ivy's Jeep can be a little full with two people and one bouncy hound dog."

"Ready when you are. I get the feeling tomorrow won't turn out to be any kind of day of rest."

CHAPTER 32

Sunday morning dawned warm and cloudy, leaving Bobby hoping the wipers on his newly purchased "gently used" sedan actually worked.

The little blue car seemed to be well-maintained otherwise. The fact that a perfectly nondescript but reliable vehicle had been on the lot waiting for him only added to his sense of getting closer to his goal.

He'd shed his comatose passengers along with their junker of a van—complete with an antiquated and expensive full tank of gas—deep in the woods about five miles outside of Hidden Springs. Turned out knowing where the extensive bicycle trails cut across the land came in handy.

By Bobby's estimate, they should be waking up about now, confused about where he'd gone and where they were. Odds were high they'd eventually figure out their location, berate themselves for the relapsed failures they were, and take advantage of the full tank and run back to Kentucky and their dubious chance at sobriety and a future.

If they made it into Hidden Springs at all, he'd be long-since departed for Lightning Gap and the real purpose of this impromptu road trip.

He didn't bother shaving, not when he was so rarely seen with even a day's growth. Not since he'd left Robert McReynolds and his scraggly teenage attempts at a beard far in the past. The surprisingly heavy shadow around his cheeks and jaw alone would make him harder to spot.

He opted for the local uniform of a new pair of brown work boots, dark blue jeans, and a navy-blue t-shirt, adding in a forest green rain jacket at the last minute.

Even if it didn't rain up in Lightning Gap, the coat and its hood would help him blend in if he needed to. Either into the cheerful tourist-friendly streets of Steph's annoying hometown, or into convenient shadows.

Half-formed daydreams and fantasies of what lay ahead shaped themselves more fully with every action he took, from an agreeably greasy roadside dive breakfast through all of his shopping and stocking up.

Bobby found his way to the quaint little local library with its free internet access and weirdly early hours, wishing he'd grabbed his laptop on the way out the door. He'd had no plans to leave Louisville yesterday, much less end up hours away in his native Virginia.

Much as he preferred to plan and have control over everything, he knew how to recognize good fortune when he found it. And good timing.

His private, anonymous browser search found no new news stories or police reports on any of his useless local associates.

Stan Phipps still dead. Eugene Hunsaker no longer mentioned anywhere, as lost or found. Dusty Atkinson so far not considered worth reporting missing on a public site.

None of that was surprising, really. Much like Bobby himself when they ran together in high school, those three weren't the kind other people worried about when they weren't around.

They caused a lot more concern when they showed up than when they disappeared.

And much like Robert McReynolds, though nowhere near as skilled, Dusty was good at not being found unless he *wanted* to be.

Unlike Stan and Eugene, Dusty sometimes showed signs of being a bit more independent-minded. More like Robert. Enough that they'd butted heads in the past, and surely would in the future.

Bobby glanced around the bland library: all white walls and ceiling, tan carpet, and pale wooden shelves and furniture. Hardly anyone was out so early on a Sunday morning. He'd spotted one other patron making a beeline for the magazine rack, and only one librarian, who looked decidedly hungover.

Perfect for the last preparations before he headed out to start his wonderful day.

Bobby pulled up the Lightning Gap High School website and clicked on the link for the faculty directory. He stopped, the pointer hovering over the link that would reveal all the teachers and other personnel in the Science Department.

Something he'd managed not to do even one time since he'd listened to Steph telling the judge all about how she'd gotten a new job teaching at a much smaller school.

No need for spousal support, not with her earning Her Own Money. Never mind that her yearly salary was a small fraction of what he brought home in one quarter.

No need for that to be brought up or counted for anything in the proceedings.

No need for contact with Bobby at all.

She'd made that even more clear with the damn restraining order.

Removing herself neatly from his life, all for his horrific crime of *words*.

Talk.

Nothing more than drawing simple mental pictures for her, truly.

He'd never once touched her in anger, no matter how clearly he watched the images form in perfect and stimulating detail in his mind.

Even that day, Bobby sat still and silent in the courtroom. Letting expensive but useless attorneys do all the talking for him.

Watching Steph stare straight ahead, never once looking him in the eye after sixteen years together, fourteen years of marriage.

Watching her walk out beside Sheriff Daddy without even a glance back at the shambles of her life.

That day marked the end of their marriage, no doubt about that.

It also marked the beginning of Bobby's determination to bring all those mental pictures into reality.

To experience what he'd only daydreamed about for far too long.

A gentle tap of his finger exposed everyone Steph worked with day to day, everyone who'd replaced his place in her life.

There she was, almost exactly in the middle of a rectangle of color photos.

Same curly red hair, shorter now. Same kind of demure, almost-dressy blouse.

Not quite the same smile, though, not like the ones he'd seen in other absurdly formal faculty photographs. Steph always looked like she was overjoyed in those images, flushed with mirth and life. Like she'd barely managed to contain shared laughter in time for the camera flash.

Now her full, red lips barely curved. Her wide blue eyes hardly acknowledged the unseen photographer. Her face read as pallid and still and nearly lifeless.

All the visible consequences of a string of bad decisions on her part.

And he couldn't avoid another change he'd expected, but hadn't yet seen in harsh, cold text.

Vibrant, happy Mrs. Stephanie Faulks had winked out of existence.

The pale, ghostly remnants of Ms. Steph Holfield had taken her place.

Bobby breathed in slowly until his throat ached, held it

until his head throbbed, and let the stale air trickle out of his lungs.

After months of passing for *normal* on his own, her absence didn't disturb Bobby as much as it once had. He no longer worried that without Steph's overwhelmingly ordinary influence, Robert McReynolds would be dragged howling and screaming into the light.

Replacing her still made sense, of course, once this situation was under control. Letting someone else—preferably someone more docile—take up the demands of maintaining the facade would free Bobby up for his own interests.

The areas where his true talents and passions awaited.

What stabbed like a thorn caught against the soft skin between his toes, or perhaps sharp bits of sand dragging across his eyes, was the idea that Steph had *chosen* this.

She'd had more than a decade with him, taken full advantage of the better-than-good lifestyle he provided. Established herself as a well-respected teacher in a prestigious school district with a bright future.

And yet she made the decision to run away to small-town obscurity and a life set on a fast train to nowhere.

He considered clicking her faculty bio page, finding out how she explained the first long stretch of her teaching career. Knowing she'd reduced all that time to a throwaway line would only fuel the fire that sustained him.

He cleared the browser's history instead, then closed it, not trusting a private browser session or the library's stated policy of enforcing protections for their patrons.

Putting a finer, more intense point on his focus could eventually cross a line into diminishing returns.

As it had on at least two occasions with Steph and a few more with others, Bobby's anger could give Robert more freedom than was good for anybody.

Instead Bobby got up and walked away, a loose plan taking shape in his mind. The front desk was empty along with the library itself as far as he could tell. He took advantage by plucking a tourism brochure featuring attractions in fabulous Lightning Gap off of a stand beside the door.

No one had seen him grab it, and no one would realize he'd be adding it to a thick book of detailed regional hiking maps he'd bought at the gas station, right after he bought the car.

He headed out into the warm, muggy morning, with a warmer ripple of excitement stirring in his full belly.

The best thing he could do for himself or anyone else was get on with the day's long-overdue business.

CHAPTER 33

Steph's regret about staying up reading half the night started when her phone chirped early the next morning. It didn't really kick in until much later.

The first few notifications didn't quite make it through into her consciousness, lodging themselves instead in uneasy half-dreams. By the time she dragged herself into bleary awareness at half past nine, she had seventeen unread messages.

Only the habit of years of insisting on at least getting coffee before she dove into the day kept her from reading all of them at once.

By the time she staggered into the kitchen—wrapped in an old purple robe that dragged the floor and with hair still tangled and bunched up from sleep—the total jumped to twenty-three.

In an annoying contrast to how she felt, both of her

parents were fully dressed and looked and sounded human. They'd left the matching sweats from the day before behind. Today the coordination of decades together led to old jeans and t-shirts faded from many washings. The remains of a hearty breakfast were still scattered across the table, along with their usual huge weekend coffee cups.

They both glanced up first, then turned back for a longer look.

"Did you get back up and finish off Ivy's blueberry hooch?" her mother said. "There's coffee in the french press, but I can make fresh."

"No on the hooch," Steph said, pulling her own oversized blue Lightning Gap High School mug out of the cabinet. "I stayed up way too late reading of all things. I can't remember the last time I did that. This coffee will be fine to start with, thank you."

"The pancakes in the oven should still be warm," her father said. "Sausage and eggs too. Nothing fancy this morning. Just fuel for whatever the hell we're all walking into."

They waited while Steph filled her mug, adding more creamer than she usually would. Three of her father's unbelievably fluffy whole wheat pancakes were still plenty warm, and those along with strawberry preservers would be exactly what she needed.

No one said a word until she finished the coffee and half of everything else. She was nothing but grateful for the respite.

"Okay, that might get my brain into some kind of working

order. Do I need to go through all the messages, or can you sum it all up?"

"I sometimes wonder if you're more his daughter or mine," her mother said, winking. "In this case, you end up a lot more on my side. After decades of transcribing every single random word and syllable, I'll take a good summary over the actual events any day. Let's see... your father should start with the bad news."

He held up his mug in a mock toast and rolled his eyes.

"Thank you for that, dear. The biggest thing is the ID photos for Bobby and Robert are undeniably the same person. He hardly made any effort on that one. Pretty much changed shirts and combed his hair different. That tells me he was careful to make sure they didn't cross paths, until he wasn't."

Steph nodded, and decided not to protest when her mother mentioned fresh coffee and headed into the kitchen. She was glad no one asked her to review the photos.

"That doesn't surprise me," she said. "Bobby was always careful when he was planning something, good or bad. But once he decided he was ready and everything was perfect, he seemed to assume nothing could possibly go wrong. I have to admit he was right most of the time. Or maybe he was just lucky."

"Well, his luck is about to run out," her father said. "Jay's friend had to dig quite a bit, but the Robert ID was created almost twenty years ago. He did do a great job on it, one of the best any of us have seen. Made sure to add in nice little touches like school records, minor moving violations, and a sprinkle of credit trouble. The best part about that is now I can mobilize more, get other departments involved without having to finesse so much."

She wasn't ready to face the unflinching reality of her ex having a secret life she'd never suspected.

"Did the guy out in Holly Creek wake up? Or did the missing one turn up?"

He shook his head. "No to all of those so far. No trace of Bobby or Robert this morning, either. If he's on the cellular network, it's with a different phone. After what he put you through and everything we've learned over the last couple of days, I know you're right. He'd keep twenty different phones if it suited his purposes."

Her mother walked back in with a newly refilled french press—the rich, earthy scent alone helping wake Steph up.

"What were you reading?" she said, filling Steph's mug. "Must have been good to keep you up late with everything that's going on."

Steph closed her eyes and shook her head, not sure if she wished for more time to sleep or more time to read.

"It was good all right. I can't say it was relaxing or any kind of escape. It's a book I found at Odds and Endings yesterday. The one that got the idea of a threat to a Lightning Gap local into my head. A bunch of kids from the Midwest go on a crime spree road trip, basically. Nothing major like murder, but a bunch of petty crimes. It was all well and good for them until they picked up a hostage in Knoxville."

Steph's father nodded and held his refilled mug close to his nose.

"I remember that. Not the novel, I haven't read that one. The kidnapping, though, that was real. Didn't end well for those kids from the outside, right?"

"I'm glad I don't remember it, since I was about five," Steph said. "I guess that depends on what you mean by well. They survived their encounter with Lightning Gap, more or less. It wasn't as bad as the ones who lost body parts out by the fairgrounds, but they had a rough time of it."

"Went to jail for a good long time, according to what I heard," her mother said, shuddering. "I don't remember much else about it. Did the book mention the weather? Enough that you could tell if it was part of the same pattern?"

"It did, actually," Steph said. "I'm guessing this part really happened, too. The kids were used to snow, growing up in the Midwest. But what they didn't understand was how much it changed at elevation, or how so many roads up in the mountains wouldn't get cleared until later, if they got cleared at all."

"That's *right*," her father said, shuddering. "They got stuck in the snow, on a side road our local boy sent them down as a shortcut. Then he backtracked through the woods to the main road while they were distracted trying to get their big van out. Ended up with some nasty frostbite by the time they were picked up and arrested."

Steph concentrated on her coffee to avoid looking at the clots of strawberry preserves still on her plate beside half a sausage link.

"Yeah, the novel gets pretty far into the details about that. They lost body parts to Lightning Gap too, but at least it was under anesthesia. Did you remember how the wind blew through that night? Dropped the temperature close to zero with the wind chill on top of it. No visibility with all that snow blowing around. They might have been fine otherwise."

Her father frowned, then nodded slowly. "I'd forgotten, but all the schools and a whole lot of businesses were closed the next day. No one was prepared, and the pipes froze solid. I guess a lot of things did."

Her mother didn't quite scowl, but she clearly didn't approve of Steph's literary choices or the conversation.

"You had a lot to worry about before you stayed up all night reading a story like that. Are you okay, Steph?"

Steph shrugged, trying to push her ornery hair away from her face.

"I'm not thrilled about any of this, if that's what you mean. I thought I'd left him and all his bullshit behind. I intended to do that, and I tried my best. Yet here he is again. Even though we don't know *where* he is. Did you send his photo out so people can look for him?"

"Of course," her father said. "The second I got confirmation of the match between the two. You know the problem as well as I do, I'm sure. This is a guy who's very good at staying under the radar, whatever his reasons, and has been for decades."

"You're right. He certainly flew under my radar," Steph said, "and just about disabled it altogether. He's an asshole, but he's not stupid. He'll be hard to catch because he won't likely *do* anything stupid. Your best shot may be when he makes his move, whatever that turns out to be."

Her father lowered his head until he was looking up at her under his eyebrows.

"I expect we can do a good bit better than that. I may be a lot older than him, but I'm hardly helpless. Neither is your mother, and I know you're not, either. In case we all get overwhelmed by sudden feebleness, we've got protection out front. Same if anyone needs to go to town, too."

Steph groaned and covered her face with her hands.

"Just what I've always wanted as a cop's kid. A cruiser out front and a constant police escort."

"Do I need to remind you again that none of this is your fault?" her mother said. "Whatever ends up happening to Dipshit, he brought it entirely on himself. Our jobs, and yours, and everyone else who was here last night, are to make sure nothing happens to you."

Steph peeked at her mother through her fingers.

"Yeah, I know. I feel guilty enough already. Any word from the rest of the Steph Holfield Special Protection Squad?"

She moved her hands and concentrated on the rest of her food. Of course she meant *everyone*. Ivy and Venus and the Seagons to go along with Kim.

Her best chance of hearing more from Kim was checking her own phone, still safely in the robe's pocket. Along with the flurry of messages that woke her.

She just wasn't ready for that much reality yet.

"Mainly more reinforcement for what we talked about last night," her father said. "Everyone who had books to go through found a stronger pattern between the weather and the violence, just like you did."

Steph's mother tilted her head. "Have you heard anything new? Maybe from Kim? I don't think I've seen anything from her this morning."

"Haven't checked yet. It seemed like a good idea to get coffee on board first. I'm sure Kim's fine."

Steph pretended the relatively dim light through the kitchen windows would hide her blush. The cloud cover had arrived, as promised.

She was relieved when her father's phone buzzed in his pocket and he excused himself. With the way her mother kept staring at her, she'd rather keep a likely embarrassing conversation between the two of them.

"Kim seems fine to me, too. How are the two of you together?"

Steph used the excuse of drinking more coffee to hide behind her mug for a second. She would have preferred a lot longer.

"I don't know, Mom. We just saw each other for the first time in years a couple of days ago, you know? We've both lived a lot of life in all that time."

"You both have, and that might not be a bad thing. I'm never going to rush you with something like this, you know that. But you two were pretty close back then. Has it been good seeing her?"

This time Steph looked into her mother's eyes without a thing to hide or be shy about.

"It's been great, it really has. Almost like we just saw each other a couple of weeks ago instead of almost twenty years. Having a friend after...after the past few years has felt really good. That was one of the things I lost in Louisville, that he took away. Friends I could talk to."

"I know you don't always like to hear things like this, but I can tell a difference in you. Even after a couple of days. Your father can too. That may be from having a close friend again. You haven't talked to Dr. Raphine since, have you?"

Steph shook her head. "Not since Wednesday. Our next appointment is Tuesday. We haven't talked about relationships all that much. New ones, I mean. She knows I dated women and men when I was younger, but that's about it. Discussions about my marriage and Dipshit took up all the air in the room, and on the video call. Any kind of new relationship hadn't crossed my mind before."

Her mother lifted one eyebrow for a second and got up, stacking the plates that weren't in front of Steph. Steph's lack of sleep showed when it took a few seconds to realize what she'd said.

"Well, if something new has crossed your mind now," her mother said, "it makes sense to talk to Dr. Raphine about it. I don't know details about your love life and I don't particularly want to. What I remember is you and Kim never had some kind of horrible screaming breakup. You just went in different directions."

She went into the kitchen, leaving Steph alone with her roiling thoughts.

Her sluggish brain didn't feel like it had space for anything more, but she'd delayed long enough. She unlocked her phone and laid it on the table.

A quick scan showed pretty much what her parents had

told her, with a few more details filled in. Her always-present weather-nerd self hoped to get a look at the Seagons' spreadsheet at some point.

The information on the cycles of violence wasn't nearly as interesting.

All the way down to an early morning one from her father, letting everyone know the photo IDs matched.

Still no Kim.

Steph let out a soft snort, wondering if Kim had gone back to the book she'd gotten so caught up in at Odds and Endings and ended up reading most of the night away, too. She tapped out a quick message.

Morning, Kim. You stay up all night too? Any interesting dreams? ;) Steph.

She finished her breakfast and her coffee, pleasantly surprised at how much better she felt. A nap wouldn't be unwelcome, assuming today didn't get as strange as the previous two had.

Her mother took the dishes out of her hands and popped them into the nearly full dishwasher. Steph held on to the coffee mug.

"Need more?" her mother said. "I don't think anyone got enough rest last night."

"No thanks, I'm good. Probably switch to tea here in a little bit."

Steph rinsed the mug out in the sink, then fumbled to get her phone out without dropping it. She frowned when she saw her mother getting hers out as well.

Probably not Kim, then.

"Ugh, notes about the autopsy," her mother said. "At least your father didn't share pictures or anything. Stan Phipps had...some kind of strange burns, like the roots of a tree."

"And ruptured eardrums? I'm sure I've heard something about both of those things before. My brain is too sludgy to catch it."

Steph switched to the web browser to search, but the phone buzzed in her hand before she started typing.

A little corner of the screen popped up with Kim's name.

"Finally. Kim usually gets up with the sun. She must have stayed up later than..."

A few simple lines of text turned everything inside Steph to ice.

My, but she's lovely, Steph.

And so considerate.

A bit too unaware of her surroundings, though.

Steph dropped the phone, grabbed her mother's arm, and screamed for her father.

CHAPTER 34

Kim parked in front of Kay's Cafe, glad she'd gotten into town in time to beat the after-church crowd. Only a few other parking spaces along the wide main street were occupied, and even fewer booths inside were. If she'd waited until eleven or later, every space inside and out would have been packed.

A lifelong habit of getting up at the ass-crack of dawn, as Steph used to say, had its advantages.

The sun hadn't quite cleared the ridge and the Lightning Stone yet, so the street and the town were still in deep shadows. Even so, the air was much warmer today, almost muggy. More like May instead of March.

The odds of some kind of storm rolling in today jumped higher in Kim's resurgent weather sense. The t-shirt and jeans she wore wouldn't be nearly warm enough in a few hours.

She glanced over at Odds and Endings, smiling at the tiny

multicolored fairy lights still clearly visible around the high turret room's windows. The first time she'd noticed them was on a dark, rainy day, when that round room packed full of kids' books was the center of the universe.

She'd gasped in wonder at what looked like glittering jewels hanging down between the elaborate latticework outside the floor to ceiling windows. All the pleasures of the blue sky painted on the domed ceiling, the fantastic frog and turtle and caterpillar lights inside, and even the books themselves had faded away to nothing.

Maybe she'd check at the hardware store in town for some, or order them online. That would be an absolutely darling touch for Auntie Venus's porch.

Maybe for the deck at Steph's house, too.

Kim hugged herself at the thought of Steph, probably still sound asleep not all that far away, and walked inside the cafe.

A young couple sat in a booth off to the right, ignoring their food so they could stare at each other. A young woman who Kim suspected was the resident writer over at Odds and Endings sat alone at a table against the back wall. Her eyes were a bit red and she had a general air of not getting enough sleep. A big robin's-egg-blue coffee mug and a rounded metal coffee pot in front of her supported that writerly impression.

A slender, dark-haired man with intense brown eyes sat at the same table by the window where Kim met Steph what felt like a lifetime ago. Looked like a typical local, with clothes not a whole lot different than hers and a good dose of five o'clock shadow going that matched his dark brown hair.

He had a phone on the table beside a cup of coffee, but he ignored both.

He watched Kim closely enough to make her vaguely uneasy, but she couldn't say why.

Kay burst out of the kitchen, her face lighting up when she saw Kim.

"Good morning sunshine! I got that to-go order of cherry cobbler all ready for you. Baked it fresh last night, so it should be just right for Stephanie today. Can I get anything else ready for you?"

Kim stared up at one of the frosted glass and blue Formica light fixtures, considering her options.

"Well, if I'm going to bring some for Steph, I suppose I really should make sure I'm not picking off her plate. How's your supply of banana pudding holding out?"

Kay laughed, shaking her head.

"You know better than to think I'd be short on *any* desserts on a Sunday morning. Just hang on for a quick minute and I'll get it all ready. Need a coffee to go?"

"That would be fantastic, Kay, thank you. I have to make a hardware store run for Auntie Venus, and the lights in that place always give me a headache."

Kim pulled out her phone and scanned the text messages. A new one from Ivy about another storm connection she'd found, but nothing from Steph just yet. That was as good a reason as any to avoid adding to the endless swarm of notifications flying around their group.

Steph had always liked to sleep later than Kim. Not that

they'd had more than a couple of occasions to test that prefer-ence out together.

A flood of sweet heat with the shiver of excitement around the edges flooded through her at the idea of working that out now.

As adults with experience of the world and other relation-ships already behind them.

No matter how long Steph needed to wait would be worth it.

Kay nearly floated back out with one of her adorable paper take-out bags and a cute two-cup coffee holder with both sides full.

"I figured it's never a bad thing to bring good coffee. It sure was nice seeing you two together again. Tell her I said good morning."

Kim grinned and headed toward the register up front.

"I sure will, Kay. Thank you."

She didn't remember the odd man until she paid, gath-ered everything up, and turned to walk out the front door.

The coffee cup still sat on his table, still nearly full.

But he was gone.

She shook her head and kept moving.

The truth was she had a few errands to run, so the coffee might not make it to Steph hot after all. Kim wasn't above letting Kay feel good about the treat, which she'd refused to add to Kim's bill.

She settled the desserts in the floorboard and one cup in each of her cupholders before she drove to the hardware store at the opposite end of town. She'd at least check for fairy lights while she picked up several short, finished shelves and brackets for Auntie Venus. Small enough to fit into her own dainty car.

Seemed a lifelong world-traveler never had enough storage, no matter how long she lived in the same house.

The parking lot around back of the sprawling brick building wasn't quite as empty as the street had been, of cars at least. No one lingered outside, obviously intent on getting their last-day-of-the-weekend supplies and getting back home.

This whole section with the hardware and a good-sized grocery store had been built while she lived away. Carved out of a vacant area on the far end of Lightning Gap, closer to the road out of town than the Lightning Rock.

She would never admit it out loud, and she did go to the cozy old establishments whenever she could. But having a couple of modern stores nearby rather than the cramped, old-fashioned one jammed into a tiny building close to the school was a huge relief after years of city living.

A modern ordering system that got things in within a day or two made a huge difference, too.

Kim took a long sip of her smooth, almost chocolatey coffee before she opened the door.

Someone shoved it closed before she could step out.

She drew back and turned, expecting Jay up hours earlier than usual himself. All she could see was a blue raincoat zipped up over brand new blue jeans.

Had the guy back at Kay's been wearing a coat? She didn't think so.

She pushed the door open again, and this time it slammed closed hard enough to rock her little car on its springs.

The man slowly bent down and looked into her driver side window, shaking his head.

He *was* the one from the cafe.

And his smile was much worse than his stare.

His smile was made of one-hundred-percent sharp and dangerous teeth.

Kim scowled, forcing herself to ignore the cold surge of fear in her belly. She waved her left hand and mouthed "what the hell?" while her right hand jabbed at the car's starter button. All the gauges on the instrument panel jumping to life let her know the near-silent electric motor was running.

Before she could slip the transmission into gear and automatically lock all the doors, the guy's hand darted forward and yanked the door all the way open.

"Kim, I presume?" he said in a calm, freezing cold voice, his wiry body blocking the door. "So nice to meet you. It was so considerate of you to pick up dessert for Steph back there. She always did have a sweet tooth."

He leaned in, his breath hot and laced with coffee and bourbon.

"Tell me, is that what she likes so much about you?" he said in a threatening whisper. "Do you taste sweet all over like she does?"

"Get the *hell* away from me, asshole!" Kim yelled at the top of her lungs.

Despite her ears ringing, she knew no one was close enough to hear. She edged her hand closer to the gear shift.

He only laughed and shook his head. His accent was clipped and Midwestern flat, but she was certain she heard a wobbly, almost slippery local twang around the edges.

"That's more spirit than Steph *ever* managed to work up around me. Well done! No wonder at all that she likes you."

Kim lowered her shoulder and tried to shove him away.

His fist crunched hard into her ear.

She cried out and tears flooded her eyes. Her whole head rang like a bell, and the delicate curves and contours exploded into white-hot pain.

Her eyes weren't watering nearly enough to obscure the long, gleaming knife he now held clenched in his right hand.

The same hand he'd punched her with.

"Now this next part is, of course, entirely up to you, Kim. I can reach a whole hell of a lot of vulnerable places without any kind of trouble. Probably make a mess in your pretty little car, though. Not to mention of your pretty little ear and nose and eyes and tits and everything else."

His Midwestern accent dropped back even more, letting the local rise and fall and slow cadence come through. He nodded slowly, with a regretful twist to his lips.

"Move one more goddamn muscle toward that gearshift and we'll see what all we can't get into before someone else shows up."

Terrifying as he was, Bobby Faulks was fading away.

She was trapped inside her own car by Robert McReynolds.

"What the hell is it you expect me to do? Sit here and let you threaten me? Fight back so we can find out if you're willing to do more than run your damn mouth?"

When he flipped the knife forward and ran the tip from the bottom of her ear, across her temple, and to the corner of her eye, she barely flinched. She'd braced herself for much, much worse.

Robert didn't break the skin. He certainly pressed hard enough to make it clear he *could*.

The question Kim wasn't sure she was willing to bet her life on was whether he *would*.

But her heart pounded so hard little black spots danced around the edges of her vision.

"Why sure, we can do either one of those things, Kim." He slipped the knife down her cheek to the corner of her mouth. "If you decide you want to test me, you go right on ahead and grab for that gearshift. Truth is, though, I don't have hardly any kind of quarrel with you. I figure you just didn't have any idea what you were getting into the middle of, did you? I can't hardly blame you when Steph probably never got around to mentioning she was a married woman."

Kim took a deep breath through her nose and got another good whiff of his booze-scented fumes for her trouble. She was still plenty damn scared, but her anger was starting to gain strength. For herself, and for Steph.

If she could stop this monster from getting to her friend, she would.

"Okay, *Bobby Faulks*. You still haven't told me what you expect me to do besides sit here and argue with you."

His hateful face broke into a broad grin, no less threatening than his smile. In fact, the fact that he was pleased she knew who he was turned the threat up higher.

And he still held the knife way too close to where her blood thrummed just under her jaw.

"Well I'll be damned. Steph *did* tell you about me! That's the best surprise I've had in a long time, maybe since she turned tail and ran off back down here to her Sheriff Daddy's house. In that case, Kim, what I want is to go somewhere we can talk. Get to know each other better. Hell, the way I see it, since we have my wife in common, we should all three get acquainted just as soon as we can."

Not Steph's words but her father's—Sheriff Daddy as this monster called him—ricocheted around Kim's head, clearing the terror keeping her mind locked solid.

Never let an attacker take you to a second location.

Never.

Fight with everything you have, because they will damn sure hurt you badly or kill you if they get you out of sight.

"There's no way in hell I'm going to take you anywhere near Steph," Kim said in a near growl.

She shot out her left hand and grabbed between his legs, squeezing as hard as she could. Her right hand gripped the shifter, pushing it toward R.

Before she could stomp the accelerator, a vicious impact behind her left ear set off an explosion of agony, and the world went black.

CHAPTER 35

Steph stared at a sharp line on the kitchen table, the spot where rich, yellow wood butted up against wood so dark she could barely see any grain or details.

Her little brother Ryan had walked them all through each and every bit of wood the day it was delivered. Describing what each piece was and where each piece came from, explaining how he'd gotten all the joins so smooth and seamless. His pride so evident in his voice, his eyes, even his hands.

Try as she might—and no matter how desperately she needed something, anything else to think about—Steph couldn't call the name for even one of those pieces of wood to mind.

All she could do was stare at it, doing her level best to wedge it permanently into her mind and memory.

If she could concentrate enough on that, maybe she could

stop the heart-wrenching words and images trying to pull her down into a sickening whirlpool of her own nightmares.

Her throat ached from her scream and with unshed tears. The anise and lemon aroma of the hot tea beside her elbow reminded her of her mother's shaking hands when she put the cup down. Her father's cold, furious voice as he paced around behind her talking into his phone.

The way her mother's voice shook when she called Venus and told her what happened to Kim.

What they *thought* happened to Kim.

What *might* have happened to Kim.

What Steph couldn't stop imagining no matter how hard she tried.

Bobby doing all the things to Kim that he'd made it so abundantly clear he wanted to do to Steph the night she left him.

And now they had no idea where Kim was or how to get to her or how to make all of it stop.

Steph regretted every bite she'd eaten and every sip of coffee too much to even consider trying the tea.

Her father stopped pacing and stood beside her, his hand resting on her back.

"They found her car, sweetheart. In the parking lot at the hardware store. Unlocked, but the door was closed. No sign of a struggle otherwise, except a puddle of puke on the ground. Not sure if that was her or him or someone else."

"But she's gone," Steph said, not moving her eyes from the seam between the two pieces of wood. "And no one saw a damn thing, right?"

"No one saw anything that we know of, yet. The deputy who spotted the car noticed two cups of coffee from Kay's Cafe in the cupholders, still warm. So she's going right now to see if Kay noticed anything this morning."

Steph's mother spoke from somewhere in front of her.

"Venus said Kim was up and out before she woke, but she does that a lot. Goes into town to do the shopping or whatever errands there are. Venus ordered shelves from the hardware store, that's probably why Kim was there."

"She never went inside," her father said. "Security footage shows she didn't even get out of her car."

"That footage shows Bobby, doesn't it?" Steph said. "Or Robert, or whatever the fuck he calls himself. But let me guess, no one could see which way he went after he took her."

Her father sat beside her without moving his hand away from her back.

"It shows him going into the store not long before Kim got there, yes. He wasn't in there for long. Then he went out and waited in his car so he could park right beside her. And no, hon, they can't tell from which way he drove off from the footage. His car is a blue Ford sedan, no license plate on the back. He probably took it off when he...before."

"Okay then, if he went inside, what did he buy?"

She wasn't sure which was worse. Wanting to know, or dreading she knew the answer. He tilted the balance to dread by staring at the table himself before he spoke.

"He bought zip ties. Not heavy duty. More like what you'd use for tying back cables, but they were long. A knife, bigger than I'd like, but better than it could have been. No duct tape or rope. The clerk said he was polite, but seemed like he was in an awful rush. That probably worked in our favor."

"So what's next?" Steph said, finally looking into his worried eyes. "He obviously has her phone. Can they trace that?"

"We can, with good accuracy as long as we have good signal to work with. You know he's smart about cellular tech. As far as we're supposed to know, *his* phone is still sitting at his house in Louisville."

Steph closed her eyes, tilting her head from one side to the other. She heard and felt the muscles in her neck creaking.

"You're telling me he turned it off. He took her, he took her phone, he used it to send that message to terrorize me, and he turned it off."

"That's exactly what he did, and yes, he sent a message to terrorize you. He has to know how smart you are, and I'm damn sure he knows how your mother and I feel about him now. So we're not going to let him draw you out where he can get to you."

Steph flattened her hands on the table, her fingers covering different colors of wood, then drew them into fists.

"I'm trying my best not to get angry, Dad. I really am. But what *are* we going to do? He *has* terrorized me, and I'm sure he knows that, too. We can't just let him do whatever the hell he wants to Kim."

The tears that had lodged in her throat since she saw that awful message threatened to force their way out. Steph pounded her fists on the table.

"He was *supposed* to come after *me!* That's what we were all prepared for, what all this research and looking for patterns and getting patrol cars out front and sending out photos was about. Hell, this is why you insisted I carry a handgun and a Taser and bunch of pepper spray and a goddamn billy club in my car. We can't just let him have her!"

Her father wrapped his hand around one of her fists before she could hit the table again, and her mother reached across and grabbed the other.

"We're not going to let him have her," her mother said, tears running down her cheeks. "Everyone knows what he looks like, what he's driving, what Kim looks like. There are only a few roads through this little town, and only one way in or out."

"And we've got that way out blocked," her father said. "He'd have to carry her over the ridge or down the mountain to get through. We'll find him."

Steph wished she shared the rock-solid certainty of his voice.

She pulled her hands away and rubbed them together.

"Then we just wait here? Hoping to hear from one of them? Or from one of the ones who's out looking?"

"They're doing everything—" her father grabbed at his phone and got up to pace again.

Steph's mother rubbed her arm while they both waited. He finally ended the call and walked back over.

"A man matching his description was in Kay's early this morning, same time Kim was in there. He never talked to her, and he left before she did. That's all anyone remembers. He paid in cash, of course, just like at the hardware. He was hardly ever here when you were married. Is there anywhere you think he might have gone?"

Steph shook her head. "You're right, he was only here a couple of times. He either stayed in Louisville or ran off to Laurel Gap. We saw the usual stuff in town. The only unusual thing is I drove him up along the ridge where Ivy lives. Not to her house, but along that road. Has someone looked there?"

"Not yet, no. That's a hell of a lot of ground, but it's worth taking a look. I'll send someone up as soon as I can. Maybe one of you can call Ivy and make sure she knows he's around."

"Already done," her mother said. "She was spitting mad enough that she could probably take him out by herself with her bare hands. If he shows his face anywhere near her, he'll be making his last mistake."

"Everyone I've talked to feels that exact same way," her father said.

A low, choppy noise Steph hadn't paid much attention to gradually grew louder and closer until the windows rattled.

"Is that a helicopter?" Steph said, managing a whisper of a smile. "You *are* pulling out all the stops."

"It is," her father said, walking toward the kitchen door. "I think a few of our neighboring counties feel guilty about not realizing he was on the move. I'll be right back. They're not landing, but I can give them the all-clear."

Steph pushed herself back from the table, determined to do something besides staring into space. Or into the nearly invisible gap between two expertly joined pieces of wood. She plucked at her robe's sleeves.

"I guess I should go get dressed. Try to clean up a little. Me dragging around here like a slob isn't going to help anybody."

"And it won't hurt anybody, either," her mother said. "Go on if it will make you feel better. But don't do it because you're worried about upsetting me or your father or anyone else."

"I don't know what could help at this point, Mom. Except finding Kim. And making sure Bobby finally gets every last thing he deserves."

CHAPTER 36

im tried to open her eyes and winced, groaning low in her throat. She had an idea she should keep quiet, but she couldn't remember why.

Her head twisted and beat and throbbed badly enough that she had no idea where she was, much less how she'd gotten there.

Something cool and kind of clammy under her cheek finally got her moving.

A sharp edge biting into her wrists stopped her, along with the sharp ache of having her arms twisted behind her back.

She forced her eyes open and rolled and pushed and struggled to get herself upright at the same time, driving a gut-twisting nausea through her head and body.

She was...in the woods? In an area packed with thickets of

rhododendron and mountain laurel and not much else besides huge trunks of trees.

She'd been laying on her side on a rough bed of rotting leaves. The metallic taste of blood lingered on her tongue, and she realized she'd bitten her cheek a good one. Her left cheek, the same side that held a badly throbbing ear and a worse throbbing skull right behind it.

That was where he'd hit her, twice.

Bobby Faulks. Robert McReynolds.

No matter what he was called, he was in Lightning Gap and way too close to Steph.

He'd been way too close to Kim, too.

The sunlight overhead was diffuse, almost impossible to pinpoint through a growing layer of light gray clouds. The fact that she could move her shoulders at all made her think she couldn't have been there too long.

The air waited heavy and still around her, and far too warm for so early in spring.

She had no idea where she was, but she still had her clothes and shoes.

The only thing missing was her cellphone.

And her car.

And her abductor, of course.

And still, the biggest problem was the considerable and painful inconvenience of her wrists caught behind her back. They were tingling and stabbing back into life as loudly as her legs had back in the basement of Odds and Endings.

She assumed her feet would do the same thing here if she

got them free. At least now she had a good idea of what kept cutting into her wrists.

Thank the gods the zip ties weren't the heavy duty, thick version law enforcement used. These were the same narrow ones she'd used herself to secure cables under desks and behind computers for years. Available at any hardware store.

Like the one she'd been parked in front of when that asshole grabbed her.

She'd used a paperclip or small screwdriver to pop those little square clasps open more times than she could remember, but enough that she hadn't bothered with a knife or scissors for years. Just as fast and not nearly as much chance of slicing the cables.

Doing that behind her back would be a hell of a trick, though. Almost as much of a trick as folding and contorting herself enough to work her hands around to the front, especially with her shoulders so wrenched. Maybe when she was a scrawny pre-teen without hips or a reasonably plump backside, that would have been possible.

Maybe back then. Or if she were as long-limbed and slender as Steph.

But as herself, and now?

Not a chance.

Kim twisted her neck and body carefully, trying not to send her head screaming back into splitting territory again.

There! One of the massive pillars of rock Steph told her about, almost directly behind her. She had to scoot around on her bottom to get a better view of it. The different angle showed another one behind and off to the side of the first.

She had to be somewhere along Lightning Ridge Road then, the several-mile-long stretch that twisted and wove through a bunch of these outcrops. Ivy's house was on this road, and the Lightning Rock at the end of it.

And Kim had no idea which direction the road was, much less the house or the huge landmark itself.

She and Steph had only been up here a couple of days ago, but from where Kim sat, it may as well have been a hundred years and she'd have the same chance of knowing which way to go.

If she could manage to go at all besides wriggling on her side or something equally ridiculous.

Wait, Steph had said something about the rocks up here, something important. She'd talked about worrying about kids falling off the cliff, which wasn't going to help Kim in the slightest.

But she'd also talked about not wanting the kids to climb on the rocks...

Because they were *sharp*, that was it. The edges would cut them to ribbons.

Kim brought her knees up as close as she could without tipping over, trying to examine the ties around her ankles.

Just because she hadn't used a sharp edge on one of these for a while didn't mean she couldn't.

All she had to do was haul herself the twenty feet or so across the soft, muddy ground, through rotting leaves and who knew what underneath. Over to the rock closest to her.

Then position herself close enough to that rock to cut the tie against one of those sharp edges.

Without cutting her wrists instead, and bleeding to death up here with no one the wiser.

All with arms again going numb from being wrenched into an increasingly painful position.

And she had no idea whether Bobby already had Steph right now, or if he was on the way back to retrieve Kim herself to use as bait.

"Come on, Kim. You're not going to let that monstrous fucker beat you."

Dreading the impact on her already agonizing shoulders, but not willing to wait any longer, Kim got ready to wriggle.

CHAPTER 37

Steph fought an intense impulse to go back into her bedroom and hide rather than help her mother get a light lunch ready.

She might have welcomed it as a chance to keep herself distracted from increasing worry about Kim if it weren't for the guests who'd be arriving any minute now.

Instead she resigned herself to fetch-and-carry duty for setting up an elaborate sandwich buffet on the broad green kitchen island. A dizzying array of bottles of condiments, jars of herbs and spices, and little round mats on the table for all the plates that would hold cheese, meat, sliced vegetables, and everything else that could possibly go between two slices of bread.

All the different kinds of bread her parents had on hand would take up a big section all by themselves.

A steady parade of deputies and other law enforcement

types passing through didn't help calm Steph's nerves one bit. Updating her father, who stubbornly refused to leave the house for any reason. Therefore, they came by for conversations that a phone call or text couldn't handle.

The biggest problem with that was every time someone knocked at the door, Steph flinched. Expecting Jay and Ivy to arrive with a heartbroken and worried-sick Venus held between them.

All because of her.

Steph wasn't about to say any of that out loud, then have to nod and listen to another explanation of how it was all her dipshit ex, not her. His choices, not hers.

She'd heard the same from her mother and father and therapist and Ivy and anyone else who knew enough to have an opinion.

Most of the time she wholeheartedly agreed, and she appreciated the reminder.

But Kim never would have crossed paths with this particular monster if she hadn't started spending time with Steph again.

When she turned around with a handful of deep orange cloth napkins that perfectly matched the floor tiles, her father stepped in through the kitchen door, a warning look in his eyes.

Right behind him walked Ivy and Jay, and they were indeed supporting Venus between them. Her silver curls hung loose and in disarray. She wore what looked like an ancient, faded blue t-shirt and a pair of green men's pajama bottoms that had to be at least twenty years old. They only skimmed her shoulders and hips, while the rest of her body swam in far too much drawer-creased fabric.

Steph was horrified to realize they had to be clothes from one of her deceased husbands, brought out for comfort on such a difficult morning.

She would swear on anyone's holy book that Kim's great aunt had aged twenty years since dinner last night.

Throwing the napkins in the general direction of the table, she crossed the room to wait in front of Venus. Scared she would yell and scream because Steph had inadvertently helped put Kim into this awful mess, and determined to let her do just that if it would help.

Venus stared at Steph for an uncomfortably long time, her eyes red and puffy, but steady. Then her face crumpled and she held out both arms. Steph stepped forward and hugged her tight, trying not to sob right along with her.

"I'm so sorry, Venus," she whispered. "We're going to find her."

Venus drew back, accepting a handful of blue tissues. The same ones Jay had offered to Steph after she collapsed crying into Kim's arms.

"Of *course* we're going to find her," Venus said, her voice loud and strong. "Then your father will simply have to turn and walk away so I can deal with the one who did this to her, and to you. Ivy tells me she has a good, long butcher knife that will be well suited to my purposes."

Ivy half-smiled and brushed Venus's hair back over her shoulder. Steph noticed BeeGirl then, pressed up against Ivy's legs with her tail wagging low.

"Once we have hold of him," Ivy said, "he'll nevermore trouble another soul. Won't have to waste money on a burial, either."

Steph stepped to the side to let Venus make her slow way to the table. She caught her father's shrug out of the corner of her eye and stood by his side. He spoke low enough for only her to hear.

"I'm not sure I'm up to standing between Ivy and Venus and what they want to get done. I don't believe I would even try in this case. You holding up okay, Steph?"

She leaned against him, grateful for his support and his arm around her shoulders.

"I don't know whether to be afraid or angry from one second to the next, but I'm okay. Have you heard anything new at all?"

"We put out an APB on all three of our missing men in all the surrounding counties. I doubt it would flush Bobby out, but if we find our third, or get information about the other two, that might lead us to him. If he *is* behind them being in Lightning Gap, he may still be working with the last one standing."

Something darted around the back of Steph's mind, but she couldn't catch the shape of it. Thinking about something else was usually the only thing that let a renegade connection like that work its way to the front of her mind.

"I know you know this," she said, "but please tell me if there's anything I can do. Right now, I'm going to help Mom get lunch on the table."

He shook his head and turned her toward the group already sitting.

"You've *been* helping, while I've been running around everywhere else. Go, sit. See if you can do anything there. If nothing else, take notes from Ivy and Venus about their techniques for later."

Steph intercepted her mother with a pitcher of lemonade on a tray full of glasses, taking it to the table herself.

Jay took over from there, distributing the glasses and pouring for everyone.

"Anything new, Steph?" he said. "Anything we can help with or make happen?"

She shook her head, still bothered by the flitting idea.

"Just an APB on all three of Bobby's Merry Men, to see if that flushes anything out. What are any of you hearing?"

"It's more what I'm *feeling*," Venus said, rotating her shoulders. "The Seagons said the same thing when I called them on the way over."

Steph moved to get up. "Are your shoulders hurting you? I can get you pain medicine."

Venus reached for her hand.

"No, it's not like that. I do have arthritis, yes. And it usually acts up when we have a storm on the way. Right now it's hurting less than it usually does on a calm hot day in the middle of the summer."

Ivy nodded, shifting her legs under the table.

"My knees and hips feel about twenty years younger. BeeGirl over there is too young for this, but I've lived with enough old dogs to know they'd be feeling better, too."

Steph glanced at BeeGirl, already sound asleep on the couch.

"I don't understand. You said the Seagons are feeling the same? What does that mean?"

"They are," Ivy said. "I'd bet your father is too. What it means is that's not any kind of ordinary storm on the way. Lightning Gap is about to get our biggest spring storm, more than a month early."

Steph turned to Jay but he only raised his eyebrows and shook his head.

"Her father will what?" Steph's dad set a plate full several shapes and colors of sliced cheese on the table.

"How's the shoulder, David?" Ivy said.

His mouth turned down and he raised his arm up and over his head.

"It feels...perfectly fine today. Like I never even injured it. That's the weather thing again, isn't it? Something about the lightning?"

Steph gasped, and she stared at her father.

"That's it, the thing I've been trying to remember. About the autopsy this morning, they said Stan Phipps had ruptured eardrums, right? And a strange burn that looked like tree roots?"

He nodded, the frown returning.

"All over one shoulder."

"He was struck by *lightning*, Dad. It causes those injuries. I was so out of it this morning I couldn't remember. I'd bet Mr. Seagon would have caught it with what Mrs. Seagon said about his habit of getting too into these weather things."

Her father had his phone out already.

"You think that's what killed him?"

"It could have been, or it may have just disoriented him. It was rainy when the hikers found him, right? He may have been struck there and the trees weren't damaged, or the damage may have been high up and not smoldering any more. Or several trees away and the strike traveled along the ground. Lightning can do some strange things even in a normal place."

"And there's no telling what it can do here," Venus said. "Or at least the people who might know keep enough of it to themselves to make things interesting. Have you been outside lately, Stephanie?"

She started to shake her head but stopped when she looked out the window. It could have easily been early evening rather than almost noon. No shadows yet, but much darker than it should have been even on a cloudy day.

Her stomach felt like it was churning as surely as the weather system developing all around them.

"Whatever Lightning Gap might do to take care of her own," Steph said, "it's on the way. And we may be running out of time to find Kim."

CHAPTER 38

Bobby shifted in the formerly comfortable seat of his new used car, trying to find a tolerable arrangement for his aching balls. That bitch Kim had surprised him, catching him in a damn vice grip worse than he'd ever experienced before, even during his youthful days of scrapping and fighting for fun.

Now the crampy sick aftereffects gave every sign of settling in for a good long visit.

The gift that kept on giving.

He took another sip of too-warm Coke, trying to settle the leaden nausea occupying his middle.

He'd managed to use the huge, detailed hiking map that covered Lightning Ridge Road—conveniently designed to tear out of the thick book and unfold—to find an old logging path a mile from the end of the long, twisting road on top of the ridge.

The car was parked at the end of the slight suggestion of tracks, close beside one of the towering hunks of rock that Steph couldn't stop carrying on about the one time she'd dragged him up here. Hidden under a thick covering of branches even with oncoming leaves only a pinkish suggestion of buds.

He doubted very much even the helicopter buzzing in lazy circles overhead would spot it in the day's dim light. Not unless he did something else boneheaded and turned on the headlights.

Bobby had very carefully walked the fifty yards or so past the car before the helicopter showed up, the way ahead overgrown with too many trees and scraggly bushes like overgrown azaleas with shiny leaves for driving.

He'd pushed through a screen of low branches and crossed the last few yards across open bare rock as quickly as he could manage. His reward, a perfect view of Lightning Gap spread out beneath him like an elaborate miniature movie set. Glittering in the occasional rays of sunlight that managed to break through the lowering gray clouds.

His vantage point out on the barren ledge was beside the even bigger rock everyone around here was so obsessed with, barely fifty feet to his right and towering more than a hundred feet straight up. But his path was well off the usual hiker's beaten tracks, and the paved road that curved away before looping back on the other side.

Even the massive Lightning Rock was obscured from his view once he got back among the thickets on the ground and interlaced branches above.

Safe enough, at least, until he could recover a bit and decide what came next.

Every time his balls or his guts twisted anew, he wished he'd eliminated Steph's new little girlfriend right there in the hardware store parking lot. Just slit her throat for her with his brand-new knife, or maybe jammed the slender blade straight into her temple.

Even better, he could have brought her out here with him, instead of dumping her couple of miles back. To the middle of the woods where no one would likely walk or drive or anything else.

Then he could have practiced all the fun and games he'd had in mind for Steph for years. Get hands-on for the first time after a lifetime of imagining every bright, hot spurt of blood and gratifying scream of pain.

Make sure he had everything right and ready for *her* when he got his hands on her instead.

Assuming he managed to get her out from under Sheriff Daddy's nose.

Sure, a practice round would have been satisfying. Finding out how many fingers and toes and ears and a nose he could remove from Kim before she lost her appeal, and her life.

This way, though—the way he'd planned when he sat in that horrid little greasy spoon cafe listening to her chat with the nosy old hag of a waitress—this was better.

This way he could use the bitch Kim's phone to torment Steph and get her right where he needed her without having to drag Kim around with him. Or put up with her smart mouth or truly vicious hands.

If she somehow managed to get herself upright and loose and down off of this blasted mountain anytime soon, she'd be too late to stop Bobby. Or to save his traitorous wife.

So it was for the best that his plan had taken over when she got past his defenses like that.

Or maybe that had been his overwhelming desire to get both of them out of sight once that evil bitch bested him.

In his wishful mental reenactment, he'd focused on her killer left hand snaking out toward him rather than her right hand grabbing for the gearshift. He'd twisted his hips to block her, then grabbed that treacherous hand and yanked her out of the car. Dislocating her shoulder in the process, of course, and stomping her head for good measure once she hit the pavement.

Instead he'd staggered back against his own car, puking his guts out in a chunky mess of greasy-spoon breakfast laced with equally fragrant brown streaks of coffee.

And she hadn't exactly been easy to drag from her car into his own even so close by. Not with his crotch and gut a gigantic white-hot cramp keeping him from catching his breath. The rest of his body a shaking, sweaty disaster, topped off by a massive lightning bolt of a headache.

By the time he'd gotten himself calmed down and following the phone's GPS up the road to the ridge above town, he didn't *want* to deal with her. Not yet.

Not until he could stand up and walk straight again, rather than letting her see how badly she'd staggered him.

Leaving her zip-tied wrist and foot at the end of another barely-there logging trail made a hell of a lot more sense.

She'd be there if he needed her.

Later.

When he was ready.

Bad reflexes and slow response time aside, it had all been worth it, and she'd served her purpose admirably. Her phone had, anyway.

Bobby had watched several turd-brown Felten County deputy cars in that toy version of the town below him, blue lights spinning, following the twisting main road to the hardware store from both directions.

Lightning Rock Road it was called, from all the way down in the valley until it dead-ended near the high school. Not all that creative, maybe, but it did coordinate nicely with Lightning Ridge Road.

Hell of a marketing gimmick in his opinion, dragging tourists up here by their wallets, all of them eager to see some kind of natural/magical phenomenon.

Too bad people who lived here seemed to believe there was more to all their manufactured hype than the endless stream of easy revenue.

That surging sewer flood of law enforcement into such a quiet sleepy town was a sure sign they'd located the bitch Kim's car, not to mention his own embarrassing spew beside it.

Bobby took a slow breath, avoiding the point of waking the beast made of hurt lurking in his abdomen, and finished the rest of his soda.

His miscalculation with Kim had gotten Sheriff Daddy's attention, and Steph's.

That might have been a mistake.

A bad one.

He hadn't been thinking clearly that morning, he could admit that now that he was hidden away and not in quite so much pain. Between hearing Steph's name out of nowhere in that cafe and realizing she'd already moved on—replaced him with a friend or lover or who knew what, but he was no less replaced—all of Bobby's logic and care and planning had vanished.

Leaving only Robert and his impulsive, often bitterly jealous actions behind.

With the way Sheriff Daddy had called in the entire county's worth of law enforcement, Bobby knew Steph would be barricaded inside that house now.

Harder to get to than he'd planned when he set off on this trip.

He'd expected to take his time. Wait and watch. Learn her routines.

The times when she put herself at risk.

A simple task, really, very much like what he'd foolishly asked the three redneck musketeers to do for him a couple of weeks ago.

Once the scouting was done, he would have been free to waltz in and catch Steph off guard and away from her overbearing ass of a father. Possibly outside the school, on the way there or on the way home.

Or *during* school if the opportunity presented itself.

Whatever it took.

Get her away from prying eyes and possible interference, then settle the unfinished business between them.

Phone number three buzzed on the dashboard, two short and one long.

A forwarded message, and from phone number two.

Robert's phone.

Bobby grabbed for it, groaning when his guts and the smoldering coals between his legs protested the quick movement. He had to enter the passcode in twice to get the voicemail to play.

Another call from the Walton County Sheriff's Office, which he'd been expecting.

The message left by the more refined variety of redneck, Larry Crabtree, on the other hand, was not what he expected at all.

Seemed Eugene's addled empty head had cleared again, and he repeated his exhortations to tell Robert. Along with mention of Dusty Atkinson—otherwise known as dusty slugs—missing man number three.

The one Bobby was most hoping to hear from.

He shifted again, determined to keep the pain and shallow breathing out of his voice.

Out of *Robert's* voice, the one Sheriff Crabtree was expecting to hear.

Didn't much matter if the sheriff heard that voice from a different phone altogether. Bobby's public phone was still nestled safe and snug in his house back in Louisville. And he had one more burner phone left if he needed it.

He closed his eyes and placed the call.

CHAPTER 39

When the blasted zip tie finally gave way, Kim forgot all her intentions to keep quiet. She let out a sobbing scream loud enough to echo.

Followed immediately by a longer, quieter moan as she inched her arms back into their normal positions at the side of her body.

Her wrists hadn't bled as much as she feared, but more than she hoped. Enough blood had trickled down her fingertips to make a little pool in the leaves underneath. Her palms and all around her fingernails were thick with congealed red.

She wouldn't stand a chance if Dracula decided to pay a visit to Lightning Gap.

Thankfully none of the wounds were deep. What they were was plentiful. Dozens of shallow scrapes and slices from the razor-like protrusion she found. A couple of good gashes around the sides and backs of her wrists.

Trying to open and close her fingers hurt worse than all the cuts put together.

Despite longing for the easy quick jab she'd used so many times to open a zip tie at work, there was no way her hands were up to the task even if she found a suitable stick or twig or something.

She tried to manage it without having to prop herself up, but in the end she gritted her teeth and used her knuckles to turn and get her hobbled ankles into position.

"Just get through this," she whispered, rolling slowly down onto her back for leverage. "You can buy yourself five brand new pairs of boots to cover up the scars."

The fact that she could actually *see* where to dig in this time instead of flailing around behind her back make it go a lot faster. Her abs and thighs still trembled and ached when it was finally done, and a few new streaks of blood decorated her calves.

On the good side, moving and straining in a different way eased the pain in her shoulders considerably. Down to a dull roar rather than a jagged shriek.

Kim pushed herself slowly onto her hands and knees, then very carefully braced against the rock to pull herself to her feet. They didn't quite feel like solid wood to her, but the prickling wakeup pains shooting up her legs were plenty bad enough.

The world only swayed a little, certainly compared to the renewed and agonizing thumping in her skull.

She leaned forward and rested her sweaty forehead against the cool mass before she kissed it.

"Thank you, thank you, thank you, rock. I'll do my best to remember where you are and come visit again. Under less bloody and terrifying circumstances."

The bare limbs creaked and clattered over her head, and the breeze lifting the damp hair from her neck was much cooler now. The sky was even less help in letting her guess the time than it had been earlier. Uneven pale whitish clouds had given way to iron gray.

They hung so low and thick Kim was sure she could just about reach up and touch them.

She didn't care if this was going to be a natural thunderstorm or the electrical apocalypse due later in the spring. She had no desire to experience it this up-close and personal.

Certainly not with Bobby still out there somewhere.

Where the hell was he?

And exactly where the hell was *she*?

Kim tested her tingling feet and ankles, then slowly walked away from her stony savior. She turned in a slow circle, desperate to get her bearings.

The forest stretched out around her, with several rhododendron thickets and a few more of the huge rocks. She followed her slithering tracks back to where she'd woken.

She spotted a barely visible old trail or trace or something about twenty feet away. Mainly because the brush was clear in a more or less straight line.

The ground was soft with recent rain, otherwise she wouldn't have seen the tire tracks in the leaf-covered path. So yeah, following that back out made sense. Odds were extremely high it would lead her right back to Lightning Ridge Road.

But she had no way to know which way to turn when she got there. Accidentally hiking out to the Lightning Rock in the middle of this growing tempest was a sure way to make her situation even worse.

Maybe even worse than walking right into Bobby, wherever he was.

Could he really have brought her all the way up here to just dump her and run?

Even if she'd never heard Steph give the barest glimpse into her marriage to Bobby and its horrible end, Kim had seen the foul, inhuman look in *Robert's* eyes. She'd heard the queasy slipperiness of his voice sliding from one dialect into another, as if he couldn't keep track of which identity he wanted to inhabit.

Whoever he decided to be for the rest of the day, he didn't strike her as the kind who would run away until he got whatever—or whoever—he came here for.

Kim brushed the remnants of leaves off her shirt and jeans, then rubbed her hands together to try to shed at least a little of the blood. She gingerly felt her ear and her skull right behind it.

Neither seemed to be bleeding or seriously damaged. Just incredibly tender and painful.

Another gust of damp, chilly wind got every bit of her attention.

In those long-ago high school science classes she hadn't paid nearly enough attention to, they'd talked about the effect of this ridge and the Lightning Rock. How the prevailing weather patterns swept along it in a predictable direction, even if the resulting disturbances were quite unpredictable according to what everyone said last night.

But what was that direction?

A longing for Steph hit Kim then, so deep and hard that it brought tears to her eyes.

Not only because she was still every bit as perfect a match as she'd been when they were seventeen. Even more so now that they'd grown up and figured a few things out about themselves.

She was only a little embarrassed to wish for Steph because she'd always known her directions and which way to go as easily as she drew her next breath.

The next gust came from the same place.

Okay.

A thousand weather forecasts flitted through Kim's mind: the notable ones that actually caught her attention when she lived away. The fronts and storms almost always moved in one direction, riding the jet stream across the continent and all the way to the Virginia coast.

West to east, unless a hurricane was in the neighborhood.

The gusts blew in from her left.

So that had to be west? It *had* to be.

Once she got back to Lightning Ridge Road, she needed to walk away from the Lightning Rock to get back toward town and away from the biggest target for the electricity she could feel building in the air.

She had to remember to turn left. And walk into that stiff wind.

A strong gust hit her then, twisting itself in all directions for a few heart-stopping seconds. Kim was certain the air from her *right* and smelled fresher, more full of ozone and an impending downpour.

Then it slowed, stopped.

And picked up from the left again.

She started a slightly unsteady walk toward the faint impression of a path. The one thing she had to go on, without either her phone or any way to see where the sun sat in the sky, was that wind.

If she couldn't trust it—or if she let herself *believe* she couldn't trust it—she'd be lost before she ever got started.

Just get to the main road.

Get to the main road and figure it out from there.

She managed about ten steps before she stumbled to a stop.

What if he'd brought her all the way up here, dumped her, and intended to come back for her later?

Steph's perverse Prince Charming had said something about wanting to get her and Steph together, and definitely not for a companionable brunch or movie night or anything the least bit friendly.

Kim still felt the cold, threatening point of that knife slipping over her skin too clearly to pretend anything like that.

He might intend to try to get hold of Steph on his own, saving Kim for use as bait if that failed.

Either way, staying here wasn't reasonable.

If nothing else, her weather sense sent out an increasing alert about the muggy air that was so unusual for early in the spring, now shot through with that cool breeze.

The breeze that still flitted around her in a jittery butterfly dance rather than anything predictable.

Normal weather patterns would tend to clear the warm air mass out with a storm.

If even a tiny bit of what they'd all been reading and learning about *Lightning Gap's* weather patterns was true, a storm after not one but two natives were targeted wouldn't be the time to be out in the open on top of this high ridge.

Which she would definitely be if she let herself get upset and confused and turned around.

Fury so rough and hot that it left her head throbbing in a whole new way twisted through her. In that moment, Kim would have happily tied Bobby or Robert or anyone else driving this living nightmare to the top of the Lightning Rock as a screaming, squirming sacrifice.

Then settled herself down with a good pair of binoculars under the roof of the huge stage at the fairgrounds and enjoyed the show.

Cheering on every bolt that struck home until she lost her voice, when she'd keep offering silent encouragement.

For now, the only thing she could think to do was follow the impressions of tires in the leafy mud. If she heard or saw a vehicle coming, she'd just have to hide the best she could.

Standing or sitting or laying here exposed to wind, storm,

and creeping psychopath, she'd be way too helpless for her taste.

Kim squared her shoulders, held her aching head high, and started walking.

CHAPTER 40

Steph was halfway back from the kitchen with a mug full of hot tea for Venus when Jay waved her over. He stood just inside the sliding doors out to the deck, and she saw her father passing by on one of his pacing circuits outside.

She set the mug in front of Venus, catching her mother's eye across the table. Steph jerked her chin toward the deck. When her mother nodded without a break in the quiet conversation, she walked away as fast as she could without drawing too much attention to herself.

Jay held his phone in one hand, turning it so she could see the display. With the way her head ached from stress and the aftereffects from hardly any sleep making her ability to read and comprehend marginal at best, she concentrated on his words instead.

"We may have just caught a break, Steph. Sheriff Crabtree

called. Apparently the mysterious Eugene Hunsaker recovered his faculties again, but only for a minute. Again."

Steph smiled, trying her best not to get impatient.

"What did the guy say?"

"He was asking for Robert over and over again, but this time he wanted to tell him something. Eugene clawed his way back to consciousness so he could tell Robert something about our other missing man. Dusty Atkinson."

"What? I mean, great that at least two of them seem to be linked to...to *Robert* now, by more than a high school class roster. I don't understand any of this."

Jay shook his head. "No, I don't either. Your dad thinks it might be what happens when a crook runs with a bunch of crooks. Sooner or later someone's going to get stabbed in the back. Sorry, I shouldn't have said that, not with him buying a knife."

"No, it's fine. That gave me a nice visual to use with my ex-husband. Did the sheriff say what the desperate message was?"

"Not to me. They think it may have been in some kind of code. But the important thing is the call. Sheriff Crabtree called Robert's old number, but Robert called back on a different phone."

Steph grabbed Jay's bicep, trying not to squeeze too hard. She opened the sliding door and pulled him through after her. He closed it without a word.

She was startled by how much cooler it was, how much the breeze had kicked up. But not startled enough to get distracted now.

"*Please* tell me they traced this new phone."

Jay nodded, and to his credit he didn't rub his arm once she finally let go.

"They did. He's up on Lightning Ridge Road, almost up against the Lightning Rock. Your dad thinks there may be some way to hike in?"

"Yes!" Steph saw her father look over and nodded. "There's an old logging path up there, hardly enough of a trail for most people to know about, but a small car could drive part of it. It ends up at the cliff edge not fifty meters from the Lightning Rock. I had a group out there in October. We can be up there in half an hour, a little less."

"Absolutely not," her father said from right beside her. "She may not even be with him. I'm going, and I'm taking at least two deputies with me. But you're staying right here with your mother."

Steph tried her holding a breath and slowly blowing it out trick, but it only added more frustration and anger when she thought she was full up.

"Or *what*, Dad? Don't worry, I know I'm speaking to Sheriff Holfield right now, and that's fine, too. I'm well over eighteen, and I'm not under any sort of detention that I know of. Bobby is a major league asshole, but he came here for me."

Jay stepped away and slipped back into the house when her father held up one hand and opened his mouth, but Steph wasn't done.

"No, let me finish! I understand all of this is on Bobby. I get that. But you have to understand that Kim wouldn't even know his name if it weren't for me. And he sure as hell wouldn't know hers. If there's any chance at all she *is* with him, we have to try. *I* have to try. He's the kind who wouldn't hesitate to use her as bait to get to me."

"I'm sorry, Steph," her father said, shaking his head. "It's too big of a risk. Thanks to you and everyone else, we know a hell of a lot more of his secrets than he thinks we do. But still, he had to know we'd be after him. He's crazy or dumb enough to be here anyway."

"*Exactly*. He's not going to do anything that might give us a chance unless he thinks he can get to me. By all means, bring your best sharpshooters and take him out the second they can get a clear shot. But please, let me make sure Kim is away from him first. I owe her that much. We all do."

He looked up at the lowering sky, then at the treetops beginning to twitch and sway. When he looked into her eyes again, his were more worried than angry.

"What will you do if I order you to stay here?"

Steph snorted out a laugh, shaking her head.

"As Sheriff Holfield or as my Dad?"

"Either way."

"Well, either way, I'll get in my car and drive myself up there. It's public land, and I'm not under arrest and haven't done anything to expect to be. I'd feel a lot better if you were with me, or at least close by. But I'll still go alone."

He nodded once.

"What I *should* do is arrest you and take you down to the jail and lock you up. Or maybe recruit the women inside to restrain you. Don't doubt for a second they could do it. If you go, you wear a vest."

"Oh come on. Bobby may be crazy, but I don't believe in a thousand years he's got a gun. That's just not...That's not how he'd do this. If he ever works up the courage, he made it abundantly clear he wants to be a lot more hands-on."

Her father swallowed hard and his face paled.

"That may be true, but I'm not giving an inch on this one. We don't know much about the locals he seems to have been working with, and one of them is still out there somewhere. Can you say for certain Dusty Atkinson wouldn't use a gun?"

"No. No, I can't. Okay, I wear a vest. But you do too."

"Done. Go get one of my sweatshirts, and one of my raincoats. That way it won't show quite so much. Besides, I think this storm everyone's been carrying on about is going to hit the Lightning Rock at about the same time we do."

CHAPTER 41

obby levered himself up out of the car, glad no one was nearby to see or hear how much it hurt him. Besides the continuing torment in his belly and balls, it seemed he'd managed to wrench his lower back quite nicely dragging that nasty *girlfriend* around.

He doubted he could pick up so much as a briefcase right now and keep a straight face. If his back didn't seize altogether first. Putting his third cell phone into his pocket in case he got another forwarded message left him gasping with tears in his eyes.

Good thing physical power wasn't what he needed right now. His brain mattered a hell of a lot more, as it almost always did.

He walked toward the front of the car, putting one foot carefully in front of the other like a crippled old man. Trying to make it out to the cliff again might not be the best idea in the world for more reasons than he allowed himself to think about.

But he felt a growing compulsion to get out there, out from under the thick canopy.

Helicopter or not, he needed to *see* what might be heading his way.

The breeze had gathered itself into a steady wind, cool and full of oncoming rain. Once that settled in, he might not be able to see a damn thing right in front of his face, much less down in Lightning Gap.

Bobby shuffled along, his feet plowing twin paths through the thick leaves.

Sheriff Crabtree might have spent a good bit of time somewhere out of Holly Creek going by the words he used and the way he used them. But he wasn't quick enough to catch on to how Eugene played him like a fiddle.

Awfully convenient how the mystery man drifted in and out of delirium like that. And when he drifted out, he got his words and his meaning across no matter how foggy and confused he might sound.

This time, he'd gotten the message to Bobby clear as the loudest church bell when all you wanted to do was sleep off your Saturday night.

The good sheriff sounded confused and even more amused.

But he'd dutifully reported that Eugene wanted to make sure Robert knew about the *slugs*.

Slugs all over the garden, gonna eat up everything before you ever know they're there.

Despite his halting progress and worry about tripping over an unseen root and making everything worse, Bobby barked out a laugh.

Of all the dumbass jokes he and Stan and Eugene and Dusty had shared, the slugs were surely bottom of the heap. So of course that had been the one to catch on and follow them well into adulthood.

After all, talking about a betrayal in progress by using snakes was awfully ordinary, even for such a...non-intellectual bunch. Damn easy for outsiders to catch on, too.

But slugs? Outside of the gardening reference, folks might think calling someone a slug meant they were lazy. Unpleasant. Pretty much useless.

So using slug to refer to a traitor instead, a backstabber, had amused them to no end back then.

While the word itself amused Bobby, the way Eugene used it didn't.

He stopped beside a towering pine tree, leaning against the scratch bark to catch his breath. A few more steps would bring him out of the cover of the trees and out onto the open cliff. He needed to be ready to move if that helicopter swung back through.

Sheriff Crabtree was careful to make it clear Eugene specifically mentioned a *dusty* slug. Over and over again, Robert's got to watch out for that dusty slug, sneaking into the garden.

Bobby had managed a breathless laugh before saying he sure wished he could help, but he had no earthly idea what Eugene might have meant by such a strange statement.

The hell of it was Bobby still wasn't sure.

He might like and respect Dusty Atkinson, and appreciate the way they so easily understood each other when it came to their more secretive hobbies. But Bobby had gotten as far as he had by making a habit of never, ever trusting anyone.

Right now, all he knew was either Eugene or Dusty were planning to betray him.

Possibly both of them already had.

But he had no idea how or why.

He couldn't hear the helicopter overhead, and standing still grabbing on to a tree wasn't going to help his various physical ailments. He held his breath for a second, then stepped through the branches and onto the cliff.

Aside from several of the streetlights winking on as he watched, Lightning Gap looked almost the same. No whirling blue lights on police cars, no evidence of strange traffic patterns for early on a Sunday afternoon.

The only strange thing was how dark the sky was for nowhere near evening. The streetlights didn't do the gray and black clouds piling up directly over his head justice.

Bobby saw plenty of huge thunderstorms in Louisville, basically the beginning of the wide open spaces of the Midwest. But he couldn't remember one moving in so quickly.

His mind shied away from the thought as soon as he had it. Yet he still had the strong impression all the masses of water vapor were concentrated directly over the Lightning Rock.

Which was much too close to where he stood.

Still, he stared up at the massing clouds, noticing disturbing streaks of red, purple, and pink higher up. Almost like he was looking at bruising flesh rather than an airborne collection of water vapor.

Phone number three buzzing in his pocket broke the mesmerizing spell. Another forwarded message, again from Robert's phone.

Bobby gasped after a thoughtless twist to grab it, then scowled at the number on display.

Well, well, well.

After days entirely out of sight, Dusty Atkinson had resurfaced at last.

A series of strong gusts that seemed to shift directions every second sent him back under the trees and away from the threatening, fascinating sky.

Bobby was glad he'd leaned against the tree by the time the message finished playing.

"Listen up, Robert, this here is Dusty. I'm real sorry I had to lay so low over these last couple days. Had a slug creeping around in my garden in the gap, had to throw a good sprinkle of magic salt on it and haul it on out of the way."

Scratchy, rough-edged laughter rang out over the phone.

Because it could have gone no other way, Eugene and Dusty had managed to get into some kind of idiotic squabble when Bobby needed them most. Then decided to try to catch him up in the middle of it.

"So to get to the point and why I'm calling now, here's the trouble. I'm bunked down right close to the house where your favorite problem hangs her pretty little hat these days. Pigs dressed all in turd brown coming and going all day, so I figured you might be in town. Then just this minute, I spotted your problem jetting out of here like her tail was on fire. Big Brown Pig Daddy right behind her, with another load of his little oinkers in his dust. Might want to watch your ass."

Bobby stopped squeezing the phone when it creaked in his hand.

That slimy scumbag fucker had put him neatly into a position where he had to decide, and right now, who to trust.

And the one thing he needed most—information—was in critically short supply.

No help for it.

If the Dusty slug was actually telling the truth, not one minute to spare.

For the first time in days of Bobby trying, Dusty picked up on the first ring.

"Gonna guess this here is Robert?"

Robert's accent didn't slip and slide over Bobby's this time. It shoved to the front without hesitation.

"Yeah, Dusty. This here is Robert. I'll need to know a hell of a lot more about what kind of spat you and Eugene got yourselves into when this is finished. Right now, I need you to get your ass up here to the Lightning Rock. Know where that is?"

"I guess I do. Just about the biggest pile of tourist trap in a hundred miles. Way ahead of you on that one. Ahead of them, too. I was a couple of long switchbacks in front of 'em when they lit out. I'm leaving out right now."

"Don't let them get past you. What I need is someone to

keep the turds occupied, maybe get 'em good and distracted. 'Cause I want that little problem right here with me where she belongs, real bad. You up for that?"

That scratchy laugh again, this time with the sound of a big, throaty engine accelerating in the background. Not some kind of delicate electric car or a hybrid, either.

Bobby guessed that was eight cylinders of pure combustion lighting it up.

"I can damn well gar-on-*tee* they won't get in front of me. As far as keeping them occupied, you know I got that covered."

"You better. We'll work out whatever it is we need to work out between us later. Now listen to where to find me, then get on it."

Not the ideal situation to deal with his disloyal wife in about a dozen different ways. He'd have to work fast instead of taking his own sweet time, assuming his wayward redneck associate managed to live up to his bluster.

But no matter how loudly his various body parts protested or how rotten the setting, if Dusty could manage to get Steph anywhere near him, Bobby would be damn sure be ready.

CHAPTER 42

No matter how much or how hard Kim wished for something, anything, about Lightning Ridge Road to let her know if she'd made the right choice, it remained silent and relentless.

Remarkably flat for running along the top of a ridge, even as much as it curved. Or at least it seemed that way to someone walking. The blacktop had been recently paved, so it didn't offer distinctive potholes or a pattern of cracks that stood out. Trees and those ever-present rhododendrons and mountain laurels peaked through the gloom. Some closer to the road, some farther away.

The sky overhead had grown much too dark for her to see the towering rock pillars out in the forest or a trace of the sun's position.

Too dark to be walking out there, and too cold and windy.

Not a shadow she could follow or judge by, either.

And that breeze, the one that she was certain went from west to east? It had devolved to a skittering tease that kept her hair constantly dancing in front of her face no matter which way she turned.

Same thing with the smell of ozone and rain poised to strike. That came from everywhere, too.

At least when it finally started raining, she'd be able to look up and collect water for her parched throat.

Ivy's house was up here...somewhere. Ahead of her, behind her, that much had to be true. But between the gleeful twists and turns of the wind and the decades since she'd followed the length of the road, she admitted she had no idea.

Even if she and Steph had driven the whole thing a couple of days ago instead of stopping, Kim wasn't so sure that would help her walking on a day like this.

To turn her worry, discomfort, and frustration up even more, the t-shirt that felt so nice when she left her Auntie Venus's house ages ago now only kept her chilled through.

She groaned, the sound lost in the rising wind. Auntie Venus had to be worried half to death. Kim wasn't sure what time it was, but enough time had passed that her disappearance would be noticed.

The choppy noise of a helicopter overhead earlier, that had to be for her, right? Those didn't randomly fly over Lightning Gap for no good reason.

She also hadn't heard that chopper noise since she got out onto the road. Not since the wind picked up in a swirling, chaotic rise, and thunder started rumbling in the distance.

And if Steph even suspected what had happened, that

Bobby had gotten himself acquainted with Kim, she'd be furious and heartbroken and terrified. Not to mention wrapped up in a guilt that Kim wished she could take away.

Her choices hadn't changed since she first woke up bound hand and foot and dumped in the woods.

Get herself free and keep herself moving.

What she thought was just another rumble of thunder slowly resolved itself behind her. That was a vehicle. Not an electric one like hers, either.

This one sounded loud enough that it couldn't have been built within the last fifty or sixty years at least.

Not anyone Kim knew and trusted, then.

Whoever was driving was a lot more likely to be on Bobby's side.

Bobby alone had almost been too much for her.

Kim stopped and spun around, then headed for the closest stand of big trees off to the side. If she could get there in time, dark as it was she should be able to disappear behind them.

She refused to think about how lightning tended to strike the highest point. How standing so close to that target wasn't smart or safe.

Letting herself end up back in Bobby's hands promised to be a hell of a lot bigger risk.

As she slipped behind two trees that grew close together, the car roared into view, headlights blazing, then slowed. She couldn't catch the make or model, but the bulky, curved shape was unmistakable.

They were called muscle cars for a reason.

The car braked harder, and Kim's heart leapt into her throat.

The driver couldn't possibly have seen her, so far off to the side and behind the trees.

The red lights flashing across the back didn't leave her much room for doubt.

Whether they'd seen her or not, they'd seen something worth stopping for.

When the car turned sharply to the left, leaving the paved road with a jounce to the suspension, Kim squatted beside the trees and covered her mouth.

Walking was taking enough out of her, especially since breakfast had to be hours ago now.

She didn't think she had enough left to run.

Instead of backing out and turning to come after her, the steel beast kept going deeper into a forest, rumbling at a low idle the whole way.

That had to be another old, almost non-existent trail, branching off in the same direction as the one she'd woken on.

But that car, it came from the *same* direction she was walking.

Kim was certain she would have heard a car that purposely loud if it had passed by in all the time she was struggling to rid herself of the horrid zip ties.

She lowered her face to her knees. Shaking her head, rubbing her eyes and cheeks across rough, muddy denim, clenching her jaws and her aching hands.

That car could have only come from Lightning Gap.

Which meant she'd been walking the wrong way all this time.

Every step taking her closer to Bobby, not farther away.

She heard the engine rev once, twice, then the rumble stopped.

No way anyone sane would drive up this mountain with a whopper of a storm building overhead, not along Lightning Ridge Road with the Lightning Rock at the end.

Bobby had to be at the end of that overgrown trail.

And Kim had just brought herself much closer to him.

A deeper rumble that shook the ground under her feet forced her to stand and head back toward the road.

After the day she'd had, she wasn't about to sit there and wait for them to find her. And she wasn't about to wait for the inevitable lightning to zero in on her, either.

She'd keep going as long as she could, and stay on the pavement unless another car came along in either direction. She'd get drenched, but maybe that would give her a little bit of protection from the bigger threat.

At least she'd be taking herself away from Bobby and however many henchmen he had on his side now.

Vowing not to think about how many steps she was retracing, Kim walked as fast as she could manage.

The fierce stitch in her side meant several minutes must have passed by the time big, freezing-cold drops of rain started pattering down around her—and on top of her already chilly head and shoulders.

Her chance to get good and pissed off about that eluded

her when she saw another pair of headlights racing along a long, wide curve toward her.

Much smaller than before, and without a trace of engine noise over the increasing wind and restless thunder. That car had to be coming from town, too.

Another set of lights loomed a good fifteen seconds behind.

Kim let out a growling whisper.

"What the *hell* am I supposed to do now?"

She started toward the side of the road, meaning to flatten herself in the leaves if she couldn't make it to the trees.

But the thought of running off and hiding again soured in her stomach and her mind.

Was that the plan for the rest of the day? Scurrying away and dropping down in the mud, while the rain and maybe hail and even sleet pounded her?

All assuming she was lucky enough to avoid the lightning?

A third set of headlights bobbed into sight behind the first two.

Okay.

If Bobby could lure that many people up here in a storm, maybe to search the ridge for her, she was done for anyway.

If that was any of the billions of people on the planet who didn't know him, she'd be better off no matter who they were.

Her heart raced in protest, and her empty stomach threatened to make her regret such foolishness.

Her hands and all of her insides trembled.

But she reversed course anyway.

Kim stood her ground in the middle of the road and waited.

CHAPTER 43

Steph gripped the steering wheel so hard her forearms ached, doing her best to watch the twisty, narrow road and the terrifying maelstrom building overhead.

In a lifetime of fascination with weather, she'd never seen a storm this vast and tall come up with almost no warning. She wouldn't have been able to see the road at all without her headlights, and even then, it was doubtful.

The bullet-proof vest her father insisted on felt like a heavy, stiff vise around her ribs, and the sweatshirt she'd rolled up past her wrists was making her exude stinking, nervous sweat.

The one battle she'd won was driving her own car.

Mainly by slipping her keys in her pocket when he wasn't looking. As soon as he finished fitting the vest, she yanked the sweatshirt over her head, grabbed the raincoat, and walked out without looking back.

Just as she'd expected, he wasn't far behind her, but he took a few seconds to bark orders at another deputy to get in with him, and another pair to follow.

By the time he got rolling, she was already out of the driveway.

He'd kept close behind her once he got going, and an irrational voice in her head insisted he meant to ram her car from behind to force her to stop. Or maybe that was the little girl who was certain she'd never be able to get away with anything as a then-deputy's kid.

She expected him to be *furious* with her, and she deserved every bit of it.

If she could get Kim back beside her, safe and unharmed, Steph wouldn't regret a second.

Once they made it to the level, curvy section of Lightning Ridge Road, her frequent trips paid off as she accelerated and pulled away. She gained an easy twenty seconds or so by the time they passed the road to Ivy's house.

She let off the gas a bit in the long curve before the trail branched off to the right. A few fat raindrops had landed on her windshield, not nearly enough to make the road overly slick. But thinking about that and just about everything else that could happen on the road was something else growing up in a law enforcement family did.

Steph had every possible aspect of driver safety drilled deep into her skull.

That training came in hand when she nearly stood on her brakes a split second later.

Kim!

That was Kim standing in the middle of the damn road.

With blood all over her arms.

The second Steph knew she wasn't going to run Kim down or go into a nasty skid, she looked in the rear view to make sure her father wasn't about to plow right into her.

She saw his headlights dip down as he braked, then drop lower and jag left and right. He wasn't close enough to have to do that to stop.

Something else was wrong.

She opened the door and heard several loud bangs. She ducked even though they weren't loud enough to be gunshots.

Then a metallic *crunch* as the second patrol car skidded into the back of her father's.

"Dad!"

The second she stepped away from her door, Kim collided with her.

"Oh my god, you have no idea how glad I am it's you."

Steph steadied her, then squeezed her tight.

Still watching to see if her father was okay.

"Steph, watch out!" he yelled. "Jackrocks!"

"Watch your feet, Kim. They may be all over the road. Are you okay?"

Before Kim could answer, another voice spoke out of the thickening darkness.

"Hello there, Problem. Got someone who's looking for you and your little friend Trouble."

Steph twisted away from Kim, reaching for the small arsenal in her front seat.

"Wouldn't do that if I were you, darlin' little girl. I got three more men out in the woods with rifles aimed right at your Daddy's head. The one in my hand is aimed at your girl-friend here."

She heard the unmistakable sound of a rifle bolt drawing back.

The sky ignited, sending a jagged electric blue bolt into the Lightning Rock.

But the deafening roar of thunder that should have come with a strike nearly on top of them was muted, distant.

Impossible.

All at once, Steph understood.

Lightning Gap would protect her own.

"Fine, we'll go with you," she said. "But you leave my father alone."

"Sure thing, sugar. Might want to explain that to him."

She could barely hear pounding feet on the pavement over the rising noise of the rain.

She still couldn't see who was talking, but she knew it wasn't Bobby's voice.

"Stay back, Dad! We're fine. It's all like the Seagons said!"

"Like hell I will!"

"You *have* to stay back!"

She turned to see him silhouetted in his car's headlights as he paused, hand on the gun at his hip.

Where she should have been able to reach for hers if she'd gotten into the habit of carrying like he wanted her to.

But she'd been too determined not to be afraid of Bobby to listen.

Now *he* had to listen to her.

"It's not safe for you out here. Remember what they said about Lightning Gap! Get back in your cars, please!"

Kim spoke into her ear, arms locked around her waist.

"No, Steph, we can't let him take us away. *Never* let them move you, never."

"Remember what the Seagons said, Kim. It's okay."

Her father stepped closer, and all at once Steph knew there were no other men in the woods. Just this one asshole who would happily drag her back to Bobby, to Robert, no matter what the protective order or anyone or anything else said.

Lightning Gap would have to take care of them all.

"Steph!" her father shouted, his voice ragged now. "You don't have to do this!"

"I *do* have to, Dad! Your car will be a lot safer. He's got men in the woods, armed men! The Seagons were right, I promise!"

"There you go," the mystery man said with a harsh, grating laugh. "Don't know these Seagons you keep carrying on about, and don't much care. Come on along back to your husband like a good girl, and we'll all feel a whole lot better soon."

"Yeah, you're right," Steph said, moving away from the car, still holding Kim close. "I think we all will too."

A huge burly man, well over six feet tall and strong as an ox, stepped forward into the headlights. He swung the rifle Steph heard around to his back.

"You're right about something else too, girl. Best place for your daddy would be safe and snug in his turd-brown pig-mobile."

He grinned, held up a phone, his thumb poised above the screen.

"*Get away from—*"

A loud SNAP—

Two gigantic bolts of lightning struck one after the other, hitting each of the patrol cars.

An instant later, explosions lifted each cruiser in gouts of flame.

Explosions from *under* the cars, not above.

In the glaring afterglow, Steph saw shadows move as her father and the three deputies surged forward and hit the pavement.

The oddly muted thunder that followed was lost in her shriek when she charged the big man in front of her, staring open-mouthed and wide-eyed at the remains of the vehicles he had not yet blown up.

He still managed to turn and catch her easily with one thick, muscled arm and put his phone away with the other.

"Here now, not so fast, pretty little thing. I'll get you back to your old man if you want him that bad. Even though I reckon you could do one hell of a lot better if you wanted."

He dropped Steph when she kicked and swung her fists at him, twisting himself neatly away.

"You sure you want to use up all that piss and fire on me? I ain't the one who wanted you spied on, or brought you up here. Ain't the one who ordered that car bomb hit on your county's finest, either."

Kim spoke from right beside her, putting one arm around Steph's waist and pulling her back.

"He's not the one who grabbed me, Steph."

"Why the hell are you *here* then?" Steph shouted.

He shrugged as if he didn't have a care in the world, but he couldn't hide the way he glanced uneasily up at the blackening sky.

"Owed him a favor, is all. Never did think he would go so far as all this."

Her father's voice yelled *bullshit* in her head, but she didn't need the reminder. She'd seen how gleeful this monster looked when he was about to detonate the bombs himself.

He flinched under the increasing rain, though.

And after those three close strikes, he knew not to trust the sky.

Or the lightning.

He simply had no idea how right he was to be afraid.

"Then let me handle him myself," Steph said, squeezing Kim's hand around her waist. "Just let me get what I need out of my car."

He threw back his head and laughed, exposing a ropy neck she could have cheerfully cut with a knife or a wire. Or her teeth.

"And let you use all Daddy's sweet little toys on me instead? No matter what Robert has taught himself to think all these years, I do have a damn brain in my head. Enough of one to get that dumbass Eugene out of the way before he acted a damn fool and got himself and probably *you* killed."

This time the whisper came from Kim, her lips warm and moving against Steph's ear.

"Don't listen to him. Listen to the storm."

Steph looked back at her father and the three other men, visible in the glow of flames the rain would soon extinguish. None of them had moved from where they'd landed.

Neither the lightning or the blasts should have been enough to kill them.

Right?

Please let that be right.

She faced the mountain of a man who had to be Dusty Atkinson.

Bobby's last ally, who at least was willing to pretend to turn against him.

"Give me your word you won't stand in my way," she said. "And tell me if he's armed."

Dusty shook his head, an unpleasant smile twisting his face.

"Aw hell, honey. Right now that boy can't hardly stand up straight, much less walk. That's why he was dumb enough to trust the likes of me. Only thing I saw was a knife, blade no longer than your hand." He looked at Kim. "You the one that put such a hurtin' on Mr. Robert Genius McReynolds, sweetheart?"

Kim raised her head and stepped away, standing on her own by Steph's side.

"Better believe it. I'll do worse this time if I get a chance."

Dusty nodded, his smile souring into a leer.

"I do believe it. Believe I'd sure like to watch whatever

either one of you want to do to him now. Best if you both do it to him at the same time, of course."

He pulled a big flashlight off his belt and waved it toward the woods. The bright white beam barely cut through the mist rising between the trees and brush, but it was a little bit better than nothing.

"Go on now, got to walk in front of me. Plenty of light for the way ahead. I reckon you'll hear Robert running his outhouse of a mouth long before you see him."

"Sounds a hell of a lot like being married to him," Steph said. "Let's go."

Ignoring Dusty's bellowing guffaws, she took Kim's hand and walked forward to finally rid herself of him forever.

CHAPTER 44

Bobby kept himself moving, walking stiffly between his car, the closest tree, the hunk of rock he'd parked beside. He kept away from Dusty's rolling intimidation of a car, afraid he'd take something and do his best to bash in the headlights and windshield and everything else he could reach if he got too close.

The one thing he made certain to stay as far away from as he could was the Lightning Rock itself.

He'd barely pretended to tolerate Steph's obsession with weather, most of the time nodding politely while she droned on and on. Usually he focused on one of his own upcoming games with a new playmate so he wouldn't look bored or actually nod off.

But he was absolutely certain lightning couldn't possibly strike close enough to him that he'd heard a sharp crack—

right before his whole world went searing blue—and then hear thunder off in the distance.

The strike had been nearly on top of him, but all his lifetime of experience wanted to tell him the storm was comfortably far away.

He pushed off from his car, terrified the metal was going to draw another blast.

A bunch of jumbled nonsense about whether cars were safe during electrical storms circled in his mind, none of it clear enough to grab hold of.

The rubber tires kept it from conducting.

The rubber tires exploded from the charge.

All the current passed right along the car's metal body, not on the inside.

The inside of the car got so hot the windshields blew out and the electronics caught on fire.

From what he'd heard when two more bolts jabbed into the ground not too far away, he half suspected at least one car had exploded when the lightning hit.

So that kept him from getting back in no matter how hard and cold the rain got, no matter how the wind seemed to turn the rain to ice against his clothes and skin.

The ache in his balls had finally started to ease up, and the muscles in his back weren't nearly as stabbing. Maybe all this wandering around was actually doing him some good.

That or the several swallows of the liquid courage he'd stashed in the back seat were working their magic on his body the same way they always did on his mind.

Taking away the fears and limitations he'd built up trying to appear normal for so many years.

Washing the thin veneer of Bobby away, leaving Robert unencumbered and ready for action.

Making it painfully clear he *never* should have trusted Dusty Atkinson this one last time.

Bobby paused, straining to hear if anyone was still shouting over the noise of the storm. It had been a few minutes since he heard the last outburst over toward the road, but that hadn't reassured him in the least.

If Dusty was going to be true to his word and bring Steph back, they should have gotten here long before now.

Something about the way Dusty rolled up with his brights on—spewing gasoline stink unusual in the era of hybrid and electric, and an ancient car that crouched like a big cat ready to strike—put Bobby's back up. Dusty proceeding to laugh his hillbilly ass off at the way Bobby had trouble walking drove that distrust home.

Then Dusty hefted a canvas bag over one shoulder, a rifle over the other, and ran off through the woods. Yelling over his shoulder.

"Just sit back down and get some rest, Gramps. I'll take care of *all* your business."

The more Bobby thought about it, the less he liked anything about this.

A hard, long gust of wind that sent all the trees clacking and groaning around him almost had him reconsider the car after all. Bobby hunched over, trying to keep some tiny part of him from getting even colder and more battered by the rain.

When he turned, a beam of light lanced through the trees back toward Lightning Ridge Road.

He tried as the light drew closer, winking in and out around unseen obstacles. He even bit his tongue and clenched his fists.

But the patience and composure required to keep quiet and wait were long gone.

"Dusty? That you?"

The distinctive voice rang out, with a vicious edge of amusement underneath.

"Oh yeah. It's me."

Bobby forced himself to stand upright and not hold onto anything at all.

"What the hell'd you *do*, man? Please don't tell me you used car bombs!"

Dusty's grating laughter cut through the droning rain and wind, the now-constant rumble of thunder from lightning that refused to strike.

A woman's voice answered, full of disgust rather than amusement.

"That's exactly what he had, *Robert*. Your friend blew up two Felten County Sheriff's Department cruisers that carried four men."

Bobby's heart and stomach dropped at the thought of that dumb hick catching him up in multiple felonies.

The rest of his insides locked up solid when he realized the voice was Steph's.

She stepped around the stone tower, her body unmistakable even bulked up from a huge sweatshirt and lit from behind.

The shape of the woman holding her hand was impossible to forget as well.

"What the hell did you bring *that* bitch for?" Bobby cried, stepping back. "I ask you to do one simple thing, and you manage to fuck that up all around! For all you love to carry on about how extra special smart you are, you're no better than those other two worthless pricks."

The two women stopped beside Dusty's car, and he opened the door to turn his headlights on, laughing the whole time.

"You know me, old buddy. Can't resist a good old-fashioned brawl of my own making, especially when the brawlers stumble right into my big, loving arms. I was gonna put you to rights myself, but this will be a hell of a lot more fun. Since one of these girls already knocked you on your ass today, I reckon the two of them will put an end to you and right quick. Damn sure past time someone did."

Bobby's overheated mind tried to make sense of Dusty's words, but they slipped right past him.

The low rumble abruptly turned itself up, as if the storm leapt from several miles distant to close enough to touch.

His crawling flesh was certain that meant close enough to touch *him*.

"Just do whatever you want to with the second one," he said, raising his voice above the din. "The only thing I ever wanted out of all this was to put things right between me and my wife."

Steph threw her head back and laughed, the joyful,

utterly dismissive sound of it tearing right through Bobby's skull.

The black and gray and purple clouds he'd glimpsed through the trees overhead strobed vivid green, outlining every contour of her face, every strand of her dripping wet curly hair.

"Nothing was ever *right* between us, *Robert*. You didn't even have the guts to marry me under your real name. Does your big, tough buddy here know how you pretend you never even heard of Laurel Gap? How hard you must have worked to lose your shameful backwoods accent so no one would ever know where you came from? How carefully you constructed Bobby Faulks so you could make sure Robert McReynolds never saw the light of day?"

Dusty slammed the heavy car door and glared at Bobby, hands on his hips.

"Is that right? Figured you'd keep us ignorant hillbillies on the hook with your bullshit games back here while you hid yourself away up there in the big city? Off where you could convince yourself you were the only one with brains enough to pull off your sorry stunts?"

Fierce red ripped across the sky without ever touching the ground, and the rumble rose up into a mighty boom.

Bobby hardly noticed.

His mind had finally worked its way through all of Dusty's words.

Wading through about a hundred different times Dusty pissed and moaned about not being in charge of their pathetic little hick gang years ago. And a few times he'd outright tried to trick or scheme his way to the top in the years since, when they'd actually been accomplishing worthwhile goals.

The deceptive little shit had just stepped out of line one too many times.

His response was pure Bobby, leaving Robert straining to catch up.

"This what you mean by someone finally putting an end to me, Dusty? Disappearing for days at a time, getting me wrapped up in fucking *car bombs* of all things? Then bringing these two along hoping they might finish the job so it won't offend your delicate sensibilities?"

"Might want to ask him what happened to your other two *good buddies*," the bitch Kim yelled. "How one ended up dead and the other all the way over in Walton County."

CHAPTER 45

Kim clutched Steph's hand for all she was worth, trying to keep her shivers and chattering teeth from shaking her to pieces. Steph promptly took the chance to walk both of them away while the two men were busy yelling at each other.

Getting an absolute beast of an old car between them and the two men helped. Especially after her own mouth ran away with her like that. She would have happily sworn on a stack of anyone's holy books that the words never got anywhere near her brain before she heard them out in the damp, charged air.

The clouds Kim could see through the trees moved fast enough to look like big, muddy bubbles coming up through the surface of a lake after someone jumped in.

Except it was all upside down and the bubbles were full of mixed colors from the storm and the sun.

Assuming the sun was still out there.

Assuming the world was going on as usual *somewhere*.

"Good thinking getting them yelling at each other, Kim," Steph said, barely loud enough to hear over the wind and rain and slow-moving thunder that somehow wouldn't stop. "We might be able to get closer now."

"Closer to what? We can't drive your car out. Not with..."

Steph shook her head sharply, sending drops of water off her hair.

"I have to deal with that later," she said. "Closer to the Lightning Rock."

Kim's mouth dropped open, but she followed when Steph pulled her a few steps farther away from the menacing car.

The men's voices erupted into shouts she couldn't ignore, even with the madness of getting closer to a gigantic natural lightning rod in the middle of the scariest storm Kim could possibly imagine.

"I guess I could have let old dumbass Eugene run with it, huh, *Bobby*? Know what he was planning to do? He figured it would be a fine idea to break into Big Brown Pig Daddy's house. Keep a *real* close eye on his little princess that way. Scouted out the yard and everything, worked out how he could shimmy right up to her bedroom window."

"Why the hell didn't you just tell me that, Dusty? That would have been too damn easy, I suppose. Made a hell of a lot more sense to what, drug him up and dump him off way over in Holly Creek? You know he told them to *call* me from there, right? Showed 'em exactly how to track me down.

That's how we got trapped up here in the middle of the biggest damn electrical storm I've ever seen!"

Bobby and Dusty had advanced on each other, standing halfway between their two cars. Fists clenched, shoulders drawn up, heads jutted forward. They looked like nothing so much as two huge birds poised for a murderous fight.

Steph pulled off a soaking wet sweatshirt that was far too big for her, revealing a bulky black vest. Kim's blurry disorientation from that punch to her head showed when she didn't realize it was a bullet-proof vest until Steph dropped it on the ground.

"They're not paying attention to us at all anymore," she said. "But we've got to be ready to run."

Kim resisted when Steph tried to pull her away from the car again.

"You can't really want to get closer to the Lightning Rock," Kim said. "Nowhere else could be worse right now."

Steph leaned closer, stroking Kim's cheek before she moved almost close enough to kiss.

"Remember what you told me, Kim. Listen to the storm. Hear how it's getting louder? I may be thinking and talking crazy, but I think that means we're doing the right thing."

"...never did drug Eugene!" Dusty yelled. "You *know* no one ever had to convince his ass to drink or drug, or did you work out how to forget everything about the *friends* you came up with, too? That was his next brilliant damn fool plan. Sneak some kind of hick blackout cocktail into the chocolate milk in your little woman's school lunch or some such shit.

When I told him what he'd manage to do was put her in the grave, he swallowed the whole thing himself."

Steph's lips drew back from her teeth, and Kim was terrified she was going to charge into the middle of the impending brawl. The thing was, Kim believed Steph would be the one to walk away unscathed. Her eyes glowed bright and furious in the headlight glow, not the least bit dimmed when the rain finally got around to a proper downpour.

"You trying to tell me Eugene somehow got himself dumped off eighty miles away?" Bobby said. "Stoned out of his mind, according to you. That must have been a hell of a road trip!"

"Aww hell, Robert. I never said he got in a car and drove. I threw him in the back of my pickup truck, him yelling and screaming about crazy shit only he could see. Yeah I dumped his ass outside Holly Creek. Seemed like far enough to let him sleep it off, keep him occupied for good long while. I never figured the dumbass would stagger into the path of a damn patrol car, then decide to fake being high as a kite for some idiotic reason. Still an improvement on what he was trying to pull off, since he didn't bust into the county sheriff's house or poison his daughter."

Dusty turned toward Steph, cupping his hand behind his ear and grinning.

"Hear that, Missus Robert McReynolds? This dipshit right here hired a real damn brain trust to take care of you. Puts a real damper on this blessed reunion, don't it? Probably 'cause he'd already proved he never could manage to take care of you himself. Not the way a *real* man could take care of you."

Kim gasped as all the hair on her arms stood on end, and not as part of the chills racing over her freezing cold flesh.

Even the heavy, soaked hair on her head stirred upward.

Steph yanked her hard, dragging her forward through the trees, yelling almost into her ear.

"Squat, but don't you *dare* put your hands down!"

As soon Kim bent her knees, the whole world blasted purple.

She had no idea how much time passed before Steph pulled her upright and shook her again. Kim had to concentrate to hear Steph's voice through the ringing in her ears.

"Kim? Please tell me you're all right. Kim?"

Kim shook her head, then covered her mouth with one hand to stop a scream from clawing its way out.

Both cars had been hit, judging by the smoking tires and scatter of window glass on the muddy ground. The blast had taken out the headlights on the antique, but she still saw light sparkling in the debris.

The boiling clouds seemed to brush the tops of the trees now, and the same purple light in nearly constant flares was bright enough to cast shadows.

Bobby and Dusty both rolled on the ground between the cars, yelling in pain and fear rather than anger.

"I don't think it's over," Kim said. "My hair is still standing on end."

"We *have* to move. I'm telling you, I keep feeling like we need to get to the Lightning Rock. This storm isn't finished with them yet!"

CHAPTER 46

Steph held her breath for an endless second, struggling to logically understand what the storm was telling her. Wanting to be certain she believed it enough to follow through.

A current of static tingling over her face and arms and hands pushed her away from thought and into action.

She stepped forward, closer to Bobby than she'd ever hoped to be again, and yelled as loud as she could.

"That strike was only the beginning! We all have to get *away* from here!"

For perhaps the first time since they'd met, Bobby didn't argue, or condescend, or try to mansplain or gaslight her. He rolled over face down in the mud, pushed to his feet, and staggered toward her.

Dusty stumbled and fell, but he was up and right behind Bobby in a second.

Steph grabbed Kim's hand and ran.

She didn't trust her memory of the cliff's edge, and she had a feeling the mobile phone in her pocket was an expensive plastic brick after being that close to two lightning strikes.

But the incandescent clouds—shifting impossibly between purple, blue, white, and even red—lit the way quite nicely.

When they pushed through the last screen of limbs and skidded to a halt on slick bare stone, but with the rain abruptly stopped, she almost lost her focus and all of her nerve.

The reality of all those colors flickering in the sky should have been beautiful. It was possible in her memory it might eventually be.

Right now, standing what could only be a few hundred yards below the clouds, Steph was terrified to her very bones.

Several inverted whirlpools twisted and roared over her head, with too many lightning bolts to count arcing between them. She'd never heard of tornadoes in Lightning Gap, and these had a much closer look to thick muddy runoff than simple air and water vapor.

The cowering lizard brain inside her head didn't care about scientific niceties.

It shrieked and moaned that they weren't safe within a hundred miles of this place.

Steph pulled Kim—looking just as stunned and gobsmacked—toward the towering Lighting Rock anyway.

Her mind could argue all day long, and probably would all night long for countless troubled sleeps to come.

A deeper part of her than her mind knew right here was the safest place on Earth for herself and Kim in that moment.

And in a lifetime of moments to come.

Shouts from behind gave them an extra burst of momentum, almost as much as a painful downpour of hail.

"Is this never going to end?" Kim cried.

"It will for them at the end of this ledge!"

Steph dared hope she spoke the truth.

They put on a burst of speed enough to pull ahead, and enough for Steph to pull Kim aside into one of the thickets of rhododendron less than ten feet from the Lightning Stone. Pushing and scraping her way through reminded her why these dense stands were called rhododendron hells.

She squatted again, pulling Kim down beside her. They were hidden enough to be missed, and close enough to the edge to still see.

"Don't touch the ground," she said, panting. She doubted Kim could hear her over the pounding hail and the howling wind, but she had to try. "Stay on the balls of your feet."

Bobby—Robert—shambled past in a more or less straight line, bawling her name. Dusty close enough on his heels that she thought they might tumble over the edge together and bring the whole horrible day to an end.

But that would not have satisfied the lightning.

The current crackling over her skin intensified. A shimmering halo rose around Kim, and both their hair stood almost straight up despite being soaked through.

The unending rumble cycled up to unbearable levels.

Kim put her face against her knees and wrapped her arms around them.

Steph held onto her own knees, but she raised her head.

She wanted to *see* this.

Both men collided with the gigantic rock, the heart and soul of Lightning Gap.

And Lightning Gap took care of her own.

Steph stopped counting after five white-hot strikes in rapid succession.

Every single one hitting dead on target.

The targets likely dead after the first devastating hit.

Even Steph could admit that was truly a mercy.

In the end, her vision carried too many afterglows for her to see the final result.

The price that had been extracted for her freedom.

She was a thousand times grateful that the sharp, fresh ozone scent covered up any aromas drifting from the base of the Lightning Rock.

It was Kim's touch, and the faint trace of Kim's voice through the lingering gong inside Steph's head, that got through.

"Come on, Steph, sweetheart. It's over. It's all over."

CHAPTER 47

Kim's heart ached when Steph knelt beside her father, still sprawled face-down on the pavement. Then she wept when Steph rested her fingers under his jaw, looked up, and nodded. Kim didn't have any trouble doing as Steph insisted, taking the chance to rest while she checked the others.

After everything that the day had brought—and the promise of countless questions on the way—neither of them might get a chance to rest for a long while.

She nearly cried again at the simple pleasure of leaning against the trunk of Steph's car. Taking a tiny bit of the pressure and strain off her feet and back.

She stared like a child first seeing a heavy overnight snow in the morning at the rapid change all around them.

The rain had returned, but no longer the pelting hard drops that were barely warmer than the frozen hailstones.

This sprinkled down a refreshing shower, a delicate promise of spring renewal ahead.

Clouds still lingered, but the massive bulk that had obscured the sun and the daylight itself was dissipating. Now she had the disorienting feeling of looking straight up at a sunrise, at fluffy cotton ball shapes transitioning from gray to blue to pink to welcoming yellow.

Kim breathed deep, hoping the fresh scent of the mountains after the storm would wash at least some of the memories away.

She knew better, but she hoped anyway.

Steph waved at her from beside the fourth man on the ground, smiling and nodding. Six of them had survived the terrifying assault of human and weather combined with far more magic than Kim had imagined existed in all the world.

Blinding light flashed through her head, overwhelming power crackled through her ears. She was surprised to wish she'd watched what happened to Bobby and Dusty rather than hiding her eyes. The reality might have been kinder than her imagination.

Maybe if she ran the worst part through her mind one more time, before it had a chance to fade as much as it ever would. While she stood in the last traces of rainfall, watching brilliant spears of light breaking through the clouds.

She wondered how Lightning Gap would look from the cliff right now, spotlit and glittering, washed clean by a spectacle they almost certainly didn't understand.

Kim doubted she'd ever be able to express any of it to another living soul besides Steph.

She closed her eyes, giving her mind free reign, aware that she'd be sorely tempted to do this again when faced with Auntie Venus, Ivy, and certainly the Seagons. They'd most likely get a watered-down version from her, if that much.

The storm's gentle, almost playful exit delighted her now as much as the unnatural speed of its arrival terrified her.

But the abrupt end of the storm, that tipped the balance into horror.

When the last nickel-sized hailstones dropped within seconds of the end of the lightning.

The end of *eleven* bolts of lightning, almost too fast and close together to count. Hearing them had been nightmare enough. Knowing Steph saw them, watched on purpose, filled Kim with a deep sense of dread mixed with respect. And more than a little awe.

She'd glanced over toward the Lightning Stone itself as she helped guide a half-blinded Steph back along the rocky cliff.

Away from a scorched black and steaming section of stone where the Lightning Rock met the ridge. Kim refused to get closer, but she was certain the middle of that shape glowed red as it flowed into new, sharp-edged contours.

A hardened, permanent memorial of the day that future visitors would never understand.

Whatever was left of Bobby and Dusty after that spectacular display must have toppled over the edge into the forest below. Far away from any roads or hiking trails, and on the wrong part of the ridge for anything to make it down to the fairgrounds below.

Thank the gods (maybe even Zeus) for small favors.

Kim jumped out of a half-sleep, her eyes opening to see three of the men sitting up on the pavement. Only Steph's father still stretched out full length, but he'd moved on to his side to talk to his daughter.

Kim stared at her wrists, the cuts still painful and raw but washed clean of blood for now.

The idea of the razor-like spot she'd used to free herself didn't sit well beside the shapes she'd seen forming on the Lightning Rock.

The dangerous formations Steph said were everywhere, all along this ridge.

Kim decided to believe that was nothing more than the result of frequent lightning strikes over countless thousands of years. Letting the idea of so many purposeful terminations into her thoughts for more than a second would change the way she felt about her home forever.

Steph shifted onto her knees to help her father stand. Kim pushed herself off the car and walked over to help.

Not because Steph needed the help, or her father from the way he easily got his feet under him. Kim wanted something else to think about until time fogged her memories a bit.

His silver-streaked hair was as unruly after the rain as Steph's, with random curls lifting in the softening breeze. He must have fallen on his face judging by the scrapes along his cheekbone and brow, and what looked like a nasty bruise rising around his whole eye. From the way Steph supported him around the waist rather than gripping his arm, he'd hurt his shoulder on the way down.

But he was alive, and paying every bit as much attention as he usually did.

"What on earth happened to your wrists, Kim?" he said when she reached for his other arm.

"I'll tell you all about it once we get down off this mountain," she said. "Once we figure out how we're going to do that."

All three of them grunted as they hauled him to his feet. After a few unsteady seconds to get his balance, he walked between them to take Kim's place against the trunk of Steph's car. The three deputies slowly moved toward them, each showing some degree of damage.

One had a badly burned arm, another couldn't walk without assistance. Seeing everyone alert and moving was more than Kim could have hoped for.

"Everything electronic in the cruisers is shot," Steph said. "Someone can check the other two cars if they want, but they're in worse shape. Mine is the only one that's roadworthy. Can't possibly fit six people, though."

"And you're entirely blocked in," Kim said. "Anyone have a working phone? I'm going to guess mine got scorched along with the cars back there."

She shivered a bit, but the mental movies were already loosening their grip. She hoped the same would be true when she tried to sleep that night.

"I don't suppose any of us are up for walking," Steph's father said with a half-smile. "I doubt I could make it the couple of miles to Ivy's house right now. My head is crackling like something shorted out, and the rest of me doesn't feel much better."

Kim nodded, reaching up to carefully touch her ear without thinking. Both Steph and her dad flashed identical scowls.

"Did you hit your head too?" Steph said, reaching up herself.

Kim caught her hand and nodded.

"My head and my ear. We'll talk about it later."

Steph crossed her arms, staring down Lightning Ridge Road, then into Kim's eyes.

"Probably everyone except me has a concussion. I could make it to Ivy's, but I don't like the idea of leaving all of you here."

"I don't think you'll have to." Kim pointed toward the ruined cruisers.

One of the deputies—the one with nothing more than cuts and scrapes that they could see—waved his arm toward something out of their sight along the curve.

Kim laughed out loud, amazed at how much worry and how much of her distress lifted at the sight of Ivy's Jeep, and the sun breaking through overhead to light the road and warm her shoulders.

And she grinned at the sound of BeeGirl's machine-gun bark.

"Should have known they wouldn't be too long getting here," Steph's father said. He tried to frown, but he couldn't manage. "I'd imagine they were just waiting for that monster storm to blow over."

Kim hesitated, but she couldn't stop herself from looking at Steph. Just as Kim expected, the two of them burst into laughter as soon as their eyes met. In a few breathless seconds, mutual amusement escalated into a proper out-of-control laughing fit, with gasps and tears and a good, hard hug.

And a desperately needed reassurance that everything really was going to be okay again.

Steph fought back straggler giggles, wiping her eyes and keeping her arm around Kim's waist.

"Yeah, that storm was a monster, Dad You have no idea. Let's just add that to the list of things we'll talk more about once we all get out of here. All I'll say right now is the Seagons will probably be curious as hell, but not surprised by any of it."

He winked as he started toward their rescuers.

"Someday, when you're both feeling better, you might just want to ask the Seagons about the lightning. Ivy and Venus, too, before you get around to your mother and me. May be a whole lot of stories there that you never even suspected."

CHAPTER 48

Before another hour passed, the brown county cars were towed out of the way, with the deputies sorted into either the tow trucks or Ivy's Jeep. Steph's father happily climbed in with her mother, who'd been following right behind Ivy.

Steph assumed arrangements were underway to retrieve the other two ruined cars, but she didn't want to know anything else about that. She was just relieved she'd eventually be able to venture out to the cliff again without seeing them.

Someday. When she was ready.

She stood off to the side when her parents saw each other, and again when Venus climbed out of Ivy's Jeep and caught Kim up in a huge, tear- and grin-soaked hug.

BeeGirl happily busied herself making sure no one was

left out when it came to love and appreciation, to go with as many kisses as she could manage. Her long red ears flopped and sparkled in the unbelievably bright afternoon sunshine.

The idea that the day had been so dark, not to mention everything she'd seen and done, was already kind of hard for Steph to get her mind around. But she was determined to remember as much as she possibly could.

At least until she could recount the entire thing to Ansou. Especially what she'd seen out at the Lightning Rock. Hopefully in person, wherever he lived now. She wanted to thank him for waking her up in that hot parking lot back in Louisville. She wanted to meet his wife and new baby.

And she wanted him to meet Kim.

The look in Kim's eyes when they decided to ride together in Steph's car made it clear she wasn't the only one who needed to get the whole day settled in her mind. Make sure it was cataloged and arranged and ready to put safely away.

Once they descended into the huge group gathered at her parents' house—a predictable and reassuring result of the small town instant communication network—Steph knew it would be a long while before the two of them had peace and quiet again.

Jay was apparently keeping everyone wrangled and organized at the house, including arranging for delivery of enough food for at least four times as many people as needed. He'd want to hear every single word as soon as Steph and Kim caught their breath, too.

The quiet in the car once the doors were closed was heavier than she expected

She looked at Kim, and winced at how red and swollen her left ear was.

"Did he do that?" she said, carefully brushing Kim's thick brunette hair back. The purpling bruise behind her ear was even worse.

"Yeah. Don't feel too bad, though. From the way my hand and forearm feel, I pretty much took him out of contention for fatherhood."

Steph managed to smile rather than fall into another glorious laughing fit.

"He miraculously avoided that ball-crunching fate for years, so thank you from me and everyone else who wanted to do the honors."

Kim shook her head and closed her eyes.

"Then the lightning took him out altogether. Did you... what did you see, Steph? Did it change things for you?"

Steph looked at her hands on the steering wheel, sorting through what she could say. How she could phrase it and not make herself sound awful.

But worrying about appearances, what other people might think, had been a huge part of what led to Bobby's madness. Before that, the same thing led to Robert's decision to bring Bobby to life.

She was determined never to do that to herself or to Kim.

"To tell you the truth, after that first strike, I saw more light than anything. That one was enough as far as taking them out, like you said. The rest... I think that was paying the price, maybe. The consequences of what he did to me and to you. Probably what Dusty *meant* to do once he goaded us into getting Bobby out of the way. All the things they both did to other people in the past."

Kim nodded, her eyes straight ahead.

"I'm not sure how to feel about all of this. I'm glad Bobby is gone, and I wasn't especially fond of Dusty in the short time I knew him. I guess it's up to your dad and Sheriff Crabtree to sort out whatever the truth is about the other one. Eugene. I can't pretend I'm not curious about it, but I doubt I'd like him much, either."

She turned and reached for Steph's hand, linking their fingers together.

"I may need a little time to work through everything. Not just the last few days, but the last few years. I really did need to make changes in my life. One thing I don't want to change is having *you* in my life, Steph. I hope we can figure out what comes next together."

Steph sighed and brought Kim's hand to her lips, careful to avoid the terrible scratches already scabbing over again. She leaned forward and kissed Kim's cheek right in front of her dreadfully abused ear.

"I've heard people talk about everything in their past being okay, because it led them to who they are now. I'm not sure I'm quite there yet. Today brought me a long way toward it. One thing I do know is all these years apart doesn't mean you and I grew *apart*. I think we grew *up* instead. Maybe we finally understand what we had in the first place."

Kim moved toward her, but instead of kissing they sat with their foreheads touching, eyes closed. The gentle contact more vital and comforting than anything Steph had known for years.

"There's nothing I *don't* want to do with you, Kim. That definitely includes figuring out how to move forward together. I can't think of anything in the world more worth getting right this time around."

CHAPTER 49

Kim sat cross-legged, feet tucked into a bronze-cushioned meditation chair, surrounded by a wonderland of rainbows, sparkles, and glittering reflections.

A row of beautiful, transparent rocks in every color she could imagine lined a set of narrow shelves hanging in front of a wall of windows to her right. To her left hung another shelf full of translucent and opaque and metallic rocks that seemed to reflect every bit of the sunlight right back into the amazing little room.

Steph had somehow managed to create a magical paradise in a tiny wedge of a closet in her geology classroom.

Even the metal and glass lab equipment she had stored higher up fascinated Kim, begging for her to pick them up and feel the cool contours.

Two delicate purple teacups Kim recognized from her

Auntie Venus's kitchen steamed away on another shelf, sending an enticing aroma of ginger through the adorable space.

Steph herself leaned against the wall in the meditation room's entry, arms crossed and smiling at Kim. The sunshine streaming through the windows glinted and played in her curly red hair, outlining the newly familiar contours of her face.

Kim struggled to put the calm, confident woman in front of her together with the tense, distressed woman who'd opened the classroom door only a few short days ago. Steph's face, the lines in her body, even the sound of her voice had relaxed somehow. Unknotted. Drifted back toward the way she looked and sounded and felt as a much younger woman when the two of them roamed these same halls together years ago.

"What am I supposed to do again?" Kim said, trying to keep a straight face. "I can't remember if I'm supposed to chant my mantra, or go ahead and hum until I levitate first?"

Steph let out a throaty, sexy laugh and shook her head.

"Yes, smartass. I made this room for levitation. It's the best way I've found to unwind between classes, and it keeps the kids in line. You better drink your tea before it gets cold. It's almost time."

Kim finally drew in a deep breath and let it out as slowly as she could, trying to calm her pre-talk jitters.

"Why did I agree to this again? These kids are going to make a career out of laughing me all the way back to Atlanta."

Steph leaned forward enough to put the warm teacup in Kim's hands and retrieve her own.

"If I remember correctly," she said, "you agreed to join us for Career Day because it was an excuse to drop by and see me. I proceeded to behave horribly and pretend I didn't know you. The next few days were totally dull and boring, nothing at all going on. And here we are."

"Ah, that's right. The weekend was pretty much forgettable now that you mention it."

Kim winked at Steph as they both sipped their tea. The ginger brew—perfectly sweetened with just a few drops of honey—warmed her all the way down and relaxed her tense muscles at the same time.

Monday through Thursday *had* been rather boring, certainly compared to the excitement of the weekend. Mainly sleeping longer than she ever had without being sick, group dinners at Steph's or Auntie Venus's or Ivy's or in town with the Seagons, listening to updates about the remaining investigations.

Kim was perfectly happy never knowing more about the remains located at the base of the Lightning Rock as long as she lived. Knowing the DNA tests would bring two more cases to a close was enough.

Hearing the story of what happened had been enough to scare Eugene Hunsaker into admitting he'd mixed up his own drug cocktail that kept him insensible for a good, long spell. Long enough for the traces to be out of his system by the time Sheriff Crabtree had him tested.

Admitted to faking after that, too, trying to stay away from Dusty, and just to see how long he could get away with it.

For now, that was enough to keep him out of the way on top of several other minor drug violations. The late Dusty Atkinson's ideas about Eugene plotting to drug Steph were likely to stay dead right along with him.

Steph's father was of the strong opinion that even after he'd served what figured to be a rather long stretch behind bars, Eugene wasn't likely to get up to much without Dusty or Bobby pulling his strings.

The best thing about the relatively calm week was the same as the overly eventful weekend: spending so much time talking to Steph. Every minute of every day left Kim more convinced that if the two of them could just sit together, talk, look into each other's eyes, they'd be able to get through anything together.

Even Steph's therapist thought that idea sounded mighty sensible after talking to both of them.

Hell, if the events up on Lightning Ridge didn't drive a wedge between them, she doubted anything ever could.

After all, the lightning had spoken.

She finished her tea, carefully set the cup down, and held out her hands to Steph. The long sleeves she'd worn to cover her healing cuts and scratches slipped back, and she didn't even care.

"Okay, I guess I'm ready as I'll ever be. Want to help me up out of this crazy chair of yours so I don't break something on the way?"

Steph helped her to her feet, hesitated for a second, and pulled her into a tight hug.

"You're going to do great," she said. "I'll be right there with you."

Kim grinned as she drew back.

"Don't play me up *too* much in the introduction, okay? Give me room to be a whole lot better than I sound on paper."

"I'll see what I can do. Watch out, or the English department might want you even more for that tech writing workshop they've been talking to you about."

Kim shivered. "Don't remind me."

Steph looked at her for a second, held tilted. "Have I told you how glad I am that you knocked on my door that day?"

"Once or twice. I think maybe if you show me, I'll be ready to face my first rowdy Career Day crowd."

Steph pulled her close again, her lips and mouth warm and sweet.

"Ready now?" she whispered.

"Ready for anything."

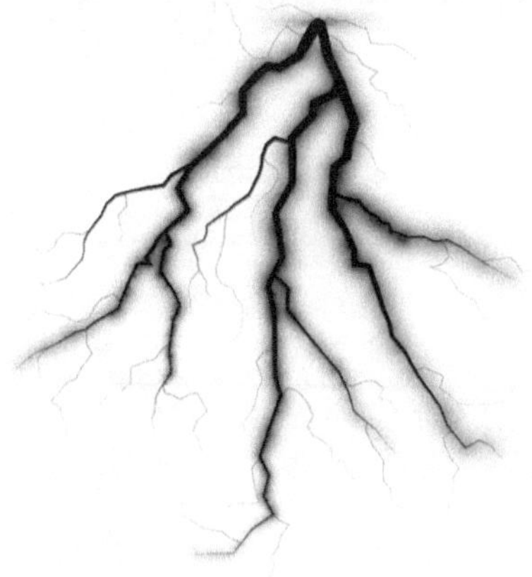

Thank you for joining Kim and Steph on their
journey home, and to each other.
For more romance from Kari Kilgore, turn the page
or visit www.KariKilgore.com/Romance.

ALSO BY KARI KILGORE

I hope you enjoyed *Protecting Her Own* as much as I enjoyed writing it.

For more tales of fantasy, check out www.KariKilgore.com/Fantasy. If you're craving more adventures from the Appalachian Mountains, and in many genres, head over to www.KariKilgore.com/TalesFromAppalachia.

For more tales with LGBTQ+ characters in almost every genre, head over to www.KariKilgore.com/LGBTQStories. If you want more of the romantic side of life, visit www.KariKilgore.com/Romance.

To dive into stories of mystery, crime, and suspense, head over to www.KariKilgore.com/Mystery.

Check out more of my fiction, including almost every genre, and be first to hear about release dates, Kickstarters and other fun projects, and exclusive e-book and print editions at www.KariKilgore.com.

Romance:

The Coffee Bomb and the Corporate Spy

The Box of Possibilities

Escape into Romance

Stories with Strong Romantic Elements:

The Voices through Time Series:

Songs in the Mountain

Secrets in the Land

Sorrows in the Earth

Walking the Ghosts

The Odd Society:

Independent by Means of Magic

Protected by Means of Magic

The Storms of Future Past Series:

Dreaming the Storm

Joining the Storm

Into the Storm

Fighting the Storm

Storms of the Heart

Storms of Future Past Omnibus

Collections:

Investigations Beyond Belief

A Tapestry of Holiday Tales

Novels:

Until Death

The Dream Thief

Hand Me Downs

The Great Gold Record Heist

Novellas:

Legacy of the Land

In the Pines

Fantastic Women: A Dark Fantasy Novella Trio

DNA Never Lies

Murder at the Fabulous Feline Emporium

Team Building Revenge

Dispatches from the Galaxy:

Restricted Species

The Becalmed

Plurapod Pathogen

The Changes Cascade

Near Future Forward (with Jason A. Adams)

Dispatches from the Galaxy: A Space Opera Novella Trio

Dangerous Days on a Pleasure Planet

Collections:

Fantastic Shorts: Volume 1

Fantastic Shorts: Volume 2

Fantastic Shorts: Volume 3

Stepping Out of Reality

Facing Down Extraordinary

Hacking Cybercrime

Passages in the Real World

Fantastic Side Trips

A Kaleidoscope of Cat Tales

Aunties Among Us

Four-Legged Heroes

Anthologies with Jason A. Adams:

Shadows Mountain Deep

Uncommon Holidays

Partnership in Crime

ABOUT KARI

Kari and her husband Jason A. Adams met in a computer lab in college in 1990 and proceeded to live out several enduring romance tropes, including rebound romance, friends into lovers, young love, and even second chance romance when they divorced and remarried, all before the end of the 90s. So it was perhaps inevitable that they'd both end up writing romance.

Kari has tremendous respect for lightning, and she prefers to enjoy the show from a safe distance. But she'd happily take the chance to see the Lightning Stone in action right up close.

Kari writes romance, fantasy, contemporary fiction, mystery, and science fiction, and she's happiest when she surprises herself. She lives with Jason, various house critters, and wildlife they're better off not knowing more about.

The Confidential Adventure Club

For Kari's exclusive free After The End stories and deleted scenes, discounts, early releases, adorable pet photos, Kickstarters and other fun projects, Spiral Publishing Exclusive Edition e-books and print books, and a whole lot more not available anywhere else, join us in The Club.

www.ingramcontent.com/pod-product-compliance
Lightning Source LLC
Chambersburg PA
CBHW032046180726
48284CB00008B/2774